*In memory of
David Griffin
1956–2021*

Chapter 1

The rain was relentless; cold and spiteful. Its stinging wetness slapped at Ruth Prendergast's face as she dashed from her car towards the shelter of the porch. After putting down the groceries she was carrying, she pulled a key from her pocket, unlocked her front door, and hurried inside.

A warm, centrally heated fug closed around her as she stepped into the hallway. Ruth felt for the light switch and flicked it on, glancing censoriously at the scuffed paintwork and gloomy wallpaper. First impressions were important, and her hallway was definitely letting the side down.

After yanking a handful of junk mail from the teeth of the letterbox and hanging up her coat, she threw open the double doors to the living room and turned on more lights to brighten things up. Except for the ticking, clicking sound of the central heating radiators, the silence in the house was absolute.

Ruth had moved to Hollybrook Close three weeks earlier, and was struggling to adjust to the suburban seclusion of her new home. Weirdly, she missed the constant buzz of the traffic-infested main road where, until recently, she had lived with the man who was now her ex-husband.

At the end of the hallway, the kitchen door stood open. She

went in and turned on the oven, threw her house keys into the half-empty fruit bowl, and went back to retrieve the shopping bags from the porch. Most evenings she enjoyed cooking a meal-for-one from scratch, something wholesome and tasty, but today's dinner would be a ready-made pizza and a large glass of Chardonnay. She'd had a long and vile day at work, made worse by the tedious and tiring trek around the supermarket on her way home.

All afternoon she'd been unable to shake off a restless, empty feeling. She felt dull and lacklustre, her vitality jaded by yet another dreary January day. Ruth was a summer person and she yearned for the end of March, when the clocks would go forward into British Summer Time. *Bring it on*, she thought. *Light nights, sunny days, warm breezes.* She could do with some of that.

Shivering involuntarily, she began to unpack the groceries. It was a loathsome but necessary chore – albeit one that was slightly easier these days, thanks to the abundance of cupboard space in her new kitchen.

When the last items of shopping had been stashed away, she unwrapped the pizza, slid it into the oven, and set the timer before going upstairs with an armful of toiletries. The silence moved with her, creeping through the house like a virus.

In the bathroom, Ruth caught sight of herself as she crammed shampoo and toothpaste into the narrow, mirrored cabinet next to the washbasin. She looked a wreck. Wet from the rain, her fringe clung to her forehead unattractively. There was no getting away from it, she'd have to blitz it with the hairdryer, possibly even the straighteners.

As she crossed the landing to her bedroom, the shriek of an animal pierced the night air. The sound was coming from the field directly behind Hollybrook Close. The cul-de-sac was on the northern edge of Bainbridge, wedged incongruously between the bustle of the lively market town and a vast expanse of open countryside. At night it was eerily quiet here and she found the

2

seclusion unnerving. Would she ever get used to living in semi-isolation? Leaving her husband, getting a new job and moving to a different town was supposed to have been a fresh start, but she wasn't convinced this house would bring the contentment she longed for.

Ruth didn't bother turning on the main light as she went into the bedroom. Its yellow glow was too harsh and made her look jaundiced. Instead, she reached across to switch on the cosier, more flattering lamp on the bedside cabinet.

That's when she saw the man, lying in her bed.

'What the …!' She leapt away, scrabbling for the main light switch. 'Who the *hell* are *you*?'

When he didn't reply, Ruth leaned over and prodded him tentatively, but still he didn't move. Her heart banged a warning against the inside of her ribcage. Instinct told her to flee, to hurry from the house and get help … but who could she call? She didn't know any of the neighbours yet, and she had no friends in the area. There was her ex, of course, but he lived miles away and they weren't exactly on speaking terms.

The man was clearly in a deep sleep, tucked under the duvet with his back to her. Ruth reached out and touched his shoulder, shaking it gently to wake him.

When he didn't respond she tiptoed around the bed and looked down at the unfamiliar contours of his face – at the thick waves in his greying hair and the kink in his nose. It was the way he was staring that chilled her bones. His eyes were green. Unblinking. That's when she knew.

The man in her bed was dead.

Chapter 2

The last thing DI Isabel Blood needed right now was a murder investigation. She was supposed to be taking two weeks' leave, for God's sake, spending time with her father who, aside from a few recent conversations on FaceTime and Skype, she hadn't seen for decades.

Isabel was on her way to pick him up at the airport when the call came through from DS Fairfax.

'We have a body,' her sergeant told her. 'An unidentified male, found in a property in Hollybrook Close in Bainbridge. The homeowner found him lying in her bed. She doesn't know who he is, and there's no ID on the victim. Sounds like a weird one, boss.'

Isabel pulled up in front of the barrier at the entrance to the airport's short-stay car park. 'Bloody hell, Dan. The timing couldn't be worse. I'm at East Midlands airport, meeting my dad.' She wound down the car window and snatched at the ticket that was spewing out of the machine.

'I realise that. I'm sorry. I didn't want to call, but the Super insisted. She's cancelled all leave … wants you at the scene, apparently.'

For crying out loud, Isabel thought. *All I want is a bit of peace and quiet and some time off. Is that too much to ask?*

4

When the barrier lifted, she took a deep breath and drove on, scanning the car park for a space. 'Are *you* at the scene yet?' she asked.

'I've just arrived.'

'OK. Well, you'll have to start without me and I'll join you as soon as I can. It's going to be at least an hour though. More likely an hour and a half.'

As she parked, she talked through the main priorities and actions with Dan, knowing she could rely on him to manage things until she got there. Once the call had ended, she leapt out of the car and raced towards the airport building. Her dad's plane had already landed. He'd be through passport control by now, reclaiming his baggage. She wanted to be in place, waiting, when he came through into the arrivals area.

She was nervous. Jittery. Eager to see him, and yet shy. Embarrassed. Until a few months ago, Isabel had been totally in the dark about her father's whereabouts. He'd walked out of her life when she was fourteen and had effectively disappeared. In the midst of her last murder investigation she'd found out he was alive and well and living in France. She'd also discovered why he'd left all those years ago.

That revelation had left the two of them with a few things to work out. Their reunion was destined to have some awkward moments but, even so, Isabel couldn't wait to see him.

Inside the arrivals area she stood shoulder to shoulder with other waiting relatives. A gaggle of taxi drivers had congregated nearby, holding up cardboard signs with surnames scrawled across them. A heady combination of excitement and apprehension was making Isabel feel sick. She took some deep breaths as she waited, trying to suppress her anxiety.

When the sliding glass doors from the customs area opened and she saw her dad walk through, her heart rate thundered into overdrive. Donald Corrington looked exactly as she remembered him, but older. Much older. His hair was white now, but at least he still had hair. He'd always been tall and lanky, but age had stooped him a little, and he was thinner, a fraction too skinny. There was a frailness about him that tugged at her conscience.

The pale blue, shining eyes she remembered from childhood were scanning the crowd, searching for her. Waving, Isabel pushed forward.

'Dad!' She surged through the crowd, desperate to reach him. 'Over here, Dad. I'm here.'

And then, there he was, standing right in front of her. Her dad. Her lovely, lovely dad.

'Isabel.' His voice was thick with emotion as he gathered her into his arms. 'It's wonderful to see you at last. I've missed you so much.'

She closed her eyes and clung to him, feeling like a kid again. Holding on tight, she breathed in the smell of his aftershave, refamiliarising herself with the forgotten contours of his shoulders and the comforting warmth of his embrace. This hug, this moment, felt like coming home. Swallowing the lump in her throat, she pulled back and smiled up at him. 'I've missed you too, Dad. More than you'll ever know. We've got a lot of catching up to do.'

It was as they stepped apart that Isabel noticed the man hovering behind her father's right shoulder. He was tall and slim, with brown hair, pale blue eyes and the hint of a swagger. Nostalgia pounded from somewhere deep inside her ribcage. This was a younger version of her dad … the man he'd been all those years ago. Instinctively, Isabel knew this must be her younger brother, Fabien. Her half-brother. What was he doing here? She hadn't been expecting him.

The man extended his arm, shaking her hand briefly. 'I'm Fabien,' he said. 'I've heard a lot about you.'

Isabel got the impression he'd chosen his words carefully, avoiding the social niceties normally used on such occasions. There was no … *it's good to meet you*, or *it's a pleasure to make your acquaintance*. Then again, Fabien was French. Perhaps his English didn't run to such stiff, British phraseology. She couldn't help wondering, though, whether his greeting had been purposefully cool. There was no kiss on either cheek. No warmth, French or otherwise.

'Hello, Fabien,' she said, her voice friendly and cheerful. '*Bonjour et bienvenue. Enchantée.*' Having exhausted her repertoire of suitable French greetings, she added: 'This is a surprise. I didn't know you were coming as well.'

Why *was* he here? Had Fabien come along solely to support their elderly father on his journey? Would he be flying back almost immediately, or did he plan on staying? Isabel had readied the spare room for her dad, but she hadn't anticipated a second visitor. Not that it was a problem. She could quite easily install the put-me-up bed in the small upstairs room they now used as a study, as long as Fabien didn't mind roughing it a little.

Her father was holding her hand, squeezing it tightly as if to reassure himself she was real. She squeezed back, her heart thumping in her chest.

Feeling uncharacteristically flustered, Isabel eyed the two enormous suitcases Fabien was dragging behind him. 'They look heavy,' she said. 'My car's over in the car park. Would you like me to drive it round to the pick-up point?'

Her father tugged her hand playfully. 'Don't worry. I'm sure Fabien can find a luggage trolley from somewhere. And I'm still quite capable of walking, you know. I may be over eighty, but I'm not completely clapped out.'

'*S'il te plaît, Papa,*' said Fabien. '*Laisse-la chercher la voiture.*'

'I have no intention of letting your sister get the car,' Donald said, rebuking his son with a tap on the arm. 'And, Fabien? Please speak English. Isabel may be one-quarter French, but her knowledge of the language is rudimentary at best.'

While Fabien went off in search of a trolley, Isabel and Donald stepped aside and waited on the concourse with the cases.

'So, Dad?' She turned to face him. 'Have you told Fabien yet? Does he know?'

Donald Corrington shrugged nonchalantly. 'The right opportunity hasn't arisen,' he said.

Since reconnecting with her father two and a half months earlier, Isabel had been mindful that her two half-brothers knew nothing about the bigamous marriage Donald had entered into with Isabel's mother back in the Sixties. Donald had promised to tell his sons the truth when the time was right, but she was beginning to wonder when that would be.

'You're putting me in an awkward position,' she said, rebuking him with a frown. 'I want to be able to talk about things openly. That's not going to be possible if Fabien still doesn't know the full story of your old life in Derbyshire.'

Donald fiddled with the handle of the suitcase, reluctant to return her gaze. 'I realise that, but I didn't think he was going to accompany me. He waited until I was checking in for the flight to announce he was coming along.'

'Why did he leave it until the last minute to tell you?'

Donald held up his hands. 'He said he wanted it to be a surprise.'

'I see,' Isabel said, not sure whether she did or not. 'I wonder why he decided to join you?'

Her father looked uneasy, his loyalties seemingly torn. 'Perhaps he wanted a chance to get to know his sister.' He opened his mouth to say more, but closed it when Fabien reappeared, pushing a trolley with a wonky wheel.

Remembering the phone call from Dan, Isabel decided to bite the bullet and break the news that she had been called into work.

She cleared her throat. 'Dad, Fabien … before we get going, there's something I need to tell you. Unfortunately, I've got to go to work this evening. I'll drop you off at my house, introduce you to Nathan, Ellie and Kate, and get you settled – but then I'll have to go out for a while. I'm really sorry. It's a hazard of the job, I'm afraid. There's been a murder, and when that happens, I'm expected to drop everything.'

'But you haven't seen our father for so long,' Fabien said. He looked annoyed. Isabel wasn't sure whether his scowl was aimed at her or the errant luggage trolley, which seemed determined to head in the opposite direction to the way Fabien was pushing it.

'Don't worry,' Donald said, patting her arm reassuringly. 'Really. It's OK. I understand. Your job's important. I'm very proud of what you do, Isabel.'

They had exited the airport building and were turning right, towards the car park. It had been a day of grey skies and heavy, wintry showers, and the damp night air bristled with a bitter chill.

'As you are not going to be around this evening, perhaps it would be better if you took us directly to the hotel,' Fabien said.

'Hotel?'

'Yes, we have reserved rooms at the local inn ... the Feathers.'

The Feathers Hotel provided the finest accommodation Bainbridge had to offer. The building itself lacked charm, but the interior had recently undergone an impressive refurbishment. The expensive restaurant served delicious Mediterranean cuisine and the bar was open to non-residents – but why the hell had Fabien booked rooms there?

'I thought Dad would be staying with us,' Isabel said, trying hard not to sound snippy. 'I've already made up the spare room for him. And, of course, you're more than welcome to stay too, Fabien. It's not a problem.'

When Isabel had arranged her father's visit, she had visualised long evenings by the fire with him, talking about the past and catching up on all the years they had lost. She'd assumed he would stay at her house. That's what she wanted. The thought of him checking into a hotel didn't sit comfortably with her. Not at all.

'We don't want to impose on your hospitality,' Fabien said. His English was good, Isabel realised. Better than good.

She shook her head. 'You're family. It wouldn't be an imposition.'

9

Her brother flashed a brief smile and held up a hand, gesturing an unwillingness to capitulate. 'The arrangements have been made. The hotel is expecting us. And as you have to go to work this evening, that is probably for the best, is it not?'

Isabel felt sneaped and disappointed. She was also annoyed, but she wasn't going to let Fabien see that.

They had reached the car, and she fumbled with the key fob to open the boot.

'Well, if you change your mind, we'd be happy to have you,' she said. 'For now, let's load up your cases, and I'll drive you to the Feathers. We can meet up again tomorrow after you've both had a good night's sleep.'

'Thanks, Issy.' Donald Corrington opened the passenger door, sat down, and swung his long legs into the front seat of the car. 'I'm looking forward to seeing Bainbridge again. It's been a while.'

Four decades, Isabel thought. In her book, that was considerably longer than 'a while'.

Chapter 3

After leaving Donald and Fabien at the hotel's reception desk, Isabel dashed home to inform her family of the change of plan and let them know that Fabien had accompanied her father on the trip.

She was greeted in the hallway by Nathan, Ellie and Kate, who had gathered to form a small welcoming committee. Even their dog, Nell, had joined the party and was wagging her tail excitedly. Behind them, in the living room, a homemade 'Welcome back to Bainbridge' banner had been strung across the top of the bookcase.

'Well? Where is he?' Kate asked, her face pinched with worry.

'At the Feathers Hotel,' Isabel said.

As she told her family what had transpired at the airport, their expectant expressions crumpled into frowns of disappointment, and the happy buzz of anticipation in the hallway fizzled out like a damp squib. They had been looking forward to this visit since before Christmas; the non-appearance of their special guest was understandably a massive anti-climax.

'So when *can* we see him?' Ellie said, rolling her eyes in the petulant way only a teenager can pull off successfully.

'Try not to be grumpy, love,' said Isabel. 'You're not the only one who's disappointed. Don't worry, we can all meet up tomorrow. Anyway … as it happens, I've got to go out this evening.'

Nathan tilted his head, questioning her silently.

'Work,' she explained. 'Dan called. I'm needed.'

She decided not to mention the murder. The mood was miserable enough as it was.

Isabel reached the crime scene ten minutes later. Hollybrook Close was a small, swanky cul-de-sac on the edge of Bainbridge, squeezed between an older residential estate and a brown, undulating stretch of ploughed fields. It consisted of five detached properties, each with sweeping, neatly trimmed front gardens. Two of the homes were enormous, three-storey, luxury residences with multi-car garages, but the body Isabel had been called to investigate had been found inside number 4, one of the smaller houses in the close. An outer cordon had been set up across the driveway and a group of vehicles was parked outside.

Isabel pulled up behind the cluster of cars and put on protective clothing, overshoes and gloves. After signing the scene log, she lifted the tape, ducked under it and then walked towards the house where DS Dan Fairfax was loitering by the front porch. His pale cheeks were almost a match for the white scene suit he was wearing.

'You OK?' Isabel asked.

'Yep, needed to get some air.' He grimaced, nodding back towards the interior of the house. 'I've just been up to see the body.'

Isabel had seen more than her share of corpses over the years and understood Dan's need for fresh air.

'It's never pleasant,' she said.

'But it gets easier, right?'

She decided to be brutally honest. 'Not necessarily.'

Offering a sympathetic smile, she brushed past him and entered the house.

In Isabel's experience, every home had its own unique smell, and this one was no exception. She breathed in an underlying scent of lemon polish combined with a whiff of new carpet. There was also the aroma of pizza, which was drifting towards her from the kitchen at the end of the hallway.

Dan had followed her inside. 'Come on then,' she said. 'Give me the low-down.'

He pointed towards a set of double doors into the room on the right, where a woman was huddled in an armchair, a tartan throw draped across her shoulders.

'That's Ruth Prendergast, the owner of the house,' he said, his voice low. 'I've done a witness interview and she was very co-operative, although there wasn't a lot she could tell me. Apparently, she came in from work and found the victim upstairs in her bed. When she realised he was dead, she called 999.'

'But she doesn't know him?'

'She's never seen him before … has absolutely no idea who the man is, or how he ended up here.'

'And you said there's no ID on the body?' said Isabel. 'No wallet? What about a phone?'

'Nothing.'

'And this is definitely a crime scene? No chance he died from natural causes?'

'None whatsoever, boss. He has a knife sticking out of his chest. Ruth Prendergast says he was tucked under the duvet when she found him. It was only when the response officer and the paramedics arrived and pulled back the covers that they realised he'd been stabbed.'

'Any indication as to how he might have got here? Into the house?'

'There's no sign of a break-in,' Dan said. 'So, either he had a key, or someone let him in.'

Isabel narrowed her eyes. 'How old is the victim?'

'Late forties, I'd say. Why don't you come and take a look for yourself?'

She followed Dan up the stairs and onto the landing, where he directed her towards one of two bedrooms at the back of the house. Isabel positioned herself on a stepping plate inside the door and looked around. The senior crime scene investigator, Raveen Talwar, was examining a section of carpet over by the window and a woman Isabel hadn't met before was examining the body. This, presumably, was the new pathologist.

'I'm Detective Inspector Isabel Blood,' she said. 'You must be Emma Willis.'

The pathologist turned to face Isabel and raised a hand. 'That's me,' she said. 'Good to meet you, DI Blood.'

Isabel leaned over to get a better look at the victim. The duvet had been folded back and she could see he was lying on his side. He was wearing a grey T-shirt, navy blue boxer shorts, and a pair of black socks. From her position on the stepping plate, she could see where the knife had entered his chest. Emma Willis had obviously removed the weapon and bagged it for evidence.

Isabel winced. 'Bit of a nasty surprise for the homeowner, coming in from work and finding a total stranger lying dead in her bed.'

'Yeah,' Emma said. 'Not what you want at the end of a long, hard day is it?'

'Or any other time for that matter.' Isabel craned her neck to get a better look. 'There's surprisingly little blood. What can you tell me?'

'He's been stabbed. The blade penetrated the heart, so he would have died within seconds. The lack of blood is down to the fact that the weapon was left in the wound. I extracted the knife a few minutes ago, but it was firmly lodged in his chest when the body was discovered.'

'No chance this could be suicide?' Isabel asked. 'He couldn't have stabbed himself?'

'Based on the angle of entry, the wound is unlikely to have been self-inflicted,' Emma replied. 'Plus, there are no fingerprints on the handle of the weapon, and the victim isn't wearing gloves.'

'This is definitely a crime scene then,' said Isabel. 'Otherwise, his prints would be on the knife, right?'

'Exactly,' Emma replied. 'The victim was discovered lying on his side under the duvet. He was probably put into that position immediately after he was killed. Based on lividity, I'd say he's been dead for between six and eight hours. I'll know more tomorrow after the post-mortem.'

'So, that would mean he died between noon and two p.m. today?'

Emma nodded. 'That's my estimate but, like I say, I'll know more when I've done the post-mortem.'

'Anything unusual about the weapon?'

'I'm afraid not. It's a standard kitchen knife with a narrow blade, the sort you'd use for filleting fish. It looks new. There are no signs of wear or scratches on the handle.'

Isabel had never filleted a fish in her life, but even so, she was familiar with the kind of knife the pathologist was referring to.

'We'll send it off to the lab for testing,' Emma added. 'Until then, there's nothing more I can tell you about the weapon.'

Raveen stood up. 'The CSIs have done an initial scan of each room of the house,' he said. 'There's no sign that the knife matches anything in the kitchen. There is a knife block down there, but nothing's missing from the set. Looks like the perpetrator brought the weapon with them.'

'Which would mean this was premeditated,' Isabel said. 'Have you found anything else, Rav? Anything interesting here in the bedroom?'

'A few hairs near to where you're standing, but they may turn out to be the homeowner's. Not much else in this room. The CSIs have started a detailed search of the rest of the house. I'll be in touch if they find anything.'

'OK, let me know as soon as you've finished. The PolSA's on

standby to bring in a search team once you guys have handed over the scene.'

Isabel retreated to the landing, where Dan was standing by the banister at the top of the stairs.

'Identifying the victim has to be our priority,' she told him. 'I'll go and have a word with Ruth Prendergast. How is she holding up?'

Dan shrugged. 'She's shocked, as you might imagine. She only moved in to the house three weeks ago. Reckons she doesn't want to stay here now.'

'Has she got somewhere she can go for a while? Friends? Family?'

'It seems not. Her parents live in Birmingham and she's new to this area. She said she hasn't made any friends yet.'

'Could she stay with a work colleague?'

'Possibly, but she only started her job a couple of weeks ago. I don't think she's had chance to get to know anyone very well.'

'Well, this is her opportunity to do just that,' Isabel said. 'I'm sure someone will take pity on her and put her up for a few nights. Or she could go to a hotel. There's a Premier Inn not too far away.'

Dan grinned. 'You're all heart, boss.'

'Are you sure she's telling the truth about not knowing the victim?'

'She seems genuine enough to me,' Dan replied. 'Go down and talk to her, see what you think.'

As Isabel made her descent to the ground floor, she noticed the carpet on the bottom stair was tattered, as though a cat had used it to sharpen its claws. In stark contrast, the beige, deep-piled carpeting in the lounge was pristine and bouncy underfoot. This was where the new-carpet smell was coming from.

Ruth Prendergast was hunched over in an armchair, staring into the unlit fire. Isabel estimated her to be in her mid-thirties. Her lank hair was an unremarkable shade of mouse, and her clothes were conservative and business-like: a pale pink blouse, charcoal grey trousers and a matching jacket. It was the sort of attire worn by someone who worked in a bank or legal setting.

'Ms Prendergast, I'm DI Blood.' She held up her warrant card. 'I know you've already spoken to DS Fairfax, but I wonder if I could ask you a few more questions?'

Ruth gripped the throw, pulling it tightly across her chest. 'Yes, of course. I'll help in any way I can.'

'I'm told that you don't know the victim. I'm sorry to push you on this, but are you *absolutely* sure about that?'

'Yes, I'm certain,' Ruth said. Her voice was soft and cultured and slightly condescending, with the hint of a West Midlands accent. 'Admittedly I didn't get a particularly good look, and the light in the bedroom isn't the best, but I got a clear view of his face. I've never seen him before in my life.'

'Might it be someone you used to know? A long time ago?'

Ruth dismissed that possibility with a quick shake of her head. 'No, I don't think so. Anyway, why would someone I know from years ago suddenly turn up dead in my bed? It wouldn't make any sense.'

Isabel conceded the point. Perhaps the victim's connection was to the house, rather than its occupant. It was time to rethink her line of questioning.

'I understand you moved here a few weeks ago,' she said. 'Did you change the locks when you moved in?'

'No.' Ruth shuddered. 'I didn't think it was necessary. I collected a set of keys from the estate agent, and there were two more sets waiting for me inside when I let myself into the house. It never occurred to me to change the locks. Should I have done?'

Isabel lifted her shoulders noncommittally. 'Frankly, I don't think many people bother. Moving house is expensive enough without the extra expense of new locks.'

Ruth smiled weakly. 'I've already spent the best part of a thousand pounds redecorating this room and having a new carpet fitted. I was going to do the hallway next, but now … I'm not so sure. I don't know if I can bear to stay here after this.'

'Do you live alone?' Isabel asked.

'Yes. I'm divorced. My ex-husband bought out my share of our old house and I used the money as a deposit for this place. New house. New town. New job. It was supposed to be a fresh start.'

'Hardly the new beginning you were hoping for,' Isabel said, offering a moue of sympathy. 'There's no sign of forced entry, so we think the victim must have either let himself in with a key, or been let in by someone else. Do you know who might have had access to the house in the past?'

'Apart from the previous owner, you mean?' Ruth plucked at the woollen throw with her right hand. 'There's the estate agent, of course. The house was empty when I viewed it, but I was shown around by a woman from the agency … Bartlett & Lee. She met me here with a key.'

'OK. Anyone else?'

'Not that I can think of, although it's not beyond the realms of possibility that the previous owner gave spare keys to members of his family.' Ruth furrowed her brow. 'He had a gardener too. A woman used to come once a fortnight to mow the lawns and keep on top of the weeds. I only know that because she called round to offer her services not long after I moved in. I've got her card somewhere. I wouldn't have thought a gardener would be given a key to the house though.'

'If you can find the card, we'll check with her.' Isabel smiled. 'You weren't tempted to hire her then?'

'I wish,' Ruth said. 'She seemed nice and she gave me loads of free advice about looking after my plants, but I can't afford a gardener.'

'What about the previous owner?' said Isabel. 'Can you remember his name?'

'Langton. Gerald Langton. He's moved to a bungalow on the

other side of town. According to the estate agent he suffers from arthritis and he was finding the stairs here a bit tricky.'

'What do you know about the neighbours?' Isabel said. 'I appreciate you've not lived here long, but do you know if anyone would have been at home earlier today, say between eleven and three o'clock … someone who might have seen the victim come to the house?'

'I've already given that information to DS Fairfax. Next door is vacant at the moment.' Ruth thrust a thumb in the direction of number 3. 'The woman who used to live there died last year and the house has been on the market for a while. I viewed the property myself, but the orientation of the garden was all wrong. North facing. Very dark.'

'I didn't notice a for-sale board,' Isabel said.

'They haven't got one. I'm not sure why. Perhaps they don't want to draw attention to the fact that the house is standing empty.'

'What about your neighbours on the other side?'

'They've gone away for a few months, overwintering in their apartment in Portugal.' Ruth gave an almost imperceptible shrug, suggesting she didn't fully approve of the reason for their absence.

'And the other two houses? The big ones further along?'

'I see hardly anything of the people who live there,' Ruth said. 'They head off to work very early … much earlier than me … and they come home late. I can't imagine any of them would have been around this afternoon.'

'For the record, what time did *you* leave the house this morning?' Isabel said. 'And when did you get back?'

Ruth rubbed her forehead. 'Look, I don't wish to be unhelpful, but I have a thumping headache and I've already given a detailed account of my movements to the other detective. He even recorded the interview … surely I don't need to go through everything again?'

'Not everything,' Isabel replied. 'Just what time you left the house, and when you got back. Please. Humour me.'

Ruth gave an exaggerated sigh, making clear her displeasure. 'I left here this morning at seven-forty-five. I normally get back at about five-thirty, but this evening I called at the supermarket en route. It was more like six-thirty when I got home.'

'You work nearby?'

'Yes. I'm an HR Manager at a telecommunications company the other side of Bainbridge.'

So, not a finance guru or a legal eagle after all, Isabel thought.

'OK, Ruth,' she said. 'Thank you for your patience and your co-operation. The forensic team are likely to be here for some time yet. Is there somewhere you could stay? Do you have friends nearby?'

'Not really,' Ruth replied, 'but I'll make some calls and see if I can arrange something. There's a woman at work I've had lunch with a few times. She might be willing to put me up for a night or two.'

'In that case, I'll leave you to it. We'll keep you informed as the investigation progresses. I would imagine they'll be bringing the body down shortly, so you might want to close the door.'

Isabel crossed back towards the hallway, her shoes springing on the thick carpet. Halfway to the door, she stopped and turned. 'By the way,' she said, 'I suggest you get someone out to change the locks.'

Ruth Prendergast looked terrified, her eyes brimming with tears. 'You don't think whoever did this will come back, do you?'

'I think it's unlikely,' Isabel said. 'But better safe than sorry.'

Chapter 4

It was nearly ten o'clock by the time Isabel and Dan got back to the incident room to brief the investigation team. Someone had been to the chip shop. The overwhelming smell of salt, vinegar and mushy peas had permeated every corner of the office.

'If you're going to stink the place out with fish and chips, the least you can do is get some for me and DS Fairfax,' Isabel said, only half joking. 'I suggest we reconvene in the meeting room. That way, we can escape the smell of trans fats.'

DC Lucas Killingworth held a chip aloft. 'We went to the Sea Fresh chippy, boss. They use locally grown potatoes, fish from sustainable sources, and there's not a trace of trans fat to be seen.'

Isabel raised an eyebrow and stared at him. 'I'm sure they're delicious, Lucas. Now finish your supper and let's get our arses into gear. It's bad enough having to work late … let's not spin things out any longer than we have to.'

Suppressing yawns and glancing furtively at their watches, the incident team trundled into the meeting room.

'I realise it's late, so I'll keep it brief,' Isabel said, when everyone had settled around the large wooden table. 'As you know, a body was found earlier this evening in a property at Hollybrook Close. The home owner, Ruth Prendergast, moved in only three weeks ago, and she doesn't know the victim … at least, that's what she says.'

'The dead man was found in the master bedroom,' said Dan. 'Ruth Prendergast came home from work and found him in her bed. Someone had even taken the trouble to tuck him under the covers.'

Lucas smiled and blew air through his nostrils. 'Did they read him a bedtime story as well?'

'If they did,' Isabel said, 'he wouldn't have heard it. The victim was stabbed in the heart with what appears to be a bog-standard kitchen knife. There was no sign of a struggle, so I don't think this was a heat-of-the-moment attack. It was planned. Thought-out. Premeditated.'

DC Zoe Piper was making copious notes and, annoyingly, looked wide awake and enthusiastic, despite the late hour.

'The victim was wearing only a T-shirt, boxer shorts and socks,' Isabel continued. 'That's a point … were the rest of his clothes found in the bedroom, Dan?'

'No,' Dan said. 'The killer must have taken them … probably wanted to remove anything that might reveal the victim's identity. I'm guessing his wallet, credit cards and phone would have been in his pockets. Someone took the lot.'

'Any significance in that?' Lucas said. 'I mean, I can understand the perpetrator taking the wallet and phone and any credit cards, but why take the clothes as well?'

'I suppose because it would have been quicker and easier to gather everything together, stuff it all in a bag and take it away,' said Dan. 'Searching through trouser pockets and jackets would have been time-consuming.'

Lucas thrust out his bottom lip. 'That suggests the killer wanted to get out of there fast.'

'That's understandable,' Isabel said. 'I wouldn't want to hang around either, not if I'd just stabbed someone.' She looked over at PC Will Rowe, one of the uniformed officers who'd made door-to-door inquiries. He was a huge, bearded, six-foot-four hulk of a man, whose towering, ursiform presence in the station had earned him the nickname Bear among his uniformed colleagues. 'Did you get anything from the house-to-house, Will?' Isabel asked.

'The properties on either side of the crime scene are unoccupied,' he replied. 'One's on the market; the owners of the other are away for the winter.'

'What about the people who live in the other two houses?' Isabel asked. 'The big posh ones?'

'We managed to speak to the residents, but none of them saw anything. They were out at work all day and didn't get in until after six o'clock. We also made door-to-door inquiries in the surrounding area, but no one could tell us anything useful.'

'Is it possible the killer was familiar with the comings and goings in the cul-de-sac?' Dan said. 'Knew there'd be no one around?'

'That would make sense,' Isabel replied. 'They would have been running a big risk otherwise.'

'If that's the case, we're looking for someone with a link to Hollybrook Close,' said Zoe. 'That has to narrow things down, surely?'

'What about security cameras?' Lucas said. 'Are there any in the area?'

'There's a security system at number 2,' Will replied. 'I've already secured the footage and taken a quick look. It captures the victim entering the close on foot at 12.54 p.m., but there's no sign of anyone else approaching the area around that time, either on foot or in a vehicle.'

'The perpetrator could have accessed the crime scene through the rear of the house,' Isabel said. 'The garden at number 4 backs on to open fields.'

'Number 5 has security cameras round the back,' Will said. 'They might have picked up something. We're trying to get hold of the homeowners in Portugal to gain access to the footage.'

'Thanks, Will,' Isabel said. 'Make sure you check all traffic in and out of the close on the day of the murder, not just around the time the victim arrived. Right now, our top priority is to establish an ID. A post-mortem's being carried out as we speak, and Forensics have promised to call me as soon as they have any news. There's no evidence of a struggle at the crime scene, and we'll have to wait for the toxicology results to find out if any drugs were administered before the fatal knife wound.'

Dan stretched his forearms across the table and splayed his fingers. 'We need to work out who the victim is, and how and why he was lured to the house in the first place, if indeed he was.'

'If we can establish that,' Isabel said, 'we'll be halfway to solving the case.'

Zoe shuffled eagerly. 'We'd better get to work then.'

Isabel shook her head. 'Not tonight, Zoe. I admire your stamina, but let's call it a day for now. We can make a start in the morning once we've received more information from Forensics.'

Dan drummed his hands on the tabletop. 'Early start then, boss?'

Isabel thought of her dad and Fabien. By now they were probably sitting by a roaring fire in the bar at the Feathers, downing a glass of red wine. Or perhaps they'd opted for an early night after their day of travelling, eager to re-energise for tomorrow.

How the hell was she going to wangle some time off? There was no way the Super would let her take any proper leave in the early stages of the investigation. The best Isabel could hope for over the next few days was a handful of snatched hours here and there. A few shared meals with her father and half-brother, and perhaps a quick trip into the Peak District one afternoon. It certainly wasn't the packed itinerary she'd had in mind for her dad's visit. *Then again,* Isabel thought, *life as a copper is notoriously unpredictable.* Her job had been the ruination of many carefully thought-out plans. This was just the latest casualty.

Chapter 5

By the time Isabel arrived home, Ellie was in bed, and Kate had gone back to her own house in Wirksworth. Nathan had waited up, and Nell was there to greet her at the door, wagging her tail devotedly. As Nathan rustled up a pot of decaf tea, Isabel took a seat at the kitchen table and sent a text to Donald.

Hi Dad, really sorry about having to dash off. I've been so looking forward to seeing you, and it's disappointing to have to be at work when I'd rather spend time with you. I hope you're not too annoyed! Nathan, Kate and Ellie can't wait to meet you. 😞 They were gutted when I told them you wouldn't be staying at our house. I have a meeting at 8.15 tomorrow morning, but I could come over to your hotel at 7 a.m. and have an early breakfast with you, if you'd like that?

'You don't get many murder cases,' Nathan said, as he poured the tea. 'It's Sod's law this has happened now, when your dad's over for a visit.'

Nell, who had been crunching dog biscuits from her bowl, skittered back across the floor tiles and sat at Isabel's feet.

'The timing couldn't be worse,' she said. 'Val Tibbet has cancelled all leave, so I'm going to have to fit Dad in around the investigation.'

26

Nathan winked. 'Or, you could try to solve the case in super-quick time.'

'Hah! I wish.' She ruffled the dog's head. 'We don't even know who the victim is yet.'

Her phone pinged. A message from her dad. She picked it up, pleased that he'd responded so quickly. Then she read the text.

Hello Isabel, this is Fabien. My father has gone to bed and is asleep. I think 7 a.m. will be too early for him, and also the hotel restaurant doesn't open until 7.30 a.m. Sorry, but breakfast will not be possible tomorrow.

Frustrated, Isabel pushed her phone aside. It seemed it wasn't just the murder investigation that was getting in the way of her reunion with her dad. Was it her imagination, or had her half-brother taken on the role of gatekeeper, controlling access to their father? She hoped she was wrong, but he seemed reluctant to let her spend time alone with Donald. Was Fabien being protective? Or plain awkward? Whatever his reasons, Isabel was determined to maintain a high level of politeness. She took a deep breath, retrieved her phone and texted back.

That's a shame, but thanks for letting me know. Ellie, Kate and Nathan can't wait to meet you both, so I hope you'll come over and have dinner with us tomorrow evening. I will text again in the morning to make the arrangements.

'It looks as though I won't be able to see Dad and Fabien until tomorrow night,' she told Nathan. 'Why is it that nothing *ever* goes to plan? I'm going to have to work long hours over the next few days. How the hell am I going to juggle things?'

Nathan squeezed her hand. 'You'll manage somehow, love. You always do.'

By eight-fifteen the following morning, Isabel and Dan were ensconced with Emma Willis, discussing the findings of the post-mortem, which had been carried out overnight.

'Good morning to you both,' the pathologist said, her voice

cheery. Despite a lack of make-up, Emma looked fresh and radiant, her smile revealing a perfect set of teeth.

'Is it?' Isabel replied, as she took a seat next to Emma's neat and orderly workspace. 'It's bloody freezing out there, I haven't had breakfast, and we have a dead body on our hands. There's nothing good about my morning.'

'Well, I'm about to change that.' Emma gave a thumbs-up. 'We have an ID for the victim.'

'We do?' Isabel felt a line form in the centre of her forehead, a tiny frown, creasing her face. 'When did that come through? Why wasn't I informed?'

Emma shrugged. 'I found out about an hour ago,' she said. 'It seemed pointless ringing you … I knew you were coming here anyway.'

'I decide whether something's pointless or not,' Isabel said, aware she was being grouchy but feeling unable to stop herself. 'For future reference, make sure you give me any updates *immediately*. Day or night.'

If Emma Willis was perturbed by the rebuke, she didn't let it show. 'Duly noted,' she said, as she opened her laptop. 'We got a match through the National Fingerprint Database. The victim's name is Kevin Spriggs. He pleaded guilty to a charge of common assault almost two years ago.'

'Right,' Isabel said. 'Thank you.'

'Do you think the murder could be an act of revenge by an aggrieved victim?' said Dan.

'Anything's possible at this stage in the investigation,' Isabel said. 'We'll need to check Kevin Spriggs' background, talk to his next of kin, and we'll have a word with the person who was on the receiving end of the assault. Get hold of the case file, Dan. If nothing else, it'll give us an insight into the victim's personality.' She turned back to the pathologist. 'What can you tell us in terms of the post-mortem?'

'It confirmed that death was caused by a knife wound, which

penetrated the left ventricle of the heart,' Emma replied. 'Kevin Spriggs was in his forties and physically fit for his age. There were no underlying health issues.'

'Any sign that he struggled, or tried to fight off his attacker?' Dan asked.

'No, nothing like that.'

'Do you think he was drugged?' said Isabel. 'Sedated, maybe?'

'We've sent off samples for a toxicology test,' Emma said. 'The results are likely to take a while, but as soon as I receive the report, I'll let you know. *Immediately.*'

Isabel nodded. 'I'd appreciate it. Thank you. Sorry if I seem cranky.'

Dan grinned mischievously. 'Get out of the wrong side of the bed did you, boss?'

'Right side of the bed,' she replied, 'just not enough sleep. A strong coffee might put things right.'

'We have a vending machine in the corridor,' Emma said. 'The coffee's not brilliant, but I've drunk worse.'

Isabel curled her lip. 'I'll wait and call in at the café on my way back to the office. What about other forensics? Have you heard anything yet?'

'According to Raveen there was very little in the way of forensic evidence. There were a few fingerprints that weren't a match to either the victim or the current homeowner. Mind you, I gather she only moved into the house a few weeks ago, so the prints Rav found could well belong to a previous occupant.'

'Thanks,' Isabel said. 'I'll arrange for someone to get prints from the previous owner, for elimination purposes.'

Dan glanced at his watch. 'Shall we go and get that coffee then, boss?'

'Lead me to it,' she replied. 'Something tells me this is going to be a double espresso kind of day.'

Chapter 6

A briefing had been scheduled for ten o'clock in the meeting room. Isabel was the first to arrive, followed shortly afterwards by Zoe and Dan. After that, the rest of the incident team seemed to drift in all at once. People scrabbled around the table, jostling to claim a chair. Soon, every seat was taken and the latecomers were forced to file in around the sides and lean against the wall.

Isabel stood at the head of the table and listened to the low murmur of voices. Worryingly, she found the steady, rumbling sound soporific. She needed to liven up. It was going to be a busy day, and she couldn't afford to let tiredness get the better of her.

Forty minutes ago, she'd spoken to Detective Superintendent Valerie Tibbet to update her on the case, which had been assigned the operational name Jackdaw. Isabel was aware that the Super was planning to put in an appearance at the briefing and, true to form, Val was the last to arrive, thundering through the door at one minute past ten. After striding over to the head of the table, she took her position, centre stage, like the star performer in a highbrow, low-budget play. Standing silently, Val waited for her audience to quieten down and pay attention.

'Operation Jackdaw,' she began, when an expectant hush had descended in the room. 'As you know, the body of an unidentified man was found yesterday evening in Hollybrook Close. I'm pleased to report that we now have an ID for the victim, which, I'm sure you'll agree, should make this investigation a hell of a lot easier. I intend to allocate as many resources as possible to the case, so that we can track down the perpetrator swiftly and bring him or her to justice.' Val paused, pointing to the photograph of the victim that had been pinned to the whiteboard. 'We need to find whoever did this.'

Talk about stating the obvious, thought Isabel. Of course they needed to find out who'd killed Kevin Spriggs – that was their job. Needless to say, what Val *really* meant was that she wanted this case solved quickly. The underlying message was that the allocation of resources cost money, and their budget was already stretched to the limit.

'I'll hand over to DI Blood to take you through what we know so far,' Val said, stepping back a fraction, but still retaining her position, centre stage.

'The victim is Kevin Spriggs, aged forty-seven,' Isabel began. 'Cause of death was a knife wound to the heart. As most of you know, he was discovered in the master bedroom of number 4 Hollybrook Close, *but* … the homeowner, Ruth Prendergast, maintains she doesn't know the victim. She discovered his body when she came home from work. There was no sign of forced entry, so we're working on the assumption that Kevin Spriggs had a key to the property, or he was let in by someone who had access to the house.'

She glanced in Raveen Talwar's direction. 'Do you want to share what you found in the way of forensics, Rav?'

Raveen had managed to grab a seat at the table, his elbows resting on its polished surface. 'Forensically speaking, there isn't a lot to report,' he said. 'That's what makes this case so interesting. We've all heard of Locard's exchange principle, right?'

It was a rhetorical question, but Zoe raised her hand and answered anyway. 'Every contact leaves a trace,' she said. 'The perpetrator of a crime will bring something into the crime scene, and leave with something from it.'

'Yes. Thanks, Zoe,' said Isabel. 'I think we're all familiar with the concept.'

Raveen slapped his hands together. 'That is precisely my point. We're familiar with it because it's the basic, fundamental principle of forensic science. However …' he held up an index finger '… we've conducted a thorough forensic search of the crime scene and found surprisingly little. The murder weapon has been photographed and swabbed and sent to the lab. We already know there are no fingerprints on the knife, but it'll be fast-tracked to see if they can discover any DNA, hairs or fibres on the handle, and they'll confirm whether any of the blood on the blade belonged to anyone other than the victim. We found a few hairs in the bedroom, and some fingerprints that weren't the victim's or the current homeowner's. However, it's possible they were left by the previous occupant, who only moved out recently. We've also taken away some fibres and some cat hairs.'

'Does Ruth Prendergast own a cat?' Isabel said.

'No,' Raveen replied, 'but the previous homeowner did. Other than that, there's nothing to report. Zilch. And that in itself, is unusual. It suggests the perpetrator may have been forensically aware.'

'Someone with background knowledge, you mean?' said Dan. 'A professional? Or a seasoned criminal?'

'Not necessarily,' Raveen said. 'These days anyone can go online and learn how to avoid leaving forensic evidence at a crime scene … and television has made everyone far more knowledgeable about CSI. All those documentaries on the true crime channel have a lot to answer for.'

'The victim could have been involved in some kind of illegal activity,' Dan insisted. 'In which case, his killer may be a criminal who's forensically savvy.'

'Are you thinking there might be a drugs connection, Dan?'

Isabel wasn't convinced. 'It's possible … but to me, the killer's MO suggests something else entirely. Something far more personal.'

'What do we know about the victim?' said Will Rowe, who was leaning his six-foot-four frame against the wall, close to the door.

'We've not had time to establish very much, but we do know that he lived here in Bainbridge, in a rented property in Lord Street,' Isabel said. 'Members of Raveen's team are over there now, conducting a forensic search. I'll be liaising with the police search adviser to arrange a detailed search of the house later on today, when Forensics have finished.'

'Any word yet on the victim's phone?' Lucas asked.

'Nothing yet,' Isabel said. 'We're trying to locate it, along with his missing wallet and clothes, but I suspect the killer will have destroyed everything by now. However, once we've confirmed the victim's mobile number, we can submit an application to the SPOC and get hold of the phone data from the service provider.'

'What about family?' asked Lucas. 'Is there a spouse or partner? Kids?'

'Spriggs lived alone,' Dan said. 'There's no live-in partner, but his neighbour informed us there is a grown-up son, who we're in the process of tracing.'

'In terms of employment,' Isabel said, 'the victim worked as a car mechanic at the Crown Garage over on Wirksworth Road. More significantly, Spriggs had a record. His fingerprints are on the database, which is how we ID'd him. Two years ago, he pleaded guilty to a charge of common assault against a woman called Sophie Tait. He was fined by the magistrate, but he wasn't given a community order. We'll be speaking to Sophie Tait, to ascertain the circumstances and find out more about what happened.'

'Was it Spriggs' first offence?' Lucas asked.

'Yes.' Isabel nodded. 'But just because he didn't have any previous convictions, doesn't mean he didn't have a history of aggressive behaviour. We need to build a clearer picture of Kevin Spriggs, find out what kind of person he was. Sophie Tait's encounter with him will give us one small piece in the jigsaw.'

'I'm thinking she could have been involved in the murder,' Dan said. 'Some sort of retaliation.'

'The assault took place two years ago,' Isabel replied. 'If Sophie Tait wanted to get her own back, why would she wait so long? And murder? Would she really go to such extremes to get revenge?'

Isabel paused, reflecting inwardly. The more she thought about Operation Jackdaw, the more unsettled she felt. Major crimes always implanted a sense of urgency in her mind, a desire for hurriedness, verging almost on panic. This type of investigation made her intensely aware of the passage of time. Minutes ticking by into hours, that spun forward into days. The longer a murder went unsolved, the less likely it was they'd ever find the killer.

Violent crimes were usually committed by someone who was known to the victim, and Isabel's gut instinct was to look for someone with a connection to Kevin Spriggs.

'In my opinion, this wasn't a chance killing in a random location,' she said. 'I suspect someone planned the whole thing carefully and used the house on Hollybrook Close for a reason … perhaps for convenience, or maybe it was chosen to communicate a message.'

'Or to misdirect us,' Dan suggested. 'It's possible the killer stumbled across a way to access the property without anyone knowing, and took the victim there because there was nothing to connect them to the house.'

'Yep, there you go.' Isabel threw up her hands. 'Another possibility for us to contend with. When you start an investigation like this, there are a hundred different scenarios as to what might have happened.'

'I agree this is a perplexing case,' Detective Superintendent Tibbet interjected. 'But let's discuss the homeowner for a minute. Ruth Prendergast is adamant she didn't know the victim and you said she seemed badly shaken by the experience. Does that mean she isn't a person of interest?'

'She says she was at work all day,' Dan said. 'We'll have to corroborate that, of course, but I reckon we can rule her out.'

'Our best course of action is to track down and talk to the victim's family, friends and colleagues,' Isabel said. 'Let's try and determine who had a reason to kill Kevin Spriggs. To work that out, we need to understand what made him tick. Firstly, was he in a relationship?' She held up her left hand, ticking things off on her fingers. 'Was he well thought of by his family and friends? Was he a reliable employee? Did he have any problems with drink or drugs or gambling? Had he made any enemies? If we can piece together a picture of Kevin Spriggs' life, we can start to work out who might have wanted him dead, and why.'

The Super pressed her hands together. 'So, what's the plan for today?'

Isabel turned to her core inquiry team, the people she would be relying on the most. 'Dan and Zoe, once we've tracked him down, I'd like you to go and talk to the victim's next of kin, his son. DC Kent has been deployed as the FLO, so liaise with her to arrange the visit. While you're out, I'd also like you to call in at the estate agency that sold the house to Ruth Prendergast. We need to draw up a definitive list of who might have had a key, or had access to one in the past. Lucas, you're with me. We'll go and see Sophie Tait and, after that, we can pay a visit to Gerald Langton, the previous occupant of number 4 Hollybrook Close. Let's see if he knew Kevin Spriggs.'

Isabel glanced around the room, addressing the other members of the team. 'I'd like the rest of you to continue with fact-checking. We need to establish the victim's mobile phone number, and can someone confirm with Ruth Prendergast's employer that she was at work yesterday, please? See if you can find out what Kevin Spriggs' movements were on the morning of his murder, and the previous evening. Find out what you can. Talk to some more of his neighbours. Check relevant CCTV around Spriggs' home. Who were his buddies? Was there anywhere he liked to hang out …

pubs, clubs … a gym maybe? We'll need to speak to his employer and colleagues as well. If he was a car mechanic, I'm guessing Spriggs owned a car of his own. Where is that vehicle now? Where might it have been recently? We've already started checking CCTV cameras within half a mile of the crime scene. Trawling through that footage is going to take time and manpower.'

Detective Superintendent Tibbet held up her hands, preparing to sum up. 'OK, folks, you have your actions for today. Let's make a start and reconvene for another briefing tomorrow at nine.'

As the meeting broke up, Val turned and left the room, PC Will Rowe close on her heels. *Exit, pursued by a bear*, Isabel thought, smiling as she watched the Super disappear along the corridor.

Chapter 7

The victim's next of kin was twenty-six-year-old Alfred Moss. The family liaison officer, DC Sarah Kent, had already informed him of Kevin Spriggs' death and offered support to the family. The purpose of Dan and Zoe's visit was to obtain background information and assess whether Alfred Moss should be considered a person of interest in the murder investigation.

'What do we know about this Moss bloke?' Dan said, as they drove towards Derby.

'Not a lot,' Zoe replied. 'Other than he lives in Oakwood with his partner. I'm puzzled as to why he has a different surname to the victim. I checked, and Kevin Spriggs and Alfred's mother were definitely married when their son was born. So why is he Moss and not Spriggs?'

'There's bound to be a simple explanation,' Dan said. 'But it's worth asking the question. Does he know we're coming?'

'Yeah, I spoke to DC Kent and she's told him to expect us. It doesn't sound as if she's having much luck engaging with Alfred though. Apparently, he and his father never had a close relationship.'

'Now that *is* interesting. I wonder what the story is?'

Zoe smiled from the passenger seat. 'Dunno. Let's ask him, shall we?'

It was the first time Dan had been to the suburb of Oakwood. Built mainly in the 1980s and 90s, it was a sprawling housing estate on the north-eastern edge of Derby, made up of an eclectic mix of starter homes, semis and larger detached properties. Alfred Moss lived in one of the smaller terraced houses, positioned at a high point on the main road that ran through the centre of the estate.

He must have been at the window looking out for them, because the front door opened before Zoe had rung the bell. Alfred was tall and skinny, with close-cropped hair. Dan noticed a tattoo of what appeared to be the tip of a feathered wing poking out from beneath the collar of his polo shirt. A bird, maybe, or an angel.

'Alfred Moss? I'm DS Fairfax and this is my colleague, DC Piper.'

'Come in,' he said, glancing at their warrant cards before pulling open the door. 'And it's Alfie. No one ever calls me Alfred.'

Dan and Zoe followed him through the entrance lobby into a compact, sparsely furnished living room. After slouching into a wooden-framed armchair and stretching his legs across the matching footstool, Alfie invited Dan and Zoe to sit on the couch on the other side of the room.

There were toys scattered across the wooden floor and a safety gate at the bottom of the stairs, but no sound or sign that any children or other adults were in the house.

'I'm sorry about your dad,' Dan said, as he sat down. 'It must have come as a shock. Is the family liaison officer not here?'

'She came round earlier,' Alfie said, 'but I sent her away. She left me her card and she's promised to keep in touch, but I told her I'm not some grieving relative who needs consoling. I was surprised about the murder, but I'd be lying if I said I was devastated by me father's death. He and I weren't close.'

Dan found this marked lack of sentiment troubling. His own father could be a grumpy bugger at times, but if Dan had received the news that his dad had died ... been murdered ... it would have cut him to pieces. Alfie, on the other hand, was displaying an air of nonchalance that suggested a cold sense of detachment. Dan was intrigued by this, and also slightly appalled. Why the lack of emotion?

Zoe was obviously wondering the same thing. 'What was the reason for your estrangement?' she asked. 'Is it a recent thing?'

Alfie leaned back against the leather headrest. 'We've never been close. Me mum and him split up when I was four. I don't have many memories of him living with us, and the ones I do have aren't pleasant. Mum left because he used to hit her. He was a nasty piece of work. We were better off without him.'

'You and your dad have different surnames,' Zoe said. 'Why is that?'

'Mum got married again when I was seven. I took me stepdad's name after that. It was easier … and Tony's a good bloke. He was the one that brought me up, really. As far as I'm concerned, he's me dad, not Kevin Spriggs.'

'Did you have any contact with your natural father as you were growing up?' Dan asked.

Alfie leaned forward and rested his elbows on his knees. 'When I was a kid we ran into him a couple of times while we were over in Bainbridge. Me mum weren't too happy about it. As I recall, he made a scene … in the street.'

There was a hint of embarrassment in Alfie's voice, his accent thickening as he recalled the encounter.

'What about more recently?' Dan said. 'Have you and your dad met up at all?'

Alfie picked up a red plastic toy train and began to spin its wheels. 'No, we didn't meet up, but he did get in touch with me through Facebook a while back. He sent me a friend request.'

'When exactly?' said Dan.

'I dunno, early last year. March maybe? Not long after me daughter was born.'

'And did you accept the request?' Zoe asked.

He nodded. 'Eventually. I ignored it at first, but then I felt a bit rotten, like.' He grinned sheepishly. 'I couldn't see the harm in becoming his friend, at least on Facebook. Not that I go on there much these days. It's more for the oldsters now, int it? I prefer Instagram meself.'

Zoe smiled. 'I bet you checked out Kevin Spriggs' profile though.'

'Course I did. Who wouldn't? There were loads of photos of him, most of 'em taken in the pub. He looked pretty wasted in quite a few of 'em.'

'And that was it, was it?' Dan found it hard to believe that either of the men would have left it at that. Surely, one or other of them would have been curious enough to make further contact.

'He did DM me a couple of times, suggesting we meet up for a pint, but I didn't reply.'

'Weren't you tempted to see him?' Zoe asked.

'Not at all.' Alfie curled his nose. 'I had zero interest in building a relationship with him. Like I said, I have a dad … Tony. I didn't need Kevin Spriggs in me life. I spent most of my childhood listening to me grandma slagging him off, so I was pretty sure he wouldn't be a positive influence. I've also got me own kids to think about. I didn't want him involved in their lives.'

'How many children do you have?' Zoe asked.

'Two. A little lad of three, and a ten-month-old daughter.'

'They're not around today then?' said Zoe.

'Nah, me partner's taken 'em out. She thought it was best. It can be a bit chaotic round 'ere when me son's running about with his toys. He's a noisy little sod – they both are.'

Dan locked his fingers together and said: 'Noisy or not, Kevin Spriggs might have enjoyed getting to know his grandchildren.'

Alfie scowled. 'I'm sure he would, but I wasn't going to risk it. Like I say, he was a nasty piece of work … at least that's what I've been told.'

'Do your mum and Tony Moss have any children?' Zoe asked.

'Yeah, I have a sister. She's the clever one in the family.' The sparkle in Alfie's eyes suggested genuine affection, as well as pride. 'She's at uni in Bristol. Went back straight after Christmas.'

'What's she studying?' Zoe's tone sounded over-friendly and intrusive, but Dan knew her enquiry was aimed at building rapport with Alfie and gaining his trust.

'Marketing? Business management? Summat like that. Like I say, she's the brains of the family.'

'Going back to Kevin Spriggs,' Dan said. 'I realise you didn't know him well, but do you know of anyone who might have wanted to harm him, or can you offer any explanation as to why he was murdered?'

Alfie turned down his bottom lip and shook his head. 'Can't say as I do,' he said. 'I don't even know who his friends were, never mind his enemies. I'd like to help, but really … I can't tell you owt. Sorry.'

'OK,' said Dan. 'If you do think of anything, please get in touch with me, or speak to your family liaison officer.' He handed over his card, feeling certain he'd end up speaking to Alfie Moss again before too long. For now though, they'd taken up enough of his time.

'One more question before we go,' said Zoe. 'Can you confirm where you were yesterday between twelve noon and three p.m.?'

Alfie jerked his head. 'Seriously?'

'Why would you think I'm not being serious?'

'Because, I'm assuming that's when me dad died … was killed,' Alfie said. 'Am I right?'

'You are,' Dan said. 'That's the approximate time of death.'

'So, are you asking because I'm in the frame for his murder?' Alfie was clearly unimpressed. 'Do you honestly think I'd get involved in summat like that?'

Zoe held up her hands. 'Right now, we're checking with everyone and keeping an open mind about who may have been responsible for your father's death. I'm sure you understand. We're confirming the whereabouts of anyone linked to the victim.

It's routine procedure, a way of eliminating people from our inquiries.'

Alfie swung his legs off the footrest and stood up. 'I don't think you've been listening,' he said. 'I wasn't *linked* to the victim. I hardly knew me dad. We were totally out of contact. As for my whereabouts yesterday, I was working.'

'Can you give us the name of your employer so we can verify that?' Zoe said, pencil poised ready to add the details to her notebook.

'I don't have an employer,' Alfie replied. 'I work for meself. I'm a plumber. I was fitting some new radiators for a woman in Hallgate all day yesterday.'

'What's the name of your client?' Zoe persisted. 'Can you give me a contact number so that we can corroborate your whereabouts?'

With a sigh of exasperation, Alfie dug around in his pocket and pulled out his phone.

As Dan watched him scroll through the contacts and read out the client's address and telephone number, one thought was running through his mind. Hallgate was only a few miles from Bainbridge. Was it possible that Alfie Moss had slipped away from his plumbing job to meet Kevin Spriggs at Hollybrook Close? And if he had, what possible reason could he have had for killing him?

Chapter 8

'He didn't tell us much, did he?' said Zoe, as they left Oakwood behind, heading in the direction of Bainbridge. Their destination was Bartlett & Lee, the estate agency that had sold number 4 Hollybrook Close to Ruth Prendergast.

'No, but at least he didn't try to hide his feelings towards Kevin Spriggs,' Dan said. 'Or perhaps I should say, *lack* of feelings. To be frank, I find it hard to fathom how someone can be estranged from one of their parents like that.' He slipped the car into fifth gear as they hit a faster stretch of road. 'I might not live close to my mum and dad anymore, but we're always in touch.'

'Well, that proves they must have been good parents,' Zoe said. 'You love them and consequently you feel a sense of loyalty and duty. Alfie Moss never had a proper relationship with his real dad, did he? He obviously doesn't have the same kind of bond.'

She was right, of course, but the notion of a family rift was still hard for Dan to comprehend. 'What about you, Zoe?' he said, thinking he should try to get to know his colleague better. 'Are you close to your parents?'

Zoe paused before answering, examining her nails as if to

buy some time. 'I suppose I'm the polar opposite to Alfie Moss. Growing up, I was always very close to Mum and Dad. They were lovely, *are* lovely, but they can be … clingy. They had me quite late in life and I'm an only one. I like visiting them and spending time with them, but I'm glad I don't live too close.'

'They live in Leicester, right?'

'Yep. It's not too far, but far enough away that I'm not obliged to go over and see them every week.' She gave him a sideways glance. 'You must think I'm awful.'

'No, not at all,' Dan said, although, in truth, he was a little surprised. 'Everyone's relationship with their parents is different, isn't it?'

They had reached the outskirts of Bainbridge. Dan navigated his way through the traffic, past the town hall and the new library, down towards the car park at the rear of the high street.

'They've been putting pressure on me, actually,' Zoe said. 'Now that they're getting older, they'd like me to move back, closer to home … get a transfer to a Leicestershire division.'

'Bloody hell, Zoe.' Dan was aware he sounded terse and irritable, but he couldn't help himself. 'You've kept that quiet.'

She gave him a dirty look. 'I'm telling you now, aren't I?' she said, annoyed.

He pulled into a parking space, switched off the engine and turned to face her. 'Sorry, I didn't mean to snap. You caught me off guard, that's all. You're a good detective and a valued member of the team. It'd be a shame to lose you.'

The smile she mustered failed to disguise her obvious unease. 'Thanks for saying that. I appreciate it, although I'm not sure DI Blood would agree with you.'

'*I* think she would.' Dan angled his head and scratched the stubble on his chin. 'So? Will you be leaving us then? Are you considering asking for a transfer?'

Zoe released a long, heartfelt sigh. 'I don't want to,' she said, 'but my dad has been quite ill recently. My mum doesn't drive and she's always complaining about having to go to the supermarket on the bus. She says carrying heavy groceries is doing her back in.'

'Fucking hell, Zoe. Is that all she's got to worry about? If it is, there's an easier solution than expecting you to up sticks and move back to Leicester. Hasn't she heard of online shopping?'

'That's exactly what I told her ... well, not the *fucking hell* bit. But I did suggest she get her shopping delivered. I *like* it here in Bainbridge. I might not stay forever, but if I move on, I want it to be on my terms. I don't want to get sucked back into my parents' lives. I love them, but I need my independence.'

'I can relate to that,' Dan said, in an attempt to reassure her. 'Everybody needs their own space.'

'When I went to uni, it was hard to untangle myself from them ... from their overprotectiveness.' Dan watched as she pushed a fingernail in the gap between her front teeth. 'My parents are way too intense, too needy. Now that I've found my freedom, I value it too much to give it up.'

'Then tell them that. Explain that you're happy here and don't want to move back. Just say no, Zoe. Stand up for yourself.'

'You're right, I know you are ... but I feel guilty.'

'You've got nothing to be guilty about.'

'I can't help it. Denying them what they want *makes* me feel guilty.' Her face was a picture of misery. 'And now, having talked to you, I feel disloyal as well. I've probably painted a horribly misleading picture of what they're like. Mum and Dad are nice, kind people. They've just got this habit of smothering me with too much love.'

Dan wasn't sure what to say, what approach to take. 'Like I said ... everyone's relationship with their parents is different,' he said. 'I'm sure they're not bad people, Zoe, but you need to tell them how you're feeling. Seriously.'

As they stepped out of the car into the January chill, Zoe pulled a scarf from her pocket and wrapped it around her neck.

'Dan?' she said. 'Don't tell the boss what I said will you … about the transfer?'

'Don't worry,' he said. 'I'll keep shtum. Now, come on, Zoe. Time to crack on. Let's go and see what the estate agent has to say.'

Chapter 9

Compared to the wintry temperatures on the high street, the office of Bartlett & Lee was stifling. It was one of those trendy, open-plan spaces designed to provoke a sense of positivity and welcoming calm. Just inside the door, a comfortable seating area formed a U-shape around a low, square table, where a selection of glossy brochures was fanned across its glass surface. Dan wondered if this was where the agents sat their clients before revealing their extortionate rates of sales commission.

A tall, elegant woman with spiky hair got up from behind one of the glossy white desks and walked towards them.

'Can I help you?' she said. 'Are you looking to buy or sell?'

'Neither,' Dan replied. 'Sorry to disappoint you. We're here about a property you sold recently. I'm DS Fairfax, and this is my colleague, DC Piper.'

'I see.' The woman managed to maintain a dazzling smile as she inspected their warrant cards. 'I'll do my best to help, if I can. I'm Kim. Kimberley Hart.' The hand she held out was decorated with a large silver ring containing a sparkling gemstone that was the same shade of green as her eyes.

'The property we're interested in is 4 Hollybrook Close,' Dan said, shaking her hand. 'The sale went through about three weeks ago. The buyer was Ruth Prendergast.'

He sensed that Kim was itching with curiosity, but doing her best to hide it.

'Are you in charge here?' Zoe said. 'Do you manage the agency?'

Kim arched an eyebrow. 'I'll have you know that I own Bartlett & Lee. So, technically, darling, I direct it.'

Out of the corner of his eye, Dan could see Zoe bristling at Kim's use of the word *darling*. He knew DC Piper wasn't a fan of such terms of endearment – either using them herself, or being on the receiving end.

'Please, take a seat,' Kim said. 'Can I get you a coffee or tea, or a hot chocolate?'

Dan was tempted by the offer, and Zoe's eyes lit up at the mention of hot chocolate, but he preferred to get on and ask his questions. Faffing about with hot beverages was always a time-waster.

'We'll take a seat, but we're OK for drinks, thanks.'

'I wouldn't mind a hot chocolate,' Zoe said, smiling at Dan defiantly.

Kim waved to her colleague, a youthful designer-clad man who looked far too self-important to make drinks for police officers. Designer-man was saved from the ignominy of doing so by a telephone call. He snatched eagerly at the receiver, leaving Kim no alternative but to trail reluctantly into a back room to prepare the drink herself.

'Has something happened at the property?' she asked, when she reappeared with a steaming mug of hot chocolate, which she placed on the coffee table in front of Zoe. 'Is Ruth Prendergast all right?'

'She's fine,' Dan said. 'There has, however, been an incident at her house. It happened while Mrs Prendergast was at work. As there was no sign of forced entry, we're working on the assumption that someone gained access to the house using a key.'

Kim pushed back her shoulders and lifted her chin. 'Now, hang on a minute ... I hope you're not here because you think someone from Bartlett & Lee has been careless with keys. If that *is* what you're suggesting, you've got a bloody nerve. I can assure you, nothing like that would happen here. We're all highly trained professionals and extremely careful about looking after any keys that come into our possession.'

Dan wondered what kind of training the haughty-looking young man on the phone had received. Certainly nothing in the way of customer service.

'Take it easy,' Zoe said, sipping tentatively at her hot chocolate. 'We haven't accused anyone of doing anything wrong, we simply need to establish what your procedures are. That way, we can determine whether anyone could have inadvertently gained access to the key.'

Kim gave Zoe a withering look. 'We keep them in a safe in the back room,' she said, adopting a steely, don't-mess-with-me tone. 'Whenever a member of staff takes a set of keys, they have to log the details, sign them out and a colleague has to co-sign the entry. It's the same procedure in reverse when the keys are returned.'

'Do you ever give out keys to potential buyers?' asked Dan.

Kimberley executed an exaggerated shake of her head, clearly horrified by his naïvety. 'Anyone wishing to view a property has to make an appointment. They're shown around by the homeowner or, if the property's empty, they're accompanied on the viewing by a member of the Bartlett & Lee team. We meet people at the house, but it's our policy to get there first and wait for them inside. At no point would we ever hand over a set of keys to a viewer.'

'Were all of your team members at work yesterday?' Dan asked, deciding to change tack.

'Yes, we were. It was an admin day. There were no accompanied viewings booked and we were in the office all day. The whole team.'

'When Ruth Prendergast viewed the house on Hollybrook

Close, was it an accompanied viewing, or did she make an appointment with the homeowner?' said Zoe.

'It was an accompanied viewing,' Kim replied. 'And please don't ask me to check because I don't need to. I was the one who met her at the property. The previous owner had already moved out by then.'

'The previous owner …' Dan referred to his notebook. 'That would be Gerald Langton?'

'That's correct.'

'Did he live there alone?'

'Yes, he's a widower.'

'Do you know how many sets of keys he might have had?'

Kim huffed. 'I'm afraid I don't. All I know is, he gave us one set for the viewings. We handed them over to Mrs Prendergast on completion day, once the sale had gone through and Mr Langton's solicitor had confirmed the purchase monies had been received. You'd have to check with Mr Langton directly about any other keys … but he's an old man and not in the best of health. It seems a shame to bother him.'

'Someone will be having a word with him today as part of our investigation,' Dan told her. 'Trust me, Kim, we're not in the habit of bothering people unless it's important. The thing is, when I said there'd been an incident at Ruth Prendergast's house, I was talking about murder.'

Kim's jaw dropped. 'Oh. My. God,' she said, her words crisply enunciated. 'I can't believe something like that would happen in such a nice part of town. Bloody *hell*.'

'Bloody hell, indeed,' said Dan. 'That just about sums things up.'

Chapter 10

While Dan and Zoe were at Bartlett & Lee, Isabel and Lucas were on their way to visit Gerald Langton. The original plan had been to speak to Sophie Tait first, but it turned out she was a college lecturer and would be teaching classes all morning. Instead, they'd brought forward their chat with Gerald Langton and would go to the college later to catch Sophie during her lunch break.

When he climbed into the passenger seat of the car, Lucas was chewing gum. The continuous smacking, salivating sound made Isabel want to scream. There was something about gum chewing that she found infuriating.

'I hope you're going to get rid of that horrible gum before we go in to see Gerald Langton,' she said, as she made a left turn into a leafy avenue less than half a mile from their destination.

Lucas's jaw froze mid-chew and he began to dig around in his pockets, looking for something to use to dispose of the offensive gum. Finding nothing suitable, he wound down the car window and threw it outside.

'Bloody hell, Lucas.' Isabel rolled her eyes. 'That's disgusting.'

He looked puzzled. 'Make your mind up, boss. Either you want me to get rid of it, or you don't.'

'I didn't expect you to throw it out of the window where it'll end up stuck to someone's shoe or pushchair wheel. Honestly! I should fine you for littering.'

'You worry too much,' Lucas said, seemingly untroubled by his actions.

Isabel was tempted to stop the car and make him go back to retrieve the slobbery piece of gum, but she didn't want to be accused of being pernickety. Plus, making a member of your team scrape a piece of chewing gum off the pavement could probably be classed as bullying, even if they *were* responsible for throwing it down in the first place.

She was saved from saying anything further by their arrival at Gerald Langton's new residence – a modern bungalow on a main bus route, situated within a short walk of a small shopping precinct and a doctor's surgery. It was the ideal location for someone looking for convenient access to all of life's essential amenities.

Lucas pressed the doorbell and they stood back and listened to the sound of Westminster chimes echoing inside. Gerald Langton appeared, wearing jeans, an old fleece, and house slippers. After the introductions had been made, he led them into a long, narrow lounge–dining room.

'You'll have to excuse the mess,' he said. 'I still haven't finished unpacking everything from the move.'

He pointed towards a collection of cardboard boxes that were clogging up the dining area. 'It's amazing how much clutter you accumulate when you get to my age. There's a lot less room here, so I'll probably end up sending a load of stuff to the charity shop.'

'I'm sure they'll be grateful,' Isabel said. 'I could do with decluttering my own house. Keeping things tidy isn't easy when you've got a teenager around.'

Gerald Langton chortled. 'I remember those days. My sons are in their fifties now and both of them are extremely house-proud, but that wasn't the case when they were youngsters. Their rooms were a tip. My late wife gave up in the end and let them wallow in their own mess.'

Isabel beamed politely, keen to move beyond this good-mannered chitchat and get down to the important questions.

'We're here today because there's been a serious incident at your old house and we need to ask you some questions.' She and Lucas sat down on a well-worn leather sofa. 'Firstly, I need to establish whether you know a man called Kevin Spriggs?'

'Kevin Spriggs?' The old man squeezed himself into an armchair, being careful not to disturb a black-and-white cat that was curled up in one corner, its head resting on a velvet cushion. 'Spriggs? Mmm … can't say that I do. It's an unusual name, so I'm pretty sure I'd remember if it was someone I'm acquainted with. Why? Has something happened to him?'

'Yes,' Isabel said. 'I'm afraid it has. Yesterday, Kevin Spriggs' body was found at your old house on Hollybrook Close.'

Gerald Langton recoiled. 'Good grief.' Wincing, he placed a gnarly-knuckled hand on his throat and drew air through his teeth. 'That's terrible. Poor man. I assume he died in suspicious circumstances if the police are involved?'

'Yes, Mr Langton. He did.'

Lucas had been gazing through the rear window of the lounge, out to the back, where a garage was located at the end of the driveway. 'Do you own a car, Mr Langton?' he asked.

'Yes,' the old man replied, sounding slightly bewildered by the question. 'I've got a little Corsa. Don't know what I'd do without it these days.'

'May I ask where you have the car serviced?' Lucas said. 'You know … MOT, repairs, that kind of thing?'

'I take it to the Vauxhall dealership,' the old man replied. 'They charge a fortune but, to be frank, I don't have any choice. The car's only two years old, so it's still under warranty and you're obliged to take it somewhere that's Vauxhall-approved.'

'So you've never used the Crown Garage on Wirksworth Road?' Lucas said.

Gerald deliberated for a moment. 'I believe I went there once, but that was donkey's years ago. Why? Is it significant?'

'That's where Kevin Spriggs worked,' Isabel said. 'I think DC Killingworth is trying to establish a possible connection … or rather an explanation as to why Kevin Spriggs was at your old house. The new owner doesn't know him you see, so it's something of a mystery.'

'I only wish I could help,' Mr Langton said.

'We'd like to know who had access to your old house,' said Isabel. 'Did you pass on all the keys in your possession when you sold up?'

'Yes.' The old man sounded very certain.

'Could someone else have had a key and decided to hold on to it?' she persisted. 'Your sons, for instance?'

'My sons?' Mr Langton looked affronted. 'My eldest did have one for emergencies … in case anything ever happened, but he gave it back to me … handed it over when I moved out. My youngest son lives in Germany, so there's no point giving him a key. He's much too far away to be able to respond quickly in a crisis.'

'Does your eldest son live locally?' Lucas asked.

'Yes. Dominic lives over in Cromford, so not too far.'

'And you're sure he doesn't still have it? The key to your old house?'

Mr Langton gave a firm and somewhat impatient shake of the head. 'Definitely not. I told you, he gave it back when I moved out. He has a set of keys to this place now, of course, but everything connected to the old house was passed over at the time of the sale. There were three sets of keys in all. I had one, plus a spare, and Dominic had one.'

Isabel heaved a sigh. This whole conundrum with the keys was like juggling with jelly. Dominic Langton could easily have had another set cut before returning the keys to his father. Then there was the estate agent to consider, and the solicitor. Theoretically, any one of them could have slipped a key into their pocket and gone down to the hardware store to get a replica cut.

'I understand you had a gardener when you lived in Hollybrook Close,' Isabel said, remembering what Ruth Prendergast had told her.

'Yes, Evelyn. She still works for me … does my gardening here, at the bungalow. I've never given her a key though; there's no need. She works outdoors. Doesn't even come inside to use the lavvy. Must have a bladder of steel.'

'Did you have a cleaner at Hollybrook Close?' Isabel said. 'A carer, maybe? Someone who needed a key to get into the house?'

'A *carer*?' Gerald Langton stared quizzically, clearly insulted. 'Do I look as if I can't look after myself? I know I'm old and arthritic, but I manage perfectly well on my own, thank you very much.'

'Sorry, Mr Langton.' Isabel thought of her own father, who was a similar age, and who would also have found such a question impertinent. 'I didn't mean to cause offence, but we need to consider all the possibilities. Was there anyone else, anyone at all, who may have had a key?'

The old man put his head on one side, thinking something through. 'There was someone,' he said, running a hand down the white bristles on his cheek. 'A lady called Katrina Mariner. She used to live next door to me in Hollybrook Close. Whenever I went over to visit my son in Germany, I left her in charge of feeding Henry here.' He reached out and stroked one of the cat's ears.

'And you gave her a key?' Lucas said. 'To let herself in?'

'I could hardly expect her to squeeze through the cat flap, now could I?' He subjected Lucas to a dubious half-frown, making it clear he thought him either naïve or stupid. 'I'd give her a key and she'd let herself in, feed Henry, water the plants and generally keep an eye on the place while I was away. Then, when I came home, she'd return it.'

'Did she ever forget to give the key back?' Isabel said.

A look of distress darted across the old man's face. 'She always made a point of returning it promptly,' he said. 'Except for the last time.'

'And what happened on that occasion?'

'When I got home from Germany, it was to the news that Katrina had died. She'd passed away only a couple of days earlier. Poor old Henry was hungry, but otherwise OK.'

Isabel stifled a grunt. It sounded as though Gerald Langton had been more concerned about the welfare of his cat than the demise of his neighbour.

'In the circumstances,' Gerald continued, 'I didn't like to pester Katrina's daughters about the key. Obviously, they had enough on their plate. They were both very distressed, understandably ... but thinking about it now, I never did get that key back.'

'So they may still have it?'

'It's possible, but it wasn't on a keyring or anything like that. If they did come across it, I don't suppose they'd know what it was a key *to*. The girls cleared the house several months ago, but I didn't like to bother them about it. I imagine it got thrown away with all the other stuff.'

'When you say "the girls", do you mean Katrina Mariner's daughters?' Isabel said.

'Yes, sorry. Stella and Heather. I'm never sure which one's the eldest.'

'They didn't live with their mother then?' said Lucas. 'They're adults?'

'Oh, yes. They left home ages ago, but if you're asking me to guess their ages, I'm afraid you're talking to the wrong bloke. Everyone looks young to me.' Glancing at Lucas, he smiled. 'Even the policemen.'

Isabel wondered whether Gerald Langton was trying to be humorous or deliberately annoying.

'OK, well, thank you for answering our questions,' she said.

'I'm afraid we'll also need to take your fingerprints for elimination purposes. I'll arrange for someone to come round and do that later on today. Is that OK with you?'

'By all means,' he said. 'As long as it doesn't mean I'm a suspect.'

Isabel smiled noncommittally. 'There were some prints at the house that we couldn't identify,' she explained. 'They could have been left by the perpetrator of the crime, or they could be prints you left before you moved out. We need to establish that.'

Gerald Langton bowed his head to show that he understood.

She pulled a card from her pocket. 'If you do remember anything about Kevin Spriggs—'

The old man cut her off. 'I told you, I don't know him. I'm not going to suddenly remember who he is, am I? I know nothing about the bloke. End of.'

'All right, I hear you,' said Isabel. 'But nevertheless, if you think of anything that might help our investigation, please give me a call on that number.' She passed her card to him and turned to Lucas, inclining her head in the direction of the door to indicate it was time to leave.

'Before we go, can I ask you something else, Mr Langton?' Lucas said. 'You said Katrina Mariner died while you were on holiday. Had she been ill? Or was it unexpected?'

'That depends on how you look at it, lad. She had been ill, but nothing physical. Katrina suffered with bouts of depression. She'd be fine for months, then she'd suddenly get a visit from the black dog. She'd been very down in the weeks running up to her death, so I don't suppose it was totally unexpected, but her daughters were devastated nonetheless. If you're planning to talk to them about the missing key, please tread carefully. You see, Katrina Mariner died from an overdose. She took her own life.'

Chapter 11

The further education college where Sophie Tait worked was a classic example of brutalist architecture. Cold and ugly, its harsh and angular concrete blocks clashed starkly with the impressive entrance block, which had been added more recently. Modern chrome and coloured glass were juxtaposed against the cold, grey walls of the older building. It was a messy mismatch of styles that Isabel found jarring.

She and Lucas marched through the main doors into a vast atrium that was filled with light and the echoing thrum of student voices. As they signed the visitor book, the receptionist rang through to Sophie Tait's office, summoning her to meet them.

While they waited, Isabel picked up a copy of the prospectus and flicked through its glossy pages. The college offered courses on a diverse range of subjects. Animal care, childcare, carpentry and construction. Hairdressing and holistic therapies. There was also a work-based apprenticeship programme linked to various vocational qualifications. Isabel hoped Ellie would study A levels and then go on to university, but she wasn't the type of mother to impose her views, especially when it came to life-shaping decisions. Isabel had seen too many parents try to live vicariously through their children, moulding and pressurising them into pursuing their own frustrated ambitions, rather than letting their kids follow their own hearts. She had no intention of doing that with Ellie. If she decided to opt for the whole university thing, then great. If not, Isabel would support whatever choice her daughter made.

When Sophie Tait hurried towards them a couple of minutes later, Isabel thought how young she looked. Skinny and fresh-faced, with shiny long blonde hair, the young woman could easily have passed for one of the students.

'I've booked us a room,' Sophie said, directing them across the atrium, striding away at a speed that was hard to keep up with.

'I hope you don't mind talking in here,' she said, as she opened the door to a small tutorial room. 'It's a bit of a squeeze for three of us. I did think about taking you to the coffee lounge, but it's rammed in there at this time of day, and I'd rather we talk in private.'

'This is absolutely fine,' Isabel said, the mention of coffee making her mouth water.

'Is it likely to take long?' Sophie said. 'Only I have to teach another class in forty minutes.'

'Don't worry, we'll be finished in plenty of time for your next class,' Isabel reassured her. 'What do you teach?'

'I'm a hair and beauty lecturer. In all honesty I'd rather still be hairdressing, but the pay's better here ... well, not great, but at least I'm employed.'

'Did you run your own business before, then?' said Isabel. 'When you were a hairdresser?'

'Kind of ... I used to rent a chair in one of the local salons. I enjoyed the work, but I opted for employment and a regular paycheque so that I could get a mortgage and buy a house.' She twirled a hand. 'So, here I am, an employed lecturer and bored out of my skull most of the time ... but don't tell the principal I said that.'

They sat on moulded plastic chairs at a small grey table. The partition wall that separated them from the main corridor had a pane of thick, frosted glass that provided both privacy and light. From somewhere beyond the opposite side of the small space, Isabel could hear the droning hum of students, their voices vibrating through the walls from the nearby refectory.

'We know you were the victim of an assault a couple of years ago,' Isabel began. 'We'd like you to talk us through what happened that evening.'

Sophie sighed. 'Do I have to?' she said. 'I gave a full statement at the time. Can't you read that?'

'We've already read your statement,' Isabel said. 'But we're trying to learn as much as we can about the perpetrator, Kevin Spriggs. I appreciate it's upsetting to talk about, and I'm sure you'd prefer to leave the experience firmly in the past, but we're investigating another crime and we need to know whether it might be connected.'

'Has he done it again? To someone else?' Sophie's face flushed red, as though she was about to cry.

'No, as far as we're aware, Kevin Spriggs hasn't assaulted anyone else, but a crime has been committed against him.' Isabel decided to hold back any further information until Sophie Tait had answered their questions.

'Serves the bastard right,' Sophie said. 'Whatever's happened to him, I'm sure he had it coming.'

Isabel glanced over at Lucas, who had flipped open his notebook, pen at the ready.

'Can you tell us what happened when Kevin Spriggs assaulted you, Miss Tait?' he said, his voice surprisingly soft and gently persuasive.

Sophie glanced at her watch and then leaned forward, placing her elbows on the table top.

'I was out in Bainbridge with some mates ... girlfriends. It was a girls' night out. We'd all had a fair bit to drink, but we weren't hammered or anything like that.'

'So just tipsy,' Isabel said. 'Merry?'

'Yeah, merry. That's a good way to describe it, actually. We'd had such a great night … never stopped laughing from the minute we met up in the first pub. There were four of us, friends I've known since school. We had an absolutely brilliant time.'

'So when did it all go wrong?' Lucas said. 'What happened?'

Sophie scoffed, self-mockingly. 'I was a stupid fucking idiot, that's what happened.' She leaned back and pulled her arms off the table so that she could rest her hands in her lap.

'It was a Friday night, so we discussed going on to a club, but two of us had work the next day, and in the end we decided to catch a late bus home.' She picked at her nails nervously. 'At the time, I lived on the other side of town to my friends. We all waited together, and their bus pulled in first. They offered to wait for the next one, rather than leaving me on my own, but I told them not to be daft. *Nothing's going to happen*, I said. It probably wouldn't have either, if I'd been patient.'

'What do you mean by that?' Lucas said.

'It was obvious my bus was running late,' Sophie continued. 'And I was hungry … you know what it's like when you've had a drink … you suddenly get the munchies, don't you?'

Tapping his pen against his cheek, Lucas smiled. 'Yep,' he said. 'I've made some of the worst takeaway decisions of my life when I've had a drink. The only time I ever fancy a kebab is when I'm pi—'

Isabel cut him off with a look.

'When I'm inebriated,' Lucas concluded. 'So, did you go and get something to eat?'

'There was a pizza place right next to the bus stop, and the smell was really getting to me. I know it was stupid, but I thought I could go in, buy a couple of slices of pizza and watch for the bus coming along the road. As I went inside, there was this bloke. He was sitting on the pavement, leaning his head against the wall. It looked like he was homeless, but he didn't ask for money.'

There was a sudden surge of voices from the other side of the partition, laughter and heckling. It sounded like one of the students was being given a hard time. Sophie waited for the noise to die down before continuing.

'While I was waiting for my pizza, I saw the bus come sailing along,' she said. 'There was no one else at the bus stop, and it hurtled right past. I think the driver was giving it some welly to try and make up time.

'Anyway, knowing that I'd missed my last bus really sobered me up. I came out of the takeaway shop carrying my pizza box, and gave it to the homeless man. I'd totally lost my appetite. The idea of walking through town on my own to the taxi rank made me really frigging nervous, but then I remembered there was a little taxi office near the bus stop, down a side alley. It was a grubby sort of place, but at that time of night, I thought it'd be safer than wandering the streets on my own.'

'And that's where you encountered Kevin Spriggs?' Lucas was leaning forward, hanging on to her every word.

'I bumped into him in the alley. I was still about a hundred yards from the taxi office, and he blocked my way. He was obviously pissed. He grabbed hold of me and asked me to go for a drink with him. He said he knew somewhere that served after hours. I told him to sod off and tried to push past him, but he grabbed hold of my arm and began to pull me down the alleyway. He told me I was being unfriendly, that I was a stuck-up bitch. God, I was scared. I started to scream, and that's when he put his hand over my mouth. He smelt of beer and sweat and I knew I was in trouble.'

None of this was news to Isabel. She'd read the case file and was already familiar with Sophie's story, but nevertheless, she empathised. It was the kind of experience that could scar you for life.

'I was terrified,' Sophie continued. 'I don't know what I'd have done if the homeless guy hadn't come to my rescue. He appeared from nowhere, grabbed Kevin Spriggs by the neck and pulled him off me. Then he threw him face-first against a wall, forced his hands behind his back and told me to call the police.'

'Bloody hell,' Lucas said. 'That pizza you gave him must have been some kind of super food.'

Isabel cringed at his tactlessness, but Sophie didn't seem to have noticed. 'I don't think he'd got around to eating the pizza,' she said. 'Turns out the guy was ex-Army. He knew how to handle himself. He'd seen me head down the alley and decided to look out for me.'

'Thank goodness he did,' said Isabel. 'Things could have turned out very differently otherwise.'

'As I understand it,' Lucas said, 'Kevin Spriggs was arrested and charged with assault, and he pleaded guilty.'

'Yes, that's it in a nutshell. It all sounds very simple and straightforward when you say it like that … as if everything was sorted out and packed away in a neat little box and tied up with a ribbon … but that's not how it felt at the time.'

Sophie gathered up her hair and pulled it forward, over her left shoulder. 'I still have nightmares about it. I live in dread of running into Kevin Spriggs. I don't know what I'd do if I saw him again. There's a part of me that would want to smack him hard across his horrible, weaselly little face, but the truth is, I'd probably run as fast as I could in the opposite direction.'

'Well you won't have to worry about that ever again,' Isabel said. 'Kevin Spriggs is dead. Someone murdered him, and we're trying to find out who's responsible.'

Sophie pulled in a lungful of air and then let it out slowly, her slender body sagging like a deflated balloon. The way her expression wavered between shock and relief suggested to Isabel that she'd been unaware of Kevin Spriggs' death, and was therefore unlikely to have been involved in its execution. But could one of Sophie's friends or a family member have had something to do with the murder? And what about the mysterious homeless man? Was he some sort of vigilante Jack Reacher type, a character who wandered the streets inflicting violence, revenging those who'd been wronged?

'I'm afraid I need to ask you whether anyone you know might have been involved in Kevin Spriggs' murder,' Isabel said.

'Say that again.' Sophie leaned forward, incredulous. 'Anyone that *I* know? Like who?'

'Perhaps a member of your family. Or someone who was badly affected by what happened to you.'

Sophie rubbed her hands up and down her face. 'I can't believe you're asking me that question,' she said. 'My family would never do anything like that. *Never.* We're not those kind of people. I'll admit my dad was pretty fucking furious when it happened, but he would never contemplate that kind of … retribution. My family, my friends … none of them would take the law into their own hands.'

'I'm sure you understand that we have to ask, as part of our investigation,' Isabel said. 'We also need you to confirm where you were yesterday afternoon, and we may need to speak to your parents as well.'

'Well, I can save you the bother,' Sophie said. She was annoyed now, fidgeting in her chair. 'My parents are away on a Caribbean cruise. They flew out over a week ago and won't be back for a few days.'

That ruled them out then. Two names that could be crossed off the growing list of possibles.

'And you?' Isabel asked. 'Where were you between noon and three p.m. yesterday?'

'Here, in the training salon.' Sophie sounded angry. 'You're welcome to check with my colleagues or any of the students I was supervising.'

Isabel would get someone to do exactly that. She couldn't afford to take anyone at their word.

'Do you have any brothers, or cousins or friends who might have decided to harm Kevin Spriggs?' she asked.

'I'm sure they would all have *liked* to,' Sophie replied. 'But none of them would. It's not who we are.'

Isabel shifted in her seat, steeling herself to change tack. To prepare for this interview, she'd scrutinised the case file on the assault, reading through Kevin Spriggs' account of the incident, as well as Sophie Tait's. Spriggs' statement had been contrite, and had presented a much more benign version of events.

Isabel cleared her throat. 'Although Kevin Spriggs admitted to the assault, his account of the incident was slightly different to the one outlined in your statement.'

Sophie folded her arms.

'I believe he also offered you an apology,' Isabel continued. 'He said he was drunk and feeling lonely and all he wanted was for you to go to the pub with him. According to his statement, he had no intention of harming you … He alleged he was only looking for company.'

'He would say that, wouldn't he?' Sophie's words were sharp and clipped. 'And, yes, he did apologise … that was something, I suppose … but it didn't excuse what he did.'

Isabel squirmed inwardly, suppressing a desire to justify her line of questioning.

'Kevin Spriggs made me feel threatened,' Sophie added. 'He put his hands on me and acted aggressively. Regardless of his intentions, that was assault. Wasn't it?'

'Certainly,' Isabel replied. 'His actions put you in fear of physical harm. There's no doubt he assaulted you. He pleaded guilty to the charge himself.'

'So why are we talking about this?' Sophie asked. 'It's like you don't believe me.'

'I don't mean to give that impression,' Isabel replied. 'I'm simply trying to establish whether Kevin Spriggs' behaviour was determined by a flawed personality, or an addiction to alcohol, or something else. Do you have a view on that?'

Sophie sneered. 'No, I don't,' she said. 'I don't care what caused him to act the way he did. All I know …' she prodded her breastbone with an index finger '… is that he attacked me, and if someone hadn't come to my rescue, I don't know what might have happened.'

'The homeless guy,' Lucas said. 'Do you think *he* could have bumped into Kevin Spriggs again and decided to take action against him?'

Mentally, Isabel awarded Lucas ten out of ten for asking the question, but the idea of a homeless man having access to the house on Hollybrook Close seemed far too unlikely to make it a real possibility.

'If you'd bothered to check properly, you'd know that the homeless man had a name,' Sophie said. 'He was called Andrew Nelson. It's the reason I know he couldn't possibly have killed Kevin Spriggs.'

'And why's that?' said Lucas.

'Because six months ago I read in the Bainbridge News that the body of a homeless man had been found in the high street, dead from a drug overdose. It was Andrew Nelson, the man who saved my neck. So, *detectives*, unless you believe in avenging ghosts, I'm sure you'll agree he couldn't possibly have been involved. Now, if you don't mind, I need to leave for my lecture.'

Chapter 12

'We should have known about Andrew Nelson,' Isabel said, as she and Lucas trudged across the college car park, back towards her Toyota. 'Why didn't anyone pick up on it? Sophie Tait made us look like a pair of bloody idiots in there.'

A weather front was coming in and the wind was getting up. It whistled around her ears, making her wish she'd worn her old padded jacket, the one with the hood, instead of her new coat, which was woollen and slightly itchy.

'Let's head straight back to the station,' Isabel said, when they reached the car. 'I want to get an update from Dan and Zoe.'

The outdoor temperature plummeted in the short time it took for them to drive back to the office. The cold spell had been forecast but, even so, Isabel wasn't happy. If it continued, it could bring snow in the north of the county, which would rule out the possibility of a trip to the Peak District. With hindsight, January probably hadn't been the best month for her dad to visit.

The inside of the CID room wasn't much warmer. There were a few pockets of tepid air next to the radiators, but the majority of the open-plan office was uncomfortably and shiver-inducingly cold.

Dan and Zoe were back already, Dan sitting with his legs stretched out, parallel to the edge of his desk. He held a mug in one hand and a peeled banana in the other. Zoe's fingers were flying over her keyboard, pausing only occasionally to extract a piece of low-calorie popcorn from the large bag that lay open on her desk. A week earlier, the DC had announced that her new year's resolution was to lose weight, and the salted and rather smelly popcorn now seemed to be her snack of choice.

Lucas retreated to his desk, and Isabel pulled out a chair.

'Bloody hell,' Lucas said, rubbing his upper arms. 'It's like a morgue in here. Any chance of turning the heating up?'

Isabel knew only too well that tinkering with the ancient thermostat was futile, so she chose to ignore Lucas's remark. Instead, she addressed Dan. 'How did it go with the victim's son? Do you think he could be involved?'

Dan sat up, put down his mug and folded the now empty banana skin. 'He certainly wasn't very upset. Then again, he hardly knew Spriggs. Alfie was only four when his parents split up, and it sounds like the marriage was a catalogue of domestic violence incidents.'

'Since then,' Zoe added, 'contact between Alfie Moss and the victim has been minimal.'

'How minimal?'

'Almost non-existent,' said Dan. 'Alfie ran into his father a couple of times when he was a kid, but the meetings were accidental. He didn't spend any time with his dad growing up. A while back, Kevin Spriggs sent Alfie a friend request on Facebook, and a couple of DMs. He accepted the friend request, but didn't reply to the messages.'

'I've been looking at Kevin Spriggs' Facebook account,' Zoe said, as she crunched on a piece of popcorn.

What is it with my team and their noisy eating habits? Isabel thought. *Why do they always have to be munching on something?*

'OK, Zoe,' Isabel said. 'When you've finished eating, perhaps you can tell us what you've found.'

Embarrassed, Zoe executed a couple of hefty chews and swallowed the popcorn. After wiping her mouth, she reached for a water bottle and took a swig before continuing.

'Kevin Spriggs has forty-eight friends on Facebook. Based on the tags in the photos, most of them are drinking buddies, but there are some work colleagues as well. Spriggs has only added two family members – one is a brother who lives in Leeds, and the other is Alfie Moss.'

'Are you saying Kevin Spriggs tagged Alfie Moss in the "family and relationships" bit of his profile?' Lucas said.

'Yes, it's a bit rich, isn't it?' Zoe said. 'Claiming him as his son on social media when he had nothing to do with his upbringing.' She stretched a furtive hand towards the bag of popcorn, but withdrew it silently as Isabel narrowed her eyes.

'Has anyone tracked down the brother in Leeds?' Isabel said. 'If not, we'll need to arrange for an officer from West Yorkshire Police to let him know what's happened, before the news ends up plastered all over social media.'

'I'll sort that,' Lucas said. 'Leave it with me.'

'Ask the FLO to pay him a visit as well,' Isabel said. 'We need to find out if the siblings were close, and what the brother can tell us in the way of background information.'

She turned to Zoe. 'The photos on Facebook, the ones with his drinking buddies, I assume they were taken in pubs? Do we know which ones?'

'There's one that features a lot,' Zoe said. 'The Sheaf of Corn. It must have been his local. It's near the marketplace. A traditional, real-ale type of pub, quite rough and ready.'

Lucas smirked. 'How would you know, Zoe? You never go in pubs.'

'I've never been to the moon, but that doesn't mean I don't know anything about it. Anyway, haven't you heard of

Tripadvisor?' Zoe raised a hand. 'No, don't answer that. It was a stupid question. I doubt you've ever been on Tripadvisor in your life. As long as a pub sells beer, I don't suppose you care what the place is like, do you?'

Isabel laughed. 'That's put you in your place, Lucas. And being as you're so concerned about Zoe's lack of knowledge of the local pubs, you can take her along with you this evening when you go to talk to the landlord and customers of the Sheaf of Corn.'

'You're joking.' Lucas rolled his eyes sulkily. 'It's Thursday, boss. There won't be many people out on a freezing cold Thursday night in January.'

'The regulars will be there,' said Dan. 'The hardened drinkers. They're the ones who're likely to have been Kevin Spriggs' mates.'

'Exactly,' Isabel said. 'Hopefully they'll be able to give us an insight into his personality. Who knows, one of them might turn out to be a suspect.'

'I suppose a pint while I'm there is out of the question?'

'Yes, Lucas, I'm afraid it is. Unless, of course, it's a pint of lemonade.'

The DC took a breath, closed his lips and exhaled, his lips flapping like a horse's. 'Pfft! Never touch the stuff. I'd rather go without than drink fizzy pop.'

Isabel turned to Dan. 'I'd like you to have a word with Gerald Langton's gardener. Ruth Prendergast gave us a business card for her, so the contact details should be on file. See if she knew the victim, and ask whether she ever had a key to the house. Mr Langton says not, but it's worth double-checking.'

'What about the sisters?' Lucas said. 'The Mariners – the ones whose mother used to feed Mr Langton's cat? Is it worth having a word with them?'

'I'm not sure they'll be able to tell us anything useful,' said Isabel, 'but one of us should talk to them. I'm going back to Hollybrook Close tomorrow to take another look at the crime scene and get a feel for the lie of the land. See if you can get hold of the sisters, please, Lucas. Arrange for one or both of them to meet me at their mother's house in the morning. In theory, the key that Katrina Mariner had is the only one that's unaccounted for, so we should follow it up.'

'We'll press on then,' said Dan. 'Make some inroads into the investigation.'

'Thanks, Dan,' Isabel said. 'I'll leave you to it.'

'Where are you going then, boss?' said Lucas.

Cheeky sod, she thought. Lucas really knew how to push his luck.

'As you may recall, DC Killingworth, I was supposed to be on leave this week. My dad's visiting, so I'm going to finish early today and spend some time with him … if that's all right with you?'

Her sarcasm was lost on Lucas. 'Righto,' he replied. 'You'll be in tomorrow though?'

'I will,' she said. 'Make sure you're all here at nine o'clock on the dot for the next briefing.'

Chapter 13

As soon as DI Blood had left the office, Lucas announced he was going to grab a late lunch from the small canteen located on the ground floor of the station.

Zoe glanced over at Dan. 'I'll hold the fort if you want to get something as well,' she said.

'No, you're all right,' he replied. 'I've just had some fruit. I'll get something else later.'

He had retrieved the gardener's business card from the file, and was turning it around in his fingers. A mobile number was printed in dark-green lettering on the front, along with a name, Evelyn Merigold. The dot above the 'i' in the surname had been replaced with a small, orange stylised flower, and the same flower design appeared on the reverse in a repeating pattern.

Dan stopped twirling the card and placed it, face up, on his desk. Picking up his phone, he dialled the number and waited, half expecting to reach a voicemail message, but the call was answered on the second ring.

Introducing himself, Dan asked whether Evelyn Merigold was free to talk to him about an incident at Gerald Langton's old house.

'Certainly, although I'm not sure how I'll be able to help.' Her accent was local, but not broad, her smooth middle-class tones mingling with a generous dollop of Derbyshire. 'I'm working in the Memorial Park on Bainbridge high street right now. I'm due a break in a quarter of an hour. Why don't you come and find me in the park and we can share a flask of tea?'

It was a more than reasonable offer, certainly the best Dan was likely to get that day.

'OK,' he said. 'I'll see you shortly.'

The memorial park was only a few minutes' walk from the station. Dan found Evelyn Merigold in the southern end, near to the bandstand. She was pruning a holly bush that was encroaching the main pathway through the park.

She was younger than Dan had expected – thirty, possibly a little older – and she looked nothing like a gardener. Her movements were graceful, and there was a delicate beauty in the smile she gave him.

'There's a seat over there.' She indicated a long, wooden bench next to an empty flower bed. 'Shall we sit down and talk?'

Dan perched on the edge of the bench, worried about bird droppings or worse, but Evelyn Merigold leaned back, unconcerned. Perhaps her easy-going attitude was down to the clothes she wore – faded jeans and an old parka that had seen better days. *When you spend all your days digging and clipping and chopping, I don't suppose you're bothered what you look like,* Dan thought. *Then again, Evelyn Merigold was the kind of woman who'd look good wearing a potato sack.*

He watched her open a flask and pour milky tea into a plastic cup, which she handed to him.

'It's got sugar in it. I hope that's OK.'

'Perfect. Exactly how I like it,' Dan replied.

'So, what's all this about Gerald Langton's old place? You said there'd been an incident?'

'A man's body was found at the house yesterday,' Dan explained. 'There was no sign of a break-in, so we're working on the assumption he was invited to the house or had access to it. We're trying to trace anyone who might have had a key to the property.'

Realising what he was implying, Evelyn stared at him questioningly.

'You mean *me*?' She gave a huff of laughter. 'You're barking up the wrong tree if you think Gerald Langton ever gave me a key. He only ever invited me into the house once.'

'Barking up the wrong tree?' Dan said. 'Is that a gardening pun?'

She smiled. 'I'd say it's more of a tree surgeon's pun.'

Steam was rising from the surface of Dan's tea, spiralling up into the cold afternoon air. 'I'm told you're still working for Gerald Langton, doing the gardening at his new house?'

She nodded.

'What can you tell me about him? What kind of bloke is he?'

Evelyn pulled at a thread on her jeans. 'He's a nice enough old guy, quite particular sometimes. He engaged me about three years ago. Before that he'd done all the gardening himself, but his arthritis was troubling him and he decided to hire someone instead. I can't say I know him well … I go round and mow his lawn and weed his garden. He pays me by the hour, so there's never much time for small talk.'

'If you've been working for him for three years, you must know something about him,' Dan insisted.

'Honestly, I know hardly anything about the man.' She turned up a palm. 'He's a retired pharmacist, I believe, and he has a couple of sons … one lives locally, the other in Germany. There's not much else I can say. If you were to ask me about Mr Langton's Australian tree fern, or the state of the cherry tree in his new front garden, I'd be able to give you a lot more information.'

'Fair enough,' Dan said. He sipped his drink, which had the odd, tinny flavour that tea always acquires when kept in a flask. 'How about Kevin Spriggs? What can you tell me about him?'

Evelyn leaned back and lifted her face to the watery, winter sun, which was doing its best to find a way through the clouds.

'Spriggs, you say? Never heard of him. The only sprigs I'm familiar with right now are the sprigs of holly that are trying to prickle me to death.' She pointed towards the half-pruned holly bush. 'This Kevin Spriggs? Is that the bloke whose body was found at the house?'

'Yes.' Dan drained his tea and handed back the empty cup. He pulled his phone from his pocket and found one of the photographs Zoe had taken from Facebook and circulated to the team. 'That's him. Do you recognise him?'

Evelyn Merigold stared at the image for several seconds before shaking her head. 'No, sorry.'

'You're sure you never saw this man anywhere near Hollybrook Close while you were working there? Perhaps paying a visit to Gerald Langton?'

'No. He was never at Mr Langton's house while I was there.' She paused. 'Look, I hope you don't mind me saying this, but if this man was killed because he was in some kind of trouble, I think it's highly unlikely Mr Langton would have known him. Gerald's an easy-going old guy who enjoys the quiet life. I don't think he'd get mixed up with someone like that.' She nodded towards the photograph on Dan's phone.

'Like what?' Dan said. 'What makes you think Kevin Spriggs was in trouble? You said you didn't know him?'

'I don't,' Evelyn replied. 'But it seems obvious, doesn't it? If the man's body has turned up and you're investigating, it's logical to assume he was in some sort of trouble … drugs, petty crime … I don't know. You're the detective.'

Dan leaned forward, twisting his head back in her direction. 'To be honest, as a detective, I'm slightly baffled by your sudden defence of Gerald Langton. You're making a real point of telling me he wouldn't be involved with anyone connected to any criminality, and yet only a few minutes ago, you said you hardly knew the guy. I hope you're not withholding information from me, Ms Merigold.'

'Not at all,' she said, throwing what remained of her tea onto the bare flower bed and screwing the top back onto the flask. 'If I'm guilty of anything, it's jumping to conclusions. You're right, I don't know Gerald Langton well enough to make any kind of assessment as to who his friends might be. And anyway, for all I know, the dead man is probably the innocent party in all this, the victim of a horrible crime. Again, I've made an assumption and, for that, I apologise. I can only reiterate what I've already told you … I don't know Kevin Spriggs, and I never saw him visit Gerald Langton's house. Those are the facts, detective. Believe them, or believe them not.'

Dan stood up and brushed at the seat of his trousers. 'OK. Well, thank you for the information and the tea. I'll let you finish your pruning before it gets dark. If I need to speak to you again, I'll be in touch.'

Chapter 14

When she arrived home, Isabel was fizzing with renewed energy and a sense of excitement. It had been agreed that Donald and Fabien would come over to the house at four o'clock. Ellie would be home from school by then, and Kate would join them later for dinner.

Nathan had offered to cook, and he was already busy prepping the veg when Isabel walked into the kitchen.

'You managed to finish work early then?' he said.

'Yes, although it's left me feeling like a kid playing truant. Guilty and a bit scared.'

'Scared? Of what?'

'Missing something,' Isabel said. 'Not being there, in the thick of it.'

'Stop worrying,' Nathan said. 'Knowing how to delegate is all part of being a DI.'

She smiled. 'What's for dinner?'

'French onion soup to start …'

'Nice. Very appropriate.'

'Quite honestly, I chose it less for its appropriateness and more for the fact that it's easy to make. Plus, it's freezing out there, and I thought a nice bowl of soup would warm everyone up.'

'What about the main course?'

'Chicken breasts stuffed with chunks of Hartington Stilton, served with a cream, brandy and mushroom sauce and a medley of potatoes and vegetables.'

'Mmm ... sounds divine,' Isabel said. 'Much better than they'd have got if I'd been cooking.'

'Did you bring a pudding?' said Nathan.

'Bollocks! I forgot.'

'Isabel.' He shook his head, exasperated. 'You only had to do one thing.'

'I know, I *know*. It's been a busy day. Don't worry, I'll nip out now and go to the Co-op. Their cheesecakes are lovely.'

In the dessert aisle at the supermarket she grabbed two large raspberry cheesecakes and a large carton of double cream. That should be more than enough to feed everyone.

As she approached the self-service checkout, she caught sight of a familiar figure at the end till. Zoe. The DC was scanning a pack of sandwiches and a large bag of crisps. Isabel scanned her own items, swiped her membership and debit cards and caught up with Zoe as she was walking out of the store.

'Hi, Zoe,' she said. 'Has Lucas sent you out for sarnies?'

Zoe looked startled, perhaps surprised at encountering her boss in a non-work situation.

'Lucas ate in the canteen,' she said. 'I didn't want much, so I thought I'd pop out for some fresh air and grab a sandwich at the same time.'

'And snacks, I see.' Isabel looked down at the carrier bag, where an enormous pack of gourmet crisps was visible. 'Given up on the diet, have you?'

'Not given up exactly,' she said, looking annoyed. 'Just having a break. Plus, I'm working tonight, aren't I? It's not easy sticking to a diet regime when you have to work long hours.'

There was more than a hint of criticism in her words. 'Yeah, sorry about that,' Isabel said, feeling like the worst boss in Bainbridge. 'And … hey, what you eat is none of my business. Apologies if I seemed rude. I was only making conversation.'

'Don't worry about it.' Zoe sighed. 'It's me who's tetchy. I'm always bad-tempered when I'm hungry.'

'I'm the same,' Isabel said. 'Although I'm going to be eating like a queen tonight. Nathan's cooking a special meal for my dad. He didn't have time to make a dessert, so I've been sent out for cheesecake.' She held up her own carrier bag. 'I'd better be getting back. Dad will be arriving soon.'

'Have a nice evening,' Zoe said.

'Thanks. I hope your visit to the Sheaf of Corn proves useful. Don't let Lucas give you any grief.'

'Aww, Lucas is all right,' Zoe replied. 'It's just banter.'

'He does tend to think he's funny,' Isabel said, a small crease appearing between her eyebrows.

'He is. Sometimes.'

'He's also very competitive,' Isabel said. 'So don't let him give you a hard time.'

Zoe paused before replying. 'It's not a problem,' she said. 'Lucas is cool. If there's anyone who gives me a hard time, it's you, boss.'

And with that, Zoe hitched her shopping bag onto her arm and walked away in the direction of the police station, leaving Isabel no opportunity to respond.

Donald and Fabien arrived at four o'clock on the dot. As Isabel hurried to answer their knock, she held on to Nell's collar, urging her to stop barking. The dog chose to ignore the command.

'Issy.' Her father towered over her on the doorstep. He was holding a large bunch of flowers: pink roses, sea holly and white lilies, surrounded by branches of eucalyptus leaves and other exotic foliage. Fabien stood behind him, clutching a bottle of red wine and a box of chocolates.

'Dad!' She breathed in the scent of lilies as she leaned in to kiss his cheek. 'Are these for me?' She touched the bouquet.

'Of course. Beautiful flowers for my beautiful girl.'

The dog was circling at their feet, barking wildly.

'And wine and chocolates too,' Isabel said, smiling at Fabien. 'I'm sorry about the dog. She always does this when we have visitors. She'll settle down in a minute once you're inside.'

The men followed her through the living room and into the dining end of the kitchen, where Nathan and Ellie were waiting.

'Dad, Fabien, this is Nathan and Ellie.'

The men shook hands, and her dad gave Ellie a long, affectionate hug. 'I can't tell you how good it is to meet you at last,' he said.

There was a pause, no one quite knowing what to say. Nell saved the day. She gave a final, short bark before giving in to her curiosity and going over to sniff Donald's shoes.

'And what is your name, little dog?' he said, bending down to pat the terrier's head.

'This is Nell,' Ellie replied. 'I told you about her on FaceTime.'

'I didn't know you had a dog,' Fabien said.

'We've only had her for a month,' Ellie told him. 'We got her from the rescue centre.'

'You're not allergic to dogs are you?' Isabel said, wondering whether she would need to lock Nell in another room.

'No, not at all,' replied Fabien. 'I like dogs very much. I have one of my own.'

That was something, then. At least they had that in common.

Together, the five of them drifted into the garden room at the back of the house, where the log burner was lit and soft lighting was making the room look cosy and welcoming. As they sat down, Nell followed them in and settled in front of the fire, drawn by its glowing warmth.

'There must have been a lot of dogs to choose from,' Donald said. 'Why this one?'

'I don't know … I thought she was cute,' Ellie said. 'Plus, her owner had died and she seemed kind of sad. She was sitting with a fluffy toy, looking sort of miserable? Then, when she saw me, she stood up and brought it over to me.'

'I notice her brows are very white,' Fabien said. 'Here on her face.' He pointed to the area above the dog's eyes.

'Yes, she's eight, so quite old. Dad says that every year of a dog's life is the equivalent of seven human years, which makes Nell roughly the same age as Mum.'

It was the right thing to say because it made everyone laugh and broke the tension in the room.

'My brows are starting to go white as well,' Isabel said, with a wink. 'But it's nothing an eyebrow pencil can't fix.'

'Why didn't you get a puppy?' Fabien said. Nell seemed to have taken a liking to him. She had sidled up to him and was leaning against his trouser leg. Isabel noticed that her brother had reached down and was gently stroking the dog's ear.

'Ellie would have preferred a puppy, but I wasn't keen,' she said. 'We compromised and got an adult dog instead. Nell was entirely Ellie's choice.'

'I looked on the website before we went and most of the younger dogs were already reserved,' Ellie explained. 'No one seemed interested in the older dogs, which I thought was really unfair. Nell's half Patterdale terrier and half Jack Russell, so her life expectancy is somewhere between twelve and sixteen years. It wasn't her fault her previous owner had died. I thought she deserved a second chance.'

'Whoever owned her before must have loved her to bits,' Nathan said. 'She's a very affectionate little dog, although she does sound pretty fierce when you first meet her.'

The conversation flowed naturally after that. Donald regaled them with his views on the Feathers Hotel – which he thought was surprisingly swish – and reported that he and Fabien had already been shopping in Bainbridge.

'The town's improved a lot since the Seventies,' he said. 'I was quite impressed, especially with the selection of coffee shops on offer. Bainbridge certainly seems to have embraced café culture. When I was here last, I recall there was only one café – a greasy spoon at the top of the high street.'

Isabel giggled. 'Josie's Café,' she said. 'I remember it well. I used to go there on Saturday mornings with my friends for strawberry milkshakes. They used to serve instant coffee, and tea from a huge metal teapot. Looking back, it was an awful place, but I remember feeling really sad when it closed down.'

'It is my belief,' said Fabien, 'that we remember these things with a sense of …' he paused, as if searching in his head for the right word '… nostalgia. It's easy to have fond memories of the things that happened a long time ago, but time can play tricks with us. We do not always see things clearly, in their true light.'

It was a long and rather unnecessary speech, and Isabel got the distinct impression her brother was referring to far more than Josie's Café. What point was he trying to make, exactly?

Fabien was proving to be enigmatic. This evening he seemed subdued. Was he shy perhaps? Did he feel like an interloper here in Bainbridge, a town that was familiar to everyone in the family except himself? Isabel thought she should make a special effort this evening, sit next to him at dinner and encourage him to come out of his shell. After all, this was her chance to get to know her brother as well as reacquaint herself with her dad.

Isabel had asked Ellie and Kate not to mention the fact that their grandfather had been married, bigamously, to Isabel's mum. She didn't like having to involve them in a cover-up, but with Fabien unaware of the family secret, she'd had little choice. At some point during the evening she would get her dad on his own and find out when he was going to tell Fabien the truth. After all, what better time than now, when father and son were together, in Bainbridge, and had plenty of time on their hands?

They ate dinner in the proper dining room at the front of the house. The meal was delicious, and the conversation relaxed and easy. Donald chatted to his granddaughters, and the girls answered his questions eagerly, their responses animated and amusing. It was as though the trio had known each other all their lives.

Fabien sat and observed the interchange silently while sipping his wine.

'Dad tells me you don't have children?' Isabel said, in an attempt to engage him in conversation.

Fabien shrugged. 'No, and as my wife and I are now divorced, this is perhaps a good thing.'

'Pascal has kids though?' Pascal was Isabel's other half-brother, eighteen months older than her and sixteen years older than Fabien.

'Yes, a son and a daughter. They are both in their twenties now. The son, Charles, will soon be thirty. He's a lawyer in Paris. My niece, Brigitte, owns a furniture shop in Carcassonne. They are both successful and content. Pascal and his wife are proud and pleased that their children are leading happy lives.'

'Isn't that what all parents want for their children? To know that they're happy?'

'Perhaps,' Fabien said. 'I wouldn't know.'

'What about you? Are you happy, Fabien?'

He smiled sardonically and took another sip of wine. 'I run a company that does extremely well. My business is successful, and success brings its own kind of happiness.'

'Perhaps.' Isabel nodded sagely. 'But in my experience, success can also be a burden. The better you become at something, the more time it demands of you. I know from my own experience that work can take over if you let it.'

'I employ people I can rely on to do a good job,' Fabien said. 'This means I don't have to work too hard myself.'

'Well then, you're lucky.'

Their conversation was interrupted by a burst of laughter at the end of the table. Fabien turned towards the sound, watching, taking it all in.

'Tell me about your mum,' Isabel said. 'What was she like?'

Fabien stared, unblinking, as though he found the question impertinent.

'She was kind, and gentle,' he said, eventually. 'She liked to cook for her family, and as she created her dishes, she loved to sing. She had a beautiful voice.'

'It sounds as though cooking was her passion,' Isabel said. 'Something that brought her joy.'

'Yes,' Fabien said, 'but she wasn't always a joyous person. There were times when she would retreat into herself. She would sit in her armchair and let her mind take her away somewhere. All we could do was wait for her to come back. Sometimes her mood would improve quickly, other times she would be distant for days or weeks.'

'That must have been hard for you,' Isabel said.

He shifted uncomfortably. 'It was what it was. She was my mother, and I would not have chosen anyone else for the role. Maman was loving and loyal, and very trusting. I'm glad she never knew about you … and your mother.'

His words felt like a slap.

Isabel swallowed a mouthful of wine. 'Can I ask you something else?' she said.

'Of course.' He stared at her, his blue eyes reminding her so much of her father.

'What did *you* think, when you found out about me?'

Fabien arranged his knife and fork on his plate, pushing them neatly to one side before answering. 'Our father told Pascal and me about you a few years ago, after our mother had died. The truth is, we were both surprised, but perhaps I was a little more surprised than my brother. You see, he remembered the years when our father spent long periods working away from home.'

Surprised. Isabel kicked the word around in her head. It was a weasel word. Ambiguous and slippery. Did Fabien mean they were surprised in a pleasant way, or did he mean they were amazed? Flabbergasted? Or did he mean shocked? Horrified even? Had learning about her existence been nasty and unpalatable, something unwanted and unwelcome?

'But how did you *feel*?' She longed for him to open up. His refusal to communicate meaningfully was beginning to make her uncomfortable. 'Were you angry?'

'I can't remember.' Fabien picked up his wine glass and swirled the contents around. Isabel watched the red liquid as it caught the light. It was dark and rich, the colour of garnets.

'I think you're being evasive, Fabien, but no matter. It was a few years ago, so your recollections are bound to be hazy.' She smiled. 'But what about when I made contact with Dad? That was only a couple of months ago … recently enough for you to remember how you felt about me getting in touch.'

Fabien stared at his empty plate, his face serious and unsmiling. 'I was concerned for him. I didn't want you to hurt him, and …' He held up his left hand, the one that wasn't holding the wine glass – a gesture that seemed quintessentially French. 'I wondered why. Why reconnect, after all these years? You have lived for most of your life without the presence of a father. Why do you need one now? Now that he is old and vulnerable?'

Isabel gripped the stem of her own wine glass, squeezing it so tightly she feared it might snap. 'I've always needed him, Fabien, but I didn't know where he was, or how to find him. And trust me, I would never do anything to hurt Dad, even though he's done things that have caused *me* pain.'

Her voice was too loud, undertones of anger making her sound harsh. The others had noticed. Their chatter and shared laughter had died away, and everyone was listening to her conversation with Fabien. Isabel glanced at her father and realised he looked sad.

'I'm sorry that I hurt you, Isabel,' Donald said. 'It was never my intention. I know you're still mad at me, and – even though he doesn't say so – I believe Fabien is angry with me too, but please don't let that spoil our time together.'

The tension in the room was now fully charged, crackling with things unsaid. One wrong word would blow everything to smithereens.

It was Ellie who saved the moment. Sweet, cheerful Ellie. 'Can we have pudding in the garden room?' she said. 'I'd like to show Grandad my art portfolio, and there's more room in there to spread out.'

Thank heavens for my daughters, Isabel thought. The evening could hardly be described as an unprecedented success, but at least it had been saved from descending into a series of hostile remarks that would have been difficult, if not impossible to recover from.

And tomorrow? Tomorrow was another day, and things could only get better. Couldn't they?

Chapter 15

As parking spaces in the vicinity of the market place were as rare as hens' teeth, Zoe and Lucas had agreed to make the short journey to the Sheaf of Corn on foot.

'I spoke to Sarah Kent earlier,' Lucas said, as they exited the police station and made their way downhill towards the centre of town. 'She was on the way back from her family liaison visit to the victim's brother in Leeds.'

'And?'

'By the sounds of it, Simon Spriggs wasn't exactly warm and welcoming. He told Sarah that he and Kevin had lost touch years back. They exchanged Christmas cards, but that was about it.'

'How did he react to the news that his brother had been murdered?'

'The same as anyone would, I guess,' said Lucas. 'It sounds as if he was shocked … upset. He admitted he'd always had a bad feeling about his brother … that one day he'd end up in over his head.'

'What did he mean by that?'

'When they were kids, he and Kevin liked to play with fire.' Lucas spun round to face her, his mouth twitching into a grin. 'I don't mean literally … they weren't into arson or anything.'

He pulled up his collar and then blew on his hands, rubbing them together. 'It sounds like the brothers used to push their luck. Simon owned up to the fact that he and Kevin both got into trouble a few times in their teens. Eventually, Simon saw the error of his ways and decided to make some changes in his life. He stopped drinking and moved away, for a fresh start.'

'It's a pity Kevin Spriggs didn't do the same,' Zoe said.

'Simon said he didn't think his brother was capable of mending his ways. Kevin was too wild, he liked to enjoy himself too much.'

'Is there any chance Simon Spriggs could be involved in the murder?'

'No, he had a routine hospital appointment on Wednesday afternoon at Leeds General Infirmary,' Lucas said, as he marched along the pavement. 'Sarah checked with the hospital, and they confirmed Simon Spriggs was having a scan at the time of the murder. So … that's one member of the family who can be ruled out. That should please the DI.'

'I saw the boss earlier, at the Co-op.' Zoe lengthened her stride to keep up. 'She was buying pudding for a dinner party. I imagine they'll be tucking into cheesecake right about now.'

'Did she actually use that combination of words?' Lucas said. '*Dinner party*? Aren't they what people used to have back in the Seventies? You know, vol-au-vent can-apes, prawn cocktails and T-bone steaks … all swilled down with a bottle of German wine?'

Zoe giggled at his mispronunciation of the word canapés. 'It's can-a-pay,' she said. 'Not can-apes.'

Lucas gave her his how-should-I-know-and-I-don't-give-a-shit-anyway look.

'In fairness, the DI didn't say "dinner party",' Zoe said. 'That was my interpretation. It's what my mum and dad always say whenever they have friends round for a meal. But even they've moved on from prawn cocktails these days, although they do still like the odd slice of Black Forest gateau.'

They were passing one of the town's trendier pubs. She peered through the window, taking in the modern, minimalist interior, which looked surprisingly cosy and inviting, but empty.

'There aren't many people about,' she said.

Lucas sucked air through his teeth. He was proud of his knowledge of the local pub scene, and always enjoyed showing off his expertise.

'It's still early, and it's midweek, Zoe. Not many people bother going out on Thursday evenings, especially at this time of year. Even I wouldn't want to freeze my nuts off going out midweek – assuming I ever got a night off, that is.'

Zoe rolled her eyes. 'Don't talk rubbish, Lucas. You get plenty of nights off – you know you do.'

'The pubs make their money on Fridays and Saturdays,' he said, choosing to ignore her challenging tone. 'The rest of the week, most places are dead as a dodo.'

'Well, I hope there are some customers in the Sheaf of Corn,' she said. 'Otherwise we'll have no one to talk to and the DI won't be happy.'

'Ah, now, the Sheaf of Corn … that's a different kettle of fish. It's a real-ale, spit-and-sawdust type of place. It's where the serious drinkers hang out.'

Zoe hoped he wasn't being literal about the spit and sawdust. 'Well, you should know,' she said. 'Although I don't suppose it's one of your haunts, otherwise you'd have said something to DI Blood. If you were a regular at the Sheaf of Corn, it follows you'd have known Kevin Spriggs.'

Lucas didn't reply and his silence spoke volumes.

'Shit, Lucas. You knew him, didn't you? Why the hell haven't you said something?'

'I didn't *know* him.' Lucas shook his head vigorously, throwing the accusation back at her like a wet dog shimmying water from its fur. 'I recognised his face, that's all. I've seen him out and about in a few of the pubs, but I never spoke to the man, 'cept once, when I told him to watch his step.'

They had reached the top of the high street and were standing on the pavement edge, waiting to cross the road and head to the marketplace.

'Are you saying you had a run-in with him?'

'He was pissed,' Lucas said. He waited for a transit van to get out of the way and then lunged across the road.

'What did he do to upset you?' Zoe said, running to catch up with him.

'He was holding a pint, swinging his arm around and some of it sloshed onto my jacket. I told him to calm down, and he told me to fuck off.'

She groaned. 'Something tells me this story isn't going to end well.'

'What're you on about, Zoe? It was nothing, all right? I took his drink off him, put it down and backed him up against the bar.' Lucas stopped for a moment and stared up at the night sky. 'Spriggs was about to kick off, so I showed him my warrant card. I told him I was off duty and didn't want any trouble, and he slunk away. He wasn't happy, but he was wise enough not to pick a fight with a copper.'

'Where did this happen? Not in the Sheaf of Corn, I hope.'

'Nah, it was another pub. The Kings Arms down on Harringdon Street. Like I say, it was nothing. I'd forgotten all about it until I saw Kevin Spriggs' photo.'

'You should have said something,' Zoe insisted.

'Why? What possible relevance could it have to Op Jackdaw?'

They were heading along a short road that shot off at an angle from the marketplace. Zoe could see a painted pub sign up ahead, golden corn tied together in a twisted bundle.

'This is it,' Lucas said. 'Let me do the talking, at least initially. As for the incident in the Kings Arms, keep that to yourself. The boss doesn't need to know about it.'

Zoe thought the interior of the pub looked like a scene from a television period drama set in the 1950s. It was shadowy, bare and austere. Black leather seating lined the walls, and dark wooden tables and stools formed pockets of space, ideal for intimate socialising. Despite Lucas's prediction about this being a magnet for hardened drinkers, the pub was almost empty. The only occupied seats were two tall stools facing the bar. The landlord stood on the other side, behind a row of pump handles, which were trimmed with logos advertising an impressive selection of real ales.

As they approached, he glanced over and stiffened. One of the men at the bar – a bald, skinny guy with a jittery look in his eyes – turned to see what the landlord had reacted to. When he saw Zoe and Lucas, he frowned.

'Ey up, lads, these look like coppers to me,' he said.

'So what?' said the other man, who hadn't bothered to turn round. 'We're not doing anything wrong. There's no law against having a pint, is there?'

The landlord folded his arms across his muscly chest. Despite the wintry weather, he was wearing a tight, short-sleeved T-shirt, chosen to best display his physique and an array of intricate tattoos.

'Can I help you?' he said.

'I hope so,' Lucas replied, holding up his ID. 'Your mate's right. We are coppers … I'm DC Killingworth, and this is my colleague, DC Piper. We're hoping you can give us some information about a customer of yours. Kevin Spriggs. We understand he's a regular here.'

The skinny man on the bar stool nodded smugly. 'Told you,' he said. 'I can spot a copper a mile away.'

The landlord straightened his shoulders and unfolded his arms. 'Look,' he said. 'Kevin Spriggs *is* a customer here, but I haven't seen him for a few days. We had words the last time he was in. I threatened to bar him if he didn't behave himself, and I suspect he's keeping away … giving me time to cool off.'

Zoe pulled out her notebook. 'Can I ask your name, please?'

'It's Robert Scaringer, and if you want to know how to spell it, I suggest you take a look at the sign above the door.'

'What did Kevin Spriggs do to upset you?' Lucas said, giving Zoe no opportunity to react to the landlord's sarcasm.

'Nothing out of the ordinary,' Robert Scaringer replied. 'Kev's always been a loudmouth. He's a total pain in the arse, if I'm being honest. Every so often, my patience wears thin and I call him out on it. He'll be back in a week or two, and no doubt he'll be on his best behaviour for a while. Then things'll go back to normal and the whole annoying process will start again.'

Zoe stepped forward. 'That's just it, Mr Scaringer, they won't.' She rested her right boot on the metal footrest that ran the full length of the bar front. 'Kevin Spriggs is dead. He's been murdered. That's why we need to talk to you.'

Lucas turned to her and wrinkled his nose, clearly peeved that she'd jumped in with the news of Kevin Spriggs' death. Zoe was aware he'd wanted to make the announcement himself, but she had no intention of standing back and letting Lucas do all the talking.

'He's dead?' The landlord ran a hand down his face, wiping away his expression. What was it he was hiding? A smirk, perhaps? A hint of satisfaction? Guilt?

'Bloody hell!' The bald, skinny man pushed his pint aside and stared at Zoe, genuinely taken aback.

Even the other bloke, the one who'd made such a point of ignoring them, had finally turned around. 'Have you caught the bastard who did it?' he said.

'Not yet,' Lucas said. 'But it's only a matter of time.'

'Can I take your names, please?' said Zoe, smiling at the two men on the bar stools.

The bald-headed man was the first to respond. 'Ethan Wenlock,' he said, spelling out his last name.

The older guy seemed cagey, shuffling on his bar stool. 'Les Crofts,' he said, somewhat reluctantly.

'So what can you tell us about Kevin Spriggs?' said Zoe, having made a note of the names. 'Did he have any enemies? Was there anyone in particular who had a problem with him?'

The landlord leaned forward, resting his fingers on the edge of the bar. 'I think everyone who knows Kev has had a run-in with him at some point.'

Zoe noticed that Robert Scaringer was still speaking of Kevin Spriggs in the present tense, as though he was having trouble absorbing the news of his demise.

'Rob's right about that,' Ethan Wenlock agreed. 'Kev's always been trouble. He was a prat. Never learned to keep his gob shut.'

'Was it usually the drink talking?' Lucas said, as he dug around in his pocket and pointed to something behind the bar. Robert Scaringer turned and pulled a packet of pork scratchings from a cardboard strip by the till. 'Did he always let his mouth run away with him?' Lucas added, as he handed over a couple of coins. 'Or was it only when he'd had a few pints?'

'Drunk or sober, he was always a cocky bastard,' Les Crofts said.

'Sounds like you didn't like him very much,' Lucas said, as he opened the bag of scratchings.

Zoe threw him a withering look, challenging him with her eyes. *Really? You're going to eat those now?* He smiled back at her, holding out the bag defiantly, offering her one of the crispy pieces of pork fat. She declined with a derisive shake of her head.

Les Crofts took a swig of his beer. 'Just because somebody drinks in the same pub as you, doesn't mean you have to like 'em. I live round the corner from here, so this is my local. It's a good pub, with proper ale, and there are plenty of regulars I enjoy having a chinwag with. Ethan here, for instance. Kevin Spriggs, not so much. He was always in 'ere though, so I often found myself drawn into conversation with him.'

'He did tend to have an opinion on everything,' the landlord added. 'And he seemed to take a controversial stance on most things. I think he did it to wind people up.'

'What kind of issues did he like to talk about?' Zoe said.

'Conspiracy theories mainly, and he had strong views on certain political and environmental issues. Kev didn't believe in global warming, for instance, or recycling. He'd also tell anyone who'd listen that a university education was a waste of time, and he didn't like what he called "creative types" ... you know, artists and poets and such like. He reckoned they were a load of namby-pambies.'

'Did his views ever get him in trouble?' Lucas said. 'Into any fights?'

The landlord shook his head. 'Thankfully, folk knew what he was like and took him with a pinch of salt. For the most part, people refused to take the bait whenever he was spouting off about his latest theory.'

'Did he have an affiliation with any particular political party?' Zoe asked.

The men looked at her as if she was talking a foreign language.

'Who did he vote for?' she clarified. 'I'll take it as read he wasn't a Liberal. So, where did he put his cross on a ballot paper? Labour? Conversative? UKIP?'

'He never said,' Robert Scaringer replied. 'His opinions tended to vary and he'd often contradict himself. He was a hard one to fathom sometimes.'

'You're right there, Rob.' Les Crofts bobbed his head in agreement. 'Although, in fairness, Spriggsy wasn't all bad. He thought the world of his dog ... used to bring it in here sometimes. He was gutted when it died.'

Zoe smothered a sigh. For all their talk, the trio were giving very little away.

'Do you know if Kevin Spriggs was in a relationship?' she said, trying to hide her frustration.

'For some reason, the ladies did seem to like him.' Ethan Wenlock looked a tad envious as he imparted this nugget of information. 'But I don't think he'd been seeing anyone recently.'

'Now that's where you're wrong, lad.' Les Crofts appeared to take pleasure in contradicting his drinking partner. 'The last time I saw Spriggsy he was telling me he was on a promise.'

'When was that?' said Lucas.

'Sunday lunchtime. In here. He seemed exceptionally pleased with himself, although he could have been making the whole thing up for all I know.'

'Did he say who this date was with?' Lucas was alert now, the bag of scratchings forgotten.

'No, all he said was she was a lot younger and she was gagging for it.' He glanced at Zoe apologetically. 'Sorry, duck. His words, not mine.'

'Did he tell you anything else about this woman?' she said.

'No, and I didn't press him either. I wasn't interested. I thought it was just Spriggsy bragging again.'

Zoe looked at the landlord and Ethan Wenlock. 'What about you two? Did Kevin Spriggs tell either of you about this woman?'

'Not me,' said Ethan. 'I've not seen Kev for over a week. Last time I saw him was on New Year's Eve. He was sitting over in that corner singing his head off. Out of tune, I might add.' He dipped his head towards the other side of the pub, to a small round table near the unlit fire. 'It was quite early on in the evening, but he was already drunk as a skunk.'

'Was he with anyone at the time?' Zoe asked.

Ethan shrugged. 'It's difficult to say. This place was heaving. Everyone comes in early on New Year's Eve to get a seat. I didn't notice whether Kev was with anyone or not. I heard him, more than saw him.'

'Do you have CCTV here in the pub?' Zoe said, addressing Robert Scaringer.

The landlord pulled a face. 'You're joking, aren't you? This isn't a brewery pub. *I* own this place, and I can't afford to install CCTV cameras.'

'These days, you can't afford not to,' Zoe said. 'Not only is

95

the footage useful if there's any trouble, the cameras themselves can act as a deterrent. You're far less likely to get drug dealing or petty theft if your customers know they're being monitored by a camera.'

'We don't get drug dealers in here,' Robert said. 'It's not that kind of place. Anyway, I'm struggling to make a profit as it is. I've no spare cash for cameras.'

'Going back to Kevin Spriggs,' Lucas said, addressing the landlord directly. 'Do you know if he'd had any run-ins with anyone recently? Apart from yourself, of course.'

Robert Scaringer pushed himself away from the bar and glowered. 'I don't like the way that sounds,' he said, his voice tetchy. 'OK, so Kev and I had words on Sunday evening. He'd been in here all day, making a nuisance of himself. I asked him to leave, and he crept away with his tail between his legs – I didn't have to physically eject him. There was no scuffle or fisticuffs. I was just doing my job.'

'I'm sure you were,' Lucas said. 'As you say, it's not easy, running a pub. These are tough times. The last thing you want is for someone like Kevin Spriggs to be scaring away your customers.'

Zoe knew what Lucas was implying and so, it seemed, did the landlord. Robert Scaringer stretched to his full height, towering over them. For a moment, Zoe allowed herself to imagine the landlord grabbing Lucas by his collar and the seat of his trousers, upending him and throwing him and his pork scratchings out onto the street. Stifling a bubble of laughter, she wondered what she'd do if her imaginary scenario were to play out. Cheer, probably.

'I'll admit Kev Spriggs was a nuisance at times, but in many ways he was a good customer,' Robert said, his muscles bulging beneath his T-shirt. 'He came in most nights. The fact that he won't be supping here anymore means my takings will go right down.'

'So where did he tend to go when you'd barred him?' Lucas

asked. 'Did he have any other favourite watering holes in Bainbridge, or anywhere else for that matter?'

'If I refused to serve him, he'd usually slink off to the Red Lion or the Flying Fish. He liked the beer in the Printer's Arms as well.'

'Kev was well acquainted with the inside of most of the pubs in Bainbridge,' Les Crofts said. 'I've seen him in the Three Horseshoes many a time, and the Kings Arms … oh, aye, and the Rose and Crown as well. Take yer pick. Kev was a familiar face in town.'

'OK, thanks,' said Lucas. 'We'll ask around.'

'For the record …' Robert Scaringer said, his voice deep and firm and brooking no argument, 'we know nowt about why Kevin Spriggs was murdered, do we, lads? We're sorry he's dead, I'm sure, and if we knew who was responsible, we'd say. I do know he'd been having some trouble at work, but that's probably because he was acting like a dickhead there as well.'

'He was a car mechanic, wasn't he?' Zoe said. 'At the Crown Garage?'

'That's right,' the landlord replied. 'And for the most part, he took his work seriously. As a rule, he didn't piss about because he knew he couldn't afford to lose his job. Something happened though, a while back, but I don't know what. You should talk to his boss about it. I'm sure he'll be able to fill you in.'

'Cheers for that,' Lucas said. 'We will.'

'Ready for a pub crawl, Zoe?'

They were making their way back across the marketplace, and Lucas was rubbing his hands together again. This time, Zoe wasn't sure whether he was trying to keep his fingers warm, or feeling gleeful at the prospect of visiting the town's vast array of public houses.

The weather was icy and clear, a night of sparkling stars. Their breath was coming out in white clouds that drifted into the air, up and up towards the distant hills. Three women were walking towards them, giggling. The sound of their heels clopping on the tarmac made Zoe long to dress up and go out with someone. Anyone. Anyone except Lucas.

He was finishing off the pork scratchings. Opening up the bag, he held it over his mouth and tipped his head back to make sure he devoured every last piece.

'God, I don't know how you can eat that stuff,' she said. 'It's disgusting.'

He licked salt from his fingers and wiped his mouth. 'What are you talking about, Zoe? It's bloody lovely. Not disgusting at all.'

'It's pig fat,' Zoe said. 'Utterly revolting. It can't be good for your arteries either.'

'I'm young,' Lucas replied. 'I can work it off.'

Zoe wasn't sure that was true, but she decided not to pursue the conversation. It wasn't as if she followed an exemplary diet herself. 'What did you make of Robert Scaringer?' she said instead.

'I'm not sure. Having made a big thing about not knowing who might have bumped off Kevin Spriggs, I thought it was weird how – at the last minute – he happened to mention the victim was having problems with his employer.'

'My thoughts exactly,' Zoe said. 'Was he trying to be helpful, do you think? Or was he trying to deflect attention away from his own skirmish with Kevin Spriggs?'

'Hard to tell. Could have been a bit of both.'

'So where are we going next?' Zoe asked.

'The Flying Fish,' said Lucas. 'Then we'll head to the Red Lion and we can decide the rest of our route from there. Play your cards right, Zoe, and I might even buy you a Diet Coke.'

Chapter 16

By ten o'clock, Donald and Fabien had gone back to the hotel, Ellie was in bed, and Kate was in the kitchen, making herself a cup of herbal tea. Isabel and Nathan were nestled in front of the television, watching the news, which was still dominated by the previous day's announcement by the Duke and Duchess of Sussex that they would be stepping back from royal duties.

'Are you OK?' Nathan said. 'You're very quiet.'

She smiled. 'I'm fine.'

They lapsed back into silence, staring at the TV screen.

'What do you think then?' Nathan said eventually.

'What?' She turned to face him. 'About Harry and Meghan?'

'*No.*' He grinned. 'About how it went this evening. Your dad's first visit to Chez Blood.'

Isabel reached for the TV remote and muted the sound. 'It was lovely to finally spend some time with him,' she said. 'I think the girls enjoyed seeing him too.'

Behind them, the door opened and Kate appeared, carrying a mug. She kicked off her shoes, sat down on the armchair and yawned.

'I think I might stay here tonight,' she said. 'If that's all right with you.'

'Course it is,' Nathan said. 'Think yourself lucky your grandad decided to stay at the Feathers, otherwise you'd be kipping down on the sofa.'

'Yeah, why was that?' Kate sipped her tea. 'What made him decide to stay at a hotel?'

'I'm not sure,' Isabel said. 'It's disappointing. I'd much rather he was here, with the family – but I'm not going to make a big thing of it. He must have his reasons. As a matter of fact, he gave me the impression it was Fabien's idea.'

'What do you make of Fabien?' said Nathan. 'The two of you were deep in conversation over dinner.'

Isabel phrased her answer carefully. 'We talked, but we didn't say very much … nothing meaningful.'

'I thought he seemed a bit aloof,' Kate said. 'Like he's not an easy person to get to know.'

'I think you're right,' Isabel replied. 'It's weird. He's my brother, so I thought there'd be an instant bond … that I'd feel a connection when we met, but there's nothing. We're strangers. Wary of each other.'

'Like it or not, he's part of the family now,' Kate said. 'But shared blood doesn't necessarily mean shared interests. The bottom line is, you're individuals with very different backgrounds. It's bound to feel strange.'

'Kate's right,' said Nathan. 'And just because you're related to someone, doesn't mean you have to love them, or even like them.'

'I know that,' Isabel said, thinking of Kevin Spriggs' fractured relationship with his son, as well as some of the other complex cases she'd worked on over the years. She understood the complicated and sometimes dangerous nature of relationships, and knew from experience that not all families were happy.

'The truth is,' Isabel added, 'I *want* to like him. I always longed for a brother or a sister when I was growing up.'

Nathan smiled. 'Be careful what you wish for, eh?'

'I'm sure it'll be fine,' she said. 'I need to work out why we haven't connected yet … That way, I'll know how to put things right between us.'

Nathan slipped his hand into hers. 'Not everything can be fixed, Isabel. Occasionally, you have to accept that some things just *are*.'

'I don't agree,' she said, smiling to play down her words. 'Fabien's my brother. I'm not ready to give up on him yet.'

Chapter 17

Isabel set off for work at eight-fifteen the following morning. In the east, the rising sun was lighting up the sky, turning it the colour of ripe peaches, and she felt her spirits lifting. *Today is going to be a good day*, she told herself.

She was silently repeating the mantra as she walked into the office, but any hopes that it might set a positive tone for the day evaporated when she saw how washed out everyone looked. Lucas was tapping a pencil on his desktop, his eyes tired and his hair uncombed. Even the indefatigable Zoe seemed subdued and unenthusiastic.

Dan had obviously opted for sustenance to keep up his strength. He was biting into an enormous breakfast cob which, from the smell of it, was filled with bacon and egg. Isabel watched as a blob of ketchup landed on the front of his shirt.

'Shit!' he said, placing the roll on his desk and dabbing frantically at the offending red splodge.

Isabel laughed. 'Serves you right for not getting the rest of the team a bacon butty.'

'Get lost, I'm not made of money,' Dan said, repelling her jibe. 'If you're hungry, you can buy your own. The café's only across the road.'

Ignoring Dan's crankiness, Isabel took a seat between Lucas and Zoe, and listened as they told her what they'd discovered the previous evening. They'd spent most of the night talking to the licensees of half of the pubs in Bainbridge, but based on the paltry amount of evidence they'd managed to glean, Isabel wasn't convinced it was time well spent.

Over the last twenty-four hours, Operation Jackdaw had generated a lot of information, but most of it was random and disconnected. It felt as though they were floundering, processing far more questions than answers.

'So,' Isabel said, summing up, 'other than confirming that Kevin Spriggs talked shite when he'd had a few pints, your pub crawl doesn't appear to have uncovered anything fresh, does it?'

'I don't think that's fair, boss ...' Lucas blustered. 'Me and Zoe did our best, but Spriggs wasn't the most popular guy around. It's not our fault nobody had much to tell us. It sounds as though everyone kept out of his way as much as possible.'

'A few people did say that Spriggs was OK when he was sober,' Zoe said. 'And one of the blokes in the Sheaf of Corn mentioned that Spriggs thought the world of his dog. He was devastated when it died.'

'What point are you trying to make, Zoe?' said Dan.

'I'm just saying ... he wasn't all bad, there was obviously a softer side to him as well.'

'Most people have at least one redeeming feature,' Isabel admitted. 'But there's no getting away from the fact that Kevin Spriggs must have seriously pissed someone off. The question is, who?'

'Simon Spriggs told the FLO that Kevin was a wild child when he was a teenager,' Lucas said. 'In fact, he admitted they both were. Seems the brothers lost touch as adults, so Simon wasn't able to shed any light on who might have wanted to kill Spriggs.'

'Is *he* in the frame?' Isabel asked.

'No, he's been ruled out,' Lucas said. 'At the time of the murder, Simon Spriggs was attending a hospital appointment.'

'I've been wondering,' Dan said, as he wiped his fingers on a paper napkin, 'is this definitely a one-off crime? Any chance it could be the start of something else?'

'Seriously? What, you think there might be a killer on the loose in Bainbridge?' Isabel frowned. 'There better bloody not be. Not on my patch.'

She crossed her legs and folded her arms. What if Dan was right? What if this was the start of a targeted crime spree? Deep down, she thought the idea was preposterous, but she hadn't fully got to grips with this investigation yet, had she?

In the early stages of a serious crime like this one, Isabel always worried that if she didn't work hard and fast enough, she'd fail to get the evidence needed to stop the perpetrator in their tracks. While ever the killer was still out there, there was a risk they might cause harm to someone else.

'Don't get me wrong,' said Dan. 'I'm not suggesting we have a crazed serial killer on our hands. I realise that's extremely unlikely, especially as this murder has more of a personal feel to it.'

'To me, it feels like a vendetta,' Zoe said. 'And Kevin Spriggs certainly had a gift for winding people up, that's for sure.'

'The more we learn about Spriggs, the more complicated this becomes, don't you think?' Isabel said.

Dan nodded. 'I agree.'

Isabel felt a pressing desire to focus. She longed for a quiet spell in her office to sit and filter the facts, but there was fat chance of that. They had another briefing in half an hour. The incident team had been busy checking data and following up leads. Fingers crossed, there might be some positive news that would push the investigation towards a satisfactory conclusion.

The full team, minus Detective Superintendent Tibbet, gathered in the incident room at nine o'clock to share information and discuss further lines of inquiry.

The forensic search of the victim's home had found nothing

of significance. There was no sign of the missing phone, although a laptop had been retrieved and passed on to Digital Forensics. Disappointingly, the police search team hadn't uncovered anything unusual, other than a couple of photographs that had been discovered stuck to the victim's fridge door.

'The pics are of two young children … a little boy and a baby,' said Matt Habgood, the police search adviser. 'It was an interesting find, given that the victim wasn't your classic family man.'

'How old are the kids?' Dan asked.

'Not very,' said Matt. 'One's a toddler, the other much younger … a couple of months old, maybe.'

'They could be his grandchildren,' Dan said. 'Alfie Moss has a son and a daughter, but he told us he didn't want Kevin Spriggs involved with them. If the photos *are* of the Moss children, how did Spriggs get hold of them?'

'He could have taken them off Facebook,' Zoe said. 'I'll check … see if Alfie Moss has posted the same images on his page.'

'Where are we in terms of checking people's whereabouts on the day of the murder?' Isabel said. 'Ruth Prendergast? Sophie Tait? Alfie Moss? Have we established where they all were on Wednesday?'

'Ruth Prendergast's employer has confirmed she was conducting job interviews all day,' said a voice from the back of the room.

'And Sophie Tait?' said Isabel. 'Alfie Moss?'

'I checked with the lecturer Sophie Tait works with, and several of the students in her class,' Lucas said. 'She's in the clear. She was definitely at the college at the time Kevin Spriggs was killed.'

'And I looked into Alfie Moss's alibi,' Zoe added. 'He claims he was working in Hallgate at the time of the murder. When I rang the client, she confirmed that Alfie was there all day. However, when I pressed her, she admitted she'd spent most of the day in her conservatory, keeping out of his way, so she wasn't keeping tabs on him. She also says Alfie took a break for lunch.'

'Can she remember what time?' Isabel said.

'Around midday, but she couldn't be sure exactly. She got the impression Alfie had gone to sit in his van to eat a packed lunch, but she agreed he could have driven away for a while without her noticing.'

'So we can't rule him out,' said Dan.

'I wonder if Alfie Moss ever did any plumbing work for Gerald Langton at Hollybrook Close?' Isabel said. 'If he did, he could have filched a key. Check it out, Zoe, and while you're at it, see if you can establish any kind of connection between Mr Langton's son and the victim. It's a long shot, but at this stage, we need to explore every angle.'

'Do you want me to speak to the firm of solicitors that did the conveyancing on Gerald Langton's house sale?' said Lucas. 'They might have had access to the house keys at some point.'

'Please, Lucas,' Isabel said. 'And while you're at it, find out if anyone working in the solicitor's office knew Kevin Spriggs. Have a look at the case file to check which lawyer represented Spriggs when he was charged with assault. It could be someone from the same law firm. We're looking for links. Any kind of link.'

'I thought I'd have a word with Jessica Moss, Alfie's mother,' said Dan. 'Her marriage to Kevin Spriggs ended decades ago, but it sounds like it was a toxic relationship, and some grudges last for years.'

'Maybe Jessica Moss found out that Spriggs had been in touch with her son through social media and wasn't happy about it,' Zoe said. 'Perhaps she was afraid Spriggs would try and wheedle his way back into Alfie's life.'

'By all means have a word with Jessica Moss, but don't waste too much time if it doesn't lead anywhere,' Isabel said. 'The Super wants us to focus our resources carefully. She won't be happy if she thinks we're going down blind alleys.'

She swallowed a sigh of frustration. It was all right telling everyone to focus, but until they'd established who the persons of interest were and whittled them down to a list of suspects, the investigation would continue to bounce around all over the place.

'Any news on Kevin Spriggs' vehicle?' she asked.

'It's been located,' said a lively young officer, who'd been drafted onto the incident team from another department. 'It was parked on the street a short distance from his house. Unfortunately, there was no satnav fitted, so we don't know for sure where the vehicle's been recently. However, we ran the reg through ANPR and it had been picked up a few times, but only on the A roads between the victim's house and his place of work.'

'What about other CCTV cameras?' Isabel continued. 'Have any images of the victim or his car been picked up on the day of the murder?'

'Nothing yet, other than the security camera on Hollybrook Close. But we are still checking.'

'We need to talk to the victim's employer, to establish whether he was in any trouble at work,' Isabel said. 'Lucas, after you've spoken to the solicitors, can you pay a visit to the Crown Garage, please.'

Lucas bowed his head. 'No problem, boss.'

'Anything you want to share, Dan?' Isabel said. 'Did you learn anything useful when you spoke to the gardener?'

'She was never given a key to Hollybrook Close,' Dan said. 'In fact, she maintains she only went inside the house once. I think we can disregard Evelyn Merigold, although …'

'What?' Isabel said. 'Don't leave me hanging.'

'I got the impression she was holding something back,' he said. 'She told me she hardly knew Gerald Langton and claimed she didn't know Kevin Spriggs … and yet, later in our conversation, she referred to Spriggs as *someone in trouble*. When I picked up on it, she backtracked … said she'd jumped to conclusions about Spriggs, based on the fact that his death was being investigated by the police.'

'I suppose it was an obvious assumption for her to make,'

Isabel said, 'but perhaps we shouldn't disregard the gardener just yet. Let's keep her on our radar for now. The fabric of this case appears to have a lot of loose threads. Let's start tidying things up.'

Isabel's own plans for the morning included revisiting the crime scene. Lucas had also arranged for her to speak to Katrina Mariner's daughters. She was meeting them at number 3 Hollybrook Close, their mother's old house. She wasn't sure what she hoped to learn from them, but the key Katrina Mariner had used for the cat-sitting sessions was the only one officially unaccounted for. As a matter of routine, they should find out what had happened to it.

'There's a lot to get through today,' Isabel said, addressing the room. 'We need to stay focused, and we need to start making progress. You all have your assigned actions, so let's get the day started. I'd like everyone back here at three-thirty for an update. Don't be late.'

Chapter 18

By ten-fifteen, Isabel was back at Hollybrook Close. The forensic and police searches of the crime scene had been completed, and the house was now uncannily quiet. Isabel was standing alone inside the bedroom in which Kevin Spriggs' body had been found. The last time she'd been here, it had been dark and rainy outside. Now the winter sun was shimmering through the windows onto duck-egg blue painted walls and casting a silver glow across the grey carpet. It seemed like a different room today, its ambience altogether more cheerful and optimistic. And obviously, the mood was greatly improved by the absence of a body in the bed.

She had followed Ruth Prendergast's journey through the house – retracing the route Ruth had taken when she'd arrived home on Wednesday evening. In through the front door. Down the hallway to the kitchen. Upstairs to the bathroom. And finally, into the bedroom.

Isabel recalled the smell of food that had lingered downstairs on the day of the murder. Ruth had explained that after unloading her shopping, and before going upstairs and making her grim discovery, she had put a pizza in the oven. In the confusion that followed, she had lost her appetite.

Everything in the house was neat and orderly now, with

nothing out of place. Isabel knew that the search team would have been thorough, but they had also worked tidily. Where possible, they had left things as they'd found them. She noted that the décor in the house was tired and outdated, but that was something that could easily be fixed. This property had the potential to be a lovely home for Ruth Prendergast, assuming she was able to overcome the horror of finding a dead man in her bed.

Now that the mattress had been stripped and the body removed, the bedroom looked innocuous and forlorn. There was nothing else it could tell her now. Even the forensic team had struggled to extract anything useful from within its walls.

Isabel went back to the ground floor and wandered into the dining room at the back of the house. From there, a patio door opened onto the garden. There was a key in the lock. She turned it, slid the handle across, and stepped outside onto a gravelled seating area that was surrounded by a low wall and a collection of terracotta pots. Although most were empty, one pot contained a sad-looking geranium in the last throes of life, and another was filled with yellow winter-flowering pansies. The flowers were lifting their optimistic faces towards the sun, which hovered low in the pale sky.

A lawn stretched beyond the patio area, up to a rear fence. On the right was a wide and profusely filled border. Most of the shrubs were brown and dead, wearing their winter garb, but Isabel recognised a hydrangea bush, and the vibrant stems of red twig dogwood.

The back garden of number 4 abutted open farmland. Someone could quite easily have crossed the farmer's field, climbed over the fence and entered the house from the rear – in which case, they were looking for someone with a key to the back door, not the front. There was also the question of footprints to be considered. The field at the rear was ploughed and it had been raining on the day of the murder. Surely, anyone crossing it would get soil or mud on their shoes? Forensics had found no muddy prints. No footprints at all, for that matter.

As she stood and assessed the garden, Isabel thought it was on the small side compared to the size of the house. It was only when she strolled onto the lawn that she realised the garden extended around to the left, beyond the eastern side of the house, behind the garage. Curious, she explored further, treading carefully on the damp grass to prevent her shoes from sinking in.

As she rounded the corner of the garage, she noticed immediately that one of the fence panels had blown down between number 4 and the house next door. The Mariner house. High winds had battered the region the previous week – the remnants of a storm blown in off the eastern coast of North America. Isabel wondered whether the fence had been a victim of the recent gales, or whether it had been down for much longer than that.

The presence of the fallen panel meant that someone could easily have accessed the rear of number 4 via the Mariners' back garden. Isabel was due to visit the house next door in five minutes. It would be the perfect opportunity to check.

Number 3 Hollybrook Close was a mirror image of number 4. The two houses faced one another, separated by their sweeping driveways and a pair of detached garages, which were off to one side, at the tip of the cul-de-sac. Whereas the sunny rear garden of number 4 was south-facing, it was the front garden of number 3 that was now bathed in winter sunlight.

Rather than knocking on the door, Isabel decided to stroll around to the right, across the front garden to the side gate. When she got there, she was disappointed to find it bolted.

By the time she'd retraced her steps to the front of the house, the door was open and a young woman was standing inside, waiting for her.

'Hello,' the woman said. 'I saw you walking up, but when I opened the door, you'd disappeared.'

'I was hoping to take a look in the back garden,' Isabel replied, as she held up her warrant card. 'As I'm sure you've guessed, I'm DI Blood. I take it you're either Stella or Heather Mariner.'

'I'm Stella,' the woman said. 'My sister's inside. Please, come in.'

Isabel followed her into the hallway, being careful to wipe her feet. They went past the empty lounge and through into the kitchen, where another woman was sitting on a stool at a central, marble-topped island.

'DI Blood, this is my sister, Heather.'

The two Mariner women were alike. Both looked to be in their late twenties, with the same tawny hair and large, doleful brown eyes, but despite their facial similarities, there was a significant difference in height and build. Stella was short and slender, whereas Heather was more solidly built and looked to be several inches taller – although it was difficult to be certain while she was sitting down.

'Thank you for seeing me,' Isabel said. 'We're trying to speak to as many people as possible in the aftermath of what happened next door.'

'We heard a man's body had been found,' Heather said.

'That's right. It's a murder investigation. I don't suppose either of you were here, at the house, on Wednesday afternoon?'

'I'm afraid we weren't,' Stella said. 'We come over and check on the place once a week, but we never stay long when we do pop in. I was at home on Wednesday afternoon. I'm a nurse and I was doing an evening shift that day.'

'Do you work locally?'

'At the Derby Royal,' Stella said.

'I was working on Wednesday as well,' Heather said. 'All day. At home.'

'Home working?' Isabel smiled. 'I like the sound of that, although it's not exactly practical in my line of work.'

'I spend most of my working week travelling around the Midlands, delivering training courses,' Heather replied. 'Thankfully, my employer lets me work from home one day a week to catch up on admin. It's bliss.'

Isabel smiled politely. 'I understand this was your mother's house,' she said. 'How long has it been empty?'

Heather scratched her chin. 'It was September when we cleared everything out, wasn't it, Stella?'

'Yes. We sorted through all of Mum's personal stuff, and then brought in a house clearance firm to take away everything that was left. We thought it would be easier to sell an empty house, but we're beginning to wonder whether that was the right decision.'

Isabel looked around the kitchen, which was modern and bright, with shiny units the colour of milky coffee. 'Has it been on the market long?'

'Nearly six months,' said Heather. 'It went onto the estate agent's website in August, just before we got rid of everything.'

'So it was on the market at the same time as next door? The house Ruth Prendergast bought?'

Stella leaned back against the kitchen worktop. 'Yes,' she replied. 'As a matter of fact, number 4 didn't go up for sale until October. It sold almost immediately, much to our annoyance.'

'I notice you don't have a for-sale sign,' Isabel said. 'Any particular reason?'

Heather tucked a strand of hair behind her ear. 'We didn't think it was a good idea,' she said. 'Security wise, I mean. We check things regularly and there's an alarm, but we thought a for-sale board might draw too much attention … flag up the fact that the house is empty.'

Isabel wandered over to the kitchen sink and peered out of the window into the garden. A roll of duct tape, a Stanley knife and a dry dishcloth had been placed on the draining board.

'Doing a spot of DIY?' Isabel asked, nodding towards the gear.

'There's a leaking pipe under the sink,' Stella said. 'Hopefully some gaffer tape will sort it, at least as a temporary measure. We're trying to avoid the expense of calling in a plumber.'

Isabel turned her back to the window and leaned against the edge of the worktop. 'I need to ask you about a key to next door,' she said, watching carefully to see if either of the two women flinched. There wasn't a flicker from either of them.

'Key?' Stella looked puzzled.

'We've spoken to the man who used to live next door, Gerald Langton. He told us your mother used to look after his cat when he was away.'

'That's right, she did,' Heather said. 'I think Mum had a soft spot for that cat. She used to let it in here sometimes and feed it tins of tuna.' She smiled at the memory.

'Mr Langton told us that when he went away, he'd give your mum a key so she could let herself in to feed the cat and water his houseplants.' Isabel paused, wondering how to sensitively phrase her next question. 'I understand that your mother died while Mr Langton was away. When he came back, he didn't ask for the key to be returned because he didn't want to bother you. So, my question is, do you know what happened to it?'

The women looked at each other, baffled. 'I've no idea,' Stella said. 'It was a difficult time for us, when Mum died. Something like that wouldn't have crossed our minds. It never occurred to me that Mum might be looking after next door's cat when she passed away.'

'And you never came across the key?' Isabel persisted. 'When you were clearing the house?'

'I certainly didn't,' Stella said. 'What about you, Heather?'

Heather shook her head. 'No, sorry. There was a tin that Mum used to keep over there.' She pointed to a long stretch of empty work surface. 'It was full of all sorts of odds and ends … you know, string, the key for the meter boxes, drawing pins. I seem to recall there were a few random keys in there, but I have no idea what they unlocked.'

'And do you know what happened to this tin?'

'I really couldn't say,' Heather said, her tone noncommittal. 'It was probably thrown away with a load of other junk.'

Isabel could feel frustration building somewhere inside her abdomen. This whole question of the key was an impossible conundrum. There were so many people who could potentially have accessed a key, or a copy of one.

She turned back to face the window, looking out at the garden, which was a larger plot of land than at number 4.

'The garden next door backs onto the fields,' Isabel said. 'What lies behind your boundary? Is it more fields?'

'No, there's a public footpath that runs along the back of the houses on this side of the cul-de-sac,' Stella said. 'It cuts between Hollybrook Close and the next housing estate along. I can show you, if you like.'

Isabel decided she would like. Very much. She waited as Stella pulled open a drawer, retrieved a key, and unlocked the back door. Isabel followed her out into the garden and, together, they walked along a central path to the top end of the lawn. Heather stayed behind in the kitchen. Understandable, given that it was freezing cold outside.

The pathway zigzagged around an impressive collection of plants and shrubbery.

'The garden's beautifully laid out,' Isabel said. 'I bet it's glorious in the summer.'

'Yes, my mum enjoyed gardening,' Stella said. 'It's all looking very neglected now, I'm afraid. The one advantage of the cold weather is that everything stops growing, including the weeds and the grass. I must confess, even when the weather was warmer, Heather and I haven't had the time or inclination to keep on top of things. That's one of the reasons we're desperate to find a buyer. By the time spring comes and everything starts to grow again, we're hoping the garden will be someone else's responsibility.'

They had reached the end of the path, where a tall eucalyptus and a bare silver birch tree stood side by side. The long, tall trunk of the birch was shiny and elegant-looking. Behind the trees was a chest-high panel fence. Isabel stood on her toes and peered over the top of it. On the other side lay a narrow, tarmacked footpath. Beyond that, a tatty fence marked the end boundary of a property on the adjacent housing estate.

Isabel turned back towards the house. 'I noticed one of the fence panels is down,' she said. 'Round the other side, at the back of the garage. The boundary between you and next door.'

'Yeah,' Stella said, sounding exasperated. 'It blew down last week during the gales. Heather and I were hoping the new neighbour would have fixed it by now.'

Heather had wandered outside. She took a seat at a small patio table by the back door and lit a cigarette.

'Perhaps Ruth Prendergast hasn't noticed it,' Isabel said, as she and Stella made their way back to the house. 'It's been so cold and wet since last week's storm … she's probably not ventured into the garden. I'm surprised you spotted it, considering the fence is round the back, out of sight.'

'It was me who noticed it,' said Heather. Turning her head sideways, she blew smoke into the air. 'You can see it from the side window in the dining room.' Then, as if to justify why she'd had reason to wander into an empty room, she added: 'That's where the central heating thermostat is. I went in to adjust it and that's when I saw that one of the panels was down.'

'I suspect whoever committed the murder may have accessed number 4 through the back door,' Isabel said. 'If so, it's possible they came along the public footpath, over the back here, through your garden and then across into next door, possibly via the gap in the fence. I'm going to bring a forensics team in to take a look.'

Heather shuddered. 'I don't like the thought of someone using Mum's garden as a route to commit a crime,' she said. 'But obviously, if you think that's what happened, you're more than welcome to bring your people in.'

'Thank you,' Isabel said. 'We've had a couple of downpours since the murder was committed, so they may not find anything, but we'll need to check.'

'Is there anything else we can help with?' said Stella. 'Only I have to leave for work shortly.'

'One last thing,' Isabel said. 'Do either of you know a man called Kevin Spriggs?' She pulled a photo from her pocket and handed it to Stella. It was a printed copy of one of the selfies Zoe had lifted from the victim's Facebook page.

'No,' Stella said. 'I don't recognise him, and I don't know the name.' She handed the photograph to her sister, who studied it carefully.

'I don't know him either,' Heather said, passing the photograph back to Isabel.

'Is he the victim?' Stella asked. 'The man who was killed next door?'

'Yes. We're trying to understand why he was at the house, and who he was seeing there.'

'What about the new owner?' said Stella. 'Doesn't she know him?'

'No, she'd never met him.'

'Urghh.' Heather shivered. 'It must have been awful for her, coming home and finding the body of a total stranger.'

'Certainly not a pleasant experience,' Isabel agreed. 'She's staying elsewhere for a while. The incident has shaken her up ... made her nervous about being in the house on her own.'

It was as she imparted this piece of information that Isabel realised that three out of the five properties in Hollybrook Close were now standing empty.

Chapter 19

Lucas was waiting to be served in the Coppa Café opposite the police station. He'd placed his order for a cappuccino, and was toying with the idea of getting a cheese and onion cob to go with it. Then, remembering he was on his way to the offices of Layton, Bradshaw & Young, he decided to opt for something else instead. He didn't want to turn up there with onion breath.

'And I'll have a sausage cob, please, with brown sauce,' he said, when the café proprietor had plonked his cappuccino-filled bamboo coffee mug on the counter. It was Lucas's own personal mug – one of those eco-friendly, reusable travel cups. Contrary to popular belief, he liked to do his bit for the environment. He also enjoyed the smug feeling of self-righteousness he got whenever he presented his recycled cup to a barista.

He carried the sausage butty to his car and ate it straight away, while it was still warm. The bread was soft and deliciously fresh – exactly the kind of grub he needed before heading off to talk to a load of hoity-toity solicitors and their flunkies. Lucas dreaded dealing with what his gran called *posh folks*. It wasn't that he thought they were better than him, or cleverer, he just didn't like the way they looked down their noses at him. It was probably his unconventional appearance that they found objectionable. Lucas knew he wasn't handsome, nowhere near, and he was well known for his couldn't-care-less attitude to fashion and haircuts. The truth was, he'd never been interested in trying to perfect the immaculately groomed look some men liked to cultivate. It was something he'd never be able to pull off successfully, so why bother trying?

Lucas was aware that he didn't compare favourably with DS Fairfax in the looks department. Dan was tall and handsome, with a coif of hair that never misbehaved. He was the type of man women considered fit and hot. Lucas slotted more into the cuddly and warm category.

In theory, Lucas should have resented the arrival of Dan with his senior rank and dark good looks. But the truth was, he thought Dan was all right. Admittedly, when he'd joined Bainbridge CID as the new sergeant, Lucas had been wary, but the DS had proved himself to be friendly, honest and decent.

The same couldn't be said of the supercilious woman who greeted him when he arrived at the offices of Layton, Bradshaw & Young. According to the engraved nameplate on her desk, her moniker was Michelle Winson and she was the office manager.

'Morning,' Lucas said, as he held up his warrant card.

Ms Winson pursed her lips, as though he was presenting her with a dead rat, or something equally distasteful. 'What can I do for you?' she said, looking at him suspiciously.

'I'd like to speak to someone in charge,' Lucas said. Two could play at power games.

'Whatever it is you want to know, you can talk to me about it,' she said. 'Although, please bear in mind that if you're here to ask about someone we represent, we're obliged to maintain strict rules on client confidentiality.'

'Let's start with an easy question, shall we?' Lucas said. 'A question about your procedures.'

'Procedures? What kind of procedures?'

'Let's say one of your clients is selling or buying a house. What's the process when it comes to the exchange of keys?'

When he'd entered the office, Michelle Winson had stood up. Now she sat down again, failing to invite Lucas to do the same.

'Before I answer your question, I'd like to know why you need this information,' she said. 'I think that's only fair, don't you?'

'Yes, of course,' Lucas replied. 'You recently did the conveyancing on a property in Hollybrook Close on behalf of your client, Gerald Langton.'

'And?'

'*And*,' Lucas continued, 'a serious crime has since been committed at the house. The new homeowner wasn't involved, and there was no sign of a break-in, so we're working on the assumption that someone entered the property using a key. *That* is why I need to know about your procedures.'

She gave him a tight smile and glanced down at her desk. 'As a general rule, we don't get involved in the exchange of keys,' she said, speaking slowly, her tone patronising. 'Let me explain how it works. On the day of completion, the buyer's solicitor will arrange for the purchase monies to be transferred to the seller's solicitor. With me so far?'

'I think so,' Lucas said, determined not to let this condescending woman get under his skin.

'The buyer normally collects the house keys from the selling estate agent, or directly from the seller,' she continued. 'Of course, the keys are only released once the seller's solicitor has confirmed that the purchase monies have been received. The process really is quite simple.'

'So it's unlikely you'd ever hold the keys to a property? Here in this office?'

'It happens occasionally,' Michelle Winson said. 'But it's rare.'

'What about the sale of 4 Hollybrook Close? Can you confirm whether your firm had a set of keys to the house at any point?'

'I don't believe we did, but let me check that for you.' She stood up, went over to a filing cabinet and pulled out a manila folder. Glancing down at the inside cover, she shook her head. 'No. There's no record of us having the keys. It says here the instructions were for the buyer to collect them from the estate agency, Bartlett & Lee.'

Lucas thought that this, at least, must be good news. It reduced the pool of individuals who'd had an opportunity to get their mitts on a key.

'Thank you for the information,' Lucas said. 'Now, can we talk about one of your firm's clients? Kevin Spriggs. He was charged with common assault a couple of years ago and, according to our records, he was represented at the magistrates' court by someone from Layton, Bradshaw & Young.'

'I really wouldn't know without checking,' Michelle replied. 'And anyway, I'm afraid I wouldn't be able to discuss the case with you. You'd need to speak to whoever represented him.'

'I believe the lawyer's name was Samuel Watling,' Lucas said, having looked up the details before he left the office.

'That would make sense,' Michelle said. 'Mr Watling was one of our criminal lawyers.'

She grabbed hold of her mouse, throttling it aggressively to wake up her computer screen.

'Was?'

'He left the firm six months ago,' Michelle said, typing something into her keyboard and scanning her screen. 'Ah, yes. As I'm sure you're aware, the client pleaded guilty. There's not a lot else I can tell you.'

'Did you ever meet Kevin Spriggs?' Lucas asked.

'I don't remember meeting him,' she replied. 'Then again, I do deal with a lot of people in my job.'

'How do I get hold of Samuel Watling if I need to speak to him?' Lucas said.

'If you let me have your telephone number, I'll call you later with his contact details. I'm afraid I'm not authorised to give out that information without checking with Mr Watling and one of the senior partners first.'

Lucas handed her a card, and she took it from him, holding it by the edges as though it were laced with poison. 'I'll be in touch,' she said, dropping the card onto her desk and giving him an unconvincing smile.

'I look forward to it,' Lucas replied. 'You have a nice day now.'

Stuck-up cow, he thought, as he stepped into the street and trudged back to his car. When he was a kid, his parents had always told him it cost nothing to be polite. It was on days like this that he realised they hadn't known what the hell they were talking about.

Chapter 20

'Henry seems to like you. You obviously have a way with cats.'

Zoe was sitting in Gerald Langton's living room, with his black-and-white cat on her knee. Its needle-like claws were kneading her lap in a steady, painful rhythm.

'To be honest, I don't have much experience with them,' Zoe said. 'But, you're right ... for some reason they do seem to like me.'

'Cats are a good judge of character,' Gerald said. 'That thing they do when they're sitting on your knee? It's a test. Henry's checking whether he can trust you.'

Despite the stinging sharpness of the cat's claws, Zoe managed to smile. 'I'm a police officer,' she said. 'I think he's in safe hands, don't you?'

The old man chuckled. 'I suppose he is. Now, how can I help you today? I've already spoken to your colleagues and told them everything I know.'

Zoe placed a tentative hand on the cat's head and stroked the space between its ears. The clawing intensified.

'When I spoke to you on the phone, you said you were going to ask your son to join us. Is he on his way?'

'He is,' Gerald Langton replied. 'He texted a couple of minutes before you arrived. There's a hold-up on the A6. Roadworks. He'll be here presently.'

As they waited for Dominic Langton to arrive, Zoe asked a question prompted by the call she'd received from the DI half an hour earlier.

'The key Katrina Mariner used when she looked after your cat,' she said. 'Can you confirm whether it was for the front door, or the back?'

'The back,' Mr Langton replied. 'That way, she went straight into the kitchen, which is where Henry's food bowls were.'

'OK, thank you.'

That would certainly fit with the boss's theory that the killer accessed the house through the back garden.

'Now,' Zoe continued, 'can you tell me whether you've ever employed a plumber called Alfie Moss?'

Mr Langton gave a dismissive shake of the head. 'I've not needed to. Everything here in the bungalow has been replaced or refurbished. It's one of the reasons I chose this place. All the fixtures and fittings are new. They should see me out.'

'What about at your old house?' Zoe said. 'Did you ever engage Alfie Moss's services while you were living at Hollybrook Close?'

'No, definitely not. That house was new when I moved in. Never had much need for a plumber, thank goodness.'

'And you've never met Alfie Moss in any other capacity?' Zoe continued. 'You don't know him socially?'

Gerald Langton threw back his head and laughed. 'What is it with you lot? The other detectives were quizzing me about someone called Kevin Spriggs, and I didn't know him either. Make a habit of this, do you? Interrogating people about complete strangers … people they've never heard of?'

'I'm hardly interrogating you, am I, Mr Langton?'

He mustered a smile. 'Fair enough. I didn't mean to be rude, but you coppers don't seem too keen on taking me at my word. When I tell you I don't know someone, you rephrase the question and ask me all over again. So … let me spell it out as clearly as I can. I didn't know the guy the other detectives were asking about, and I don't know any Alfie Moss. Professionally or socially.'

'What about your son? Could he—'

She was interrupted by the sound of a key in the door.

'Here he is now.' Gerald Langton leapt up. 'You can ask him yourself while I make a hot drink. Is tea OK, or would you prefer coffee?'

'I'm all right, thanks. I had a coffee before I left the station.'

She turned as Dominic Langton strode into the room. He was in his fifties, doughy-faced and tall, like his father. He looked rather cross and impatient, as though he was being put to an almighty inconvenience.

'Hello, Dad,' he said. Then, turning to Zoe, he added: 'I'm Dominic Langton. You're DC Piper I assume?'

'I am. Thank you for coming, Mr Langton.'

'I thought I'd better. After all, it's not every day you find out your father's being questioned by the police.'

'You make it sound very sinister,' Zoe said. 'He's simply helping us with an inquiry we're conducting, and I'm hoping you'll do the same.'

'You can sit in my chair, Dom,' Mr Langton said. 'I'm going to go and make us a cuppa. I'll leave you to it.'

Catching sight of Dominic Langton, the cat jumped off Zoe's knee and scurried into the kitchen with its owner. Clearly, Henry wasn't fond of Mr Langton junior.

'I'm sure your father's already spoken to you about our investigation,' said Zoe.

'He's told me a little.' Dominic pulled at the knees of his trousers as he sat down in his father's armchair. 'He was rather baffled about why you're asking him questions. I'm even more mystified about why *I'm* being questioned.'

'As I'm sure you know, the body of a man has been found at your dad's old house,' Zoe said, thinking that the facts spoke for themselves. She didn't feel the need to offer any further justification for her inquiries.

'Yes, I'd gathered that much.' He brushed at a speck of fluff on his trouser leg. 'But what's that got to do with us?'

'We're speaking to everyone who has a recent connection to the house,' Zoe told him.

'Why? Surely you don't think we were involved?'

'We're simply pursuing routine inquiries,' Zoe said. 'Talking to people to find out what they know.'

Dominic fidgeted, tugging at a cushion that was wedged into the small of his back. 'Well, I can tell you now, I don't know anything. Neither does my father.'

'Even so, I do need to ask you some questions. At this stage, we're trying to build a picture of what happened to the victim, and why. Conversations with people like you and your dad can often throw up important leads.'

He huffed, looking unconvinced. 'If that's what you believe, then get ready to be disappointed. I doubt there's anything my father or I can tell you … but, go on … I'll play along. What do you want to know?'

'First of all, do you still have a key to number 4 Hollybrook Close?'

Dominic folded his arms. 'That's easy enough to answer. No. I don't.'

'But you had a key, until recently?'

'I did. I gave it back to Dad on the day he moved.'

'And you didn't get a spare cut?'

'No. Why on earth would I do that?'

To retain access to the property? Because you were planning to use your dad's old house to commit a murder? Zoe was aware that her instinctive dislike of Dominic Langton was in danger of clouding her judgement. The man was arrogant, certainly, but that was probably all he *was* guilty of. She forced herself back to her intended line of questioning.

'Can I ask whether you know a man called Kevin Spriggs?'

'That's the man whose body was found in Hollybrook Close?'

'That's right. Can you answer the question, please?'

'With pleasure.' He forced his lips into an unctuous smile. 'I don't know anyone called Kevin Spriggs, but perhaps if I saw a photo, I may know the man by sight.'

Zoe pulled out her phone and showed him a photograph of the victim.

'He does look vaguely familiar,' Dominic said, 'but, no. Sorry. I don't know him.' He gave a firm shake of the head.

'He was a regular at the Sheaf of Corn,' said Zoe. 'Perhaps you recognise him from there. Have you ever been to that pub?'

Gerald Langton had wandered back into the room carrying two mugs and a pack of shortbread, which was tucked under his arm.

'You used to go there when you were a youth, didn't you?' he said, as he placed the drinks on the coffee table. 'Or was that your brother?'

'When he was young, Neil hung out in almost every pub in Bainbridge,' Dominic said. 'The Sheaf of Corn was never my scene. I did end up in there on a couple of occasions … years ago. It was a dingy little place as I recall. A real dive. These days, if I'm going to have a drink, I like it to be somewhere more upmarket.'

'For all you know, the Sheaf of Corn might have had a makeover and gone all trendy,' said Gerald.

'Trust me, it hasn't,' Zoe said. 'Being generous, it's probably best described as authentic.'

'Some people love places like that,' Dominic said. 'They travel miles for a touch of what they consider to be *authenticity*. They sit on uncomfortable furniture and order their pints of real ale and tell themselves they're experiencing the real deal. If you ask me, they're deluding themselves.'

Even though she agreed with him, Zoe couldn't bring herself to say so. Instead, she pressed on with her next question. 'Kevin

Spriggs worked at the Crown Garage here in Bainbridge,' she said. 'Have you ever taken your car there?'

Dominic Langton looked horrified. 'Certainly not,' he said. 'I have my car serviced at the BMW garage. Establishments such as the Crown Garage are all very well if you drive an older vehicle, but I wouldn't dream of letting some backstreet mechanic get his hands on my motor.'

Zoe added snobbery and pretentiousness to Dominic Langton's list of faults. There was also a touch of misogynism in his automatic assumption that a car mechanic would be male.

'What about Alfie Moss?' Zoe asked. 'Ever heard of him?'

'No,' Dominic said.

'He's a plumber. Do you think he could have done any work for you in the past?'

'I have no idea. That's not the kind of information I carry around in my head. When you hire a plumber, you're not necessarily going to remember his name, are you?'

'Or her name,' Zoe said. She really didn't like Dominic Langton, not at all, and she was glad to be able to draw the interview to a close.

'If you do remember anything at any stage, please give me a call,' she said. 'For now, I'll leave you to your tea and biccies. Thank you, gentlemen.'

She stood up, certain that when she left, the Langton men would stir their tea and whinge about how she'd wasted their time. Zoe couldn't wait to get back behind her desk to log on to her computer. She preferred technology over difficult people any day.

Chapter 21

In terms of the allocation of actions in this investigation, Lucas was beginning to think he'd drawn the short straw. Having dealt with the snooty woman at Layton, Bradshaw & Young, he was now off to the Crown Garage, where he would no doubt get short shrift from some greasy mechanic, answering questions reluctantly from under the bonnet of a car.

The garage was at the end of an industrial estate off the main A6 road. He pulled into the forecourt and, grudgingly, headed inside.

At the customer service desk he was directed towards an office at the back, the domain of the garage owner, Carl Redport. Contrary to any preconceptions he might have had, the office was a surprisingly calm and quiet space. A thick partition wall deadened the sound of revving engines and dropped spanners in the workshop, although the smell of oil and fumes and Swarfega had somehow managed to infiltrate its walls.

Lucas had called ahead and had already brought Carl Redport up to speed on the purpose of his visit. During that conversation he'd gleaned that Spriggs had been on leave on the day he was killed, the third of three days he'd booked at short notice.

Lucas parked himself on an uncomfortable upright chair. 'You told me on the phone that Spriggs was on holiday on Wednesday,' he said, getting straight to the point.

'That's right,' Carl Redport said. 'He booked Monday, Tuesday and Wednesday off. Said he'd decided to take a long weekend to use up some holiday. It was a last-minute arrangement.'

'Any idea what he was going to do with his time off?'

'I got the impression he was having a few lazy days,' Carl said. 'As far as I know, he didn't have anything special planned.'

'Tell me about Kevin Spriggs,' Lucas said. 'What kind of bloke was he?'

The garage owner leaned back in his chair and filled his cheeks with air. 'Where do I start?' he said. 'Kev was a complicated individual, but a great mechanic. Most of the time anyway.'

'Had he worked here long?'

'Yeah, even longer than me,' said Carl. 'My dad bought this place in the mid-Seventies and he took Kev on as an apprentice in the late Eighties. I started here a couple of years after that, and when my dad retired fifteen years ago, I took the business over.'

'And was Kevin Spriggs a good employee? Was he reliable? Honest and trustworthy?'

Carl leaned forward, looking a little uncomfortable. 'Kev's never been the most popular member of the team,' he said. 'There have been a few issues over the years. I imagine you already know he was found guilty of an assault charge a couple of years back?'

'Spriggs pleaded guilty to the charge,' Lucas said, setting the record straight. 'How did that affect his situation, here at work? He obviously kept his job.'

'By the skin of his teeth,' Carl said, huffing air through his nostrils. 'If it wasn't for the fact that he'd worked here for over thirty years, I probably would have let him go. I thought long and hard about sacking him but, in the end, I decided to keep him on. I didn't think it'd do Kev any good to add unemployment to his list of problems.'

'How did that decision go down with your other employees?'

'Not well at all. They weren't happy. They gave Kev *and* me the cold shoulder for a while afterwards.'

'So, why did you choose to keep him on?'

Carl Redport shrugged. 'It boiled down to the fact that he was my best mechanic. Kev was a highly skilled worker and, at that point, he hadn't given me any real cause for complaint … about his technical abilities, at any rate. More recently though, he let himself down. Badly.'

Lucas pricked up his ears. 'Oh, yeah? What did he do to blot his copybook?'

Carl shuffled awkwardly, seeming reluctant to reveal the nature of Kevin Spriggs' misdemeanour. 'I wouldn't want this to be common knowledge,' he said. 'We have our reputation to think about, but now that Kev's dead, I don't suppose there's any harm in telling you about it.'

Lucas waited.

'Kev messed up.' Carl leaned forward to emphasise his next two words. 'Big time.'

'Messed up how?'

'Do you want the technical details, or a straightforward explanation?'

'I'll go for the straightforward version,' Lucas said. He'd listen to a more detailed explanation if and when necessary, but why make this investigation any more complicated than it already was?

'About six months back, Kev was doing some repair work on a brake system … something he'd done thousands of times over the years. Long story short, he cocked it up. Thankfully, another member of the team picked up on the problem before the customer came to collect the car. If he hadn't, well … let's just say the motor wouldn't have been safe to drive.'

'No harm done then, really?' Lucas said. 'I mean, even the best people make mistakes occasionally. I can understand you being annoyed, but why was it such a big deal?'

'Because …' Carl leaned forward and lowered his voice. 'Kev

had been drinking. Actually, no. I promised you the straightforward version, so I won't mince my words. He was drunk. Pissed. It's a sackable offence and he was extremely lucky to keep his job. I'd already given him a second chance after the court case fiasco.'

'So, effectively, you gave him a *third* chance,' Lucas said. 'That was very generous of you.'

'Or stupid,' Carl said. 'Depending on how you look at it.'

Lucas frowned. 'Was that the first time Kevin Spriggs had turned up for work drunk?'

'Yes. Give him his due, up to that point Kev had always taken his work seriously, and I know he valued his job. Occasionally he'd roll up with a hangover, but never anything that impacted on his ability to work safely. Kev liked a drink more than most – he'd had a problem with alcohol for most of his adult life – but, when it came to his job, he wasn't in the habit of pissing about. In fact, he was proud of being a good mechanic. It was one of the few things in life he'd managed to get right.'

'Was he drinking at work?'

'God, no! If I'd found out he'd brought alcohol in here, to the garage, I'd have sacked him on the spot. I know he didn't have any booze on him, because I checked. I even made him open his locker, and there was nothing there either. He'd been out at lunchtime though, and I can only assume that's when he'd had a drink. A *lot* to drink.'

'Did he go to the pub? Or to an off-licence?'

'I don't know for sure, but he only had an hour's break, so he wouldn't have had time to drink many pints. It's more likely he bought himself a half-bottle of spirits and downed that.'

'Or went to the pub and had a few whisky chasers?' Lucas suggested.

'Yep, that's possible. Anyroad, we'll never know now, will we?'

'Why would he behave like that?' Lucas said. 'From what you've said, it seems out of character. I mean, why risk his job? Was there something bothering him?'

'I asked him that. I thought if something earth-shattering had happened, it would at least excuse his behaviour … to some extent anyway. Something or someone *must* have got to him, but other than saying it was to do with his lad, he refused to give me any details. Kev was a tough cookie. If he was upset, he never showed his emotions … in fact, I'm not sure he knew how to express his feelings. Something had happened though, I'm sure of it.'

'What about his colleagues? What did they have to say about the situation?'

'I got one hell of a load of grief about it,' Carl said. 'Kev wasn't well liked, even at the best of times. He didn't know how to play nice, if you know what I mean. Anyway, when I let him off with a written warning after the drinking incident, the other lads accused me of being soft.'

'Is there any one member of staff who had a particular problem with the situation?'

'Not especially,' Carl replied. 'In fairness to them, the lads and lasses at Crown Garage tend to stick together and no one bears a grudge for very long. At the end of the day, and despite everything, Kev was still one of the gang. Don't get me wrong, he could be infuriating, a total pain in the arse, but he was *our* pain in the arse, if you know what I mean? The lads had a way of overlooking his foibles. You have to, don't you? When you work with someone, you're obliged to make the most of things.'

Lucas thought of Zoe. She certainly had a few quirks, but he didn't mind them. The truth was, he liked her and he wouldn't have her any other way. Getting along with Zoe must be an absolute breeze, compared to working with someone like Kevin Spriggs.

Carl placed his elbows on his desk. 'If you've come here looking for someone with a grudge against Kev … someone you can pin his murder on, you're looking in the wrong place. We're a small team, but a happy one. The guys out there' – he pointed to the main workshop area – 'they're good people. Polite and law-abiding. Admittedly, some of 'em might not be the brightest lights on the Christmas tree, but nobody in my employment is dumb enough to bump off a co-worker.'

This bloke is a loyal boss, I'll give him that, Lucas thought. *Was there a reason he felt the need to defend his employees so vigorously?*

Lucas decided on a different approach. 'What about the customer?' he said. 'The one whose car Kevin Spriggs cocked up? Did he ever find out what had happened?'

Carl Redport gave him an old-fashioned look. 'Thankfully not, and I'd like it to stay that way. Like I said, the problem was discovered before the customer collected the car. No one was ever in any danger of driving on dodgy brakes.'

'When I spoke to some of Spriggs' drinking buddies, they said he'd been concerned about something at work.' Lucas scratched his chin and stared at Carl Redport. 'Do you think it was his mistake with the brakes that was worrying him? The whole being-drunk-at-work thing?'

'I hope to God he didn't tell his mates about his shoddy workmanship.' For the first time in the conversation, Carl sounded angry. 'Times are tough enough as it is. The last thing I need is for word to get around that the Crown Garage can't be relied upon to do a good job.'

'I wouldn't worry too much about that. As far as I know, the people I spoke to knew nothing about the brake debacle,' Lucas said. 'But are you sure that's what was troubling Spriggs? There wasn't anything else going on, here at work?'

'No, there was nothing else,' said Carl, rubbing his nose quickly. 'Other than the incidents we've discussed, Kev's work life was pretty unremarkable.'

'What about his love life?' Lucas said. 'Do you know if he was seeing anyone?'

'Search me. Kev's encounters with women were always shrouded in mystery. There were times when I wondered if his supposed conquests were all in his imagination.'

'So there was no one special in his life?' Lucas said. 'No one he was seeing regularly.'

'Not that I know of. And if they *were* going out with Kev, they would have been very *special* indeed. It would have taken a strong woman to put up with his antics.'

Lucas smiled. 'OK, well … thanks for your time, Mr Redport. I'll be in touch if I need to ask you anything else.'

Leaving behind the relative peace of the office, Lucas wandered back through the noisy repair shop. One of the mechanics was hammering a piece of crumpled bodywork, and someone else was using a power drill to screw in a set of wheel bolts. Lucas nodded at them as he walked past. Outside, a young mechanic in a pair of green overalls was sitting at a plastic-covered driving seat, revving the car's engine. As Lucas strolled by, he took his foot off the accelerator.

'You're a detective then,' he said. It was a statement, rather than a question.

'Yes,' Lucas replied. 'I am. DC Killingworth. You are?'

'Dylan,' the lad replied. 'Dylan Brewster. Penny said you're here about Kevin Spriggs.'

'Penny?' said Lucas.

'The receptionist.' Dylan tilted his head towards the customer service desk.

'Ah, yeah, right.' Lucas nodded his understanding.

'Have you found out who killed him yet?' Dylan asked.

'No, but we're working on it. Is there something you want to tell me? Do you have any thoughts on the matter?'

'Me?' The young mechanic looked startled, like a young buck caught in the headlights of an approaching truck. 'Thoughts? What kind of thoughts?'

'Do you know if Kevin Spriggs had any enemies? Had he upset anyone recently?'

Dylan pulled a face. 'He was always upsetting people. He wasn't much liked around here – I'll tell you that for nowt.'

So much for Carl Redport's assertion that his employees were a 'small but happy team'.

'We put up with Kev because we had to,' Dylan continued, 'but I'm a hundred per cent certain no one's gonna miss him. Especially Penny. She *really* didn't like him.'

Lucas stopped and turned, swivelling around to face the garage again. 'Is that right?' he said. 'Thanks, Dylan. Perhaps I should have a quick word with Penny before I go.'

Chapter 22

'I hear you weren't exactly Kevin Spriggs' biggest fan,' Lucas said. 'Want to tell me about it?'

The receptionist, Penny, was sitting behind the customer service desk, riffling through a catalogue of car parts.

She looked up. 'And who told you that? Young Dylan, I bet. I saw you two chatting. You don't want to believe everything he says. He's young. Naïve.'

'Are you saying you *did* like Kevin Spriggs?'

She slapped the catalogue shut and pushed it bad-temperedly to the other side of her desk. 'No, I didn't like him, but I wasn't the only one who felt that way. Kev wasn't the easiest person to warm to.'

'Did you have a problem with him for any particular reason?'

She placed her forearms on the counter and leaned forward.

'Look, I've worked here long enough to grow accustomed to the ways of that lot out there. When you sit here day after day, you can't help but overhear their swearing and belching and stupid comments. They can be a right bunch of heathens, but despite their uncouth ways ... deep down, they're OK. They're respectful to me ... kind and polite, and I wouldn't swap them. Kevin Spriggs? Well, he was a different animal altogether. He was full of himself, always took things too far. There were times when he made my flesh crawl.'

'What did he do to upset you?'

She pulled back and stood to her full height. 'He kept asking me to go out for a drink with him. I thought he was joking at first. I mean, he knew I was married, and he'd be in trouble if my husband found out he was giving me grief, but he wouldn't let it go. It got to the point where I didn't like being on my own with him.'

'And did you tell your husband that he was hassling you?'

'Yes, and a fat lot of good it did me. He told me I was being oversensitive. Said it was probably a case of Kev being Kev, and that I shouldn't take it seriously.'

Lucas was confused. 'Your husband knew Kevin Spriggs?'

The tinkling sound of Penny's laughter sounded inappropriate to Lucas's ears. 'Of *course* he knew him,' she said, her voice teasing. 'I'm Penny Redport, Carl's wife.'

Chapter 23

There was no sign of Dan or Lucas when Zoe got back to the office. It was chilly out, but even colder in the CID room. After she'd hung up her coat, she pulled on the ancient woollen cardigan that was permanently draped over the back of her chair. Folding it around herself, she plucked absent-mindedly at the fuzzy bobbles on the pilled sleeves and stared into space, trying to think laterally about the case.

Whoever killed Spriggs had known that no one would be in at number 4 Hollybrook Close at the time of the murder, which meant they must have had prior knowledge of Ruth Prendergast's schedule.

How had that knowledge been gained?

Had the perpetrator watched the house? Or had Ruth talked to someone about her job and inadvertently let slip her working hours. Or perhaps, despite her assertion that she didn't know him, Ruth Prendergast was somehow connected to Kevin Spriggs' death. She'd been in interviews all day on Wednesday, but she must have broken for lunch at some stage. Was it possible she could have slipped away during that time and gone back to Hollybrook Close?

The best way to get answers to those questions was to ask Ruth directly. Picking up the phone, she dialled her number.

Fifteen minutes later, Zoe knocked twice on the glass partition that separated the DI's office from the rest of the CID room.

'Can I talk to you, boss?' she said, pulling at a strand of hair and twirling it around her finger.

'Of course,' DI Blood replied. 'What's up. You look anxious.'

'I can't get hold of Ruth Prendergast. Her phone's switched off.'

'Maybe she's busy, or in a work meeting.'

'That's just it,' Zoe said. 'She isn't *at* work. She seems to have gone AWOL.'

'AWOL?' DI Blood sat up. 'What makes you say that?'

'When I couldn't get her on her mobile, I rang through to her office and her boss said she's taken the day off.'

The DI's shoulders relaxed. 'That's hardly surprising. Perhaps she's had a meltdown about discovering the body and needs some time to herself.'

'I thought the same, initially,' Zoe said, 'but then her manager gave me a number for the colleague Ruth's been staying with … someone called Leanne.'

'OK … and what has this Leanne said that's got you in such a tizzy?'

'Leanne's also taken the day off. She and Ruth are supposed to be going away for a couple of nights.'

'Together?'

'Yes, some kind of walking weekend. They've booked rooms in a hotel in Hartington for tonight and Saturday. They were due to set off at midday. However, at eleven o'clock this morning, Ruth announced she was popping back to Hollybrook Close to get her walking boots and some waterproof clothing for the trip. She hasn't come back.'

The DI touched the screen of her phone to check the time. It was half past two.

Zoe folded her arms. 'I know she's only a couple of hours or so overdue, but Ruth doesn't come across as the sort of person who would go off grid like this. And why is her phone switched off? I've tried the number several times, and Leanne's been calling her since noon.'

'Do you think she's disappeared on purpose? That she was involved in the murder, or she's hiding something ... not telling us everything she knows? Or are you worried she might have harmed herself?'

'I don't believe she had anything to do with the murder,' Zoe said. 'I double-checked with her boss ... Ruth was conducting job interviews all day on Wednesday and, although she did break for an hour, she spent the whole of that time eating a buffet lunch with the interview candidates. She never left the building.'

'So what are you thinking?' said DI Blood.

'What if she saw something, or knows something about the perpetrator?' Zoe said. 'Something she's only now realised is significant?'

'She'd get in touch and tell us, surely?'

'What if she's not in a position to get in touch? What if she's confronted someone and inadvertently put herself in danger? What if that *someone* is the killer?'

'Bloody hell, Zoe, that's a lot of "what ifs". Dan and I spoke to Ruth not long after she found the body. She was helpful and co-operative. I certainly didn't get the impression she was holding anything back. However, if your gut's telling you something different, you should follow it up. Start by sending a patrol car round to Hollybrook Close to see whether Ruth is still there.'

Chapter 24

Dan had driven over to Pentrich, to the home of Jessica and Tony Moss. They lived in a stone-built cottage in the centre of the village, a couple of hundred yards from the local pub. The property's mullioned windows were small and, consequently, the interior of the house was dark – but it was far from gloomy. The room they were sitting in was homey and snug, cheerfully decorated, with brightly coloured furnishings and an open fire burning in the grate. The sweet smell of woodsmoke tickled the back of Dan's nostrils. He liked a real fire. It reminded him of his gran's old house.

'As part of our investigation, we're trying to build a picture of Kevin Spriggs … a character profile, if you like,' he said. 'If we can understand the kind of person he was, it'll help us determine who might be responsible for his death.'

Jessica and Tony Moss exchanged a worried look. They were sitting in cushioned armchairs on either side of the fireplace, but neither of them looked comfortable.

'I've not had any contact with him for years,' Jessica Moss said, clearing her throat nervously. 'The Kev I divorced wasn't a very nice person.'

'But you must have liked him once,' Dan said. 'When you married him?'

'He was always a bit of a tearaway … but yes, I liked him well enough in the beginning,' she said. 'It was when he started drinking heavily that his personality changed.'

'Aye, alcohol can do that to a person,' said Dan.

'We were really young when we got together,' Jessica said, her large brown eyes shining as she recalled that earlier period in her life. 'Kev was funny in those days. Funny ha ha, that is. Not funny peculiar. He knew how to make me laugh and he looked out for me. We never had much money, so we didn't do anything exciting with our lives, but he was kind to me at first and … yeah, I was happy enough. No doubt the relationship would have run its course eventually, but then I got pregnant.'

'And so you got married?' Dan said.

'Yeah, my mum insisted we get hitched. She was old-fashioned like that.'

'Your mum liked Kevin then?'

'On the contrary,' Jessica said. 'She never had a good word to say about him, but I guess she thought he was better than nothing. She didn't want me to end up as a single mother.'

'If you don't mind me saying so, that doesn't sound like a good reason to get married,' said Dan.

'It wasn't,' Jessica replied. 'I had my doubts, but I went along with it to keep the peace. There'd been an almighty bust-up a few years earlier when my sister got pregnant, and I didn't want history to repeat itself.'

'So when did Kevin's drinking start to get out of hand?'

'He always liked a drink – something else that my mother disapproved of – but it was after I had Alfie that it started to become an issue. Before that, Kev and I used to go to the pub together, and I like to think I kept him in check. When Alfie was born, he started to go out on his own on Friday nights. Without me to keep an eye on him, he'd come home worse for wear. Then, gradually, he started going out midweek as well as the weekends. It made things hard, because we were already struggling financially.'

143

Dan sat back, nodding occasionally, allowing Jessica Moss to tell her story at her own pace.

'One night, he came in after midnight, stinking of beer and barely able to stand up. Alfie had colic, and I'd been struggling all evening to cope on my own. When I saw the state Kev was in, I lost it. I told him to get out if he didn't want to be a father. That was the first time he hit me. He was mortified afterwards and he said it'd never happen again, but of course it did.'

Tony Moss reached across and patted his wife's knee.

'You don't have to talk about this, Jess,' he said. 'Not if you don't want to.'

'It's fine,' she said, shrugging wearily. 'It's all in the past. I got over it a long time ago.' She looked at Dan, leaning forward in a gesture of appeal. 'I hope you catch whoever did this, because even though Kev ended up being a right bastard, I want you to know he wasn't always like that. He lost his way ... went down the wrong path, but that doesn't mean he deserved to be murdered.'

'We'll do everything we can to find whoever killed him,' Dan assured her.

'Thank you,' she said. 'Kev led me a merry dance, but my luck changed when I left him. After the divorce, I met someone who was kind, someone I could trust. *This* man, right here.' She pointed at Tony Moss and smiled.

It was a touching scene, and Dan hoped his next question wouldn't spoil the mood. 'Did you know that your ex-husband had contacted your son through Facebook?'

Jessica nodded. 'Alfie told me at the time. I have to admit, I wasn't keen on the two of them reconnecting, but my son's a grown man. He makes his own decisions.'

'You're right about that,' said Tony. 'Alfie's always had a mind of his own, even when he was a nipper.'

'Alfie told me he didn't reply to the messages,' Dan said, 'but he did befriend Spriggs on Facebook.'

'That's correct,' Tony said, dipping his head in agreement. 'There's no harm in that, is there?'

Dan thought about the numerous ways social media accounts could be used to find things out about people. Tony Moss seemed oblivious to the opportunities Facebook, Twitter and Instagram offered for online prowling.

'Can I ask where you're going with all these questions?' Tony added, beginning to look irritated. 'Kevin Spriggs was a bad lot and he gave my wife a hard time but, like she said, that's old news. What does their past relationship have to do with what happened to him this week?'

'At this stage in the investigation, we're trying to gather as much information as we can,' Dan said. 'I know you lost touch with Alfie's dad years back, Mrs Moss, but I need to know whether you've had any contact with him more recently.' He swept his eyes in Tony's direction, including him in the question. 'You too, Mr Moss.'

'Of course not,' Tony said, looking bewildered. 'Why would he want to get in touch with us?'

Dan turned his gaze onto Jessica. 'And you, Mrs Moss? Have you had any contact with Kevin Spriggs in the last few years?'

'No. I've already told you that. Anyway, he wouldn't have known how to get in touch. Neither me nor Tony are on Facebook, or anything like that. We're not into all that social networking crap. It's a load of tripe, if you ask me. If I want to keep in touch with my friends, I pick up the phone and have a natter with them, or we meet up for a coffee. I certainly don't rely on social media.'

'So Kevin Spriggs didn't know where you lived?'

'I doubt it,' she said, her tone uncertain. 'I know Alfie wouldn't have told him.'

Tony Moss leaned towards the fire and selected a poker from the brass-handled companion set on the hearth. He began to prod a piece of charred wood, pushing it closer to the centre of the flames. 'Jess and I are both sorry about what's happened to Kevin Spriggs,' he said dismissively, 'but there really is nothing else we can tell you.'

Clearly, he was doing his best to bring the conversation to an end, but Dan wasn't having any of it. He continued with his next question. 'Did your ex-husband have any other close relatives, Mrs Moss?'

'I know he lost both his parents ages ago,' she said. 'He had a brother, Simon, but I never met him. He moved up north a couple of years before Kev and I got together. He was a fair bit older than Kev, and the two of them weren't close. There was a cousin as well that Kev was quite friendly with for a while, but I heard she died about ten years ago.'

'Do you know if he's had any other partners since you and he split up?'

She laughed bitterly. 'He had a few *before* we split up. As well as knocking me about when we were together, Kev was seeing other women. I think most of them were one-off encounters. He never was any good at developing meaningful, lasting relationships, but who knows? He might have met someone special after we divorced … I really couldn't say.'

The fire was roaring now, and Dan was beginning to roast. He wished he could move his chair away from the flames, but there was no space in the tiny room to retreat to. Thankfully, he only had one more question to ask and then he could get out of there, back into the fresh air.

From his inside pocket, he pulled a copy of the photographs found on Kevin Spriggs' fridge. The pictures of the two kids. He smoothed them out and handed them to Jessica.

'Can you tell me if you recognise either of these children please, Mrs Moss.'

She took the photos and stared at them, a line forming between her eyebrows. 'Where did you get these?' she said.

'Do you know who they are?'

146

'They're my grandchildren,' she said. 'These are Alfie's kids. Can I ask why you're carrying their photos in your pocket?'

'They were found during a search of Kevin Spriggs' house, pinned to his fridge.'

Jessica Moss looked across at her husband and held up the photographs with a shaking hand. 'There's no way Alfie would have sent them, so how the hell did he get hold of them?' she asked, her voice shrill.

'He may have downloaded the photos from Alfie's Facebook page,' Dan said. 'Spriggs could have saved the images and had copies printed out.'

'No,' Jessica said vehemently, shaking her head. 'Alfie and Becky don't post photos of the kiddies on Facebook or anywhere else online. They're both very careful about it.'

'You're sure about that?' Dan said.

'Positive,' Jessica said, pushing her fingers through her hair. 'I remember Becky telling me that one of her friends had posted a photo of my grandson on Instagram … or somewhere. Becky was furious. She made her take it off.'

'Becky? Is that Alfie's partner?'

'Yes,' Jessica replied. 'Do they know that Kevin had pictures of the kids?'

'I'm not sure,' Dan said. 'We haven't talked to them about it yet.'

Tony Moss was prodding the fire again and placing another log on top of the pile. The temperature in the small room was becoming intense. Dan wondered whether he was stoking up the heat on purpose, to drive Dan out. If that *was* his strategy, it was working. If Dan didn't get out of there soon, he thought he might faint, or end up melting like a Salvador Dalí watch, folding over the chair and dripping onto the carpet.

Jessica handed back the photographs, her expression calmer. 'Now that Kev's gone, I don't suppose it matters where he got these from,' she said. 'Thinking about it, I'm quite touched he cared enough to put them on his fridge. Perhaps, deep down, there was still some trace of the real Kev left, eh? The old Kev. The young lad *I* once knew.'

Dan thought Jessica Moss was deluding herself, but it wasn't his place to disabuse her. 'Perhaps there was, Mrs Moss,' he said instead. 'It'd be nice to think so.'

Chapter 25

'We're not getting anywhere,' Isabel said. 'Everything's too nebulous and disconnected.'

It was mid-afternoon and she was standing by the window in the CID room, where several members of the incident team had congregated. Their expressions were, for the most part, despondent.

'We've succeeded in building a picture of the victim,' said Dan, who had filled them in on his interview with Jessica Moss. 'The trouble is, no one seems able to tell us anything substantial or significant, and they're certainly not admitting to anything.'

Isabel gazed out of the window at a huge, iron-grey cloud that was sliding listlessly across the horizon. The weather was an exact match for the mood and pace of Operation Jackdaw: cold and dull and sluggish. She and her colleagues had spent the last twenty minutes sharing information and relaying the details of their inquiries, and it had got them precisely nowhere. They were going round in circles.

Despite hours spent trawling through CCTV footage, there had been no sightings of Kevin Spriggs' car on the day of the murder. Further door-to-door inquiries with Spriggs' neighbours had revealed very little. No one had admitted to knowing him well, and he hadn't been spotted leaving his house on the day he was killed.

'It rained nearly all day on Wednesday,' Isabel said. 'Why didn't he take his car when he went over to Hollybrook Close?'

'He could have been planning on having a drink when he got to his destination,' Lucas suggested. 'I'd imagine he'd need his driving licence for his job, so I don't suppose he'd want to risk a drink driving charge.'

'Drinking in the middle of the day?' Isabel pursed her lips. 'Probably not unusual for Kevin Spriggs, based on what we've learned about him – but if he was hoping for a booze-up, that suggests he was meeting someone socially.'

'Maybe it was a secret liaison,' Dan said. 'Perhaps Spriggs was having an illicit relationship with someone.'

'How long would it take to walk from Spriggs' house over to Hollybrook Close?' Isabel said.

'It's right over the other side of town,' said Theo Lindley, the young DC who'd spent most of the day checking the CCTV cameras. He was bright and smart as a whip, but even his natural effervescence seemed to be on the wane. 'I'd say a fast walker could do it in thirty minutes, thirty-five tops.' He rubbed his eyes. 'However, we've checked the cameras on the most direct route, and there's no sign that Spriggs made the journey on foot.'

'In that case, he must have got a lift, or a taxi,' Lucas said. 'I'll check with the local cab firms, see what I can find out.'

'Bear in mind the security cameras in the cul-de-sac captured him *walking* into the close and approaching the house on foot,' Zoe said. 'If he did get a taxi, it must have dropped him off on the main road.'

Isabel scratched her head. 'We keep coming back to the same questions. Why there? Why Hollybrook Close? And who was he meeting?'

'Do you think it could have been Penny Redport, Lucas?' Dan said.

'I'd say it's highly unlikely,' Lucas replied. 'She said Spriggs gave her the creeps. Not a great basis for a relationship.'

Zoe laughed. 'Is that the excuse *your* girlfriends use when they break up with you, Lucas?'

He opened his mouth to retaliate, but Isabel interjected. 'I'm still wondering why Carl Redport wasn't totally honest with you, Lucas. Why didn't he mention that Spriggs had been hitting on his wife? Why keep quiet about it?'

'Pride?' Lucas suggested. 'Maybe Redport was embarrassed.'

'If it was me,' said Dan, 'I'd be annoyed, not embarrassed. Hell, I'd be furious – certainly pissed off enough to have had words about it.'

'Maybe he did tackle Spriggs,' Isabel said. 'Or he chose not to, for some reason.'

'Perhaps he didn't care,' said Zoe. 'Or possibly Carl Redport was scared of Kevin Spriggs.'

'Or Spriggs had something on his boss,' Lucas said. 'Information he could use against him. Perhaps that was how he managed to hold on to his job, despite his misdemeanours. I'll give Redport a call, follow it up.'

Isabel crossed the room and stood in front of the whiteboard. 'All this speculation is fine, but it seems so trivial. Gossipy. We've yet to find anyone who liked Spriggs, but so far I've heard nothing to suggest that anyone had reasonable grounds for murdering him.'

'Jessica Moss did say that Kevin Spriggs was a nice enough guy, once upon a time,' Dan said. 'It's sad when you think of the way alcohol changed things for him. It sounds like he became a deeply unhappy and lonely man.'

Isabel studied Dan carefully, a bemused expression stamped across her face. 'Are you all right, DS Fairfax? It's not like you to be sentimental.'

He smiled. 'I'm trying to be open-minded, boss. See things from both ends of the tunnel.'

'I'm only joshing,' Isabel said. 'You're right about not making judgements, but we mustn't forget that Kevin Spriggs assaulted Sophie Tait. In my book, that makes him an unpleasant and potentially dangerous individual.'

'Aye, well, however dangerous he was, in the end he was no match for his killer,' said Dan.

Isabel turned back to the whiteboard. 'What we need is a breakthrough,' she said. 'Can someone chase up the digital forensics as a matter of urgency. I'm hoping the laptop will give us something we can use to move Op Jackdaw forward.'

PC Will Rowe had strolled through the door. He leaned his broad shoulders against the wall, and his presence made the room feel suddenly crowded.

'Anything to report, Will?' Isabel asked.

'I've been over to Hollybrook Close to check on Ruth Prendergast.' He stood up straight and folded his arms. 'Her car is on the driveway, but there's no sign of her inside. I looked through the windows and knocked several times, but no one answered.'

'She can't have gone far if her car's still there,' Zoe said.

'I was over at the property myself this morning,' said Isabel. 'There was no sign of Ruth at ten-forty-five when I left. However, given that her car's at the house, her phone's switched off, and no one's seen her since eleven o'clock, I think Zoe's concerns are well founded. Head back to the house with another officer, Will, and search inside the property. We can go in under a Section 17. Thankfully, we're still in possession of a key, so there'll be no need for a forced entry. Let me know what you find. If Ruth isn't there, I think it's time to officially report her missing.'

Chapter 26

When Dan wandered into her office twenty minutes later, he had a beaming smile on his face.

'Digital Forensics have been in touch,' he said.

'Go on.'

'They've retrieved a couple of things of interest. Firstly, they found some emails between Kevin Spriggs and a solicitor. Seems he made a will a few months back. We're following that up, and should have the details soon.'

'I wouldn't have thought he'd be the kind of guy to have much to leave to anyone,' Isabel said. 'What else? You said there were a couple of things.'

'They discovered some messages linked to Kevin Spriggs' Facebook account, sent to him through Messenger about six months ago.'

Isabel could tell from the tone of Dan's voice that this was important. She stood up. 'From?'

He leaned his head to one side, his mouth firmly closed. What did he want her to do? Guess?

'Come on, Dan. Spit it out. This isn't some stupid bloody game show.'

He straightened up and lowered his eyes. 'Becky Siddall,' he said. 'Alfie's partner.'

'Is that so?' Isabel sat down again and stretched her legs. '*Very* interesting. And what exactly was the nature of these messages?'

'There were only three, all of them pretty innocent,' Dan said, handing over a piece of paper.

Isabel spluttered. 'They may seem innocent, but no one's beyond suspicion when a man's been killed,' she said, snatching eagerly at the printed sheet of messages.

The first one was the longest.

Hello, Kevin. It's Becky here, Alfie's partner. I know you've messaged him and you're waiting for an answer, but I wanted to let you know that Alfie isn't going to reply. I'm really sorry. I know you two have been out of touch for a long time, but you are still his dad. For what it's worth, I told him he should contact you, but he's being his usual stubborn self. He was dead upset when you got in touch. Quite angry, in fact. Anyway, please don't send any more messages, and don't keep hoping for a reply from him, because there isn't going to be one. When Alfie makes up his mind about something, he doesn't change it.

Kevin Spriggs had replied.

Cheers, Becky. Thanks for letting me know. I'm sorry that Alfie doesn't want to see me, or speak to me. I can't say I blame him. I was a pretty crap dad to him when he was a lad, and time hasn't improved me any. I regret losing touch with him, but I'm sure he had a happier childhood without me in it. I've spent my whole life screwing things up, and I doubt I'll ever change for the better. The reason I messaged him was because I thought it was time, that's all. I'm getting older (if not wiser) and it would be nice for us to meet up. I see from one of Alfie's posts that you both became parents again recently. Congratulations. It's a shame I'll never get to know my grandkids. I realise it's a big ask, but would you send me a photo of them?

The final message was short and to the point.

I'm sending a photo of Leo, and one of Serena, but please don't tell Alfie that we've been in touch, because he wouldn't be happy. I really do wish you all the best but, PLEASE, leave us alone. Don't message me or Alfie again.

'So, that's how he got the photos,' Isabel said. 'Why didn't we pick up on this before? Zoe checked Facebook, didn't she? How come she didn't notice that the victim was friends with Becky Siddall? I assume they were Facebook friends, if they were messaging each other?'

'Actually, they weren't,' said Dan. 'You don't have to be friends with someone to send them a message, providing they haven't blocked you that is.'

'I see,' Isabel said. 'I'm not on Facebook, so I wouldn't know.'

'Are you not into social media then, boss?'

'God, no.' She rolled her eyes. 'I don't feel the need to bare my soul online, thank you very much. Plus, I'm much too long in the tooth to upload one of those pouting selfies, even one that's been put through a photo filter.'

'How do you know that's what people post if you're not on Facebook?'

'I've seen Nathan's page … not that *he* posts pictures of himself pouting, mind you.' She grinned. 'My son's on Facebook and Instagram. Nathan signed up to keep track of what he's been up to on his travels.'

Dan smiled. 'What are we going to do about Becky Siddall? Does this mean she's a suspect?'

'It certainly makes her a person of interest.'

'It's only a few messages, though,' Dan said. 'Like I say, innocent enough on the face of it.'

'At first glance, maybe,' said Isabel. 'But what if Kevin Spriggs didn't leave it at that? What if he tracked Becky down? Started making a nuisance of himself?'

'Based on what I've heard, I wouldn't put it past him,' Dan said. 'I'm also fairly sure Alfie Moss doesn't have a clue about any of this … the photos and the messages. What do you want to do?'

Isabel glanced at the clock. 'Let's head over to Becky's place and see if we can catch her in,' she said. 'Can we drive there in separate cars? I want to head straight home after we've spoken to her.'

'OK. Fine with me.'

'Come on then, Danny boy,' Isabel said. 'And grab your coat. It's freezing out there.'

Chapter 27

Zoe's phone rang thirty seconds after Dan and the DI had dashed out of the office. When she picked up, the first thing that struck her was how deep and soothing Will Rowe's voice was. If he ever gave up his job as a policeman, Zoe was sure he'd be able to make it as a voiceover artist.

'We've completed a primary search of 4 Hollybrook Close,' Will told her. 'There's no sign of Ruth Prendergast in the house or garden. We did find a holdall in the hallway though … it contains warm weather gear, a waterproof jacket, and a pair of walking boots.'

Clearly, Ruth had had time to gather together the items she needed for her trip … but what had happened after that? Where the hell had she gone?

'Can you try and get hold of the security cameras at number 2,' Zoe said. 'They should be able to tell us whether Ruth left the close on foot.'

'I'm not sure the homeowners will be home yet,' Will said. 'But I'll come back later if I have to. I'll knock on some doors as well, find out if anyone's seen anything.'

'You'll be lucky to find anyone about in Hollybrook Close.

We've already established that the cul-de-sac is all but deserted during the day.'

'I'll try anyway,' Will said. 'I'll let you know how I get on.'

Zoe ended the call and rested her elbows on her desk. This whole thing with Ruth Prendergast was weird. Had she dropped out of sight on purpose? Was she planning to harm herself? Or was there something more sinister at play here? Had someone hurt her, or abducted her?

Zoe flicked through her notebook. On her employment file, Ruth's parents were listed as her next of kin, and Ruth's boss had given Zoe their number. The last thing she wanted to do was alarm them unnecessarily, but the time had come to make them aware of what was happening. There was even a remote possibility that Ruth might be there, with them. Admittedly, the chances were slim, given that they lived in Birmingham, and Ruth's car was standing in Hollybrook Close, its engine cold.

'Is that Mr Charlesworth?' Zoe said, when her call was answered.

'Yes. Who is this?'

'My name's DC Zoe Piper from Bainbridge CID. I'm trying to get hold of Ruth Prendergast.'

'I'm her father. Is Ruth all right?' he said, his voice ragged and breathy. 'Has something happened?'

'She's not there then, with you?'

'No … no, she's not. Why would you think she's here?' He sounded alarmed and impatient. 'What's this about?'

'I've been trying to contact your daughter since early this afternoon, but her phone's switched off,' Zoe said. 'No one knows where she is … We're concerned for her safety.'

There was an audible sigh of relief on the other end of the line.

'There's no need to be concerned,' Mr Charlesworth said. 'My wife and I spoke to Ruth last night. She told me she was going to the Peak District with a friend for a few nights. The incident at her house on Wednesday upset her, and she said she wanted to get away for a while. She's probably switched her phone off.'

He sounded so certain, so confident. Relieved. In Mr Charlesworth's mind, his daughter was safe and well. Zoe didn't want to be the one to have to disabuse him.

'Unfortunately ...' she said, her voice hesitant, '... the friend Ruth was going away with ... she doesn't know where your daughter is either. Ruth went back to Hollybrook Close at eleven a.m. this morning to collect some clothes for her trip, and didn't come back. We've checked the house – her car is there, but Ruth isn't.'

'Oh, God.' Mr Charlesworth gave a strangled cry. 'Do you think something's happened to her?'

'We don't know. Has she ever done anything like this before ... taken off without telling anyone where she is?'

'No. Never.'

'What about her mental health?' Zoe asked. 'Do you know if she's been depressed lately?'

'She's recently been through a divorce, but I wouldn't say she was down about it,' Mr Charlesworth replied, his vocal cords trembling. 'Quite the reverse, in fact. Ruth's move to Bainbridge is a fresh start. She's been feeling upbeat about it. Admittedly, the discovery of a body at the house has tainted things somewhat ... It's unnerved her, but I certainly wouldn't say she's depressed.'

Ruth's positive state of mind considerably reduced the probability of self-harm or suicide, but the flip side of that coin was that it increased the likelihood that she'd fallen victim to an accident or crime.

'Can't you track her phone or something?' Mr Charlesworth said.

'Not when it's switched off,' Zoe replied. 'Because Ruth's out of touch, and given her recent connection to an ongoing murder investigation, I'm going to report her missing – but, please, try not to worry.'

'That's easy for you to say,' Mr Charlesworth replied, his voice thick with emotion. 'For God's sake! You can't tell me my daughter's missing and expect me not to worry. What can we do? Shall we come over there? Try to look for her? Tell me what to do.'

'You should stay put for now,' Zoe said. 'There's every chance Ruth will turn up within the next few hours. I'll keep in touch and update you regularly. If she turns up at your house, or gets in touch with you, please let us know immediately. I'll text you the number you should call should you hear from her.'

Where are you, Ruth? Zoe thought, as she ended the call. *More to the point, who are you with?*

Chapter 28

As Isabel and Dan waited at Becky Siddall's front door, they heard the sound of a child crying inside. When she answered their knock, Becky looked stressed. She held a sleepy child in her arms, and an older, red-faced toddler was clinging to her right leg. There were tears on his cheeks but, thankfully, the arrival of two strangers seemed to have silenced him.

'Becky Siddall?' Isabel said. 'I'm DI Blood and this is DS Fairfax.'

The little boy – presumably Leo Moss – was staring up at them, hiccupping, clearly intrigued about who they were. Becky, on the other hand, looked flustered and annoyed.

'I'm sorry, but my partner's still at work.' She shifted her arm, shushing her daughter who was in the process of falling asleep. 'He'll be in later. You'll need to come back and speak to him then.'

'It's not Alfie we want to speak to this time,' Isabel said. 'It's you we'd like to have a word with.'

Becky ran a hand through her dishevelled hair. 'It's not a good time,' she said. 'As you can see, I've got my hands full. Can't you come back later when Alfie's here?'

'Yes, we can do that if you prefer,' Isabel said, her tone friendly and co-operative. 'In fact, it might be a good idea. I'm sure Alfie will be interested to hear what you have to say about the messages you sent to Kevin Spriggs.'

'And the photos, boss,' said Dan. 'Don't forget the photos.'

Becky had tensed and, as if sensing her anxiety, the little boy began to whine again. It was crying of the mardy, half-hearted variety – aimed more at getting attention than to signal any real distress.

Grudgingly, Becky stepped back and held open the door. 'You'd better come in,' she said, yielding to their less than subtle pressure.

As Isabel and Dan filed into the room, the little boy peered at them from behind his mother's legs.

'I need to put my daughter down for her nap,' Becky said. 'Do you mind keeping an eye on Leo while I take her upstairs.'

'Not a problem,' Isabel said. 'I've had three kids of my own, so I know what it's like trying to juggle things. We'll wait here and look after Leo.'

The child watched his mother's feet disappear up the open-tread staircase. Then, realising he was stuck with the two unfamiliar guests, he turned and gave them a charming smile.

'My name's Leo,' he said, a slight lisp making him sound even cuter than he looked. He twizzled shyly with one hand behind his back, pointing to Dan. 'What's your name?'

'Me?' Dan pointed at his own chest. 'My name's Daniel, but my friends call me Dan.'

Leo spun in Isabel's direction. Stepping forward, he tapped her on the knee. 'What's your name?'

She winked at him. 'Isabel, but my mum and dad sometimes call me Issy, for short.'

'I'm Leo,' the child repeated.

'Yes, you said. I don't suppose you can shorten your name, can you?'

The clacking of Becky Siddall's shoes sounded on the stairs as she came back down to the living room.

'Sorry about that,' she said, sitting on the leather armchair

162

and pulling Leo onto her lap. 'If she doesn't get her afternoon kip, she gets very grizzly.'

'No worries,' Isabel said. 'I'm sorry we didn't agree a time with you in advance, but in our line of work, some things can't wait.'

Becky seemed unimpressed by Isabel's apology. 'Go on then. What do you want to talk to me about?'

Dan leaned forward. 'When I spoke to Alfie, he told me that Kevin Spriggs had been in touch through Facebook. He said he didn't reply to the messages … was adamant he didn't want anything to do with Spriggs, and he didn't want him involved in your children's lives either.'

Becky stroked her son's hair, but said nothing.

'Today,' Dan continued, 'we discovered that *you'd* been in touch with Kevin Spriggs through Messenger and that you sent him photographs of your children.'

Becky pressed her lips together and buried her face in the top of Leo's hair.

'I take it Alfie doesn't know about this?' Isabel said.

Reluctantly, Becky lifted her head and shook it.

'Can you tell us why you sent the messages please, Becky?' said Dan.

'I only contacted him a couple of times, after he sent the second message to Alfie.' She sounded nervous, desperate to excuse her actions. 'Alfie grew up being told all sorts of bad stuff about his real dad, mostly by his grandma. I'm sure she had her reasons, but I tried to tell Alfie that there are always two sides to every story. I told him he wasn't thinking straight when he decided not to reply. I thought he should meet this Kevin Spriggs, even if it was only once. I thought he owed him that.'

'But Alfie didn't agree?' Isabel said.

'Not at all – in fact, I got my head snapped off for suggesting it. Alfie didn't think he owed Kevin Spriggs anything. If you must know, he said he wouldn't piss on him if he was on fire. I don't think he had any feelings for him, not positive ones anyway. He certainly wasn't interested in meeting him, and I felt bad for Kevin.'

'So you decided you'd send him a message yourself?' said Isabel.

Becky winced. 'I wanted to let him know that Alfie wasn't going to contact him. I thought it was the polite thing to do. I didn't want him hanging around, checking his messages, hoping there might be one eventually. I told him that Alfie wasn't going to get in touch, and I said I was sorry.'

'Why did you feel the need to apologise?' Dan asked.

'I suppose I was saying sorry on Alfie's behalf,' Becky replied. 'And that's what worries me the most about Alfie finding out. He'll be annoyed that I went behind his back, but he'll be bloody furious if he knows I apologised.'

'You sent the photographs with a second message?' Dan said.

'Yes, but only because Kevin asked for them. He replied almost straight away … said he regretted losing touch with Alfie. He said …' She covered the child's ears and lowered her voice. 'He said he'd screwed up his own life and that he was sorry he wouldn't get to know his grandchildren. He ended the message by asking me to send photos.'

'And you went ahead and did that, even though you knew Alfie wouldn't approve?' Isabel said, doing her best not to sound judgemental.

'Yes. It was stupid of me. I realise that now. I sent a photo of Leo and one of Serena, and I told him not to get in touch again. I asked him to leave us alone.'

'And did he respect that?' Dan asked.

'He did.' Becky nodded. 'I never heard from him again, and I didn't think Alfie would ever find out. How was I to know that Kevin Spriggs would get himself murdered? If I'd known the police would end up digging around in his personal life, I wouldn't have sent the messages, never mind the photos.'

'Was that the extent of your contact with Kevin Spriggs?' Isabel said. 'You didn't meet with him, or communicate with him in any other way?'

'*No.*' Becky looked horrified. 'No way! Look … I know I was an idiot to message him, but that's all I did. I never met him or called him or contacted him again.'

'Even so,' said Dan, 'can you confirm where you were on Wednesday afternoon?'

Becky hugged her son. 'Here,' she said. 'Looking after me kids.'

Leo seemed mithered by his mother's display of affection. He pulled away and slid to the floor, where a pile of Duplo Lego was waiting for him, scattered across the rug. He lay on his stomach, propped up by his elbows, and began to construct something with the plastic bricks.

Becky looked pale and shaken. 'Does Alfie have to know about this?' she said. 'Will you tell him?'

'We may have to,' Isabel said. 'Depending on which way the investigation goes.' *If it turns out Becky Siddall was involved in Kevin Spriggs' murder, Alfie's going to have a lot more to worry about than a few photographs,* she thought.

In many ways, Isabel felt sorry for Becky. If the young woman was telling the truth, her actions had been those of a considerate and kind person, someone who valued the importance of family.

'The thing is,' Dan said, 'Alfie's mother already knows that Kevin Spriggs had photos of your children on his fridge door. I imagine she'll tell Alfie about it and, when she does, I'm sure they'll work things out for themselves.'

'DS Fairfax is right,' Isabel said. 'You should probably tell Alfie yourself. Best coming from you, eh?'

Becky put her head in her hands and groaned. 'You've not left me much choice, have you?' she said. 'I'll tell him when he gets home.'

'Is it possible he already knows?' Dan said. 'Could he have found out somehow and decided to challenge Kevin Spriggs about it? Warn him off?'

Becky was gazing wide-eyed at Dan, rendered speechless by his suggestion.

Isabel decided to push Dan's point to the ultimate level. 'Do you think Alfie could have had anything to do with Kevin Spriggs' murder?' she said.

'No! God, no.' Becky's voice had grown shrill, panic putting her on edge. Leo had noticed. He toddled over to his mother and handed her a piece of Lego.

'Will you play with me, Mummy?' he said.

'In a minute, sweetie. When I've finished talking to these people.'

'Don't worry, Leo,' Isabel said. 'We'll leave your mummy in peace in a minute, as soon as she's answered our question.'

'Alfie had nothing to do with what happened,' Becky said. 'He's too gentle to do something like that. He's a big softie really. If you knew him, you wouldn't be asking that question.'

She'd begun to cry. Emotion was tugging at her lips, twisting and wobbling them against her will. 'Anyway,' she added, 'if I had any inkling that Alfie *had* done something, do you really think I'd tell you? What kind of person would that make me, grassing on me own partner?'

'Precisely.' Isabel stood up. 'Which leaves me wondering whether you're telling us the truth, or covering for Alfie. We'll leave it at that for now, but we might need to talk to you and Alfie again at some point, possibly down at the station.'

Outside it was almost dark and a whipping wind was blowing low clouds across a murky sky.

'What do you reckon?' said Dan. 'Do you think either she or Alfie could have been involved?'

'I honestly don't know, Dan, but we have to consider them as suspects. We've already established that Alfie's alibi doesn't stand up to scrutiny. However, the MO of the killer … that seems more like a woman to me.'

'Becky?'

'Possibly, but if she was off committing murder and not looking after her children like she said she was, who *was* taking care of the kids?'

'So, what do we do? How can we prove or disprove their involvement?'

'I'd like you to go back and talk to them again later, once Alfie's home and Becky's had a chance to confess her little secret. Take Zoe with you. Tensions will be running high between Alfie and Becky, which makes it the perfect time to make some more inquiries.'

Chapter 29

Alfie Moss looked far from happy when he opened the door to Dan and Zoe at ten past seven that evening. He stood with his feet apart, arms folded, bracing himself.

'What do you want?' he said, his voice cold and unwelcoming. 'Come to stir up more trouble, have you?'

'We're just doing our job,' Dan said. 'We've got a few more questions for you and your partner.'

'I'll bet you have.' Alfie stood firm, filling the doorway. 'I gather you asked more than enough questions when you were here earlier. You've upset Becky; now you're upsetting me. I'm asking you to leave us alone.'

'Sorry,' Dan said, even though he wasn't. 'Can't do that, I'm afraid. We won't keep you long, but we need to step inside. Unless, of course, you'd prefer to have a conversation here on the doorstep … let your neighbours listen in?'

Alfie turned down the corners of his mouth, expressing reluctance, but stepped aside anyway and let them in. Becky was sitting on the couch, biting a fingernail. Her eyes were red and her cheeks blotchy.

Zoe sat next to her. 'Have you talked to Alfie?' she said. 'About what was discussed earlier?'

Becky nodded, fresh tears brimming in her eyes. 'I didn't have any choice. Your colleagues made sure of that.'

On the other side of the room, Alfie threw himself into the leather armchair. There was no sign of the children.

'Are your kids not here?' Zoe asked.

Becky shook her head. 'Alfie's mum came and got them. They're having a sleepover at her house tonight. We thought it was best … you know, give us some time to talk.'

Alfie sat up, his knee jigging as he glared at them. 'You think you're clever, don't you?' he said. 'Happy are you? Now that you've put the cat among the pigeons?'

'If you're referring to us asking Becky about the messages she sent to Kevin Spriggs, our intention wasn't to be clever,' said Dan. 'Far from it. We found out she'd been in touch with him, so naturally we were obliged to ask her about it. It's hardly our fault she hadn't told you about the messages.'

'Well, she's told me now,' Alfie said, his voice strong and blustering. 'I can't say that I'm happy about it, but we've discussed it, and I know Becky … so I understand why she did it.'

'Why's that then?' said Dan.

'Because she's got a kind heart and she felt sorry for him. Becky cares about people. It's one of the things I love about her, as a matter of fact. So, if you've come here thinking you've managed to drive a wedge between us, you can think again.'

'It was never our intention to cause problems between you,' Zoe said. 'And I'm glad you've talked things through.'

'Don't patronise me,' Alfie said. 'I don't care whether you're glad or not. What I want to know is, why have you come back? What do you want now?'

'To ask Becky whether anyone can confirm that she was here, at home, on Wednesday afternoon.'

Becky wrapped her arms across her body and began to rock gently. 'I told you,' she said. 'I was on my own.'

'Is there anyone at all who could vouch for you?' Dan said. 'A neighbour, perhaps? Someone who called round to the house?'

'No.' Becky snatched at the cuffs of the fleece she was wearing, pulling them down over her hands. 'The neighbours on both sides are out at work all day. Besides, even if they had been around, they wouldn't have spotted me because I didn't go out. It was pissing it down all day on Wednesday, so I stayed indoors. I made some lunch and watched the telly while I ate it, and then I played with the kids for most of the afternoon.'

'What did you watch?' said Zoe. 'On TV?'

'*Bargain Hunt*,' Becky replied, without missing a beat. 'Then the news, and after that I put the cartoon channel on for Leo.'

'You know what?' Alfie stood up and pushed his hands into the pockets of his jeans. 'You're seriously winding me up now. Why does Becky need someone to vouch for her? Do you honestly think she could have had anything to do with the murder?'

'Whenever we're investigating a crime of this nature, we have to ask some unwelcome questions,' Zoe said. 'You may not like it … but I'm afraid that's tough. You should understand better than anyone why we're asking. We're trying to find out who killed your dad.'

'I know that – I'm not thick – but I don't expect you to go accusing me partner.' He went and sat on the other side of Becky and put his arm around her. 'You're out of order. And I told you, Kevin Spriggs wasn't me dad. Not in the true sense.'

Dan decided to deliver the startling piece of news he'd been given earlier. A member of the investigation team had managed to get hold of a copy of Kevin Spriggs' will, and it had made for interesting reading.

'I accept that you didn't have any emotional attachment to Kevin Spriggs,' Dan said, 'but he must have cared about you.'

'How d'ya work that one out?'

Dan watched Alfie and Becky carefully, ready to gauge their reaction to what he was about to say. 'We've found out that, six months ago, Kevin Spriggs made a will. He's left everything he had to his grandchildren, to be split equally between them.'

The look that Alfie and Becky exchanged was one of genuine astonishment.

'It seems that sending the photos of Leo and Serena was a wise move on your part, Becky,' Dan said.

Alfie's anger had melted away. 'I hope you're not suggesting that's why she did it,' he said, his voice surprisingly meek and unsteady. 'We didn't know anything about this ... and anyway, I doubt he had much to leave anyone.'

'That's where you're wrong,' said Dan. 'His house was rented, so you won't cop for that. But he's got a nice car that he owned outright ... a Lexus, which now belongs to you – or, rather, to your kids. He also had almost twenty grand in savings, so that will go to Leo and Serena too.'

Alfie whistled weakly. 'Bloody hell!' He squeezed Becky's hand.

'I'm sure it'll be useful when they're older,' Zoe said. 'It's going to help, especially if they go to uni. They may be young now, but they'll grow up soon enough. Thanks to Kevin Spriggs, it looks as though they'll have some financial security to look forward to.'

Dan hated the word *gobsmacked*, but it was the most accurate way to describe the expressions on Alfie and Becky's faces. They looked stunned, as though they'd received a stinging slap in the mouth.

'That kind of money ...' Dan said. 'Some might say it could be a motive for murder.'

Rendered momentarily speechless, the couple leaned into each other, mute and subdued.

'We knew nothing about this,' Becky said, eventually.

'How the hell did he manage to save up that kind of money anyway?' Alfie said, his manner suddenly suspicious and cynical.

'According to his employer, Kevin Spriggs was a hard worker,' said Zoe, feeling it was time to say something positive about the victim. 'He'd obviously stashed quite a lot of money away over the years.'

'If he hadn't made the will, it would all have come to you, Alfie,' Dan said. 'As his only child, you would have inherited the lot.'

Alfie leaned back and rubbed his face. 'You know what?' he said. 'I'm glad he left it to the kids. *That* I can accept. I'll admit it'll be a help when they're older. There might even come a time when we're grateful to him, but … if he'd left it to *me* … I wouldn't have been comfortable with that. No way. It's not that we couldn't do with the money, but I wouldn't want *anything* from him. Not with the way things were between us.'

Dan wasn't entirely convinced by Alfie's words. Surely anyone would welcome a decent inheritance, especially if they didn't have much financial security themselves. A flash car, a Lexus no less, would have been useful for Alfie and his family. As it was, Dan wondered whether the vehicle would have to be sold as part of the assets of the estate. Presumably, some kind of trust would need to be set up for Leo and Serena, until they were old enough to receive their legacy.

'Besides,' Alfie added, 'if there hadn't been a will, the money wouldn't necessarily have come to me. Not all of it.'

'Why's that then?' Dan said.

'Because I'm not Kevin Spriggs' only child. He's got another kid out there somewhere, although I don't know whether he was aware of it.'

'Hang on,' Dan said. 'You're saying Kevin Spriggs had another child?'

'Yep. I got the impression he'd sown a lot of wild oats over the years, so it didn't come as a huge surprise when I found out.'

Dan took a deep breath and pulled out his notebook. 'I think I'd better sit down,' he said. 'You can tell us all about it.'

Chapter 30

Donald had texted Isabel to say he'd booked a table for six at the Feathers restaurant for seven-thirty. His treat.

At twenty past seven, she pulled the front door behind her and set off on foot with Nathan, Kate and Ellie. Kate had driven over from Wirksworth and was staying overnight again, so that she could have a drink with dinner. They were meeting Donald and Fabien in the hotel reception area.

Nathan set a fast pace into the cold wind, which nipped at their faces. They entered Queen Street, climbing uphill, past the Co-op, towards the top of the high street. Isabel knew that if she looked over her shoulder, she would be able to see the top floor of the police station. She was itching to turn around, desperate to check whether the lights were still blazing in the CID office, but Nathan was holding her hand. He'd soon work out what she was up to if she stopped. This was her night off. Time to spend with her family. And her dad.

Halfway along the high street they turned right and then left, into the sweeping car park of the Feathers. This was the family's favourite place to eat, and they were looking forward to the meal – Ellie especially so.

'I'm going to have the goat's cheese starter,' she declared, as they pulled open the hotel's glass-panelled door and stepped into the warmly lit entrance lobby. 'And then I'm going for the chef's special chicken for the main.'

'They might have changed the menu since we were last here,' Isabel told her. 'They do that from time to time, depending on what's in season.'

'The chef's special chicken is always on the menu,' Ellie said confidently.

'Bloomin' heck, sis,' said Kate. 'There's plenty of time to decide what we're going to eat. Anyway, we're not here for the food, we're here to see Grandad and Uncle Fabien.'

'I know we are,' Ellie said. 'But I'm here for the food as well.'

Donald was sitting in the reception area, reading a newspaper. Fabien was next to him, studying his phone.

'Hi, Dad. Hi, Fabien,' Isabel said. 'I hope we're not late.'

Donald folded his paper, and thrust it to one side. 'You're right on time, as arranged,' he said. Standing up, he gave Isabel, Kate and Ellie a hug, and offered Nathan a warm handshake. Fabien put his phone away, and smiled.

'We're looking forward to this,' Nathan said. 'The food's amazing here. It's our restaurant of choice for family celebrations.'

'We're coming again next week for Mum's birthday,' Ellie said. 'Will you still be here for that, Grandad?'

'Of course I will,' he said. 'I wouldn't want to miss your mother's birthday now, would I?'

'You've missed the last forty-two of them, Dad.' Isabel laughed to soften her words.

Donald looked slighted. 'I never missed the first fourteen though, did I?' he said. 'We were always together on the fifteenth of January, come what may.'

Isabel laughed. 'True enough. We always had fun on my birthday. Mum would make a cake and you'd insist on singing "*joyeux anniversaire*", even though you're tone deaf.'

Fabien stood up. 'Shall we head into the restaurant?' he said, his tone pithy. 'We don't want to lose our table.'

Ignoring the look of irritation on her brother's face, Isabel linked arms with her dad and together they strolled over to the restaurant. As they walked, she leaned in and whispered into his ear. 'Have you told him yet?'

'Not yet,' Donald said. 'But I will. Soon.'

Chapter 31

'Did you not think to mention this to us before?' Dan said, as he settled alongside Zoe on the couch. Becky had gone into the kitchen to make a brew, and Alfie was back in the armchair.

'To be honest, it didn't occur to me. I found out about it last year, but nothing ever came of it … so it kind of slipped my mind.'

'You're not in touch with this person then?' Zoe asked.

Alfie was jigging his knee again. 'No, I don't even know their name.'

'This other child of Kevin Spriggs' – is it a woman or a man?' Zoe said.

'I couldn't tell you.'

'So how did you find out this person existed?' said Dan. 'Start at the beginning. Tell us everything you know.'

'They got in touch,' Alfie said. 'Messaged me.' He edged forward, his body rippling with nervous energy. 'About a year ago, I signed up for this website. *Tree of Life* it was called … one of those genealogy sites that lets you trace your ancestors. Not that I was interested in the Spriggs side of the family, you understand.' He flicked a hand, waving aside any possibility that he might be curious about his paternal heritage.

'So why did you sign up?' Zoe asked.

'It was a couple of days after Christmas,' Alfie explained. 'I'd taken a few weeks off and I got this email offering me free access to the site for three days. I must have been bored or summat, because I logged in. Anyway, within a couple of hours, I was hooked … ended up signing up for the full membership. There was all sorts of stuff on there. Censuses. Marriage information. I was interested in finding out about the ancestors on me mum's side, who came over from Ireland in the nineteenth century.'

'And how did you find out you'd got a half-sibling?' said Zoe.

'Ah, now that's where it got *really* interesting. At the end of me first month's membership, I was sent a discount code for a *Tree of Life* DNA kit. I did a cheek swab, sent it back and waited to get the report about my ethnicity. You get to learn where your ancestors originated from … you know, which geographic region.'

'But how does that tie in with discovering you had a half-sibling?' said Zoe. 'How did that come about?'

'After about four or five weeks, I got an email to say my ethnicity report was ready. I read it, showed it to Becky and me mum, and that was that. Fascinating stuff … if you're interested in that sort of thing. Anyway, as part of the deal I was matched with other people on the site who shared the same DNA. To access that information, I had to log on to the site, and I didn't bother at first.' He shrugged. 'That side of things didn't interest me. Besides, by the time the ethnicity report came through, I was back at work and really busy. I didn't have time for any more of the genealogy stuff and, for a while, I lost interest. It was a few months before I logged on to the site again. That's when I saw I'd got a close match, DNA wise, and a message.'

Now they were getting to it. Finally, a new lead.

'What did it say?' said Dan.

'I can't remember the exact wording.' Alfie pulled a face, suggesting he'd found the whole experience disagreeable. 'I was suspicious at first. The message had come through the *Tree of Life* site, so whoever sent it was obviously a member, but I noticed their username wasn't their real name, just some letters and numbers. There was no profile photo either. It all seemed a bit dodgy to me. I had no intention of answering … but then I read the message.'

'Which said?' Zoe was getting snappy, clearly impatient for information.

'Let me think …' Alfie puffed up his cheeks and puckered his brow. 'It said something like they were getting in touch because we were matched in the "Close Family" category. The message said our DNA match meant that I was either this person's half-sibling, uncle or nephew. They explained they didn't know anything about their dad's side of the family, but that would be how we were linked – on the paternal side, you know?'

A rush of adrenaline had increased Dan's heart rate. He felt energised and animated. Surely, they were onto something here? Despite engaging with a wide pool of people in connection with Op Jackdaw, the team had so far failed to identify any likely suspects. Could this long-lost child of Kevin Spriggs be the person they were looking for?

Alfie continued: 'They said they wanted to know more about their family history on their dad's side and wondered if I'd be willing to help. They also asked how old I was … said my age would allow them to work out how we were connected.'

'And did you reply to the message?' said Zoe.

'Yeah, I said I was twenty-five, which I was at the time.'

'And after that?' asked Dan. 'Did this person contact you again?'

'Almost immediately. They seemed to think we were half-siblings, and they asked me about me dad. About Kevin Spriggs, I mean. This person said he was his or her dad an' all, you see, and they wanted me to tell them about him.'

'Why was this person so sure Kevin Spriggs was their biological father?' said Dan.

'We shared something like twenty-three … twenty-four per cent of our DNA. I was too young to be an uncle and too old to be a nephew … so that meant we must be half-siblings.'

'And how did you feel about that?' Dan was wondering where this was going, desperately hoping it was relevant to the investigation.

'I wasn't exactly jumping for joy,' Alfie said. 'Quite honestly, I didn't give a monkey's.'

Becky had come back into the room carrying a tray containing four mugs. She lowered it, letting Dan and Zoe take their drinks.

'Didn't you feel curious?' said Zoe, as she blew on her tea. 'I'm sure I would have.'

'That's what Becky said.' Alfie smiled at his partner. 'She loves watching all those family reunion programmes on the telly ... always cries at the end, when the long-lost family members meet up.'

Becky looked embarrassed. 'It gets me every time,' she said. 'Always brings a lump to me throat. Alfie takes the piss when I start blubbing. He's not sentimental like that, are you, duck?'

'Hardly,' Alfie said. 'I get emotional about me own kids, but I've got no interest in other people ... people I don't know.'

'So what did you tell this half-sibling?' Dan said. 'About Kevin Spriggs?'

'I didn't reply straight away. I waited a few days, gave it some thought. In the end, I decided to be honest. I said I was estranged from me biological father, and that he was a bad lot. I offered to put them in touch with him if that's what they wanted, but I made it clear I didn't recommend it. *He wasn't a nice person.* That's what I said. I mentioned he'd done some unforgivable things in the past and that, sometimes, it's better to let sleeping dogs lie. *Not every family reunion has a happy ending,* is how I put it. If you ask me, people are naïve. They have this sentimental view of what their long-lost relative is going to be like. Their emotions take over ... There's too much thinking with the heart instead of with the head.'

'Well, I certainly don't think anyone could accuse *you* of being sentimental, Mr Moss,' said Dan, with a wry smile. 'How did this person respond to what you told them?'

'They didn't,' Alfie said. 'I never heard from them again. I assumed they'd taken on board what I said and decided to leave things be. I felt slightly guilty about putting them off, but it was for the best. No good would have come of meeting Kevin Spriggs. I doubt whether he'd have been interested in meeting up anyway.'

'Did you tell this person his name?' Zoe said. 'Or your name?'

'I think I signed the message with my first name, but I certainly didn't reveal Kevin Spriggs' name, or anything else about him.'

'Other than that he was a bad 'un,' Zoe said, her tone disapproving.

Alfie curled his lip. 'As far as I was concerned, that's all there was to say about him.'

'We'll need to see the messages,' said Dan. 'Do we have your consent to access to your *Tree of Life* account?'

'Sure.' Alfie held his hands in the air. 'I can give you my login details and password … whatever you need, but me membership expired last month. Sorry.'

'Don't worry about that,' Dan said. 'We can arrange for the membership to be renewed. What was your username?'

'AlfredMoss1993, and I've got the password written down somewhere. As I say, it was a while back when I last logged in. I'm too busy with me own kids these days to worry about who me ancestors were. Plus, after I received those messages … it felt like I was opening a can of worms. There are some things you're better off not knowing.'

'I realise it was a while ago,' said Zoe, 'but can you recall what your half-sibling's username was? You said it was some letters and numbers. Do you remember what they were?'

'Not really,' said Alfie. 'I seem to think it was something stupid, you know, like 12345 and some letters. Initials maybe?'

'Can you try and remember what those letters were, Mr Moss?' Dan urged. 'It could be important.'

Alfie put a hand over his face and closed his eyes, concentrating.

'Do you think this person had something to do with the murder?' Becky said, watching as Alfie searched through his memory archive.

'There's no way of knowing at this stage,' Dan said. 'But we have to explore all possibilities.'

'E.' Alfie was suddenly alert and clicking his fingers. 'E and possibly an N, or an M. Or it could have been a W.' He scrunched up his mouth. 'Sorry, I can't recall exactly. I might be wrong at that.'

'But you definitely remember an E?' Dan said. 'So, EN, EM or EW? Does that sound familiar?'

Alfie grimaced. 'I dunno,' he said. 'Possibly. I can't say for certain.'

'If you can find the password, we'll look into it,' Zoe said. 'With your permission, we'll log into the site and find out who it was that contacted you.'

'I'll dig out the password now,' Alfie said. 'But if you ask me, you're wasting your time. I didn't give out any information, so how could they possibly have traced Kevin Spriggs?'

'You'd be surprised,' Dan said. 'When someone's determined enough, it can be a lot easier than you might think.'

Chapter 32

Ellie got her favourite main course, but goat's cheese was no longer on offer as a starter. The choices, if anything, had improved since the last time the family had eaten in the Feathers restaurant. Everything was delicious, the service was first class and the place was packed.

'I thought we could go out tomorrow,' Isabel said. 'The weather should be reasonable. It'll be cold, so we'll need to wrap up, but there's no snow forecast. I thought we could go to Bakewell … show Fabien around. Or we could see if Haddon Hall is open. What do you think?'

'That sounds like a splendid idea,' Donald said. 'Are we all going?'

'Yes, we'll have to take two cars. Ellie can travel up with Kate, and you, me, Nathan and Fabien can go in our car.'

Ellie was unhappy with that decision. 'I want to travel with Grandad,' she said.

'Well, tough, because you're going with Kate,' Isabel said, trying not to sound bad-tempered.

'I can travel with Kate, if Ellie prefers to be in the same car as my father,' Fabien said.

Our father. Isabel was tempted to correct him, but knew it would sound petty.

'Thanks, Uncle Fabien,' Ellie said. 'Are you sure you don't mind?'

'It's fine,' Fabien said, seeming temporarily disconcerted at being addressed as 'uncle'. 'I'm sure Kate is a very good driver.'

Nathan laughed. 'I wouldn't be too sure about that,' he said.

Kate, who was sitting next to her dad, thumped his arm playfully.

'Ow!' Nathan said. 'OK, I take it back. I was only joking. Kate's the safest driver in the family … not the fastest mind you, but definitely the safest.'

'Why am I thinking that wasn't meant as a compliment?' Kate said, with a shake of her head.

Donald smiled. 'That's settled then. Will you pick us up here at the hotel, or would you like us to walk over to your house?'

'We'll pick you up here,' Isabel said. 'How does ten-thirty sound?'

'It sounds perfect,' said Donald. 'I'm sure we'll have a lovely day.'

After the meal was over, they went back to the hotel lounge for a final nightcap. Isabel had set her phone to silent to eliminate the risk of their family meal being disturbed, but while Nathan and Fabien were at the bar, she managed a surreptitious glance at the screen. There was a text from Dan.

We've discovered that Kevin Spriggs had another child – sex and ID unknown at this point. I know you're going out for the day tomorrow, but can you give me a call in the morning, before you head out? There's no evidence that this person is involved in the murder, but worth looking into, don't you think?

Isabel kept her phone under the table as she rattled off a quick reply.

Sounds promising. Look forward to hearing more tomorrow. Don't call me, I'll drop into to the office at about 8.30 in the morning for a quick catch-up. Can you be in by then, with it being Saturday?

His reply pinged back almost immediately.

I'll be there. No such thing as a 'weekend' when you're a copper. ☺

Chapter 33

Dan pushed his phone into his pocket and pulled out his car key. 'The DI's going to drop in to the office in the morning. At eight-thirty.'

'That's early for a Saturday,' said Zoe, as she climbed into the passenger seat of the car. 'I thought she was taking the day off, spending it with her dad.'

'She is,' Dan said. After sliding the key into the ignition, he started the engine and pulled away from Alfie Moss's house. 'It must be awkward for her really. She's obliged to make time for her dad, but she also needs to keep tabs on Op Jackdaw.'

'Does she want me to work tomorrow?'

'She didn't say, but I think you should. We ought to crack on, yeah? Now that we've got a new lead.'

They drove on in silence for a while, leaving Oakwood behind and heading north, back to Bainbridge.

'Here I am again,' Dan said, after a while. 'Working Friday night, and due in on Saturday as well. If someone had told me ten years ago that my social life was going to be so dire, I'd never have believed them. It's a bit shite sometimes, being a copper. Don't you think, Zoe?'

'I don't mind it,' she said. 'I've never been one for parties and suchlike. Not even when I was young.'

'What d'ya mean, *when you were young*?' Dan laughed, scorning her seriousness. 'You're *still* young, Zoe.'

'I'm nearly thirty.'

'So what?' Dan glanced at her with mock sternness. 'Haven't you heard? Thirty's the new twenty. Age is just a number. It's how you feel in your head that counts.'

Zoe turned to stare out through the passenger side window, at the long row of cottages they were passing. 'In that case, I'm probably about fifty,' she said, her tone unhappy and self-deprecating. 'My social life is non-existent, and I'm not sure it'll ever improve.'

Dan liked Zoe, but sometimes he found her hard to fathom. Most of the time she gave the impression of embracing life as a loner, but occasionally she vacillated between seeming content with her lot, and being subdued or dissatisfied. There were times – like now – when she looked at him with sad eyes, appealing to him silently for God knows what. Whenever it happened, Dan felt inadequate, as though he was letting her down – but what could he do? His own personal life wasn't exactly a barrel of laughs. How could he help Zoe if he couldn't even get his own life in order?

'I sympathise,' Dan said, deciding to level with her. 'But it's the same for me, you know. Since I moved here last year, it's been nothing but work, work, work. As for the whole dating malarkey … I find it all a complete bloody nightmare. Most women aren't interested when they find out you're with the police. We make notoriously bad partners, apparently.'

'I thought you were going to hook up with that girl from the Ecclesdale Drive case,' Zoe said. 'Amy, wasn't it? Amy Whitworth? What happened there?'

They had pulled up at a junction. Dan leaned on the steering wheel briefly and sighed, before pulling away.

'I messed up,' he said. 'I thought I'd leave it a while, with her being a witness, you know? I thought about contacting her in mid-December, but I always think it's weird, starting to go out with someone a few weeks before Christmas.'

'Weird?' Zoe said. 'In what way?'

'Well … do you buy them a present? If so, do you go the whole hog and get them something expensive to try and impress them, or do you keep it low-key so as to not scare them off? Then there's the whole question about whether you're going to spend Christmas Day together. It makes things awkward and complicated … so I decided to leave it.'

'And?'

'Then New Year's Eve was looming, wasn't it? Again, not the best time to hook up with someone. I mean, they're bound to have plans for seeing in the new year. Anyway, I decided to wait. I finally rang her a few days ago.'

'I'm assuming she wasn't best pleased to hear from you?'

'She was, as a matter of fact – very pleased – but unfortunately, she told me she'd already started seeing someone. Met him on Boxing Day. So, there you are. I missed out, should have made my move sooner.'

Zoe groaned sympathetically. 'Sounds like a classic case of crap timing,' she said. 'You know what? I think you're right, Dan. Being a copper is a bit shite sometimes.'

He grinned. 'Ah, now. Finally. You're coming round to my way of thinking.'

'So, are we finishing for the day when we get back to the station?' Zoe asked. 'Or are we carrying on looking into this *Tree of Life* thing?'

'Let's keep going for a couple of hours, shall we?' Dan said. 'We can call for some chips on the way back, if you like? Eat them at our desks.'

She frowned. 'Chips? I'm supposed to be on a diet. Can we go for a Chinese takeaway instead?'

'Aye, I suppose so,' Dan said. 'It does sound a lot healthier – and I need to keep in shape, don't I? If I'm going to find myself a woman.'

'It's me that needs to worry about my shape,' she replied. 'I don't think you'll have any problems getting a girlfriend, Dan. Not if you put your mind to it.'

They ate beef chow mein, chicken in black bean sauce and egg fried rice from foil takeaway containers. Dan had also ordered prawn toast, which Zoe refused on the grounds that it was too fattening.

'I see you've logged on to the *Tree of Life* site,' he said. 'What have you found?'

'Not a lot. I've managed to get to Alfie's login screen, but it's asking for credit card details, which means I can't read any of the messages. I'll get hold of someone in the Intelligence Unit to arrange for the membership to be renewed.'

'At least that's something that can be easily sorted,' Dan said. 'Getting access to the messages on Alfie's account will be a useful starting point, but our main priority has to be getting information about the person who sent them. That could be tricky. It'll mean getting in touch with the owners of the website.'

'Yep. Could take a while,' Zoe said, as she speared a piece of chicken with her fork. 'The owners of the *Tree of Life* site are based in the States.'

Dan grimaced. 'That's bad news. It means I'll have to make contact with UK Interpol so they can put in a formal request with their counterparts in the US.'

'How long's that going to take?'

'I don't know,' Dan said. 'The site owners might not release the details without a warrant … and even if they do agree to forego a warrant, it could still take several days.'

Zoe had finished her share of the chicken and had moved on to the chow mein. 'What I *can* see from Alfie's *Tree of Life* account is that he's uploaded a profile picture,' she said, twirling noodles with her fork.

'Is that significant?'

'It could be,' she said. 'He told us he didn't give any information about Kevin Spriggs when he replied to the message, but maybe he didn't need to.' She spun her computer screen around so that Dan could see it better. 'Alfie's user name on the site is his real name. First name, last name. The person he messaged could easily have searched for him on the main social networking sites. Let me show you …'

She logged into Facebook and typed 'Alfie Moss' into the search box. At least fifty Alfie Mosses appeared in the results.

'Surprising how many there are,' Dan said. 'I wouldn't have thought the name was that common. How would this mystery sibling have known which was the right one?'

'Have a look,' Zoe said, scrolling through the various Alfies until she found the one she was looking for. 'The profile picture on Alfie Moss's *Tree of Life* account is the same one he uses for his Facebook profile. All they needed to do was find the right photo.'

Zoe opened up Alfie's Facebook page. There were no recent posts, but when she clicked on the 'About' tab and then on 'Family and relationships', there it was. *Kevin Spriggs. Father.*

She clicked the link through to Kevin Spriggs' page, which was populated with an array of photographs and information.

'Kevin Spriggs' security settings were set really low,' she said. 'Anyone can see his profile information and photos.'

'So even though Alfie didn't disclose any details to his half-sibling, they could easily have worked it out for themselves?'

'Precisely,' Zoe said. 'Spriggs is tagged in tonnes of photos, loads of which include a location. The Sheaf of Corn pops up several times, of course. It's obvious it was Spriggs' local. Anyone could have gone in there and picked him out of the crowd, based on his Facebook photos. Simple as that. You don't need to be a detective to work it out.'

'No, but it does help.' Dan smiled. 'Good work, Zoe. Let's hope Interpol can persuade their counterparts to get the *Tree of Life* people to release the personal data we need.'

'If the site's hot on data protection and confidentiality, they might not co-operate.'

'Actually, I read somewhere that the US cops have a good relationship with genealogy sites,' Dan said. 'They've even used them to help solve crimes. There's a case in the media at the moment ... the Golden State Killer ... the perpetrator was at large for decades, until the American police tracked him down through familial DNA on a genealogy site.'

'There you are then, the fact that we're dealing with a murder case might swing it for us. The detection of a serious crime must surely outweigh any issues around confidentiality.'

'You'd think so, wouldn't you? I'll get in touch with Interpol tonight, get the ball rolling. Then, it'll be a matter of waiting and being patient.'

'A thought did occur to me,' Zoe said. 'And I'm sure you've considered it as well ...'

'Go on.'

'Alfie Moss's recollection of the username of his half-sibling ... he said he thought it was made up of the letters, EN, EM, or EW. If they're someone's initials – and I'm not saying they are – but ... well, we do know someone with the initials EM, don't we? Someone you've already spoken to.'

'You mean Evelyn Merigold?' Dan furrowed his brow. 'I must confess, I did think about her, but it's quite a stretch. I'd say Evelyn was about your age, Zoe, maybe a few years older. And how old was Kevin Spriggs?'

'Forty-seven,' Zoe said.

Dan looked dubious. 'Spriggs would have had to have been a teenager when and if he fathered Evelyn Merigold. Fifteen? Sixteen? Seems unlikely.'

'Unlikely,' Zoe said, 'but not impossible.'

'OK. Fair point. Let's run it past the boss tomorrow, see if she wants us to talk to Evelyn Merigold again.'

'What the DI will want is full access to the mysterious half-sibling's *Tree of Life* account. She'll want to know who paid for the membership, what their address is, and she'll expect us to bring them in for questioning ASAP. Trouble is, we aren't going to get that kind of information overnight.'

'In that case, perhaps we should have a word with Evelyn Merigold anyway,' Dan said. 'Ask her straight. Was she Kevin Spriggs' daughter?'

'I'm not sure she'd tell us if she was.'

'She might, if we tell her we'll know for certain anyway in a matter of days.'

'It'd be good to rule her out before then, if we can,' Zoe said. Pointing to the foil container balanced on top of a box file on his desk, she added: 'Do you want the last of that rice?'

'Nah, you're all right. You can have it. I'm going to the incident room to get the ball rolling with Interpol. Then I'm going to head home and I suggest you do the same. I'll see you in the morning … unless you've got other plans for tomorrow?'

'This is me we're talking about,' Zoe said. 'I'll be here.'

'Then you should probably go home too. Get some rest. It's been a long day.'

'I might stay a bit longer,' Zoe said. 'I'd like to get a better idea of how the *Tree of Life* site works.'

Dan rolled his eyes. 'Suit yourself. Be a glutton for punishment if you want to be. It's your choice.'

He stood up and pulled on his coat. As he reached the door, he turned and looked back at his colleague. She was staring at her computer, the foil tray of rice in her left hand and a spoon in the other. As she scanned the screen and scooped rice into her mouth, she looked strangely happy. Content.

Dan shook his head. He really did worry about her sometimes.

Chapter 34

At six-thirty on Saturday morning, Isabel prised her reluctant body from the warmth of her bed and pulled on her running gear. Quietly, she closed the front door behind her and ran out of the driveway onto the streets of Bainbridge, her footsteps heavy on the icy ground. The cold gnawed at her nose and the freezing air seeped through her clothing, forcing her to run faster to keep warm.

As she upped the pace, her breathing quickened, the frost crunching beneath her feet. She ran along empty pavements, past shuttered shops, and thought about Kevin Spriggs. So far, no one had said anything positive about the man, but that didn't mean he didn't deserve justice. He may not have been popular, or even very nice, but being a wazzock wasn't grounds for murder. If it was, half the population of Bainbridge would be at risk.

According to Dan, Spriggs' ex-wife was the only one who'd said anything remotely pleasant about him. She'd spoken nostalgically of the young Kevin Spriggs; the man he'd been before his drinking had spiralled out of control and played havoc with his personality. It was sad to think of someone's potential being obliterated by alcohol. Would Spriggs' life have been better if he'd chosen a different path, or at least sought help for his addiction?

Isabel speculated on what it was he'd done … what sin he had committed to cause someone to drive a knife through his heart.

Would the discovery of Kevin Spriggs' long-lost child provide them with the answers they sought? And what about his missing phone? They'd been able to confirm the number and had applied to obtain data from the phone service provider, but would that information prove useful, or be yet another waste of time?

When she reached the halfway point in her circular route, Isabel slowed her pace. Heading home, she reflected on the fact that she was trusting her colleagues to press on without her today. She didn't normally let family commitments get in the way of work, but her dad and Fabien had been in Bainbridge for three days now, and she hadn't spent nearly enough time with them. Even though her dad insisted that he understood, she knew he must be disappointed, and she didn't want to hurt his feelings. Today's trip to Bakewell was important. She hoped it would be a day to remember, a time for her fragmented family to bond.

The rest of the household was still asleep when she got home, so she used the downstairs shower room to avoid waking them.

After feeding the dog and downing two large mugs of black coffee and three slices of wholemeal toast, Isabel pulled on her coat and slipped out of the house for the short drive to the station. She was keen to talk to Dan and Zoe to find out more about what they'd discovered the previous evening. The team was due a piece of luck to help them move Operation Jackdaw forward, and the discovery of Kevin Spriggs' long-lost child could be the breakthrough they'd been looking for.

She got to the office at eight-twenty. Five minutes later, Zoe arrived. Quietly and concisely, the DC updated her on the previous evening's conversation with Alfie Moss, and outlined the actions they'd put in motion to gain access to the *Tree of Life* accounts.

'And what about Ruth Prendergast?' Isabel said. 'Any news on her whereabouts?'

'Nothing yet, but she's now officially a missing person, so the wheels are in motion to try and find her. Do you think her disappearance is connected to Op Jackdaw, boss?'

Isabel frowned. 'Unfortunately, I think it probably is. The only other alternative is that she's harmed herself in some way. Her marriage broke up recently, and the discovery of a body in her new home must have been a huge setback. If she wasn't depressed before, she's likely to be now.'

'Not according to her dad,' Zoe said.

'In that case,' said Isabel, 'maybe she's encountered the person who killed Kevin Spriggs.'

Their musings were interrupted by the arrival of Dan.

'I'm not late, am I?' he said. 'You did say half eight?'

'I did,' Isabel said. 'Zoe and I were early, that's all. She's already filled me in on Alfie Moss's contact with his half-sibling through the genealogy website.'

'I'm going to check with the Intelligence Unit again, to see if anyone's managed to renew Alfie's membership,' Zoe said.

'Ask them to make it a priority,' said Isabel. 'Even more important is getting the personal information on whoever sent the messages to Alfie in the first place.'

'I'll give UK Interpol another call in a minute, to find out how it's going,' Dan said. 'I only put in the request last night though, so it's too early to start making a nuisance of myself. Did Zoe mention that Alfie Moss thought the username of this mystery person could have included the initials EM?'

'She did,' Isabel replied. 'How sure was he about that?'

'Not very,' Dan said. 'It's over six months since the messages were exchanged, and he hasn't logged on to the site since. His recollection was sketchy, but Zoe and I have been speculating on whether EM might be Evelyn Merigold? Could she be Spriggs' long-lost daughter?'

Isabel considered the possibility. 'It's a long shot,' she said. 'But worth checking. Have another chat with her, see if you can rule her out – and take Zoe with you. While you're at it, get the FLO to call Simon Sprigg … see if *he* knows anything about his brother having another child.'

'No problem,' said Dan.

Isabel looked at her watch. 'What else can you tell me about this genealogy website, Zoe? The *Tree of Life*.'

'It's a subscription site,' Zoe replied. 'For ten pounds a month you get online access to birth, death and marriage records and census information. You can also build an online family tree, based on any research that you do. Users can choose to make their trees available to other members of the site and, if they do, people can get in touch to share information and photographs … although details of anyone who's still alive are hidden from other members.'

'Did Alfie Moss create a family tree?' Isabel asked.

'He said not. He did some research but, as far as I can tell, there aren't any trees associated with his account.'

Genealogy wasn't something that held any appeal for Isabel. She realised why it might be of interest to some people, but it wasn't for her. As far as she was concerned, tracing your lines of descent was a pointless exercise. She'd always believed in plotting her own unique journey through life – what could she possibly gain from studying ancestors whose lives had been determined by a totally different set of rules and circumstances? The past was history, and the future unknown and not guaranteed. It was the here and now that mattered. At least that's what she told herself.

To some extent, her reluctance to research her ancestors had been influenced by the fact that her family history had always been shrouded in mystery. She knew nothing about her paternal grandparents, and her maternal grandmother had died before she was born. She did have a vague memory of sitting on the shoulders of her maternal grandfather, her small hands clinging to a head thatched with thick grey hair. The opportunity to create more of those memories had been snatched away when her grandad died suddenly, the week Isabel was due to start school.

Despite her lack of knowledge and interest in her own heritage, Isabel appreciated that some people were fascinated by the idea of tracing their descendants – uncovering what their ancestors did for a living, where they lived and, in some cases, how they died.

Ellie loved to watch those soppy programmes on TV about long-lost families being reunited, and Isabel had occasionally watched them with her, swallowing the hard lump in her throat that appeared whenever an emotional meeting took place. Common sense told her to despise the sentimentality of it all – but, deep down, a tiny part of her had longed for her own, tear-jerking reconciliation with her own father. Now, finally, she had achieved that – initially through the wonders of FaceTime and Skype and, this week, in person at the airport. It was a marvellous feeling, even though Isabel sensed that she and her dad were still holding back, keeping their emotions in check. She wasn't sure why that was. Perhaps they were both afraid of being overwhelmed by the release of a dam of pent-up feelings.

Dragging her thoughts back to Operation Jackdaw, she said: 'I'm a bit surprised that Alfie sent off his DNA.'

'Millions of people across the world have done the test,' Zoe said. 'I'm even considering buying one of the kits myself.'

'You wouldn't catch me doing one,' said Dan. 'I've no intention of letting my DNA be used by a genealogy site for commercial purposes. From what I've seen, they use the data they hold as a promotional tool, promising matches with potential relatives. You've got to ask yourself what you're opening yourself up to. There could be all sorts of skeletons in the cupboard.'

'It's highly unlikely in my family,' Zoe said. 'We're much too boring. You've got a point though. I'd be more interested in the geographical side of things … like Alfie Moss was … finding out which parts of the world my ancestors came from. I'd be a lot less keen on being contacted by some stranger saying they're my fourth cousin, once removed.'

'The whole thing is pretty staggering when you think about it,' Isabel said. 'These people are submitting their DNA willingly. If the police want to collect a DNA sample, we have to have a bloody good reason, and we're obliged to follow strict procedures on how and if the data can be processed and stored.'

'That's the difference, isn't it?' Dan said. 'DNA as a commodity, versus DNA as evidence.'

Isabel held her hands above her head and stretched. 'Why wasn't Alfie able to tell you the name or even the sex of this "close match"? Are you telling me that people can remain anonymous on the site, even though they're getting in touch to ask potentially life-changing questions?'

'That appears to be the case, boss,' Zoe said. 'I checked, and messages through the *Tree of Life* site don't include someone's real name, unless they use it as their membership username – which is what Alfie Moss did. You'd imagine, wouldn't you, that someone sending that kind of message would at least sign it? Alfie said the messages he received were unsigned, so presumably the person sending them was being cautious.'

'Or intentionally underhand,' said Dan.

'Wouldn't they have had to include an email address?' Isabel asked.

'No.' Zoe shook her head. 'You can, if you're comfortable with doing that and want to encourage whoever you're contacting to correspond with you directly. Otherwise, any contacts go through the *Tree of Life* messaging system.'

'I totally get why people might not want to share their email details,' Dan said. 'You might be distantly related to these people, but at the end of the day, you're still strangers.'

'I don't consider a half-sibling to be a distant relative,' Isabel said, thinking about her own half-brothers. 'If I was contacting someone about the possibility of that kind of relationship, I'd want to be up front about who I was. It's common decency, isn't it? People are far more trusting and willing to engage if they know who they're dealing with.'

Zoe was chewing the end of a pen. 'Alfie said this person had a blank profile as well,' she said. 'No photograph. No family trees. Even more reason to be suspicious. I'm surprised he bothered to reply at all.'

'He did wait a few weeks before sending a response,' Dan said.

'Let's hope we don't have to wait that long to find out the identity of the person behind the *Tree of Life* account,' Isabel said. 'More to the point, when we do find out, let's hope it's not another dead end.'

Chapter 35

'I'd better not drive too fast,' Nathan said, 'otherwise Kate won't be able to keep up with us.'

They were heading up the A6, approaching the traffic lights near the Sainsbury's supermarket in Matlock. Donald was in the front passenger seat next to Nathan, and Isabel and Ellie were in the back. Since pulling out of the car park at the Feathers Hotel, Ellie had been talking pretty much non-stop.

'I'd forgotten how hilly it is round here,' Donald said, taking advantage of a brief pause in Ellie's monologue. 'There's something slightly brooding about it, especially at this time of year.'

'How does it compare to where you live, Dad?' Isabel said.

He seesawed his head from side to side, considering his answer. 'It's much colder here,' he said. 'The winters are very mild in Carcassonne, and the architecture is different there too. Of course, when people think of Carcassonne, it's the castle in the medieval citadel that springs to mind – and that's understandable. It is magnificent, standing tall and proud, overlooking the new town across the river. But there's far more to Carcassonne than its castle.'

'Do you live in the new town, Grandad?'

'Yes, Ellie, I do – although it really isn't very new at all. It's a fine place to live – its buildings stand together, shoulder to shoulder, like old friends. There's something gently chaotic and unplanned about the part of the town where my house is ... as though the buildings have gravitated towards each other organically, drawn together by a mutual sense of belonging.'

'There are parts of Derbyshire where you could say the same thing,' Nathan said.

'True,' Donald replied, 'but Derbyshire is bleaker, darker, but perhaps all the more beautiful because of that.'

'Which do you like best,' Ellie said, 'Derbyshire or Carcassonne?'

'Don't ask me that, child,' he replied. 'I don't like to make comparisons. Each place is wonderful in its own way ... but, please, don't make me choose.'

'Come on,' Ellie persisted. 'You must have a favourite.'

'No,' Donald said, with a shake of his head. 'Really, I don't. That is like asking me which of my children I prefer. There's no answer to that, because I love them all equally.'

'But Mum's your only daughter ... she's got to be your favourite, surely?'

'Ellie!' Isabel gave her a warning nudge. 'Stop bugging your grandad. Let's be quiet for a while and let him enjoy the scenery.'

Donald chuckled. 'I don't mind answering your question,' he said. 'I can confirm that Isabel is definitely my favourite daughter. Just don't ask me to tell you who my favourite son is.'

There was a lull in the conversation, and Isabel thought that Ellie had finally piped down. She was wrong.

'In the summer, can we fly out and visit you, Grandad?' Ellie said. 'That way, we'll be able to see Carcassonne for ourselves.'

'There's nothing I would like more,' Donald said. 'I'll give you a guided tour. I'm sure you'll love it.'

Nathan was staring through the rear-view mirror. 'Ah-oh,' he said. 'Looks like we lost Kate and Fabien at the lights. Shall I pull over and wait for them to catch up?'

Isabel turned and peered through the back window of the car. Sure enough, Kate's red hatchback was stuck at the traffic lights, waiting for them to turn green. Kate could never be accused of being an amber gambler.

'Keep going,' Isabel said. 'We always park in the same place and she knows the way. All she has to do is follow this road.'

'Serves her right for being slow,' said Ellie.

'When you're old enough to drive and have a licence of your own, Ellie, you'll be in a position to criticise,' Isabel said. 'Until then, keep it zipped.'

They entered Bakewell along the A6, driving past the imposing, three-storey Rutland Arms Hotel, turning right at the roundabout, and making their way along Bath Street towards the River Wye. When they'd crossed the bridge, they turned right into Station Road and entered the town's main car park.

As Nathan reversed into the first parking space he could find, silence descended in the car's heated interior.

'Kate won't be far behind us,' Nathan said, as he put the handbrake on and turned off the engine. 'Come on, Ellie, let's go and get a ticket.'

'No thanks. I'll stay here, where it's warm.'

'You're going to have to get out of the car in a minute anyway,' Nathan insisted. 'Let your mum and grandad have a few minutes without you squawking in their ears.'

'I don't squawk.'

Nathan laughed. 'That's a matter of opinion. Now come *on*. You can help me with that horrible ticket machine. I never can work out how to use it.'

'Dad, you're the most technically savvy person I know,' Ellie said. 'You don't need my help.'

'Ellie.' Nathan's voice was firm. 'Don't argue. You can keep an eye out for Kate … give her a wave when she arrives.'

Pouting, Ellie pulled the zip of her coat tight under her chin and got out of the car.

'Are we being given some time alone for a reason?' Donald

said, as Nathan and Ellie weaved through the parked cars towards the ticket machine.

'I think Nathan's trying to give your ears a rest. Ellie can talk for England when she gets started.'

'I like listening to her. She's amusing and bright … She reminds me of you when you were her age.'

'Actually, Dad,' Isabel said, her voice solemn, 'by the time I was her age, you'd already left.'

Donald sighed. 'Perhaps so, but that's how I remember you back then … the last time I saw you.'

Isabel leaned forward, grasping the back of the seat in front of her.

'Have you told Fabien yet? Told him everything?'

'No, not yet. I'll speak to him this weekend.'

She released a sharp, irritated groan. 'Will you? Really? Or are you going to find another excuse to put it off?'

'Please, Isabel. I don't understand why you're being so impatient … so *insistent*. And I really don't see what good will come of me telling Fabien about my marriage to your mother.'

'Your *illegal* marriage. Your *bigamous* marriage.'

Donald turned away, towards the car park entrance, where Kate's car had pulled in and was approaching them slowly.

Isabel watched her daughter drive by, Fabien next to her in the passenger seat, his face serious and inscrutable.

'Quite honestly, Dad, I don't understand why you wouldn't want to tell Fabien.'

Donald let his head drop for a moment, and then spun round to face her. 'Because I'm ashamed. OK? Fabien has always looked up to me, respected me … I don't want to destroy that. I realise you'll consider me selfish and proud, but I'm afraid of what he'll say … what he'll *think* of me.'

Isabel felt temporarily stunned. Was she being unreasonable, demanding that her father tell Fabien and Pascal the whole truth about his long-ago life in Derbyshire? Would it really make her feel better? Or serve only to make her brothers feel worse?

She gazed into her father's sad, blue eyes. His face was old, careworn and brittle, his pale vulnerability a stark reminder that one day she would lose him again, and the next time it would be for good. The prospect terrified her.

If she had a more generous nature, she would smother her anger and let go of the past – but she'd been hurt too deeply to be tender-hearted. There were still days when she found herself nursing a bitter ache of indignation, curling into it like a physical pain.

She knew that, deep down, her father was a good man, but by refusing to divulge the true extent of his double life to Fabien and Pascal, he was preserving a lie – and that was something she couldn't condone.

'I know you think your marriage to Mum is ancient history,' Isabel said. 'But it happened, Dad, and I need you to acknowledge that by telling your sons the truth. I'm sorry, but I must insist on it.'

Donald shifted his legs, fidgeting, as if desperate to escape the confines of the car. 'Isabel, you must understand this isn't easy for me. I'll never forgive myself for how I betrayed you and your mother, and I can't expect you, or Fabien and Pascal to forgive me either – but if I disclose the full details of how badly I behaved, I fear the revelation will drive a wedge between us all.'

Isabel stifled a sigh. 'Look, Dad, I don't want to make unreasonable demands or cause you anguish, but you've got to realise how important this is to me. It's wonderful to have you here and for us to be together again … and I'm looking forward to getting to know Fabien, but I don't want to build a relationship with him that's based on a lie.'

'You haven't lied, Issy. I'm the one who's hidden the truth from him.'

'That's not strictly true, is it? You're expecting me and my family to maintain the pretence, which means we're lying by omission. That's not on, Dad. I love you, and I don't want you to have to pay an emotional forfeit to have me in your life – but this is something that's non-negotiable. You need to be honest so that we can focus on the future.'

Donald pushed a time-weathered hand through the gap between the headrests. 'I'm an old man. I'm not sure how much future I have,' he said.

'All the more reason to do the right thing,' Isabel said, hardening her heart to stem the tears that were welling in her eyes.

She stared at his hand. It was freckled with liver spots, and the veins stood out beneath the skin. She should reach out. Grasp it. Hold it. Squeeze his fingers reassuringly.

But was that all he was offering? A hand? He certainly hadn't promised to do as she'd asked. He was being characteristically stubborn. Her father was an obstinate bugger. Always had been.

The outstretched hand hovered, waiting patiently. How could she ignore the gesture? If she snubbed him now, what kind of a person would that make her?

She hesitated, battling internally with her own mulishness – and then the moment was broken when Ellie banged on the car window, making them jump.

'Come on, you two,' she shouted. 'Kate and Fabien are here. Let's go into town.'

Chapter 36

Evelyn Merigold lived about a mile outside of Bainbridge in a converted stone barn. A couple of chickens were strutting around the extensive front garden, pecking the ground. There was a coop, which Dan assumed was where the hens spent the night and laid their eggs, and next to that was a large, reedy pond. A small poly tunnel was located at the far end of the garden, along with a shed, a collection of raised beds and a wooden structure, which he thought must be a beehive. The scene was like something from the pages of an organic gardening magazine.

By the front door, a long stone trough had been filled with herbs, which were now decidedly winter-ravaged. Handwritten labels had been stuck into the soil alongside each of the frost-bedraggled plants. Marjoram. Thyme. Sage. Lemon balm.

When she answered the door, Evelyn Merigold looked surprised and not altogether pleased to see them.

'Hello, DS Fairfax,' she said. 'What are you doing here?'

'I have a couple more questions for you, in connection with the murder investigation we spoke about the other day. This is my colleague: DC Piper. May we come in?'

'Certainly, although I do have to go out shortly.'

'Don't worry,' Dan said. 'This shouldn't take long.'

The inside of the house was remarkably bright and spacious, the conversion from barn to home having been achieved sympathetically, with a nod to modernity. An open-plan kitchen and living area filled the long, central part of the building, and a wide section of bi-fold doors filled the wall directly opposite the front door. Dan peered through them, out to the rear garden, which backed onto a small meadow. Beyond that lay a copse of fir trees. Standing there, it was easy to imagine that the house was located in the middle of nowhere, not a mere one-mile drive from town.

'Tea, coffee?' Evelyn asked, as she pulled out chairs so that they could sit around the enormous farmhouse table that dominated the kitchen.

'No. Thanks anyway,' Dan replied. He squinted at Zoe, daring her to contradict him. 'This may seem an odd question, Ms Merigold, but have you ever signed up for a membership to the *Tree of Life* website?'

'*Tree of Life*?' Evelyn said, her forehead wrinkling. 'No. Not that I recall. Is it a gardening site?'

'It's a family history website,' said Zoe, who had taken off her jacket and was hanging it on the back of a chair. 'Genealogy. That sort of thing.'

'I can assure you I definitely wouldn't have signed up for anything like that,' Evelyn said. 'That kind of research doesn't interest me. Never has.'

'You're sure about that?' Zoe said.

'Absolutely. Why would I say otherwise?'

'Is that lack of interest because you already know everything about your family?' Dan said, as he pulled his notebook from his pocket. 'Your mum, and your dad?'

Evelyn flinched, her eyebrows huddling together warily. 'Sorry, but why are you asking about my family?' Her eyes scanned his face. 'I don't wish to be rude, but what does that have to do with you? Or with the case you're investigating?'

'We're following a lead,' Dan said. 'You don't have to answer my questions, of course, but it would help our inquiries. We're trying to establish the identity of a member of the *Tree of Life* website who may have had a connection to the victim. We're in the process of formally obtaining the relevant data from the owners of the site, so we'll have an answer soon enough – but that confirmation may take a few days to come through. We're asking questions now to try and speed up the investigation.'

'I'll help if I can, but I still don't understand what it is you're asking me.'

'We're here to confirm whether you've ever visited the *Tree of Life* website—'

'I've already answered that question.' She folded her arms.

'—and whether or not you have a close relationship with your parents?' Dan continued. 'More specifically, with your father.'

Evelyn stared at him, her face expressionless. Dan got the impression she didn't want to answer, but knew how such a refusal might be interpreted.

'I'm going to assume your question is important,' she said.

'We wouldn't be asking otherwise,' said Zoe.

'OK.' Evelyn unfolded her arms but continued to glare. 'It's fair to say that I don't have a close relationship with my parents. Not anymore.'

'But you did?' Dan clarified. 'At one time?'

'Yes,' she said. 'I had a happy upbringing. Unfortunately, my parents' attitude changed towards me when I refused to tow the middle-class line. They wanted me to become a doctor. Something *professional*, was how they put it.'

'And that kind of career didn't appeal to you?' asked Dan.

'I wasn't cut out for it. I got into medical school, but I quit after a year and went travelling around Europe. As you might imagine, my parents were livid. I worked in a vineyard in France for a while, and then I ended up working in a park near Florence. When I eventually came back to the UK, I started to work as a gardener, and I took a part-time horticultural course at college.

My parents didn't approve, of course. They accused me of being eccentric and avant-garde.'

'Really?' Dan said. 'Why's that then?'

Evelyn rolled her eyes. 'I wasn't conforming to their idea of a what a daughter should be. They expected me to be compliant and conventional, and I refused to play along.'

'It sounds as if they have an outdated attitude,' Dan said. 'It's a shame, because you seem to enjoy your job.'

'I do. I love it. But even though I'm happy, my parents can't bring themselves to accept my chosen career. It doesn't help that I'm into organic growing and self-sufficiency. They think I'm some sort of new-age hippy.' She smiled, but Dan could see hurt lurking in her eyes.

'So you and your parents aren't close?' said Dan.

'Not anymore,' Evelyn said again. 'I still see them, but not often. We've drifted apart emotionally.'

'I'm sorry to labour this point,' said Zoe, 'but your dad is your dad, isn't he? He not your stepdad or anything? You're not adopted?'

Evelyn laughed contemptuously. 'Sadly not. They're my flesh and blood, which makes it worse.'

Dan glanced sideways, taking in the look of disappointment on Zoe's face. He knew why she was unhappy. Evelyn Merigold was estranged from her parents, but she clearly had no doubt about who her father was. There was no ambiguity in their relationship. She wasn't Kevin Spriggs' long-lost daughter.

'In that case,' Dan said, 'you're not the person we're looking for in connection with the *Tree of Life* site.'

The look Evelyn gave him was rather sour. 'I did tell you that. You should have taken me at my word. It wasn't necessary for you to delve into my personal life.'

'This is a murder investigation,' Dan said, his voice stiff. 'Which means we sometimes have to ask what might seem like irrelevant questions, but I can assure you we're only doing our job. It's a shame we've had to bother you on a Saturday, though. I'm sure you've got better things to be doing than talking to us.'

'Not really,' Evelyn admitted. 'Nothing exciting. A bit of retail therapy, that's all.'

'Well, before you head off to the shops, there is one more thing I'd like to ask,' Dan said. 'The last time we spoke, I got the feeling you were holding something back from me. Am I right?'

She shrugged. 'Even if you are, what makes you think I'm suddenly going to open up to you now?'

'Perhaps in the spirit of co-operation?' Dan said. 'Because you're helping us with our inquiries?'

Evelyn scooped her hair behind her ears and stared at him for a moment. 'You've got good instincts, Detective, I'll give you that. You're right. There is something I've not told you, but it has nothing to do with your case.'

'You can let me be the judge of that,' said Dan.

With a sigh of resignation, Evelyn placed the palms of her hands on the tabletop and wiggled her fingertips. 'When we met, I failed to mention that I knew Gerald Langton's neighbour.'

'Katrina Mariner?'

She smiled. 'Katrina and I were friends. I met her one day when Mr Langton was away and she came round to feed his cat. I was cutting the lawn, and we got chatting. She made me a cup of coffee in Mr Langton's kitchen and we sat and talked for a while. Katrina was a lovely person. I really liked her. When I spoke to you the other day, I told you I'd only been inside Mr Langton's house once, but that wasn't strictly true. There were other times, when he was away and Katrina invited me in. I didn't like to say anything because … well, it wasn't her house was it?'

'Surely Gerald Langton wouldn't have minded?' said Zoe.

'Probably not, but as I still work for him, I thought it best to say nothing. I wouldn't want him to think I'd overstepped the mark by guzzling his coffee in his absence. It only happened a few times anyway. Once Katrina and I got to know each other better, I went to see her in her own house. She enjoyed gardening. It was one of the things we had in common.'

'Katrina Mariner died last year, didn't she?' Zoe said. 'She took her own life.'

Evelyn pressed her lips together. Nodded briefly.

'You must have been shocked when you found out?' said Dan.

'I was sad and distressed.' Evelyn took a deep breath to steady her voice. 'But I don't think I was shocked.'

'So it wasn't unexpected then?' Zoe said. 'You knew she was depressed?'

'Of *course* I knew, although I didn't think she was suicidal. If I'd known that, I would have stepped in … got her some help.'

'Do you know what caused her depression?' Dan asked.

'Whatever it was, she didn't like to talk about it,' Evelyn replied. 'Admittedly, I only knew Katrina for a short while, but she was beginning to trust me. I believe, given more time, she would eventually have confided in me, and then I could have helped her. I only wish I'd had a chance to get to know her properly.'

Evelyn held her hands in front of her face, inspecting them, front and back. 'When I'm gardening,' she said, 'I wear thick gloves to protect myself from the weeds and roots and brambles. Even so, a sharp thorn will occasionally pierce the thick canvas of my gloves and draw blood. It's inevitable. A hazard of the job. When I met Katrina, I had the feeling *she'd* wrapped a thick layer around herself, as protection from the scratches of what she perceived to be a prickly and cutting world. I didn't know what had happened to make her think that way, but she was vulnerable. She hid behind the shield she'd created for herself because it made her feel safe.'

'You make her sound very … inaccessible,' Zoe said. 'It couldn't have been easy, getting to know her.'

'It wasn't,' Evelyn said, her voice laced with sadness. 'Being Katrina's friend was hard work at times, but I felt drawn to her.

Maybe I recognised her as a kindred spirit, or perhaps I'm a sucker for lame ducks. It doesn't really matter now, does it?'

'So, you gardened together?' said Zoe.

'Yes, I advised her about choosing some new plants. Her garden was north-facing and she'd been trying to grow sun-loving flowers, wondering why they didn't thrive. Why they were dying.'

'And you helped her choose the right kind?' said Dan. 'Plants that were more suitable for her garden?'

'Yes. In some ways, it felt like I was doing more than just improving her garden. Katrina was a lot like a sun-loving flower, you see ... and she was in a dark place. She needed transplanting, looking after ... nurturing.'

'And were you hoping that you'd be able to do that?' Zoe said. 'Through your friendship? Look after her? Take care of her?'

'Maybe,' Evelyn said. 'I'm a loner by nature. I don't have any siblings or many friends, so that made our relationship all the more valuable to me ... but then Katrina died and our short, but beautiful friendship died with her.'

'I'm sorry you lost your pal,' Dan said. 'But I'm glad you told me about it, otherwise I'd have been wondering what you were hiding. There's nothing else you haven't told me, is there?'

Evelyn laughed. 'There's *lots* I haven't told you,' she said. 'What do you want? My life story?'

'Far from it,' Dan replied. 'Only the things that might be relevant to our ongoing murder investigation.'

'In that case ...' Evelyn folded her hands together. 'I think we're done. Sorry to disappoint you, but there's nothing I can tell you. I'm not sure what you were hoping to discover about me or my family, but whatever it was, you're digging in the wrong place.'

Dan grinned. 'Is that another one of your gardening puns?'

'No, it's my way of telling you that you're wasting your time with me.' She raised her eyebrows. 'Move on, detectives. You won't solve a murder sitting here.'

'Fair enough,' said Dan. 'Thank you for talking to us anyway. Enjoy the rest of your day.'

He slipped his notebook into his pocket and stood up. Zoe scraped back her chair and pulled on her jacket.

As they walked out of the front door, one of the chickens scurried past, flapping its wings bad-temperedly.

'Do you think she's telling the truth?' Zoe muttered, when they reached the car.

'If she isn't, we'll find out soon enough. We *will* trace whoever messaged Alfie Moss through the *Tree of Life* website – it's only a matter of time. Come on, let's head back to the station and chase it up. I'm going to call in at the café on my way back. Do you fancy a hot chocolate?'

Zoe grinned. 'Have you ever known me turn one down?'

Chapter 37

With their car parking tickets fixed to their windscreens, the six members of the Blood-Corrington clan set off on foot, crossing back over the river and onto Bridge Street. Their first port of call was the visitor centre and, from there, they hit the shops, moving through the streets of Bakewell as a group. Occasionally, two or three of their party would break away and wander into a gift emporium or clothes shop for a spot of browsing. Nathan bought a truckle of cheese from the wine and cheese shop, and Donald bought a tea towel featuring Derbyshire scenes.

Inevitably, they gravitated to the Bakewell Pudding Shop where Fabien showed interest in the town's famous puddings.

'They *are* delicious,' Isabel told him. 'The pastry melts in your mouth … so puffy and buttery.'

'What's inside the tart?' Fabien asked.

'There's a layer of strawberry jam at the bottom,' Kate explained. 'On top of that is a soft, custard-like filling … I think it's made with ground almonds and eggs and sugar. Absolutely gorgeous with a nice cup of tea.'

'I'll go in and buy one,' Isabel said. 'We can take it home and have it later.'

'There's a restaurant on the first floor,' said Nathan. 'We could go in for a bite to eat.'

Donald didn't seem keen on the idea. 'If you don't mind, I quite like the idea of some proper fish and chips for lunch.'

'Yeah, I fancy some chips,' Ellie said. 'We could eat them by the river.'

'I don't mind having chips,' Isabel said, 'but I draw the line at sitting outside to eat them. It's far too cold.'

'There's a really good fish and chip place on Water Street, where you can eat in,' Nathan said.

Fabien pulled a disgruntled face. 'Many times I have heard about your fish and chips, but I've never eaten them.'

'Why not, Uncle Fabien?'

'Because, Ellie, I cannot understand why the British insist on battering their fish.'

Isabel suppressed an overwhelming urge to laugh, as an image of someone whacking a fillet of fish with a blunt instrument flashed across her mind.

'Actually, I have tried the chips, without the fish,' Fabien continued. 'I found them bland and much too chunky. They were … stodgy?'

'You should have had them in a pea mix,' Ellie said.

'Pea mix?' Fabien looked mystified.

'Chips with mushy peas,' Ellie explained. 'With salt and vinegar.'

'*Sacre bleu!*' Fabien said. 'You batter your fish, you chunk your chips and now you are telling me you mush your peas?'

His words, and the look of horror on his face, made them all laugh. Even Fabien yielded a grin.

'Fish and chips are brilliant,' Kate said. 'You don't know what you're missing.'

'And you really shouldn't knock them until you've tried them at least once,' Isabel said. 'Come on, Fabien, live dangerously. Let's go to the chippy on Water Street and see if we can get a table for six.'

As they waited to cross the road, Isabel stood next to her father.

The traffic was flowing freely and Nathan, Fabien, Kate and Ellie took advantage of a gap in the cars, dashing across to the other side. Donald hung back, and Isabel stayed with him.

'Either the vehicles on the road are going too fast, or I'm not as quick as I used to be,' he said. 'Let the others go ahead, Issy. We'll catch up with them in a minute.'

They let another line of traffic roll by. 'I'm enjoying today,' Isabel said. 'Even Fabien seems to be unwinding.'

'Oh, trust me, he doesn't need to unwind. There is no one more relaxed and laid-back than Fabien. What is it people say? *If he was any more relaxed, he would be horizontal.* Did I say that right?'

Isabel nodded, although she wasn't convinced it was a phrase that could be applied to her brother. From the moment he'd arrived at the airport, he'd seemed tense and formal. She wanted to warm to him, wanted to *like* him, but she was finding that difficult, and it bothered her. Fabien was, after all, her own flesh and blood. She'd assumed that when they met, they would bond automatically. She couldn't work out why that hadn't happened. Why were they both holding back?

'I know the Feathers is a lovely hotel, and I'm not sure we could offer the same level of comfort, but I'd really like you and Fabien to come and stay with us, Dad.' She linked her arm through his as the road cleared and they stepped off the pavement to cross over. 'It makes sense. I'm having to go into work most days … if you were at our house, you could spend more time with Ellie and Nathan, and you'd be there when I got home. We could stay up late and talk into the early hours without worrying about getting you back to the hotel.'

Donald patted her hand. 'I will talk to Fabien about it,' he said.

'That's fine … and if Fabien wants to stay on at the hotel, that's fine too. Obviously, I'd like him to come and stay with us, but I'll understand if he prefers not to. But *you*, Dad – I insist that you stay at the house. It's what we talked about when we made the plans for your visit.'

They had reached the other side of the road, where the rest of the family were waiting, stamping their feet to fend off the cold. 'Like I say,' Donald replied. 'I'll talk to Fabien this weekend.'

'OK,' Isabel replied, not in the least bit convinced he would do so. 'It sounds as though the two of you have a lot to discuss this evening.'

Chapter 38

'There you go, Zoe. One hot chocolate, as requested.'

Dan placed the cardboard cup next to Zoe's keyboard, and carried his own coffee over to his desk, along with the brie and cranberry panini that had been the Saturday special at the Coppa Café.

'Your timing's impeccable,' Zoe said. 'While you were out, I got word that Alfie Moss's *Tree of Life* membership has been renewed. I've been able to access his account and I'm printing out the messages now. You can read them while you drink your coffee.'

Dan pumped his fist. Progress at last. The printer was away to the side of his desk and, as it whirred into life, he wheeled his chair over and waited for the printed sheets to emerge.

'What have we got then, Zoe?' he said, after he'd wheeled himself back into position behind his desk. 'Bring your drink over and talk me through it.'

Zoe did as instructed, pulling her chair to Dan's side of the office. 'There are only four messages,' she said. 'The first is the initial message to Alfie, from EM5678.'

'So it was EM,' Dan said. 'Any significance in the numbers? Could it be a date of birth? Fifth of June, 1978?'

'If it is, it's not Evelyn Merigold. I checked. She was born in

1989. Anyway, the numbers could well be random and have no significance whatsoever. Five, six, seven, eight …'

'Who do we appreciate?' Dan grinned.

'That's two, four, six, eight,' Zoe said, seeming to take pleasure in correcting him. 'Five, six, seven, eight are easy numbers to remember though, and fractionally more secure than one, two, three, four.'

Dan read the first message.

From: EM5678
To: AlfredMoss1993
Date: 2 May 2019

I'm getting in touch because we have a match in the Close Family category. Our shared DNA means we're either half-siblings, or you're my uncle or nephew. I think we must be linked on the paternal side, because I know nothing about my dad or his family. I WOULD like to know more, and I wondered if you'd be willing to help. Can you tell me how old you are, so that I can work out how we're related? Many thanks.

'It's exactly like Alfie said … no name. It's a short message and quite abrupt.'

'I agree,' said Zoe. 'If someone sent that to me, I don't think I'd bother answering it. I mean, common courtesy costs nothing, does it?'

Dan turned to the next message. 'It looks as though Alfie gave as good as he got. His reply is blunt, to say the least.'

From: AlfredMoss1993
To: EM5678
Date: 30 June 2019
Hey, thanks for your message. I'm twenty-five.
Alfie

The next message had been sent the same day. Again, there was no signature, which was staggering considering it claimed such a close family relationship.

From: EM5678
To: AlfredMoss1993
Date: 30 June 2019

 Thanks, Alfie. You're too young to be my uncle and too old to be my nephew, so you must be my half-brother. I realise this news will come as a surprise, but it looks as though you and I have the same dad.

 I've never known who my father is, so I'm hoping you'll be able to tell me about him and possibly put me in touch, assuming he's still alive.

 Looking forward to your reply.

Alfie had waited five days before responding. His message was short and brutally honest, cutting directly to the point.

From: AlfredMoss1993
To: EM5678
Date: 5 July 2019

 Thanks for your message. It's weird to think I have a half-sibling out there somewhere. The truth is, I'm estranged from my biological dad – just like you are. My mum and him split up when I was five and he and I haven't kept in touch. Truth be told, our dad was a bad lot. Not a nice person. If you really want to get in touch with him, I'll do my best to help, but I honestly don't recommend it. He did some nasty things in the past and, although time may have improved him, there's no guarantee. If you've had a happy childhood, you might be better off letting sleeping dogs lie. Not every family reunion has a happy ending and I honestly don't think you've got anything to gain from getting in touch with me dad. Anyway, have a think about it and send me another message if you do want more information.

Alfie

'And that's it?' said Dan, holding up the last sheet of paper. 'EM5678 didn't bother sending any more messages?'

'No, there's nothing else. Again, quite rude, wouldn't you say? The least they could have done was thank Alfie for his reply.'

'Now that you've got access to Alfie's account, have you been able to find out anything else about the EM5678 account?' Dan asked.

Zoe shook her head. 'Nothing. The membership has expired. I tried searching for any family trees linked to EM5678's username, but drew a blank. We'll have to wait for the *Tree of Life* website to get back to us to find out who the account belongs to.'

Dan picked up his panini, which was going cold. 'It's bloody frustrating,' he said. 'I only hope, when it does come through, the information is worth waiting for.'

Chapter 39

'The *Tree of Life* website administrators are playing hardball,' Dan said later that afternoon. 'They're saying they won't release the information without a warrant.'

Zoe was updating her case notes. 'You're joking, aren't you?' she said, letting out a wail of frustration.

'I only wish I was,' said Dan. 'But you can chill, Zoe. Interpol are confident the US police will be able to negotiate with the site owners. I've texted DI Blood, to keep her in the loop.'

Zoe picked up a pen and began to tap it against the side of her nose. 'How about we leave aside *who* might be responsible for Kevin Spriggs' death … at least for now?' she said. 'Isn't it time we turned our attention to the details of *how* he was killed.'

'I must confess, I have been wondering about that,' said Dan. 'How the hell does anyone get up the nerve to pull off such an audacious murder?'

'I've got a theory,' Zoe said. 'Do you want me to tell you about it?'

'Let me make another coffee first,' Dan said. 'I always work better with some caffeine inside me. Is Lucas coming in at all today, do you know?'

'I don't think he was planning to, but I can ring him and ask him to pop in if you think it'd help.'

'Yeah, do that, Zoe. Three heads are better than two. And ask him to bring some biscuits or cake in with him. A sugar rush might get the brain cells going.'

Lucas arrived twenty minutes later carrying a box of caramel doughnuts from the local bakery.

'There you go,' he said, opening up the box and placing it on Dan's desk. 'Don't say I never give you anything.'

'Cheers, mate. They look delicious.'

'Where's the DI?' Lucas asked, as the trio pulled their chairs in front of the whiteboard. 'I bought her a cake, thought she'd be here.'

'She's gone out for the day,' Zoe said.

Lucas curled his lip and rolled his eyes.

'Don't pull that face, Lucas,' Zoe said. 'DI Blood was supposed to be on two weeks' leave. Her dad's over from France, and she hasn't seen him in over forty years. This case has really put the kibosh on his visit.'

'All right, keep your hair on,' Lucas said. 'Your defence of the DI is admirable, but she isn't around to hear it, so you can turn the volume down.'

Zoe stuck her nose in the air and gave Lucas the silent treatment.

'Anyway,' Lucas continued, 'how come she hasn't seen her dad for so long?'

'It's a complicated story, and one we haven't got time for right now,' Dan said. 'We're here to discuss the MO of the killer. How did he or she pull off this murder? Why didn't Kevin Spriggs fight back?'

He stared expectantly at the two DCs, hoping they'd unleash a volley of ideas. Instead, they were biting into their doughnuts, their faces a picture of contentment.

'Bloody hell, you two. Come on! Never mind stuffing your faces … talk to me. We need to come up with something that makes some sense.'

Lucas sucked his sugary fingers. 'Here's one scenario for you,' he said. 'The victim was invited to the house and, bearing in mind he was found in the bedroom, it must have been a romantic liaison that went wrong.'

'So, someone who wasn't the homeowner invited him round for a shag?' Dan looked sceptical. 'Are you suggesting the murder wasn't planned? That it was a spur-of-the-moment thing? A lover's tiff that got out of hand?'

'Hey, you asked for ideas,' Lucas said. 'All I'm trying to do is jump-start the discussion. Feel free to come up with a more convincing scenario.' He pushed the remaining half of his doughnut into his mouth and sat back, his cheeks bulging.

'In my opinion, the whole thing was planned meticulously,' said Zoe. 'I mean, why else would someone have a knife in the bedroom?'

'Zoe,' Lucas said, through a mouthful of cake. 'You've got cream round your gob.' He pointed to the left-hand corner of his own lips, and then pointed in her direction.

She frowned and pulled a tissue from her sleeve, wiping her mouth before continuing. 'As I was saying … this was premeditated. You saw the crime scene, Dan. Did it look like a crime of passion to you?'

'Quite the opposite. Everything looked …' Dan grasped for the right description. 'Neat. Far too neat for my liking. There was no struggle, no blood spatters. And, of course, his clothes and other belongings had been taken. So, yes, I think you're right. It was definitely planned.'

'Do we think the perpetrator was a woman?' Zoe asked.

'It seems likely,' Lucas replied. 'But it could have been a man.'

'Right, so our killer was either a woman or a man … nice

one, Lucas.' Dan grinned. 'I do think you're right about one thing though …'

'Cheers.' Lucas pulled a face.

'The victim was in bed, half-dressed,' Dan continued. 'That suggests he was probably anticipating or participating in some form of sexual activity.'

'As far as we know, Kevin Spriggs was straight,' Zoe said. 'So, let's assume the killer was a woman. She lured Kevin Spriggs to the house – we don't know why *that* house – but then what? She took him upstairs?'

'It seems logical,' said Dan. 'Let's extrapolate … try and sketch out a scenario that would fit the circumstances we found at the crime scene.'

'It still doesn't make sense to me,' Lucas said. 'Let's say the victim lay on the bed and the killer got on top of him … what then? Did she pull out a knife hidden under the pillow? If so, why didn't Spriggs push her away? No one would lie there and allow someone to push a knife into their chest without putting up a fight.'

'He wasn't drugged,' Dan said. 'We got the toxicology report yesterday. It came back clean.'

'There you are then,' said Lucas. 'In what other circumstances would someone willingly lie there and let themselves be stabbed?'

'What if Spriggs didn't know he was about to be stabbed?' Zoe said.

'You'd have to be blind not to see a blade coming at you, Zo,' Lucas said.

'Or blind*folded*,' replied Zoe. 'What if they were playing a sex game? You know … handcuffs, blindfolds.'

Lucas smirked. 'Sounds a bit kinky to me.'

Zoe scowled. 'Grow up, Lucas.'

'Zoe's right,' Dan said. 'We've not come in on a Saturday to piss about. We need to focus.'

He went over and grabbed a folder from his desk. 'Crime scene photographs.' He held the folder in the air. 'The headboard on the bed is padded ... upholstered. If it had been one of those metal ones, with a row of vertical bedposts, I might have gone along with your theory, Zoe. However, it wouldn't work with this type of headboard. There's no way the killer could have fastened the victim's hands to the bed.'

Dan dragged his own hands down his face. He was tired. Tired of going around in circles and getting nowhere.

'Top marks for imaginative thinking though, Zo,' Lucas said, ruffling his hair.

Dan frowned. 'Let's leave it for now,' he said. 'If you do come up with a feasible scenario, please run it past me. In the meantime, can one of you find out the latest news on Ruth Prendergast? It's nearly twenty-four hours since anyone saw or heard from her. If her disappearance is connected to Operation Jackdaw – and it seems highly likely – she could end up being the next victim.'

Chapter 40

After they'd finished looking around Bakewell, the family drove back in convoy via Pilsley, calling in at the Chatsworth Estate Farm Shop, and then dropping down, past the church at Edensor. They had swapped things around in the cars. Donald was travelling with Kate and Ellie, and Fabien was with Isabel and Nathan. They drove through the Chatsworth Estate at a sedate pace, so that Fabien could catch a glimpse of Chatsworth House.

'It's magnificent,' Fabien said, twisting around in the passenger seat and craning his neck to get a better view of the stately home of the Duke of Devonshire. 'Can it be visited by the public?'

'Yes. The house is stunning, and the gardens are spectacular too,' Isabel said. 'It's the sort of place you need to spend a full day exploring.'

'Perhaps I'll go there on my next visit,' Fabien said, facing forward again when the house had slipped out of sight.

'So you plan on visiting us again?' Nathan said. 'That's good.'

'This is a scenic part of the UK,' Fabien replied. 'I can see why my father was drawn to it.'

'It wasn't the scenery that brought him back here time and again,' Isabel said. 'He had a family here.'

'Yes,' Fabien said. 'I realise that.'

Seconds later, her brother had changed the subject, asking Nathan about the Derwent Valley mills. Isabel sat in the back and listened, feeling ungracious that she couldn't muster the will to contribute to the conversation.

By the time they arrived back in Bainbridge, it was getting dark. Inside the house they gravitated to the garden room, gathering around the log burner, where they drank tea and ate generous slices of Bakewell tart.

'It's been a long day,' Donald said, as he declined a second cup of tea. 'I think we'll go back to the hotel now, so that I can take a rest.'

'But you'll come back in the morning?' Isabel said. 'And stay for Sunday lunch? I'm cooking.'

'In that case,' Donald said, 'I wouldn't miss it for the world.'

A proper Sunday roast was something they rarely bothered with, so cooking a huge joint of beef and making Yorkshire puddings made the next day's lunch feel like a special occasion.

Nathan collected Donald and Fabien at eleven-thirty, and the family sat in the living room while Isabel finished preparing the meal. Fabien volunteered to help, which she thought was a kind gesture, but she turned down his offer. Isabel was a good cook, but a chaotic one. She needed plenty of elbow room, space to do things her own way.

After lunch, they took a short walk around the town before heading back to play cards and watch TV. For Isabel and her father, it was a pleasant interlude and an opportunity to discuss some of the highlights of the last forty years.

The fly in the ointment was that Donald obviously hadn't talked to Fabien, and there was no mention of when or if they might move out of the hotel and stay at the Blood residence. Isabel wasn't going to kid herself – she was disappointed and frustrated. She'd made clear her position in the car park at Bakewell: she wanted her dad to tell Fabien the truth. Admit to it. Acknowledge it. His lack of action was infuriating.

On the other hand, she was trying not to let her desire for an airing of the truth dominate her father's visit or unsettle her. Forcing aside her disquiet, she did her best to enjoy their time together.

In the late afternoon, after consuming a heavily iced and sugary cupcake, Isabel decided to fend off any potential cavities by going upstairs to clean her teeth. As she stood in front of the mirror in the en suite, the cold-water tap running noisily as she brushed, Ellie poked her head around the door.

'Blimey, Ellie. You made me jump.'

'Mum, you'd better come down. It's all kicking off.'

'Kicking off? What's kicking off.'

'Fabien's found out … about Grandad's marriage to Gran. There's a row going on. You'd better get downstairs.'

Isabel felt her heart rate accelerate. 'If your grandad and Fabien are falling out, I'm not sure I'm the one who should intervene,' she said, feeling an irrational reluctance to get involved.

'It isn't Grandad and Fabien who are falling out,' Ellie said, grabbing her arm and pulling her towards the bedroom door. 'It's Grandad. And Dad.'

Chapter 41

There appeared to be a stand-off in the living room. Nathan was hovering near the fireplace, and Donald had risen out of the armchair he'd been sitting in, his hands on his hips. Each of them appeared to be waiting for the other to make a move.

Fabien was on the settee, looking decidedly unimpressed as he gazed up at his father and brother-in-law. The dog, sensing that something was wrong, was standing with her ears back, alert.

'What's going on?' Isabel said, inserting herself between the combatants. 'Tell me what's happened.'

'Ask your husband,' Donald said, pointing a finger at Nathan.

'Nathan?' She pushed her own hands into the pockets of her jeans, to stop her fingers from trembling. 'Whatever it is, you both need to calm down. Take a seat, the pair of you … and then tell me what's happening here.'

Reluctantly, the two men lowered themselves into a sitting position. Nathan parked himself on the edge of the armchair, his body coiled.

'Nathan?' she said again. 'Do you mind explaining what this is all about?'

'I told Fabien about your mum … the fact that she was married to Donald,' Nathan said.

His betrayal was a gut punch.

'Why?' She turned on him, dark eyes flashing. 'Why would you do that? I thought we agreed …'

Nathan stood up again. 'No, we didn't. You told us not to say anything; that's not the same thing at all.'

'It wasn't your secret to tell,' she said, through clenched teeth.

Nathan had opened a Pandora's box of recrimination. Isabel was furious – and yet, at the same time, she felt a quiet sense of relief that, finally, the truth had surfaced.

She looked at Fabien, who was staring at Donald with angry eyes.

'I'm sorry you had to find out like this, Fabien,' she said, placing a hand on his arm. 'Dad promised me he'd tell you himself. It wasn't my place to say anything, and it wasn't Nathan's either.'

Nathan glared at her defiantly. 'Your dad was never going to tell him – can't you see that? And I wouldn't have said anything at all, if it hadn't been for Fabien's attitude.'

'Attitude?' Fabien turned to direct his anger at Nathan. 'What do you mean by that?'

'You know exactly what I mean,' Nathan replied. 'You obviously resent being here. You've had a face like a wet weekend since you arrived.'

Isabel wasn't going to contradict him, because she knew he was right, but she wished he wasn't being so openly critical and antagonistic.

Nathan glared rebelliously. 'I was talking about your mother living out in Spain,' he explained. 'When I mentioned Barbara's name, Fabien couldn't hide his animosity … The scowl on his face was enough to curdle milk. When I asked what was bothering him, he told me he didn't want to hear about someone who'd knowingly formed a relationship with another woman's husband.'

Isabel covered her ears. This was exactly what she'd been trying to avoid. Her father's stubbornness was to blame for this. His silence had created a festering sense of rancour and resentment, whether he liked to admit it or not. Dragging her hands away from her face, she cast an I-told-you-so look in Donald's direction.

'I told him Barbara had done no such thing,' Nathan continued. 'I explained that she hadn't known about Jeanne, and had been under the impression Donald was married to no one but herself.'

Donald was becoming agitated. 'You had no right to say that,' he said.

'And you had no right to marry Barbara when you were already married to someone else,' Nathan countered, his face white with rage. 'Can you not see how on edge Isabel has been since you and Fabien arrived? She asked you to do the decent thing and tell your son the truth, but you're too much of a coward, aren't you? Too bloody selfish by half.'

'Nathan!' Isabel held up her right hand. 'I know you're trying to defend me, but please stop. Don't make this situation any worse than it already is.'

The atmosphere in the room was volatile and tempers were running out of fuse. Isabel turned to Ellie and Kate, who were huddled together in the window seat, bracing themselves.

'Girls, can you give us a few minutes, please? Go and make us all a fresh brew.'

Kate stood up. 'We'll make one, Mum,' she said, her voice quivering. 'But it's going to take more than a cup of tea to fix this.'

When her daughters had filed past on their way to the kitchen, Isabel turned to her brother.

'I'm sorry, Fabien, but what Nathan said is absolutely true. Mum was pregnant with me when she married Dad. That was in 1962. She had no idea he was already married. She didn't find out until 1977, which is when Dad left us both. I never knew what had happened to him, or where he was. Mum didn't tell me the truth until recently. The shock of what she told me was overwhelming, and I'm sure you must be feeling the same way right now.'

Fabien turned to her, as though seeing her properly for the

first time. '*Je suis désolé*,' he said, his voice thick with contrition. 'I am the one who must apologise. When I think of how I have behaved, I am embarrassed. When our father told us about you, I assumed you and your mother knew about Maman, and Pascal and me. I thought neither of you cared that Papa had betrayed his family, but I realise now that I was wrong. You were innocent of the things I have accused you of … here in my head.' He tapped his forehead. 'I didn't trust you, and for that I am sorry. So very sorry.'

What a bloody mess, Isabel thought. *Dad should have bitten the bullet and told his sons the truth, no matter how unpalatable.* His refusal to speak had only made a bad situation worse, and she wasn't sure she could forgive him for that.

'You've been kept in the dark, Fabien,' she said squeezing his arm, 'but please don't stay angry about it. The truth has finally come out. Now, we can move on properly … as a family.'

'That is easier to say than to do,' Fabien said. 'Right now, I am very angry … not with you, Isabel. With him.' He thrust a stiff finger in Donald's direction but refused to meet his eye.

Turning to face Donald, but continuing to address her brother, Isabel said: 'Dad's behaved badly. He's been foolish and selfish and stupid. He should have told you himself, a long time ago.'

'She's right, Fabien,' Donald said, sounding utterly browbeaten. 'I should have been honest with you and Pascal.'

'Then why weren't you?' Fabien said, his face lined with anger. 'You have had many opportunities to speak the truth … but for you, it's always easier to say nothing, isn't it? Nathan is right – you are a coward and you are weak, and you should be ashamed. Your deceitfulness allowed seeds of doubt to grow in my mind and made me suspicious of my own sister.'

Isabel looked into her brother's eyes. 'Is that why you came here with Dad?' she asked. 'Because you didn't trust me? Is that the reason you booked the hotel? Because you didn't want to stay here, with us?'

Fabien gave her a sad, weary smile. 'You believe it was me who made those decisions? I can see why you might think that, but you are wrong. It was Papa who asked me to travel with him, and it was he who decided to book a room at the Feathers. You see, Isabel, I'm not the only one who has been kept in the dark.'

'*What?*' His words were an unexpected sideswipe. She felt winded. Her father had lied to her. Again.

Placing the flat of her hand on her ribcage, she pressed against the dull ache of regret she had carried for so long, an ache she thought had gone away for good.

Donald tottered to his feet. 'Issy … I can explain.'

'I'm sure you can.' She shrank from him, scoffing contemptuously. 'I thought we said there would be no more lies. You promised, Dad.'

'I know I did, but I can explain—'

Isabel held up a hand to halt his words. 'No. Not tonight,' she said. 'You need to go back to the hotel. I don't want to listen to your excuses.'

'But, Issy …'

'No, Dad,' she said, feeling scorched by her father's betrayal. 'I've had enough. I've got work tomorrow and I need to get some sleep. I haven't got the energy to spend the rest of the evening going over old ground with you. I'm tired. I can't take any more crap today. We'll talk again tomorrow.'

'She's right, Papa,' Fabien said, his face cold and angry. 'You've given us all a lot to think about. We should give Isabel some time alone. You and I can talk when we get back to the hotel. You have a lot of questions to answer … a lot of explaining still to do. And don't think this can be brushed away. You always taught me to be accountable for my actions. Now is the time for you to be accountable for your own.'

Isabel spun away, dashing at the tears forming in the corners of her eyes. She'd thought her heart was immune to any more emotional wounds, but she was wrong. Her father's words and deeds still had the power to hurt her.

'I'll drive you back to the hotel,' Nathan said.

'I think that would be a good idea,' Fabien replied, his voice stiff.

'No.' Donald got to his feet. 'I'd prefer to walk.'

Isabel turned on him, snapping impatiently. 'Stop being so bloody stubborn, Dad. It's dark and it's freezing cold out there.'

'The fresh air will do me good.'

'Come on, Donald, be sensible,' Nathan said, his voice conciliatory. 'Isabel's right. It's icy. It could be slippy underfoot. I'm sorry about earlier. Please. Let me take you back to the hotel in the car.'

Donald put his shoulders back and lifted his head. 'No, really, I'd like to walk. It's when I do my best thinking. And please, don't apologise for what you said. You were defending your wife, and I am in no position to criticise you for that.'

Chapter 42

Isabel arrived at the station the next morning feeling exhausted and out of sorts. She and Nathan had talked into the early hours, going over the events of the previous evening. Isabel wasn't sure who she was more angry with: her dad, Nathan, or herself. Strangely, she felt no hostility towards Fabien. He'd had to face the ignominy of being exposed to the family secret, and she knew how much that hurt.

Now that the truth was out, the best she could hope for was that they would be able to smooth out their wrinkled relationship and move on. Whether that was possible would be determined by whatever happened over the next few days.

Her lack of sleep was now dragging her towards lethargy and bad temper. She was doing her best to fight off a dark mood, but it was a battle she was losing.

On her way to her office she called in to the incident room to talk to the team. At least being back at work would help take her mind off the turmoil within her own family.

'Morning,' she said. 'Any more sightings of the victim or his car on CCTV? Or anything suspicious? Who's been checking the footage?'

A DC put up his hand. He'd been seconded from Derby, and

Isabel was ashamed to realise she couldn't remember his name.

'We've been taking turns to trawl through it,' he told her. 'We've got the car reg number, but there's a lot of footage and a lot of traffic. It's not exactly the most exciting job.'

'It might not be exciting,' said Isabel, 'but it's important. Keep looking, and let me know if you find anything. What's the word on Ruth Prendergast? Does anyone know if she's turned up?'

'Not yet,' said DC Lindley. 'We managed to get hold of the security footage from one of the neighbours. It clocked Ruth Prendergast driving into the close at ten past eleven, but unfortunately the camera doesn't point in the direction of her house, so there's no record of her movements into or out of number 4. There's no sign of her leaving the close, either in her car or on foot.'

'What about other vehicles? Any sign of anyone entering or leaving the close around that time?'

'Stella and Heather Mariner drove into the close within a few minutes of each other, around ten o'clock, and your own car is on camera arriving at ten-fifteen a.m. The footage shows your car leaving at ten-forty a.m. Stella Mariner left about five minutes after you, and Heather Mariner drove out of the close at midday.'

'Give Heather a call,' Isabel said. 'She left after Ruth arrived. See if she saw anything suspicious.'

Retreating, Isabel moved along the corridor, into the CID office, where Dan was at his desk.

'Anything from Interpol about the genealogy website, Dan?'

'Nothing yet,' he replied. 'They keep chasing it, but the guys over in the US are taking their time.'

'Do they know that our inquiry relates to a murder investigation?'

'They know, but it hasn't made a blind bit of difference. It's bloody frustrating.'

Isabel sighed. 'Looks like we'll have to exercise a little more patience then,' she said. '*Finis coronat opus*, and all that.'

'Say again, boss?'

'It's Latin.'

'Sounds like double Dutch to me.'

'It means, the end crowns the work. In other words, the end goal gives value to the work that produces it.'

Dan looked at her, bewildered.

'Getting the data from the *Tree of Life* people might seem like an uphill struggle now, Dan, but hopefully it'll be worth it when we get the results back.'

'Oh aye, I see what you mean. Why didn't you say that in the first place? No need to show off with the Latin, boss.'

'Watch your step, Fairfax,' Isabel said, as she headed towards her office. 'I'm not in the mood for backchat.'

Dan assumed a look of mock horror. 'What's wrong with you this morning?' he said. 'Has something happened?'

'I don't want to talk about it,' Isabel replied. 'Now, unless you need me for anything urgent, I'm going to sit at my desk for a while and catch up on the case notes.'

'Have you read the messages I texted to you?' Dan said. 'The ones between Alfie and the EM5678 person?'

'Yes, thanks for sending those,' she said, inching closer to the sanctuary of her office space. 'I downloaded them first thing this morning. Good work, Dan.'

'It's Zoe who deserves the credit,' Dan said. 'She's the one who managed to retrieve them.'

'Right. Well, when she comes in, you can thank Zoe on my behalf.'

'It might be better if you did it yourself,' said Dan. 'Let her know she's appreciated.'

'Are you telling me how to do my job?'

'I'm just saying it wouldn't do any harm to let Zoe know that you value her.'

Isabel regarded him suspiciously. 'Has Zoe said something to you?'

'She has, but she spoke to me in confidence. If you want to

know what's bothering her, you'll have to speak to her yourself.'

'Sod that, Dan. I'm asking *you* to tell me.'

He buried his hands in his pockets. 'I'm not sure I can do that.'

'Yes, you can. I'm your boss. Tell me what she said.'

He pulled his hands out of his pockets and folded his arms. 'She's thinking of getting a transfer. And if you want my view on that, I'd say it'd be a disaster. I wouldn't want to lose her. Zoe's a hard worker, a key member of the team.'

'I agree,' Isabel said, giving a swift and decisive nod. 'Don't worry, I'll have a word with her. Now … unless the building's on fire or an alien spaceship lands on Bainbridge marketplace, I don't want to be disturbed.'

'Not even if we do a coffee run to the café?'

She cracked a reluctant smile. 'For that, I would make an exception. I'll have a latte, please.'

By ten-thirty, Isabel was beginning to feel better about things, and far more organised. Progress on the case was slow, but at least everyone was keeping on top of the admin. Small mercies.

Detective Superintendent Tibbet had been on the blower for an update, and had offered to step in to pull some strings and move things along with the *Tree of Life* request, if nothing was forthcoming by the end of the day.

As well as the latte, Isabel had drunk two cups of strong tea and eaten a couple of chocolate digestives. The biscuits had been the highlight of an otherwise unremarkable morning.

She heard a soft knock and looked up to find Dan hovering in the doorway.

'What are you hanging around outside for?' she said, beckoning him in and turning back to her computer.

'You looked deep in thought, boss. I didn't want to disturb you.'

'I don't mind being disturbed, providing you've got some good news.'

'I have, as it happens.'

When she looked at him again, Isabel realised her sergeant was supressing a grin.

'Go on then,' she said. 'Don't make me wait for it.'

He sat down in the visitor's chair next to her desk and leaned forward. 'We've finally heard back from the guys at the *Tree of Life* site.'

'And?'

'We know who Kevin Spriggs' other kid is. It's someone we've already spoken to. Want to guess who it might be?'

'No, I don't want to *guess*, thank you. Don't mess with me, Dan. Tell me who the hell it is.'

'Turns out that EM stood for Estella Mariner.'

'Stella Mariner?' Isabel pushed her hands behind her head, leaned back and let out a low whistle. At last, the pieces were falling into place. All they had to do now was follow the evidence and see where it took them.

'It does make sense,' she said. 'Her mother had a key to the house next door. Stella must have held on to it.'

'She told you she didn't know where the key was.'

'Well, she would, wouldn't she? Come on, Dan. We've been looking for someone with a link to both the victim and the house, and now we've found it. If Stella Mariner *isn't* the killer, this is one hell of a coincidence.'

'That's true, but what about motive?' Dan said. 'If Kevin Spriggs was her father, why would she want to kill him?'

Isabel stood up and pulled on her jacket. 'We'd better ask her, hadn't we? Bring her in for a voluntary interview. I'm going to go down and see the Super, tell her what's happening. Come and get me as soon as Stella Mariner arrives.'

Dan had put the suspect in interview room one. When asked whether she wanted a solicitor, she had declined, saying she didn't need one, that she'd done nothing wrong.

Despite strong overhead lighting, the grey-painted walls of the interview room made it feel cold and grim. Isabel took a seat at the table, and Stella stared back at her from the opposite side, solemn-eyed and wary.

'OK,' Dan said, after he'd switched on the recording device and asked Stella to confirm her name. 'As I've already told you, you're not under arrest and you can leave at any time. Is that clear?'

'Perfectly,' Stella said.

'I'm also going to remind you that this is a voluntary interview,' Dan said. His voice was courteous but professional as he cautioned Stella and asked her to confirm she understood.

'Yes,' Stella said, her voice unsteady, 'I understand.'

Isabel paused for a moment before posing her first question. She knew she had to tread carefully. Other than the *Tree of Life* account, there was no evidence to link Stella with Kevin Spriggs, let alone with his murder.

'Thanks for coming in to talk to us, Stella,' she began. 'Or, should I say, Estella? That's your full name, isn't it?'

'Yes …' Stella seemed bewildered.

'And yet, when you confirmed your name for the tape, you said *Stella* Mariner. Why was that?'

'The only person who ever called me Estella was my mum,' she replied, her face pale and confused. 'To everyone else, I'm Stella.'

'And your mum was Katrina Mariner,' said Isabel. 'Am I right?'

'Yes.' She knitted her brow, obviously wondering where this was going and why she'd been brought to the station.

'What about your dad?' Dan continued. 'What's his name?'

'Why? Why are you asking me that?'

'Just answer the question, please, Ms Mariner,' Dan said, eager to press on.

Stella hesitated. 'Colin Mariner,' she said. 'He died five years ago.'

'You're sure about that?' said Dan.

Stella screwed up her face, letting her irritation show. 'What? That he's dead?'

'That he's your father,' Dan clarified. 'Your *real* dad?'

She paused, studying Dan's face. 'Colin Mariner wasn't my biological father, but he was the only one I've ever known.'

'Fair enough,' Isabel said. 'I understand what you're saying, but we do still need you to confirm the name of your biological father.'

Stella looked at her hands. 'I don't know his name,' she said. 'I've never met him, and my mum told me nothing about him, other than he was a one-night stand. I'm not sure if *she* even knew his name.'

Their line of questioning seemed to be making Stella uncomfortable, but she wasn't flustered. The answers she gave were delivered calmly and eloquently. Was she telling the truth, or was she an accomplished liar?

'I'd now like to ask you about your membership of a website called *Tree of Life*,' Isabel said. 'We know that you signed up last year, and that you messaged someone called Alfie Moss, with whom you had a DNA match.'

'Yes, I joined the *Tree of Life* website,' Stella said, after a moment. 'You've obviously checked all of this, so I'm hardly going to deny it, am I? Anyway, why would I want to? I took a DNA test in the hope of finding relatives on my paternal side. More precisely, I hoped to find my father. There's no law against that, is there?'

'I understand that Alfie Moss was flagged as a "close match",' Isabel said, ignoring Stella's remark. The woman was here to answer questions, not ask them. 'What's your understanding of what that means? How would you define a "close match"?'

Stella pushed away a strand of hair that had fallen across her eyes. 'It meant that he was either a half-sibling, or my nephew or uncle. Obviously I was interested to know how we were connected, so I messaged him to ask how old he was.'

'And what conclusions did you draw from his reply?' said Dan.

Stella swivelled her eyes in Dan's direction. 'He said he was twenty-five … which was only a few years younger than me, so he was unlikely to be my uncle or nephew. He had to be my half-brother.'

'And how did you feel about that?' Dan said. 'Were you pleased to have made contact?'

'Initially I was elated.' The memory brought a flash of happiness to her face. 'But then ... when I sent a second message, the reply I got was disappointing, to say the least.'

'In what way?' Isabel said, asking the question even though she already knew the answer.

Stella was becoming truculent. 'Do I really need to explain?' she said. 'I'm assuming you've accessed the messages between me and Alfie Moss, so you must already know what he said.'

Isabel opened the file in front of her and retrieved the printed record of the *Tree of Life* messages. She handed a copy to Stella.

'For the purposes of the tape, can you please read out the highlighted section in the second message from Alfie Moss.'

Stella scanned the sheet of paper in front of her, her lips bunching from side to side. 'It says: *I'm estranged from my biological dad – just like you are.*' Her voice broke for a moment, and she coughed to clear her throat before continuing. '*My mum and him split up when I was five and he and I haven't kept in touch. Truth be told, our dad was a bad lot. Not a nice person.*'

'I can understand why you were disappointed,' Isabel said.

'I don't need your understanding. Please don't pretend to care. And anyway, how is any of this relevant? I assume you're asking about this in connection with your murder investigation? Has my biological father committed a crime? Is he the killer?'

'No,' Isabel said. 'I'm afraid he's the victim.'

Chapter 43

Stella Mariner placed a hand across her mouth and then dragged it down onto her neck, where she held it under her chin. 'The victim? The man they found in Hollybrook Close – that was my *dad*?'

If she was acting, she deserved an Oscar. Her face was bone-white, drained of all colour. Her shock appeared to be genuine, and Isabel began to feel prickles of doubt. Had they jumped to the wrong conclusion? What if Stella Mariner's connection to the victim *was* a bizarre coincidence and she wasn't who they were looking for?

'Kevin Spriggs,' Dan said. 'Your dad's name was Kevin Spriggs – but then, you knew that already.'

'No! No, I didn't.' There was a shrill edge to Stella's voice, a hint of panic. With a shaking hand, she pushed her copy of the printed messages back across the table. 'I didn't know his name. My mum never told me and Alfie Moss didn't either. Take a look for yourself.' She prodded the sheet of paper. 'There's no mention of his name in these messages.'

'That's true,' Dan said. 'But you could easily have found that information another way. Through social media, for instance.'

'No, I'm telling you, I didn't do that.' She ran her fingers up and down the sides of her temples. 'After I got that second

243

message, I was gutted. I don't know what I'd been expecting ... an emotional and joyous reunion, I suppose ... certainly not the news that my father was a *bad lot*. It wasn't what I wanted to hear – that's for sure.'

'It seems to me you were more than willing to take Alfie Moss at his word,' Isabel said. 'If I'd been in your position, I might have been tempted to get in touch with Kevin Spriggs anyway – to find out for myself whether Alfie was telling the truth. The whole truth.'

When Stella answered, her voice was shaky and halting. 'I ... I did think about it ... about contacting him. In fact, I thought about nothing else for days – but every time I'd end up asking myself the same question. *Why would Alfie lie about his own father?* The conclusion I came to was that he wouldn't, that Alfie Moss was being honest with me.'

Isabel placed the sheet of messages back into the file and placed her hands on top of it.

'We'd like to confirm your biological connection to Kevin Spriggs,' she said. 'Would you be willing to give a DNA sample so that we can compare it to the victim's?'

'Yes, OK. I have no problem with that.'

'Thank you,' Isabel said. 'We'll arrange for a swab to be taken before you leave.'

'Can I ask what happened after you'd received the messages from Alfie Moss?' Dan said. 'What did you do next?'

'Nothing.' Stella shrugged. 'I didn't contact him again ... in fact, I completely abandoned the search for my father.'

'Just like that?' Isabel said. 'Even though you'd wondered about him for years? Why give up so easily?'

'I was disenchanted,' Stella said, her tone melancholy. 'I'd always had this dream of what my dad would be like, you know? I imagined a kind, generous, intelligent man who'd be thrilled that I'd finally managed to track him down. Listening to myself now, I realise how ridiculous that sounds.'

'Not really,' Isabel said. 'It's understandable.'

'Anyway, Alfie's message completely shattered my naïve vision of a happy-ever-after. The things he told me put me off. I think I was scared of meeting my natural father and being horribly disappointed. My mum had already passed away by the time Alfie replied to my message, but I remembered how furious she'd been when I told her I'd done a DNA test, and that was playing on my mind as well – so I decided to walk away from the whole thing.'

'Why was your mother upset?' Isabel asked.

Stella wrapped her arms around herself and shuddered. 'I don't know for sure. Her mental health was always fragile. She suffered with depression throughout most of her adult life, and the news that I was trying to track down my father plunged her into a particularly low mood.'

'Did it fall to you and your sister to support your mother when she was depressed?' Isabel asked.

'We'd rally round and do our best, but it was never easy. My dad ... my stepdad ... he was the one who always looked after Mum whenever she was ill. He knew how to lift her spirits and keep her on an even keel and, after he died, Mum was never the same. The gaps between her bouts of depression got shorter and shorter, and towards the last few years of her life she was living in a state of almost constant hopelessness. It got to the point where my sister and I didn't know what to do about it. Then, as we were reaching the end of our tether, Mum suddenly started to smile again. She went back to working in her garden, and she made a friend. Life was on the up for her. And then I told her about the DNA test, and put all of that in jeopardy.'

'That friend,' Dan said. 'Was it Evelyn Merigold?'

'Yes,' said Stella. 'She and Mum used to go out for lunch together and visit open gardens. It was an odd friendship, really. Mum was at least fifteen years older than Evelyn, but they had a lot in common and enjoyed each other's company. For once, Mum seemed happy and upbeat. That's why her suicide was so hard to understand.'

'Tell me how she reacted to the news that you'd done the DNA test,' Isabel said.

'It distressed her. She was upset and worried and nervous. Then, when I got the results and told her I'd found a close match, she became distraught. It seemed to affect her physically as well. She stopped eating. She wanted to know why, why I was pursuing my search. *I didn't even know the man,* she said. *Why go looking for him now? What do you hope to gain?*'

'Did she ask you to stop?' Isabel said. 'End the search?'

'She didn't ask, she *begged*. But, of course, by then it was too late. I'd already done the test and sent a message to Alfie. Even though I hadn't received a reply at that stage, Mum reacted badly. She was signed off work, and a few days later she took an overdose of sleeping tablets.'

'That must have been extremely upsetting for you and your sister,' Dan said.

'It broke my heart,' Stella said, a film of tears shrouding her eyes. 'I blamed myself. Deep down, I knew that the search for my biological father was what had driven her to take her own life. So, as well as a sense of grief, I found myself dealing with a terrible weight of guilt.'

Had that sense of guilt been at the root of Kevin Spriggs' murder, Isabel wondered? Had the death of her mother triggered an uncontrollable sense of rage in Stella, a need for revenge? But why attack Kevin Spriggs when it wasn't clear if he'd even known of Stella's existence? Had she seen it as retaliation for some perceived wrong? If so, what was it she wasn't telling them?

Isabel eyed Stella closely. She was pale, but composed, neither frightened nor particularly resentful of their questions. 'Assured' was the adjective that jumped into Isabel's mind. Stella Mariner was confident, unruffled and level-headed. Was that because she was innocent, or because she was sure she could get away with murder?

'Alfie Moss didn't reply to your message until several weeks after your mother's death,' Dan said. 'How did you feel when he finally contacted you?'

Stella deliberated for a few seconds. 'I was beginning to come to terms with losing Mum, so Alfie's reply was a real setback. His message disturbed me. The things he said, combined with Mum's devastating reaction to my search for my natural father … it made me wonder.'

'About what?' said Dan.

'About the circumstances of my conception. Perhaps it was more complicated than Mum said.'

'She told you she got pregnant after a one-night stand,' said Isabel. 'Why would she have said that if it wasn't true? What reason would she have to lie?'

Stella clutched the bottom of her chair.

'I did wonder whether she'd had an affair with someone … a married man, for instance.' She let go of the chair and folded her arms, hunching forward defensively.

'That would account for why she didn't want you to go looking,' Isabel said.

'It's certainly one explanation,' Stella replied. 'Mum always made a point of telling me it was a one-time thing, but I'm sure there was more to it than she was letting on. I guess I'll never know now.'

'You must have tried to talk to her about it?' Isabel said. 'Why do you think she was so reluctant to open up?'

Stella sighed. 'I think getting pregnant traumatised her. Her parents were furious when they found out. According to Mum, they were ridiculously straitlaced … didn't believe in sex outside of marriage.'

'That sounds like a very Victorian point of view,' Isabel said.

'Quite.' Stella smiled feebly. 'Mum didn't tell me much, but from the few things she let slip, I got the impression her mother was completely unreasonable … a total control freak.'

'Are your grandparents still alive?' said Dan.

'I've no idea. Heather and I have never had anything to do with them. When Mum told them she was having a baby, they threw her out. They never even came to see her when I was born. Eventually, Mum moved to Bainbridge and met my stepdad and he promised to take care of her – and that's what he did, right up until the day he died.'

'I appreciate you answering our questions,' Isabel said, staring into Stella's large brown eyes. 'You've been very candid. Before you go, can I clarify a few things?'

'Of course.'

'You maintain that, until we told you today, you didn't know the name of your biological father?' Isabel said.

'That's correct.'

'And, after you received Alfie Moss's replies to your messages, you abandoned the search for your dad.'

'Yes.'

'You didn't do any detective work on social media? Try to track down Kevin Spriggs through Alfie Moss's Facebook account?'

'No. I'm not on Facebook. I prefer Twitter.'

Dan leaned forward. 'Tell me,' he said, his tone curious, 'what about Alfie Moss? He's your half-brother … aren't you interested in meeting him? Getting to know him and his family?'

Stella was beginning to look exasperated. She screwed up her nose and scowled at the question. 'I was looking for my father. I already have a sister who I'm close to. I wasn't interested in acquiring another sibling. I'm sure Alfie Moss is a nice enough man but, quite honestly, I've no desire to get to know him.'

'That surprises me,' said Dan.

'Why? I wish him all the best, really I do, but I doubt he and I have much in common. More to the point, if I did meet Alfie, he'd probably want to share all the gory details of our wayward father – and that, quite frankly, is information I can live without.'

'So, what? You decided it was best to draw a line under that strand of your life?' Dan said.

'Yes, and now that I know Kevin Spriggs is dead, it's something I'll never have any reason to resurrect.'

'Did Alfie Moss know your email address?' Isabel asked. 'Would he have known how to get hold of you, if he wanted to?'

'No,' Stella said, with a quick shake of the head. 'And that suited me perfectly. I was extremely careful about how much information I put onto the *Tree of Life* site, and I made sure my communication settings were at the highest level of security. It meant I was able to contact Alfie through the site's online message feature, but other members – including Alfie – wouldn't be able to see my email address.'

'Any particular reason you didn't want to share that information with him?' Isabel asked.

'I'm a very private person. I don't like sharing my details online. I might have chosen to share it with him eventually, but I wanted to sound him out first. Then, after his crushing revelation, I was glad I hadn't. It meant I could stay anonymous and beat a hasty retreat.'

'Without leaving any trace, you mean?' Isabel leaned forward. 'Tell me, why did you feel the need to be so cautious?'

For the first time, Stella looked uncomfortable, as if she'd been wrong-footed.

'I'm a naturally cautious person.'

'And yet you were quite happy to send off your DNA kit?'

'Well … yes, but I did have my reservations.' She chewed her lip. 'Don't get me wrong, those DNA tests offer amazing opportunities for people like me, but they also have the power to wreak havoc. I was aware I risked barging into my biological father's life uninvited … virtually speaking. For all I knew, he could have been happily married with a picture-perfect family – and I didn't want to rock any boats. I was mindful that the news of my existence may have been unwelcome.'

'But you didn't know your biological father's name? You didn't try to trace or contact him?'

'How many more times do I have to say it? No.' Stella leaned forward. 'Can I ask … *was* he married? Did Kevin Spriggs have a wife? Any other kids?'

'He never married again after the divorce from Alfie's mother,' Dan replied. 'And, as far as we know – apart from yourself – he only had the one child. Alfie.'

Isabel waited for a moment, letting Stella absorb the information.

'For the record,' Isabel said, aiming to catch Stella off guard, 'can you confirm that you had no involvement in Kevin Spriggs' murder?'

'Definitely *not*.' Stella's hands curled into fists. 'And *for the record*, I had no idea that the man whose body was found in Hollybrook Close was my dad.'

'You have to admit, if what you're saying is true, then this is one hell of a coincidence,' said Dan. 'Your biological father turns up dead in the house next door to where your mother once lived … a house that she had a key to. Are we expected to believe it's some weird quirk of fate?'

'You can believe what you like,' Stella said, her words clipped and sharp. 'And please, don't bring my mother into this. She's dead. It's not as though she's come back from the grave to bump off my father to keep him out of my life, is it?'

'Is that what she would have wanted, do you think?' Dan persisted. 'To keep him out of your life?'

Stella glared. 'Now you're trying to put words into my mouth.'

'Hey,' said Dan. 'I think you'll find I was merely repeating back what you said. I can rewind the tape if you don't believe me.'

'Can you answer the question, please, Stella?' said Isabel.

'I'm pretty sure I already have,' Stella said, her voice stroppy. 'I've told you that Mum wasn't happy about me trying to find my dad … and, yes, she tried to stop me … but she knew me well enough to know that once I get an idea in my head, no one and nothing will prevent me from following it through. I'm stubborn like that. Who knows, maybe it's a trait I inherited from Kevin Spriggs.'

Stella pushed back her chair. 'I'd like to go now,' she said. 'I'm free to do that, right? You said this was voluntary.'

Isabel held back a sigh. This case was getting to her. From the outset, her gut instinct had told her they were looking for someone with a connection both to the house and the victim. In Stella Mariner, they had established those connections – but there was still no firm evidence to put her at the crime scene, or suggest a motive. Unless, of course, Stella was lying to them and knew more than she was letting on.

'Before you go, can you answer one more question?' Isabel said. 'Did you tell anyone else about the messages you sent to Alfie Moss?'

Stella stood up, but kept her head down. 'I've co-operated with you and answered your questions,' she said, pulling on her coat, 'but I've had enough now. I want to go home.'

'OK, Stella,' Isabel said, knowing she had no option but to let her go. 'DS Fairfax will escort you out and arrange for a DNA swab to be taken before you leave. Thanks for coming in. You're free to go. For now.'

'What do you reckon then, boss? Did she do it?'

Dan and Isabel were back in the CID room, their hopes of bringing the case to a swift conclusion having floated away with the clouds that were drifting past the window.

'She seems like the obvious suspect,' Isabel replied. 'But perhaps too obvious.'

'I must confess, she looked genuinely shocked when we told her the man found at Hollybrook Close was her dad. She was white as a sheet, and that's hard to fake.'

'I agree,' said Isabel. 'She seemed utterly stunned by the news. She was also exceptionally communicative about her mother. If she was guilty of murder, I'd expect her to be a lot less forthcoming.'

'Maybe Stella *is* innocent,' Dan said, 'but there's no denying she *is* the link ... that connection between the victim and the house.'

'She probably showed those messages from Alfie to someone else,' said Isabel. 'In which case, we'll need to widen our net. She's close to her sister. Perhaps she shared the messages with her.'

'Possibly. The only thing I know for certain is, this isn't over yet. Not by a long chalk.' Dan went to stand by the whiteboard, his hands in his pockets. 'Even if Stella Mariner *is* guilty, we're stymied. We can't arrest her without some proof to link her to the murder.'

'Get someone to check CCTV to see if we can spot Stella or someone else within a half-mile radius of the crime scene at the time of the murder. She said she was at home, and that she worked an evening shift at the hospital that day. Let's see if we can catch her out.'

'I'll get onto it, boss.'

'And talk to Digital Forensics,' Isabel added. 'See if there's anything on Kevin Spriggs' phone yet ... anything at all that might place Stella Mariner at the scene.'

Chapter 44

'I've just finished speaking to Raveen, boss,' Dan said, an hour later as he poked his head into Isabel's office. 'Three pieces of good news. First of all, the CSIs found a partial print in the kitchen that doesn't belong to Ruth Prendergast or Gerald Langton.'

Isabel was unimpressed. 'It could have been there for ages and belong to anyone,' she said.

'I don't think so,' Dan said. 'It was on the worktop … a chance impression. Let's face it, those kinds of surfaces get wiped down every day. At least, they do if you're not a lazy sloven – which Ruth Prendergast doesn't strike me as being.'

'Presumably this partial print doesn't match anything on the database?'

'No, unfortunately not. However, as Raveen pointed out, it's evidence we can use if the print turns out to be a match for someone we go on to arrest.'

Isabel lowered her head. 'Hit me with the second and third pieces of good news,' she said. 'I hope you've saved the best till last.'

'I have,' Dan said. 'The phone data is back from the service provider. Plus, Theo has tracked down some CCTV footage from a camera positioned near the path that runs at the back of the Mariner house. He's looking through it now.'

Isabel thought of the unlit stretch of narrow lane she'd observed when she'd peered over the top of the Mariners' rear fence. The quality of any CCTV images from that kind of location would be dark and fuzzy at best. Plus, if the perpetrator *had* accessed the crime scene via the Mariners' back garden, they would surely have covered their face.

'I admire your optimism, Dan,' she said. 'But we both know the quality of some of the CCTV footage we're expected to use as evidence. It's as good as nothing. Worthless.'

'True, but if we do find something, it would at least confirm the route the killer took to get to the crime scene.'

'You said the phone data's in?' Isabel said, pinning all her hopes on the final piece of good news. 'Please tell me it includes something of interest.'

'It does,' Dan said. 'The SPOC copied you in.'

Isabel reached for her keyboard and logged in to her internal emails. In the absence of the victim's phone, the report on the data had been obtained from the service provider. Opening the email attachment, she scanned the list of recent texts and phone calls. Remarkably, there weren't many texts. The dearth of close family and friends in Kevin Spriggs' life meant that the majority of the messages were from service companies. There were several from couriers, advising when various packages would arrive, and a few notifications that his phone bill was available to view online. There were also routine messages from other companies – one from Green Flag recovery service to confirm that his breakdown cover had been renewed, and another from his energy provider offering a new tariff. The newest texts were from Spriggs' employer, Carl Redport. The first was sent on Thursday 9 January at 9.20 a.m., the day after the murder.

I was expecting you in today, Kev. I thought we agreed three days' leave. Where the hell are you? We're snowed under with work. I need you here, mate.

An hour later, Carl had sent another message.

What are you playing at, Kev? And what's happened to your phone? Where are you? Why aren't you at work? Get yourself in ASAP.

Carl Redport had presumably given up after that, because he'd sent no more messages.

'Check out the text sent in the first few minutes of New Year's Day,' Dan said.

Isabel scrolled through the messages to one from an unregistered number, sent at 12.06 a.m. on 1 January.

This is my number. Make sure you call me. I'll be waiting. xx

'Who the hell sent that, then?' she said.

Dan shrugged. 'It's an unregistered pay-as-you go.'

'But you think it's the killer?'

'I do.'

'Didn't Lucas say one of the guys from the pub saw Spriggs in the Sheaf of Corn on New Year's Eve?' Isabel said. 'Do you think this person met him there?'

'I'm sure of it. The timing of the first message certainly fits in with that. From the tone of it, I'd say she, or he, was desperate to hook up with Spriggs … or pretended to be.'

Isabel scanned through the list of calls and texts. On Saturday 4 January at 11.03 a.m., Spriggs had sent a message to the unregistered number.

Sorry I've not been in touch. Had one hell of a hangover on New Year's Day!!! I was going to ring you the next morning, but couldn't believe someone as lovely as you could seriously be interested in little ol' me. ☺ If you still fancy meeting up, give me a call. If I don't hear from you, I'll assume you were wearing your beer goggles when I saw you at the pub.

At 11.06 a.m. on the same day, a call lasting four minutes and thirty-five seconds had been made to Spriggs' phone from the same unregistered number.

Fifty minutes later, at 11.56 a.m., Spriggs had sent another text message.

Enjoyed talking to you earlier. Still can't believe you want to see me. I'm off work on Monday, Tuesday and Wednesday, so I'm free to come over whenever suits you best. I'll bring a bottle of something classy. Let me know when and where. REALLY looking forward to it. xx

The following day, the unregistered caller had rung Spriggs at 3.03 p.m. The call lasted eight minutes and twelve seconds.

At 3.24 p.m., Spriggs sent a text.

Wednesday at 1 p.m. it is then. I'm still having to pinch myself. Don't forget to text me your address. Can't wait to see you again. xx

At 3.27 p.m., a final text had been received from the unregistered number.

Yep, should be good. I can guarantee we'll have fun. ☺ Address is 4 Hollybrook Close, Bainbridge. See you on Wednesday. xx

Isabel clicked her tongue. 'So, this is the killer setting up the meeting,' she said. 'Who do you think it is, Dan?'

'If you're going to force me to guess, I'd have to say Stella Mariner,' he said. 'But it's going to be nigh on impossible to prove.'

'The use of a burner phone supports our theory that everything was planned meticulously. The killer had no intention of being traced.'

'Do you think whoever sent the text could have accidentally given the wrong house number?' Dan asked. 'Typed in number 4 instead of number 3?'

'I doubt it,' said Isabel. 'Number 3 is empty. Kevin Spriggs would have smelled a rat if he'd turned up there. In my opinion, he was definitely expected at number 4.'

'Maybe the partial print will tie Stella Mariner to the crime scene,' Dan said. 'Providing she *was* there.'

Isabel's face clouded. 'You obviously have some misgivings,' she said. 'Speak up if there's something on your mind.'

Dan moved a cardboard box off the visitor's chair and sat down. 'Stella Mariner has strenuously denied being involved. What if she's telling the truth?'

'I agree she seemed credible, but it's a big *if*, Dan. If Stella murdered Kevin Spriggs, she's got nothing to lose by lying to us.'

'And motive?' Dan said. 'Why would she want to kill a man she didn't even know? A man she'd gone to great lengths to find.'

'She might not have been tracking him down to establish a relationship. Perhaps she wanted to find him to bring about his downfall. As for motive, I suspect there's more to her mother's story than she's letting on.'

Dan leaned forward and rested his elbows on his knees. 'Another possibility is that she started her search for Kevin Spriggs with the best of intentions, but changed her mind later on, after her mother took her own life. Stella seems riddled with guilt over her mother's death. She admitted that doing the DNA test pushed Katrina Mariner over the edge.'

'You mean the guilt she felt in the wake of her mother's death flipped her feelings about her natural father?'

'Yep, and rather than blame herself for her mother's suicide, she decided to turn her anger on Kevin Spriggs,' said Dan. 'She killed him to avenge her mother.'

Isabel placed her hands on her desk and drummed her fingers to the rhythm of a military march. 'I can think of at least two other people who might have wanted to avenge Katrina Mariner's death. Heather Mariner and Evelyn Merigold.'

Dan stuck out his bottom lip and nodded. 'If Stella *is* telling the truth, that would put Heather and Evelyn firmly in the frame.'

'Heather seems the most likely alternative to Stella,' said Isabel. 'I'm not sure whether the friendship between Evelyn Merigold and Katrina Mariner would have been strong enough to warrant Merigold taking such a drastic step.'

'Perhaps they were more than friends,' Dan said. 'Evelyn may have been in love with Katrina. I've heard you say more than once that love is a strong motive for committing a crime.'

'And what greater love than two overprotective daughters for their vulnerable mother?'

'So, what? We focus on the Mariners for now?'

'I think so. I'm sure we're on the right track. The person Stella is most likely to have shown Alfie Moss's messages to is her sister. Maybe Stella wasn't the only one who believed the *Tree of Life* shenanigans were what drove her mother to suicide.'

'Fair point,' Dan said, 'but Katrina Mariner's suicide happened a couple of months before Alfie Moss got in touch. Strictly speaking, it was *Stella's* actions that tipped Katrina over the edge … her stubborn insistence on looking for her father. If Heather wanted to avenge her mother, wouldn't she have chosen to punish Stella, rather than Kevin Spriggs?'

'I don't think so. I've seen the sisters together, and they appear to be extraordinarily close. If Heather *is* involved, it's my opinion she would have held Kevin Spriggs responsible for Katrina Mariner's frame of mind.'

'Rather than speculating, we need to establish whether Stella told anyone else about the messages from Alfie Moss,' said Dan.

'You're right. Bring both of the sisters in for questioning. If one of them *is* guilty, I doubt she'll stand by and let her sister take the blame.'

Chapter 45

Stella Mariner pulled her car onto the driveway at Hollybrook Close and switched off the engine with trembling fingers. The visit to the police station had shaken her. She'd done her best to maintain a calm façade, but she'd been alarmed by some of the things they'd asked about. She'd had no choice but to tolerate their insidious probing, but she was worried about where their investigation was heading.

Her mobile's piercing ring tone made her jump. She retrieved the phone from her bag and declined the unknown caller. Right now, what she needed was some quiet time alone to think things through. Life was getting complicated.

She looked up at the house through the passenger side window. God, she hated this place. There was something drab and oppressive about it. Her mother had never really been happy here. Then again, happiness wasn't something that had come easily to Katrina Mariner.

How much longer would it take to find a buyer? The house was a money pit. Even though it was standing empty, the council tax and utility bills still had to be paid. She and her sister were currently sharing the burden of that expense, but neither of them could afford to keep shelling out forever.

There had been loads of viewings when the property first went on the market, but the number of appointments had dwindled as winter and Christmas approached. Now that the new year was here, there might be a flurry of renewed interest. She hoped so.

They'd already dropped the asking price to something that was more than reasonable. *Priced to sell* was how the estate agent had put it. In theory, the house should have been snapped up ages ago. What was wrong with the place? Did it have a bad aura? Was the ghost of her mother still lingering in its walls?

Stella's pulse quickened as she caught sight of a blue Nissan in the rear-view mirror. Her sister's car, turning into the cul-de-sac. What the hell was Heather doing here? She wasn't due to check on the house until later in the week. Stella had assumed she'd have the place to herself. Heather was the last person she wanted to see right now.

She fumbled with the passenger door and got out. There was a film of ice on the driveway and her heeled boots began to slip beneath her feet. Shrugging the strap of her handbag onto her shoulder, she teetered over to the front door, reaching it just as Heather parked her car behind Stella's Mini, blocking her in.

Heather was out of the car in seconds, her own sensible boots making short work of reaching the front porch.

'Hey, sis. What are you doing here?' Heather said.

'I was about to ask you the same thing,' Stella replied. 'Why aren't you at work?'

'I'm owed a few days. I need to use up some leave before the end of March.'

'Haven't you got anything better to do than hang around here? I can check the house. Why don't you go clothes shopping or something? Or get your nails done? I see you've broken one.' Stella indicated the car keys clutched in Heather's right hand. The red-painted nail on her index finger was broken, snapped off at a jaunty angle.

'I've already spent a fortune in the sales,' Heather said. 'I can't afford to go shopping until I get paid again. As for this …' She held up the offending nail. 'I'm booked in for a manicure next week. It can wait until then.'

Stella turned to face the door and slipped her key into the lock. 'Even so, I'll check the house if you want to head off.'

'I'm here to finish sorting that leak under the sink,' Heather said. 'I'll tell you what, why don't *you* go home? You can come back at the weekend. The estate agent rang me earlier and they've got a viewing lined up for Saturday. We might have more luck if someone's here to show potential buyers around.'

'A viewing? That's good news.' Stella twisted the key and opened the door. 'Wouldn't it be great if we could finally sell this bloody place? It depresses me, coming here. Makes me think about Mum.'

'All the more reason for you to go home,' Heather said. 'I'll move my car so you can head off.'

'I'll go in a minute … There's something I need to ask you about first.'

Stepping inside, Stella marched along the hallway, leaving damp footprints on the wooden floor. Her sister followed, close on her heels.

'What's so urgent that it can't wait?' Heather said, grabbing her arm.

'Ouch!' Stella said. 'Let go of me. That hurts. What's the matter with you today? Anybody would think you didn't want me here. You've not got a bloke hidden in the upstairs cupboard, have you?' She began to laugh. Then, remembering what had happened to Kevin Spriggs, she let the smile slip from her face.

'If you really want to talk, I can come round to yours this evening,' Heather said. 'I'll bring a bottle of wine and some nibbles and we can watch something on Netflix. Whatever it is you want to discuss, it can wait until then.'

'It can't actually. I've just come from the police station. I've been questioned again by that detective. It was awful. They put me in an interview room and cautioned me. They told me the man they found next door was my biological father.'

'*What?*' Heather's face had lost its colour. 'How the hell did they come to that conclusion?'

'Let's go and sit in the kitchen and I'll tell you about it.' Stella set off again but, when she reached the kitchen door, she paused. 'What was that?'

'What?'

'A noise. From upstairs.'

'I didn't hear anything.'

The sound came again. A soft, metallic rattle, like the gentle vibration of a radiator.

'It's probably the heating playing up again,' Heather said. 'I'll have to call the plumber out. More sodding expense.'

Stella was about to accept the explanation, when another sound floated down the stairs. A faint, muffled gurgle.

'What was *that*?' she said. Staring at the red flush on her sister's neck and noticing her guilty expression, she added: 'What have you done, Heather? What the fuck have you done?'

Chapter 46

'Stella Mariner's not answering her phone,' Dan said, 'and neither is her sister. I've sent officers to both of their home addresses, but there's no one at either property.'

'Stella's probably gone to work,' Isabel said. 'Have you tried to get hold of her at the hospital?'

'I have, and she's not there either. The person I spoke to on her ward said she's not on shift until later. I've also done some digging on Heather Mariner. Turns out she works for a company called Westwoods.'

'Is that significant?' Isabel said.

'The firm's based in Chesterfield. They offer health and safety training, and they're also a supplier of PPE. Personal protective equipment.'

'I know what PPE is, Dan.'

'Heather Mariner delivers food hygiene and safety courses, including modules on deep cleaning and disinfection, and the use of protective gloves and clothing. It occurred to me that she would be pretty adept at knowing how to avoid contaminating a crime scene. Plus, she has access to protective workwear ... the ideal get-up for someone who's planning to commit murder and doesn't want to leave a forensic trail.'

Isabel nodded. At last, the pieces were beginning to fall into place. 'Have you rung Westwoods? Is Heather Mariner at work today?'

'I have, and guess what?'

'Not guessing games again.'

Dan laughed. 'I spoke to Heather's boss and he said she rang in sick today. Heavy cold, apparently.'

'Heavy cold?' Isabel's eyes widened. 'I only saw her the other day, and she was fine then.'

'It's the usual excuse, isn't it, if you want to throw a sickie?'

She raised an eyebrow. 'Is it now? I'll remember that. Get hold of Heather's vehicle registration – she travels a lot for work, so I'd imagine it'll be a company car. Let's see if we can locate her … put a marker on the vehicle and see if it triggers the ANPR. And send someone over to 3 Hollybrook Close. If the Mariners were responsible for Kevin Spriggs' murder, it's a fair assumption they're somehow involved in Ruth Prendergast's disappearance. We've got CCTV of Ruth driving into Hollybrook Close, but there's no sign that she left. She could have gone next door, to the Mariner house.'

'I'll send a patrol car round there now,' Dan said. 'In the meantime, we'll keep trying Stella's phone.'

Chapter 47

'What the hell are you doing?' Stella said. 'Heather … tell me what's happening here.'

'I've turned off my phone, and you need to do the same.' Heather held out her hand and snapped her fingers, indicating that Stella should surrender her mobile.

'For God's sake, *why*? What's going on? You need to tell me.'

Heather clicked her fingers again and, reluctantly, Stella opened her bag and passed her phone to her sister. Heather turned it off and placed it on the worktop.

'If you really want to know what's happening, it's best if I show you,' Heather said. 'But before I do, what was it you were so desperate to ask me about?'

Stella pushed her fingers through her hair and pressed the heels of her hands against the top of her skull. 'My head's thumping,' she said. 'You're scaring me, Heather.'

'Scaring you? Why? You don't have to be afraid of me, I'm your sister. I'd do anything for you.'

Rather than reassuring her, Heather's words made Stella more anxious. Her legs were beginning to shake, so she pulled out one of the stools and lowered herself onto it. 'That detective woman, she asked me whether I'd told anyone about the messages I received through the *Tree of Life* website.'

'What did you say? Did you lie?'

Stella sat up, an angry glint in her eye. 'I'm not going to lie to the police, Heather. Not even for you.'

'So you told them? That I'd seen the messages?'

'No, I didn't. Rather than lie, I chose not to answer the question.'

Heather smiled. 'Thanks, sis.'

'I don't want your thanks. I was hardly going to drop you in it, was I? Although I'll admit I was tempted. When they asked me who I'd shown those messages to, everything clicked into place. You killed that man, didn't you? You killed him because he was my biological father.'

Heather walked over to the kitchen window. 'You're wrong on so many levels, Stella,' she said. 'That man's not dead because he's your biological father, he's dead because he was the reason Mum killed herself.'

'That's not true,' Stella said, tears welling in her eyes. 'If anyone was to blame, it was me. I was the one who went searching for him. She begged me not to, but I went ahead anyway.'

'You don't get it, do you?' Heather spun around and charged back towards the centre of the kitchen, her face crimson with fury. 'It wasn't the search that bothered her, it was what would happen if you tracked him down. The very thought of that man terrified her. He was a monster.'

'Monster?' Stella shook her head to fend off the word.

'It's true,' Heather said. 'I went round to see Mum after you'd signed up for that stupid website. She was in a right state. It took me ages to calm her down, and when I did, I forced her to tell me what was bothering her.'

Another sound came from upstairs. Fainter this time.

'Who's in the house, Heather?'

'I said I'd show you, and I will,' she replied. 'But first, you're going to sit and listen to what I have to say. Mum told me her story first-hand, and I want you to hear it too.'

'Story? What *story*? What are you talking about?'

'I'm talking about what happened to her ... what he did to her. Think yourself lucky you don't have to witness the pain and despair that was in Mum's eyes when she told *me* about it. Like it or not, Stella, I'm going to tell you everything, and you *are* going to listen. You need to hear the truth.'

Chapter 48

While Isabel waited for her team to locate Heather and Stella Mariner, she sat and cogitated on the perplexities of the case. She felt stressed, and had to resist the temptation to lay her head on her desk and give in to a growing wave of exhaustion. She knew they were close to the truth, but they still needed to sort the facts from the multitude of irrelevancies they'd come up against over the last week. This case felt like panning for gold, shaking things back and forth and side to side, sifting through the dross for a shining flash of truth. Right now, they were at the stage where they had to proceed carefully and gently, so as not to wash away the very thing they were looking for.

Isabel pondered on which of the sisters was most likely to be guilty, or whether they were both in it together. Luring Kevin Spriggs to a meeting at 4 Hollybrook Close had been a risky undertaking. The killer must have let herself into the house through the back door … but how had things unfolded after that? What had happened when Kevin Spriggs came calling? And what would the killer have done if Ruth Prendergast had been at home that day?

Feeling the need to talk things through, Isabel wandered into the main office. The only person at her desk was Zoe. The winter sun was streaming through the window, lighting up her blonde hair and making her face glow.

'Is Dan still in the incident room?'

'Yep,' Zoe replied. 'As is Lucas. They're on the trail of the Mariner sisters. Oh yes, and Lucas asked me to give you a message.'

'What's that?'

'He spoke to Carl Redport. Turns out Carl has been having an affair, and Kevin Spriggs knew about it. That's the reason he was given so many chances at work.'

'Are you saying Spriggs was blackmailing his boss?'

'Not blackmailing exactly,' Zoe said. 'I'd say it was more a case of putting pressure on him. I don't suppose it's relevant now. It was a loose end though, which is why Lucas wanted me to tell you.'

'Thanks.' Isabel plonked herself down in Lucas's chair and leaned across his desk. 'I've been thinking about the day of the murder. About how things must have unfolded.'

'And what conclusions have you come to?' Zoe said.

'That the perpetrator knocked on Ruth Prendergast's back door to check the house was empty before letting herself in with a key. I can't help but wonder though … what would have happened if Ruth Prendergast had been home?'

'I've wondered the same thing, but it's immaterial now, isn't it? Ruth wasn't home, and the killer must have realised that … known she'd be at work.'

'But what would have happened if Ruth had been ill and taken the day off unexpectedly?'

Zoe thought for a moment. 'If Ruth *had* answered the door, I guess the killer would have made an excuse for being there. If it was one of the Mariner sisters, they could have come up with any number of reasons to be calling round. They were neighbours, after all. Well … sort of.'

'And if Ruth had been home, what would have happened at one p.m. when Kevin Spriggs came knocking?'

'I suppose he would have assumed he'd gone to the wrong address, or had been ... strung along. Why does it matter? We know Ruth Prendergast wasn't there, and that the killer gained access to her house and let Kevin Spriggs in.'

'And now Ruth Prendergast has disappeared from the same property,' Isabel said, her voice strained with worry. 'Any news on whether the Mariner house has been checked yet? My gut's telling me that's where Ruth is.'

'There was no sign of her yesterday during the door-to-door inquiries, and no sign of the Mariners either. Dan sent a patrol car round to the house a few minutes ago to have another look.'

'You were right to be concerned about Ruth,' Isabel said. 'I'm worried about her safety.'

'Me too. She's not been seen for three days now,' Zoe said. 'I hope to God she's all right.'

'You've got good instincts, Zoe, and that's not something that can be learned. Your gut feeling about Ruth Prendergast, for instance ... I have faith in your judgement.'

'Thanks.'

'Now probably isn't an ideal time, but I do need to have a word with you.'

'Is there a problem?' Zoe wrinkled her forehead. 'Am I in trouble?'

Isabel smiled frustratedly. 'Why do you always assume the worst? You're quite a worrywart on the quiet, aren't you?'

'Not especially,' Zoe replied. 'Not about work, anyway. I think I'm pretty good at my job.'

'I agree,' Isabel said. 'Which is why I don't want to lose you from the team.'

Zoe's shoulders dropped. 'I assume Dan's been talking to you?' she said, glancing towards the DS's empty desk. 'He had no right to do that. I told him not to say anything.'

'In fairness to Dan, I did have to prise the information out of him. All he said was that I should show you more appreciation, which tipped me off that something was wrong. I *made* him tell me the rest, dragged it out of him. That's when he told me you were thinking of getting a transfer.'

'You must think I'm stupid,' Zoe said, 'giving in to my parents.'

'Your parents? How do they fit into this?'

Zoe put her hands over her face for a second. Then, sweeping her hair back from her eyes, she stared across the desk at Isabel.

'Dan didn't mention your parents,' Isabel said. 'Are they the reason you're thinking of leaving Bainbridge?'

Zoe nodded. 'They're putting pressure on me to move back to Leicester.'

'I see. That's a shame. I thought you liked it here.'

'I do. I haven't decided anything yet. It's not a done deal.'

'Well, that gives me some hope.'

'Really?' said Zoe, a disbelieving look in her eyes. 'I wouldn't have thought you'd be bothered either way.'

The comment stung. Isabel knew her management skills weren't exactly textbook, but she was ashamed to think she'd made a member of her team feel undervalued.

'I'm sorry if I haven't always shown my appreciation, Zoe,' she said. 'You're an important part of the team, and I'd be very sorry to see you go. You're bright, and you have a promising career ahead of you.'

Zoe's cheeks turned red.

'If it's a quick promotion you're after, then I can understand why you might need to go elsewhere. If, on the other hand, you're leaving because of anything I might or might not have said or done, then I'd ask you to reconsider.'

Zoe heaved a sigh. 'It's not you,' she said. 'Not really. I wouldn't even be considering moving on if it wasn't for my mum and dad. Then again, when I analyse my life here in Bainbridge, I do sometimes wonder. Work's fine … I love my job, but it's about the *only* positive thing in my life right now.'

'Isn't that a good reason to hang on to it?' Isabel said. 'You seem settled here. The rest of it – your personal life – that's just as likely to fall into place here in Bainbridge as anywhere else.'

'I suppose so.'

'Hang on in there, Zoe. Be patient. And try to make some more connections locally. I've been saying for months you need to liven up your social life. It's a new year … a good time for a fresh start.'

Zoe cringed. 'I know you mean well, but I don't find it easy to socialise. I'm not what you'd call a gregarious person. You're right though – I know you are. I'll try and make more of an effort.'

'And moving to Leicester?' Isabel asked. 'Is that still on the cards?'

'Probably not. I imagine you'll be stuck with me for a while.'

'That sounds good to me,' Isabel said. 'I'm sure Dan will be relieved too. This place wouldn't be the same without you.'

Their tête-à-tête was brought to an abrupt end by the arrival of Dan and Lucas, who hurried into the main office as if pursued by an angry bull.

'We've heard back from the patrol car we sent in to Hollybrook Close,' Dan said. 'Both Heather and Stella Mariner's cars are parked at number 3. The officers haven't approached the house yet; they're awaiting your instructions.'

Isabel stood up, hurried into her office and grabbed her car keys and coat.

Dan followed her and leaned on her office door. 'Are you going over there? To Hollybrook Close?' he said.

'Of course I am,' she replied, barging past him. 'And you're coming with me.'

Dan rubbed his hands together. 'Lead on, Macduff,' he said, standing back and letting her go ahead.

'Don't misquote Shakespeare at me, Dan,' Isabel said, as she put on her coat.

He pulled a face. 'I wasn't aware I was. I didn't even know it was Shakespeare.'

'It's from *Macbeth*,' she said. 'And it's *lay* on, Macduff.'

Out of the corner of her eye, Isabel could see Lucas wobbling his head from side to side, his mouth moving as he silently mimicked her.

'I can see you, Lucas,' she shouted, as she hurried out of the office.

Chapter 49

'I'm not sure I want to hear the truth,' Stella said. Her legs felt weak and her pulse was racing. She was trying to close her mind to what her sister might have done, because the thought of it horrified her.

'Is that why you abandoned the search for your dad?' Heather said. 'Too scared to face up to the awful truth?'

'I was told he was no good. His own son warned me against him. Why would I want to meet someone like that?'

Heather huffed cheerlessly. 'You've always been a scaredy-cat,' she said. 'When we were kids, it was me who was the daring one, even though I was the youngest.'

'That's true,' said Stella. 'You're braver than me. Fearless.'

'I am, and I think Mum knew that too. It's why she felt able to talk to me, after she found out you'd sent off that DNA test.'

'She didn't *find out*,' Stella said. 'I told her.'

'Whatever.' Heather shrugged. 'All I know is, sending off that DNA kit sealed Mum's fate. It's what made her decide to take her own life – but first she needed to unburden herself. She wanted someone to know the truth, and it was me she chose to confide in.'

'Why you?' said Stella. 'She could have talked to me, or both of us.'

'She didn't want to tell you in case it freaked you out.'

'Why would I be freaked out?' Stella was gripping the bottom of the kitchen stool to stop her hands from shaking. Another sound came from upstairs. She should go up there ... face whatever or whoever it was, but Heather was right. She was a scaredy-cat. She had a habit of shying away from anything unpleasant.

'There was a reason Mum was so fragile,' Heather said. 'It was because of your father and what he did to her.'

'What?' Stella could feel her heart pounding. 'What do you mean?'

'He raped her.'

Feeling the breath freeze in her lungs, Stella shook her head. 'No. That's not true. He was a one-night stand. She told me that herself.'

'She told you that to protect you. Dad, *my* dad, knew the truth. He was the only one she ever told, apart from me ... at the end.'

Stella hugged her arms to her chest, shielding her body from her sister's words.

'She never told her parents what happened,' Heather continued. 'Mum said our grandparents were evil, the pair of them. They were teetotallers and they didn't like Mum going to pubs or clubs.'

Stella had begun to shiver. 'She obviously didn't pay them any heed. I've seen loads of photos of Mum when she was young, posing in clubs with her friends. She and her mates were party animals – she used to say that herself.'

'They were. She was a rebel, but all that stopped for Mum when your father attacked her.'

'I don't believe you,' Stella said, her words little more than a whisper.

'There you go again,' Heather said, flipping a hand in Stella's direction. 'In denial. Running scared. It's what you always do.'

'That's not fair.'

'Yes, it is. You might not like it, but what I'm about to tell you is the truth.'

'Go on then.' She steeled herself. 'I'm listening.'

'Mum was in a pub,' Heather began. 'It was packed and she got separated from her friends. She told me she got talking to this bloke at the bar, and he seemed nice. He bought her a drink and they had a laugh, but it was getting late, so Mum told him she was going to go and find her mates. He persuaded her to stay with him for one more drink.'

The heating had come on, but Stella still felt chilled. She was trying not to shiver, and the effort was making her muscles ache.

'Mum didn't even know the bloke's name,' Heather continued. 'She was just being friendly, she said, chatting to him. He was quite nice-looking, but older than her, and she wasn't interested in seeing him again. Eventually, she left him at the bar and wandered away to find her mates, but they'd disappeared. She was pissed off that they'd left her there, on her own. Later on, she came to the conclusion they must have seen her talking to the bloke at the bar and assumed she'd copped off. Anyway, Mum left the pub and went to find a taxi.'

Stella felt sick. Hadn't she always had a sixth sense about this? She thought of her mother's unwillingness to talk about the circumstances of Stella's conception, and her own innate acceptance of that reluctance. Was this what she'd been afraid of? Her own subliminal fear? Was it the *real* reason she'd abandoned the search for her biological father?

Heather's words flowed, her dispassionate tone of voice at odds with what she was saying.

'She saw a taxi turn at the end of the street. Its light was lit, so she knew it was available, and she remembered feeling relieved. She was about to lift her arm to flag it down, when someone grabbed her from behind. It was the man from the pub. He pinned her arms against her sides as the taxi rolled by, then put his hand over her mouth, and dragged her across the pub car park to the sports ground. That's where he raped her.'

'Stop!' Stella said, placing her hands over her ears. 'Why are you telling me this?'

'Because it's time you knew,' Heather said, her voice acidic. 'You might not like it, but you need to hear the truth.'

'No, I don't.' Stella held up a palm in a plea for silence, but Heather ignored the gesture.

'Afterwards,' she continued, 'when he'd run away, Mum got up and walked home. It was nearly two miles, but she didn't care. She couldn't bring herself to get into a taxi. She said that, strangely, she was no longer afraid of walking through the streets, because the worst had already happened.'

'Did she report it to the police?' Stella said, common sense telling her that Heather couldn't be making this up.

'No. She told no one.'

'Why the hell not? Why didn't she tell her parents?'

Heather snorted. 'You're joking aren't you? They already disapproved of Mum's socialising; they'd warned her that no good would come of what they termed her *gallivanting*. Mum didn't think they'd believe her … either that or they'd make her feel like it was her own fault. She'd talked to the man. He'd bought drinks for her. No matter what she told them, her parents wouldn't have trusted her version of events.'

'But it wasn't her fault,' said Stella. 'Accepting a couple of drinks from someone doesn't mean you're consenting to have sex with them. She should have reported him.'

'So you do accept that I'm telling the truth?' Heather said. 'You don't think I'm making all this up?'

'I believe you,' Stella said, pressing her lips together to stop herself from crying.

'Mum stopped going out after that,' Heather said. 'She lost contact with her friends and, for a while, she was in her parents' good books. But then she found out she was pregnant.'

Stella felt bile rise up in the back of her throat. She was glad her mother had never told her this, because she wouldn't have known what to say. Had her mum thought about that bastard every time she'd looked at her? When Stella had smiled at her mother, had it been the same smile the rapist had given her as he handed over the drink he'd bought her?

'She didn't want to tell her parents what had really happened,' Heather continued. 'So instead, she said she'd had a one-night stand. Of course, they were furious. They said her behaviour disgusted them, and they threw her out. You know the rest of the story … she moved away and cut all ties with her family. Then she met Dad and, eventually, they got married. But Mum said she was never the same after it happened. Kevin Spriggs stole her peace of mind.'

Stella put a hand over her mouth and took deep breaths through her nose. 'So, you *do* know his name,' she said. 'Even though I abandoned my search, you decided to pursue it, didn't you?' She felt sick to the stomach. She loved her sister … always had, but no matter what Kevin Spriggs had done, she could never condone murder.

'I might have let the whole thing go,' Heather replied, 'but then, as if it was meant to be, Alfie Moss got in touch with you, and you showed me his messages.'

Stella twisted her fingers. 'Which, as I recall, were short and to the point and lacking any detail. There were no names or email addresses. How the fuck did you find out about Kevin Spriggs?'

'It was easy,' Heather said. 'The one snippet of information those messages did include was your half-brother's name. I found him on Facebook and worked it out from there.'

'And then what? You decided to avenge Mum's death? You tracked Kevin Spriggs down and killed him?'

'You're only half right,' Heather said. 'I tracked him down, but I didn't kill him.'

278

Chapter 50

It felt as if all the air had been syphoned from her lungs. With Heather's words pounding in her ears, Stella clutched her throat and tried to drag oxygen through her windpipe. All she wanted was for this nightmarish conversation to end.

If Heather was telling the truth, and she *wasn't* responsible for killing that man, then her sister wasn't yet beyond redemption – but it didn't alter the fact that she was complicit in his death.

'If you didn't kill him, then who did?' Stella said, not sure whether she wanted to hear the answer.

'You really are very curious today, aren't you?' Heather said, a disparaging sneer playing on her lips. 'And you know what curiosity did, don't you?'

A soft thump came from upstairs. It sounded like an elbow banging against the floor, the sharp point of a funny bone connecting with a hard surface.

'Do you really think I'm going to tell you who did it?' Heather thrust her face into Stella's. 'All you need to know is … it wasn't me.'

Stella reached for her mobile. 'We need to call the police. You can talk to that detective—'

'You've got to be kidding.' Heather snatched at the phone and threw it across the kitchen. It crashed against one of the cupboards and ricocheted along the tiled floor. 'That nosy bloody cow? No way, and I don't want you talking to her either.'

'For Christ's sake!' Stella said, fear creeping up her spine, into the back of her neck. 'She's not nosy. She's doing her job – and she won't stop doing it until she gets to the truth. DI Blood will find out what happened eventually, whether I say anything or not. You *have* to go and see them, Heather. Tell them what you know and explain how you're involved. And you need to tell me who's upstairs.'

'Why don't I show you instead?' She grabbed Stella's arm and pulled her towards the door. 'Come on, sis. I could use some advice on what to do. You always were the sensible one.'

When they reached the hallway, Heather pushed Stella ahead, onto the stairs.

'Go on, up you go.'

Anxiety had formed a hard lump in Stella's throat. 'Where am I going?' she said. 'Which room?'

'The main bathroom,' Heather said, keeping a firm hand on Stella's back.

When she reached the landing and turned right, Stella thought she was going to pass out. Blood whooshed in her temples and she stopped for a moment, not wanting to face whatever or whoever was up here.

'Being a scaredy-cat again, Stella?' Heather propelled her forward, through the door and into the bathroom.

A woman lay on the floor, grey duct tape around her ankles and knees, and across her mouth and nose. A gap near her nostrils was allowing her to breath, but Stella could see that the woman was struggling for air. Her arms were behind her back, bound together at the wrists. The same tape had been used to attach the woman to the tall and solidly built radiator on the wall. There was a desperate look in her eyes, and a strong smell of urine, indicating she had been there for quite some time.

Stella dropped to her knees and looked into the woman's eyes. She thought she might have seen her somewhere before, but it was difficult to tell because most of the lower half of her face was covered in tape.

Stella touched her arm. 'It's OK,' she said. 'You're going to be all right. We'll sort this out.'

The woman whimpered, shaking her head feebly, her eyes bulging and terrified.

Stella pushed herself upright and grabbed her sister's upper arms, shaking her furiously. 'What the hell are you playing at, Heather? What are you trying to do?'

'Isn't it obvious?' Clearly, Heather had convinced herself that her actions were logical. 'I'm stopping her from going to the police.' She pointed a toe at the prostrate woman with no hint of remorse. 'I let something slip … said something I shouldn't.'

'I don't care if you gave her a full fucking confession,' Stella said. 'Who is she anyway? How long's she been here?'

'It's the woman from next door,' Heather said. 'From number 4. She came round here on Friday. I couldn't let her go … she'd have rung that detective.'

Realising where she had seen the woman before, Stella bent down again and placed a hand on her arm. 'I'm so sorry about this. Don't worry, I won't let her hurt you.'

It wasn't Heather's lack of emotion or abnormal sense of calm that terrified Stella the most, it was the fact that her sister seemed convinced her actions were those of a rational human being.

'For God's sake,' she said. 'You must see how ridiculous this is. What exactly are you planning to do with her?'

Heather shrugged. 'I haven't worked that out yet.'

Channelling her status as elder sibling, Stella made a bid to take control. 'The poor woman can hardly breathe, and she must be thirsty as hell. Go downstairs *now*. Get something to cut through this tape and bring one of the mugs up so that we can give her some water.'

'I'm not sure I can do that,' Heather said. 'I won't—'

She stopped abruptly, silenced by the sound of someone banging on the front door.

Chapter 51

Outside, Isabel stood next to Dan on the front step, her hands in her pockets. Two uniformed officers were waiting behind them on the driveway.

The weather was cold and gloomy. A dreary mist was chilling Isabel's bones and dampening her spirits.

The cul-de-sac was preternaturally quiet, as though it was asleep, or pretending to be. Isabel had parked her Toyota on the driveway of number 3, behind a blue Nissan and a grey Mini. Over at number 4, Ruth Prendergast's car was still parked in front of the garage door, but there was no sign or sound of life.

'They're obviously here,' Dan said, nodding towards the Mariners' vehicles. 'I wonder what's keeping them?'

'They've probably seen it's us and don't want to talk,' said Isabel. 'Knock again. Louder this time.'

Dan banged his lower right arm against the door. The sound echoed around the uncanny emptiness of the close, but the door remained closed.

He leaned down and looked through the letterbox. 'No sign of anyone,' he said.

'Give it another go,' said Isabel, nodding again at the door.

Dan lifted the knocker, striking it against the metal plate as loudly as he could. When that failed to provoke a response, he bashed the end of his fist against the uPVC door panel.

'Shall I go round the back?' Dan said.

'I think you're going to have to. The gate's round that side, but it might be locked.' She inclined her head towards the side of the property, and the wooden gate she'd tried herself only a few days earlier. 'I'll stay here.'

Dan and one of the uniformed officers disappeared around the corner of the house and Isabel waited, praying that, if Ruth Prendergast was inside, no harm had come to her. Behind her, a blackbird called out a warning as it launched itself from one of the trees in the Mariners' front garden.

She turned and squinted across the cul-de-sac, towards Ruth's house. Was it her imagination, or was the mist growing thicker and greyer, more cloying? The murkiness of the day felt appropriate somehow, reminding her of the fog that continued to cling to this investigation, making it impossible to decipher anything clearly. It was time to cut through it and get to the truth.

Chapter 52

The knock on the door seemed to do something to Heather. It was as though someone was rattling hard against the side of her head, rather than at the door. Her body jerked, like she'd been jolted out of a deep sleep. Stella crossed her fingers, hoping the sound would knock some sense into her sister's fuddled brain and bring her back to reality.

Running a hand over the top of her head, Heather looked around, her eyes settling on the woman on the floor, as if seeing her for the first time.

The banging downstairs came again, louder this time. The sound of a fist pounding on the door reverberated through the empty house.

'Whoever it is,' Stella said, 'it doesn't sound as if they're going to go away.'

Heather stood silently, her hands hanging limply on either side of her body. For the first time today, Stella thought she detected fear in her sister's eyes.

'You must see that this is wrong, Heather. You need to give me your phone so that I can call the police and an ambulance.'

Stella held out a hand, praying that Heather would do the right thing.

Chapter 53

As Isabel waited by the door, her mobile rang. It was Dan.

'No sign of life round the back either, although I can see a bag on the worktop in the kitchen.' He paused. 'Hang on … I can hear someone moving around.'

As Dan's words drifted into Isabel's ear, she too heard a sound. Footsteps. Heels on the hallway's wooden floor. A second later, the door was unlatched. It opened a fraction and a pair of brown eyes peered through.

'It's DI Blood,' Isabel said, holding up her warrant card. The face looking out was pale and scared, but she couldn't tell whether it belonged to Stella or Heather. 'I'm here with my colleagues. We need to come in.'

The door opened wider. Stella Mariner was standing on the other side.

'Thank God you're here,' she said. 'Your timing couldn't be better.'

Stepping back, she allowed Isabel to enter the house.

As she did so, Isabel spoke to Dan, who was still on the phone. 'Come round to the front,' she said. 'I'm inside with Stella Mariner.'

Ending the call, she followed Stella along the hallway and up the stairs.

'Is your sister here with you?'

'Yes, she's in the bathroom, and so is the woman next door.'

'Ruth Prendergast? Ruth is here?'

'Yes,' Stella replied, as she reached the landing. 'I called the police before I answered the door … and an ambulance.'

'Ambulance?' Isabel experienced a flash of alarm.

'Ruth Prendergast came round here on Friday … my sister's been keeping her here, against her will.'

'Why did she do that?'

'I'll let her tell you that herself.'

Stella crossed the landing, and Isabel followed close behind. The scene that greeted them in the bathroom was both shocking and bizarre. Ruth Prendergast was lying on the tiled floor, bound at the ankles, knees and wrists, and tethered to a tall, wall-mounted radiator. A large quantity of tape had been wound around her mouth.

'What the hell?' Isabel dropped to her knees and dug around in her pocket, pulling out a bunch of keys. Among them was a small penknife, hanging from the keyring. Opening out its tiny blade, she cut through the tape at the side of Ruth's face. 'Don't just stand there,' Isabel said, angry at the inaction of the Mariner women, who were standing, watching. 'Help me get this off.'

The welcome sound of Dan bounding up the stairs echoed through the upper floor of the house.

'Bloody hell,' he said, when he reached the bathroom door. 'What's happening here, then?'

'False imprisonment,' said Isabel, pulling back the tape from Ruth Prendergast's mouth. 'Who did this to you, Ruth?'

Ruth lifted a weak finger and pointed at Heather Mariner. 'She did.' Her voice was weak and dry, almost inaudible. 'She threatened me … with a knife … and she knew about the body being found in my bed.'

Isabel stood up. 'You two are coming down to the station,' she said, addressing the Mariner sisters. 'Dan, do the necessary.'

As Dan arrested and cautioned both of the women and ushered them downstairs, Isabel helped Ruth Prendergast to a sitting position.

'There's an ambulance on its way,' she said. 'I'll take a statement from you when you're feeling better.'

'I'm fine, a bit tired and thirsty, that's all,' Ruth said. 'I don't want to go to hospital … I need something to drink.'

'I'll go and get you some water.'

Isabel went downstairs and searched the empty cupboards until she found a pair of mugs. She half-filled one of them with water and carried it back upstairs.

'Take a few sips for now,' Isabel said, as she knelt down and handed over the mug. 'When the paramedics get here, they'll get you properly rehydrated. You really should go to the hospital and get checked out by a doctor. How long have you been here?'

'Since late Friday morning,' Ruth said, as she drained the mug. 'I came over to talk about the fence … wanted to get it fixed … It's a shared boundary. There was a car on the drive, so I knew someone was in. That woman … she invited me inside.'

'Heather Mariner,' Isabel said. 'The woman who's been keeping you here?'

Ruth gave a slow nod. 'Yes … we got talking. She told me she'd heard that a body had been found in my house.'

She paused to take some deep breaths.

'Take it easy,' Isabel said. 'You can tell me this later, when you're feeling better.'

Ignoring her, Ruth continued to speak. 'She seemed nice, sympathetic … she said *it must have been awful for you, coming in and finding him there, in your bed.* I told her I planned on sleeping in a different room when I moved back in … and then it dawned on me … what she'd said.'

'About the body being found in your bed?' said Isabel.

'Yes. DS Fairfax had asked me not to talk about the case, and I knew the police hadn't released many details either, so I challenged her … asked her how she knew. There was a knife on the draining board … like a box-cutting knife. The next thing I knew, she'd grabbed it and was pointing the blade at my throat. She forced me up here and bound me up with tape.'

Tears spilled from the corners of her eyes.

'You should probably rest now,' Isabel said. 'We'll take a more detailed statement from you when you're feeling better.'

The sound of a wailing siren announced the arrival of the ambulance.

'The paramedics are here,' Isabel said. 'Let them take care of you, Ruth. You deserve to be looked after. You've had one hell of a week.'

Ruth managed a weak smile. 'I know. Is it always like this round here?'

'Believe it or not,' Isabel said, 'Bainbridge is usually a nice, quiet town. I do hope you'll give it a second chance.'

Chapter 54

Heather Mariner was sitting in interview room two, alongside the duty solicitor. Her DNA and fingerprints had been taken by a member of the detention staff, who was arranging for the latter to be checked against the partial print found at the crime scene. Isabel was keeping everything crossed for a match.

As she sorted through her notes, Dan switched on the recording equipment.

'Ruth Prendergast tells me that you held her at 3 Hollybrook Close against her will,' Isabel said, once Dan had repeated the caution. 'You threatened her at knife-point and imprisoned her because you'd disclosed information that exposed your involvement in the murder of Kevin Spriggs. Is that right?'

The solicitor leaned in and whispered something in Heather's ear.

'Are you asking me to confirm that I held that woman at my mum's house, or are you asking whether I killed that man?'

'Both,' Isabel said, 'but I accept my question was ambiguous. Let me start again … did you assault and falsely imprison Ruth Prendergast at 3 Hollybrook Close?'

Heather turned again for another hushed conversation with her brief. After receiving a nod from the solicitor, she gave them her answer.

'Yes, I did.'

'And can you tell us why you did that?' said Dan.

'Because I accidentally said something I shouldn't have,' Heather replied. 'And I didn't want her to go blabbing to you lot.'

Isabel glanced down at her notes. 'According to Ruth Prendergast's preliminary statement, she came over to discuss the repair of a fence panel with you. During your conversation, you mentioned she must have been shocked to find a body in her bed. Is that true?'

Heather nodded.

'Can you answer the question, please,' said Dan. 'For the tape.'

'Yes, that's what I said … the thing I accidentally let slip.'

'How did you know the body we found at 4 Hollybrook Close was discovered in the bedroom? In bed?'

'Someone must have told me.'

'That's not possible,' said Dan. 'We didn't disclose that information to anyone.'

'DS Fairfax is absolutely right,' Isabel said. 'So, try again. How did you know where the body was found?'

Heather remained silent.

'I put it to you that you knew exactly where the victim was because you're the person who murdered Kevin Spriggs. And that's the conclusion Ruth Prendergast came to, isn't it? That's why you threatened her and held her against her will.'

'I admit to keeping the Prendergast woman at the house,' Heather said. 'But I didn't kill that man.'

'Well, you must have been involved somehow,' said Dan. 'You know things only the killer could know. That suggests either you *are* the killer, or you know who is.'

The solicitor wagged a finger to silence Heather. 'My client has told you she wasn't responsible for the death of …' He glanced down at his notes. 'Kevin Spriggs. She has admitted to the assault and false imprisonment of Ruth Prendergast, so I suggest you charge her with those offences and let me get on with making a bail application.'

Isabel gave Dan a sideways glance before looking back at their suspect.

'We're not finished with your client yet,' Isabel said. 'Nowhere near.'

Dan leaned forward. 'Heather, do you know who was responsible for the death of Kevin Spriggs? Was it Stella?'

'No! Stella had nothing to do with it. Leave my sister out of this.'

'So who was responsible?' Dan asked. 'Do you know?'

'I do,' she replied, 'but I've got no intention of telling *you* who it was.'

'Were you involved in planning and executing the murder?' Isabel said.

Heather glanced at her solicitor before turning back to face Isabel and Dan. 'No comment.'

'If you co-operate with us now, Heather, it will stand you in good stead with the judge,' Dan said. 'On the other hand, if you choose to withhold information, it'll go against you.'

'Let me be clear on this,' Isabel added, sounding more confident than she felt. 'We *will* find out who was responsible for Kevin Spriggs' murder. Whatever it is you're involved in, it's all unravelling now. We'll be talking to your sister next. Are you expecting her to keep quiet in order to protect you?'

Heather gave an impatient shake of the head.

'Stella's bound to have split loyalties,' Isabel said. 'After all, you're holding back important information about the murder of her biological father. How do you think she's going to feel about that?'

'Stella won't care. She wasn't interested in meeting him. She told me so herself.'

'So, you admit the two of you discussed the search for her natural father?'

'We discussed it. Briefly.'

292

'Come on now, Heather,' said Dan. 'Why don't you tell us what you know? I mean, it's better coming from you, isn't it? It would save your sister having to give evidence against you.'

Heather said nothing.

'DS Fairfax is right,' Isabel said. 'Why put Stella through that? She's bound to feel torn between her loyalty to you and doing what's right. If you're not willing to co-operate with us, then we'll have no choice but to question your sister, which will put her in a difficult position. My guess is, she'll talk to us … and then spend the rest of her life feeling guilty about snitching on her little sister.'

Heather leaned forward, her face a picture of indecision. She stared, first at Isabel and then at Dan. As she considered her reply, her expression hardened.

'No comment,' she said.

Zoe was waiting for them as they came out of the interview room.

'You wanted to know whether either of the Mariners were a match for the partial print found at the crime scene, boss?'

'I did,' Isabel said. 'What's the verdict?'

'Sorry.' Zoe grimaced. 'It didn't match either of them.'

Chapter 55

Stella Mariner was back in interview room one. She'd been cautioned and, with a certain air of bravado, had once again turned down the offer of a solicitor.

Isabel and Dan had spent the last twenty minutes talking to her about what had happened earlier that afternoon, after she'd arrived at Hollybrook Close. She'd shared her sister's revelation about their mother's allegation of rape, and told them Heather had admitted to tracking down Kevin Spriggs. She'd also made it clear that Heather had denied being responsible for his murder.

'Your sister's got herself into a right mess, hasn't she?' said Dan.

'I'd say that's an understatement,' Stella replied.

'We're charging her with the assault and unlawful imprisonment of Ruth Prendergast, which she's admitted to,' Dan said. 'We now need to establish the extent of her involvement in the murder of Kevin Spriggs.'

'Even if she didn't wield the knife herself, she could still be facing a murder charge, or a charge of intentionally encouraging or assisting an offence,' Isabel said. 'You've told us yourself that Heather traced Kevin Spriggs, and we think she was involved in planning the murder. She may even have assisted his killer – all of which begs the question: *who is the killer?* You seem like an obvious candidate.'

Stella's body sagged, her bravado melting away. 'What?' she said. 'You can't be serious?'

'If you aren't responsible, then who is?' Isabel persisted. 'Come on, Stella. Help us out here.'

Stella thrust out her chin. 'Look, I've told you everything I know. I've been totally honest with you … and I'm telling you the truth now when I say I don't know who killed Kevin Spriggs.'

'You must have some idea,' Isabel said.

'No, I haven't.' Stella swung her legs to the side of her chair, preparing to get up. 'I'm sure you'll agree I've been very candid. I've answered your questions. I had nothing to do with the crime you're investigating … now I'd like to go home.'

'I'm afraid you can't do that this time,' Isabel said. 'This isn't a voluntary interview. You've been arrested. I'd also like to remind you that this investigation relates to the murder of your biological father. Don't you want to help us find whoever did it?'

'Of *course* I want to help, but I don't know what more I can tell you.'

Isabel tapped her fingers impatiently. 'You're asking us to believe you weren't involved in the murder of Kevin Spriggs?'

'Yes, because it's the truth.'

'If that's the case,' Isabel said, 'you need to help us understand who *was* responsible, and to do that, you need to answer a few more questions.'

She turned to Dan, nodding for him to continue.

'Is your sister in a relationship?' he said.

As if resigned to her fate, Stella swung her legs back to the forward position and leaned her elbows on the table. 'Not that I know of,' she replied. 'Then again, Heather's always been cagey about her romantic entanglements.'

'That surprises me,' Isabel said. 'You two seem very close.'

'In many ways we are, but we're not in the habit of sharing

the intimate details of our love lives. We tend to keep that sort of information to ourselves.'

'What about friendships?' Isabel asked. 'Does your sister have any close friends? Someone who would be willing to help her … or act on her behalf?'

'By committing murder, you mean?' Stella looked at them cynically, refusing to blink. 'That's an awfully big ask, even from the best of friends.'

'We're asking you to work with us on this, Stella,' Dan said. 'Who is it your sister's protecting?'

Stella rested her chin on her hands and gave the matter serious consideration. 'I don't know,' she said, eventually. 'There's no one who springs to mind.'

'Whoever it is would probably have known your mum,' Dan said. 'Been close to her even.'

'Heather and I weren't in the habit of taking our friends round to Mum's. You never quite knew what mood she'd be in … she could be difficult with people she didn't know or trust …' Her voice tailed away and she lowered her eyes.

Isabel had been processing some thoughts of her own. She wondered if the conclusion she'd come to was the same one that was now flitting through Stella Mariner's mind.

'How about Evelyn Merigold?' Isabel suggested. 'She was good friends with your mum. Was she also friendly with your sister?'

Stella blinked. 'Yes, Evelyn got on well with both mum *and* Heather, but I wasn't aware the friendship had continued after Mum's death.'

'But it could have done?' said Dan.

'Perhaps.'

'Do you think it's possible that Heather and Evelyn Merigold decided to work together to avenge your mother's death?'

Stella sighed. 'I've no idea,' she said, putting her head in her hands. 'Why don't you ask them?'

Chapter 56

Dan and Lucas pulled up outside Evelyn Merigold's house less than twenty minutes later.

'Do you think she did it?' Lucas said.

'Yes, mate, on balance, I do.'

He nodded across the garden, towards a hooded and suited figure leaning over the wooden beehive.

'Take a look at that,' he said.

'Is that her?' asked Lucas.

'It's difficult to tell, but I think so,' Dan said. 'The bee suit looks a lot like a scene suit, don't you think?'

'You're not suggesting she wore that to commit the murder?'

'Nah, not the bee suit,' Dan said. 'But Heather Mariner would have been able to get hold of a proper body suit from her workplace. When we get back to the station, give Heather's employer a call. Find out what PPE she's requisitioned recently, specifically whether she's requested a body suit. It'd be the perfect gear for committing murder. Someone wearing one of those wouldn't have to worry about leaving forensic evidence at the scene.'

Lucas scrunched up his nose. 'True, but if Kevin Spriggs was at the house to get laid, he wouldn't have been impressed with that sort of get-up. When someone says they're going to slip into something more comfortable, a body suit definitely doesn't fit the bill.'

Dan laughed. 'Depends what you're into, I guess. Come on, let's go and arrest Ms Merigold. We can ask her all the questions we need to down at the station.'

Evelyn Merigold sat with her hands neatly folded in front of her, and her solicitor by her side. After the tape had been switched on and Evelyn had been cautioned, she sat quietly, waiting for the questioning to begin.

DI Blood kicked things off, going straight to the heart of the matter.

'We've spoken to Heather Mariner,' she said. 'We know she was involved in the murder of Kevin Spriggs, but she denies killing him.'

Evelyn stared back at them, silent and solemn.

'We believe Heather planned the murder with someone else, and that person struck the fatal blow.' DI Blood's tone was cool and professional. 'Was it you who pushed the knife into his chest, Evelyn?'

The suspect raised her eyebrows. 'Is that what Heather told you?'

'On the contrary, your friend has been extremely reticent.'

'I wouldn't class Heather as a friend,' Evelyn said. 'It was me and her mum who were mates.'

'Let's not split hairs, eh?' Dan said. 'Heather has admitted that she tracked down Kevin Spriggs, although she's not said anything to implicate you or anyone else in his murder.'

'In that case,' said Evelyn, 'I'm hardly going to implicate myself, am I?'

'Don't you see?' said the DI. 'By taking that approach, you're dropping Heather right in it. She vehemently denies killing Kevin Spriggs, but without anyone else in the frame, things don't look good for her. As things stand, she could end up taking the blame for something she didn't do.'

'The last time I checked, citizens in this country are innocent until proven guilty,' said Evelyn. 'I take it that hasn't changed?'

'No, but we do have a certain amount of circumstantial evidence,' said Dan. 'It points towards Heather having had the means, motive and opportunity to commit the crime. Unless, of course, you want to contradict that and put us straight about what really happened?'

Evelyn looked at her solicitor and rolled her eyes.

'You must think I was born yesterday,' she said. 'I'm not going to contradict something that you have no real proof of.'

Dan sensed the DI was getting restless. She'd folded her arms and was scrutinising the suspect with an unblinking stare. 'What do you think Katrina Mariner would say if she were here now?' she said, her voice stern and disapproving. 'How do you think she'd feel about her daughter being left in the lurch, taking the rap for something she didn't do?'

Evelyn shuffled uncomfortably. 'No comment.'

'We know what Kevin Spriggs did to Katrina Mariner,' the DI said. 'His actions ruined her life. I wonder what Katrina would think if she knew Heather was facing a stiff prison sentence … and all because of Kevin Spriggs?'

'Heather Mariner has been loyal to you,' said Dan. 'Now's the time for you to return the favour. Tell us the truth about what happened on the eighth of January.'

Evelyn lowered her eyelids and covered the lower half of her face with her hands. They waited, watching as she turned and murmured something in her solicitor's ear.

'My client and I would like some time alone,' he said.

Chapter 57

Having agreed to a forty-five-minute break before continuing the interview, Isabel and Dan had wandered down to the staff canteen for a takeaway coffee and a snack.

'Do you think she's going to tell us what happened?' Dan asked, as he chose a sandwich from the scant selection on offer. 'I mean, there's no question it was her. Is there?'

'Not in my mind,' Isabel said.

'So, do you think she'll cop for it?'

'Let's hope so. If loyalty to Katrina Mariner drove her to commit murder, then surely she won't stand by and let Katrina's daughter take all the blame. I'm pretty sure the two of them formed an allegiance. They were in it together, Dan.'

'That makes sense,' he said. 'Pulling off that kind of murder would have been difficult for someone working on their own. I only hope Evelyn takes the full three-quarters of an hour with her brief.'

'Why's that?' said Isabel.

Dan grinned. 'If we're called back in early, there's a danger I won't have time to eat this sarnie, and I'm bloody starving.'

* * *

'Evelyn Merigold is a match for the partial print found in the Hollybrook Close kitchen,' Lucas said, when they returned to the office.

'At last,' Isabel said. 'Something tangible in the way of forensic evidence.'

'She could say it's an old print,' Dan said. 'She's already admitted to having been inside the kitchen, in the days when she did the gardening at the house.'

'She's not done the gardening there for months,' Isabel said.

'No, but Ruth Prendergast did say Evelyn Merigold had called round more recently to offer her services. She could claim the print was left then.'

Isabel shook her head. 'It was found on the edge of the main work surface, which has got to be where Ruth Prendergast prepares her meals. She seems like a fastidious woman, the sort who'd wipe everything down carefully every day.'

'Shall I check with her, boss?'

'Please, Lucas, and while you're at it, ask Ruth about the conversation she had with Evelyn Merigold. Find out if her working hours were mentioned during their little chat. Something tells me Ms Merigold's visit was less about finding a new gardening client, and more about gathering information on Ruth's schedule.'

It was after six by the time they returned to the interview room. Keen to bring Operation Jackdaw to a satisfactory conclusion, Isabel and Dan resumed by disclosing the information they'd received about the fingerprint match.

Lucas had also had a telephone conversation with Ruth Prendergast, who was recovering back at her friend's house. Ruth had confirmed she was in the habit of wiping down the worktop daily, after preparing her meals. The last time she'd done so was after making breakfast on the day of the murder. She also told Lucas she'd engaged in ten minutes of small talk when Evelyn

Merigold had called round to her house – a conversation that had included the name of her employer and her working hours.

Despite being late in the day, Zoe had managed to get hold of someone at Westwoods who had checked the PPE inventory. Heather Mariner had requisitioned a body suit four weeks earlier.

Isabel was in no doubt now that Evelyn Merigold was responsible for the murder of Kevin Spriggs, assisted by Heather Mariner. Unwilling to waste any more time, she cut to the chase with her first question.

'Evelyn Merigold, did you, on the eighth day of January 2020, murder Kevin Spriggs at 4 Hollybrook Close in Bainbridge?'

Evelyn looked up for a moment, as though seeking divine intervention. Then, without flinching, she said: 'Yes, I did.'

'Can you tell us why you killed him?' Dan said.

'Because of what he did to my friend.'

'Your friend being Katrina Mariner?' said Isabel.

Evelyn nodded. 'Katrina and I weren't just mates, there was a connection between us. We were kindred spirits. She'd struggled with her mental health for most of her adult life, and when I found out what Kevin Spriggs had done to her, I finally understood why. She'd carried that secret around with her, and only ever shared it with one other person – her husband. When he died, she was left to bear the burden of truth on her own.'

'But she told you about it?' said Isabel.

'No. It was Heather she confided in.'

'So when did Heather share that information with you?' Isabel asked.

'In the aftermath of her mother's death. She was beside herself with grief and needed someone to talk to.'

'Why choose you?' Dan said. 'Why didn't she talk to her sister about it?'

Evelyn cast a scornful look in his direction. 'That would have meant telling Stella that her father was a rapist. She didn't feel she could do that.'

'Well, she's done it now,' Isabel said. 'She told her sister all about it earlier today.'

Evelyn sighed. 'I didn't realise that. Katrina spent her whole life protecting Stella from the truth, and I thought Heather intended to do the same. If she's told her, she must have had no alternative.'

'I suspect Heather's sudden candour had to do with the fact that she'd falsely imprisoned someone, and Stella found out,' Isabel said. 'Did you know about that? Did Heather tell you she was holding a woman against her will?'

Evelyn looked confused. 'No, that's news to me and, quite frankly, I find it hard to believe. I can't imagine Heather being capable of doing something like that. When we talked about killing Kevin Spriggs, she was adamant she couldn't do the deed herself.'

'So, you admit that you and Heather Mariner planned the murder together?' Dan said.

Evelyn paused for a moment, leaning in to consult with her solicitor.

'Heather and I were both still grieving for Katrina, and we were very, very angry. When Stella heard from her half-brother, Heather used his details to trace Kevin Spriggs and we decided we'd make him pay for what he'd done. We wanted him to know that actions have consequences.'

'That's a lesson you'll be learning yourself, soon enough,' Isabel said.

'Can you tell us what happened on the day of the murder?' Dan said. 'Talk us through your plan and how it was implemented.'

'OK, but first, I want to make it clear that Stella had nothing to do with any of it. None of this is her fault.'

'Duly noted,' said Isabel.

Evelyn nodded before continuing. 'Stella showed Heather the messages she'd received through the genealogy site, and Heather used that information to trace Kevin Spriggs. We spent ages refining our plan before we finally contacted him. I suggested we lure him to Katrina's old house, but Heather said that would make it too easy to connect Spriggs with her and Stella. Besides, they'd got rid of all the furniture by then, and the bloke would have been suspicious if he'd turned up at an empty house.'

'So, you decided to use the property next door for the rendezvous?' said Isabel.

'Yes, Heather had found a key from when Katrina used to feed Mr Langton's cat. As far as she was concerned, there was nothing to connect her or Stella to the house next door. When the new woman moved in, I sussed her out by calling round on the pretext of offering my services as a gardener. We had quite a chat. I told her what I knew about the garden, and she talked about her job and even told me her working hours.'

'So, you knew when the house would be empty?' said Dan.

'Yes. Heather kept tabs on the other residents in the close as well. We knew the couple at number 5 were away in Portugal and the people in the other houses worked long hours. It was the perfect set-up. We had the cul-de-sac to ourselves, so we made our move.'

'Why did you choose to kill Spriggs at the house?' Dan said. 'Why not wait for him to come out of the pub on a dark night?'

'We were aware of how much CCTV there is in Bainbridge these days. The house provided a much more private and controlled environment. It meant we could plan everything carefully, and anticipate what might go wrong.'

'Why the bedroom?' Isabel asked. 'Why take him upstairs?'

'Kevin Spriggs came to the house in broad daylight. There was little chance of anyone seeing us, but we didn't want to risk it. The master bedroom is at the back of the house, looking out over open fields. There was no chance of anyone looking in and seeing anything.'

'Tell me,' Isabel said, 'was it Heather who hooked up with Kevin Spriggs, or you?'

'Heather. Pretty much everything else was down to me. When

it came to the nitty-gritty of getting rid of Spriggs, she was surprisingly squeamish.'

'So how did Heather engineer a meeting with him?' Dan said.

'Why don't you ask her yourself?'

'We will,' Dan replied. 'Right now, I'm asking you. I'd like to hear your version of events.'

Evelyn leaned back. 'We'd seen on Facebook that he frequented the Sheaf of Corn, so she went there on New Year's Eve. It's the one night of the year when every pub is guaranteed to be packed, so she was able to blend in … just another face in the crowd. I'd also done a recce, and we knew there was no CCTV in the pub. There were plenty of photos of Kevin Spriggs online, so he was easy for Heather to spot.

'She loathed having to pretend to be interested in him. When she let him kiss her at midnight, she said she wanted to gag. It was only the thought of getting revenge for her mum that kept her focused. The truth is, I think Heather was afraid of Spriggs, worried he might do to her what he'd done to Katrina. She was careful to keep him at a distance for a while. They exchanged phone numbers …'

'The number she gave him was unregistered?' Dan said.

'Yes. We bought a pay-as-you-go phone so that the texts and calls couldn't be traced back to us. Heather strung him along for a while … suggested they meet up for some no-strings sex. She spoke to him a few times, kept him dangling for a few days, and then agreed a time to meet him.'

'And the address she provided was 4 Hollybrook Close?' Dan asked.

'Yes. She didn't give him the address until she was certain he'd turn up on the right day, at exactly the right time.'

'You were obviously confident that Ruth Prendergast wouldn't be at home on the day of the murder,' said Isabel. 'What would you have done if she'd rung in sick that day?'

'Heather went round to the back of Ruth's house through the

gap in the fence. She knocked on the door and waited. If Ruth had answered, she'd have made up some story about fixing the fence. But Ruth wasn't there, so Heather let herself in with the key. I followed shortly afterwards.'

'We checked CCTV from some of the other properties in the cul-de-sac,' Isabel said. 'There was no sign of your car, or Heather's car on the day of the murder.'

'Heather took everything over to number 3 a few days before-hand … the PPE, the knife. We walked to the neighbourhood on foot in the early hours of the morning on the day of the murder, but we avoided the cul-de-sac. We climbed over into the garden of Katrina's old house from the footpath at the back.'

'Someone's in the process of checking CCTV from that foot-path,' Isabel said. 'Now that we know the timeframe, I'm sure we'll be able to find you.'

'We covered our faces,' Evelyn said. 'However good the quality of your CCTV, you'll be hard pushed to recognise us.'

'What did you do then?' Isabel said. 'Wait inside number 3?'

'Yes. At about twelve-thirty, Heather went round to number 4, and I followed five minutes later. Before she let herself into the house, Heather took off her shoes, and put on gloves and a face mask. Once she was inside, she was careful not to brush against anything … she didn't want to leave any evidence.'

'You obviously weren't so careful,' Isabel said. 'Clearly you weren't wearing gloves when you were in the kitchen, otherwise we wouldn't have found the partial print.'

'I put the body suit on in the kitchen when I got there, along with a pair of gloves and a face cover. Heather told me not to touch anything, but I must have brushed against the worktop accidentally. It's not easy to get into one of those suits without flinging your arms around.'

'What did you do once you were kitted out in your PPE?' said Isabel.

'I went upstairs with the knife and waited in the bedroom.

When Kevin Spriggs knocked at the door, Heather took off her gloves and face mask, and let him in. As soon as he stepped inside, she led him upstairs. On the landing, she let him go ahead of her, into the bedroom, where I was waiting. When he walked in, I took him by surprise. As I stabbed him, I told him "*This is for Katrina*" and he stared at me with a curious look on his face.'

'Was Heather in the room when this happened?' Dan asked.

'No, she stayed out on the landing. I put Spriggs onto the bed, took off his shoes and most of his clothes, and stuffed them into a rubbish bag along with his phone and the half-bottle of Jack Daniel's he'd been carrying in his pocket. I covered him over and then Heather and I went downstairs, with the bag of stuff. Heather put her gloves back on, wiped the front door handle to remove any fingerprints, and then we got out of there, back the way we came. I took the bag of clothes with me and burned them in my garden. Heather said she'd get rid of the phone. As for the bottle of Jack Daniel's, I took that with me and opened it later to toast a job well done.'

'Zoe's theory about the fluffy handcuffs was a mile wide of the mark then?' said Lucas, when Isabel and Dan had updated the team.

'With hindsight, it's obvious it had to be the work of two people,' Zoe said. 'It would have been a risky, if not impossible undertaking for someone acting alone.'

'Both Evelyn Merigold and Heather Mariner have been charged,' Isabel said.

'I know they wanted revenge,' Dan said, 'but they must be asking themselves whether it was worth it. They're facing years in prison.'

'They were confident they'd get away with it,' Isabel said. 'I doubt they gave any thought to what would happen if they got caught.'

'Well, they'll certainly have plenty of time for reflection now …' said Zoe, 'now they're in custody.'

'I'll ask the FLO to go and see Alfie Moss,' said Dan. 'Put him in the picture.'

'Thanks,' Isabel said. 'Plus, as a courtesy, I think someone should go and see Stella Mariner. Considering how this has turned out, I'd imagine she's feeling utterly devastated right now.'

'She strikes me as being pretty resilient,' Dan said. 'Hopefully she'll be able to come to terms with everything that's happened to her.'

'I hope so,' Isabel said. 'I really do.'

Chapter 58

Having congratulated the incident team on bringing Operation Jackdaw to a satisfactory conclusion, Isabel set off for home, calling to buy a takeaway on the way. She knew her dad would be waiting to talk to her at the house, and it wasn't the sort of conversation that could be had on an empty stomach.

She entered the living room carrying a brown paper bag. Donald and Nathan were watching television, looking mildly sheepish, and she wondered whether they had managed to patch up their differences.

'Hello, Dad.' She held up the carrier bag. 'I'm guessing you guys have already had dinner? I got myself a curry. We'll talk once I've eaten. I'm ravenous, so it shouldn't take long.'

She walked through into the kitchen, where she found Fabien sitting at the table, drinking a glass of red wine.

'Hi, Fabien,' she said. 'What are you doing, sitting here all on your own? Where's Ellie?'

'Upstairs. She said she was going to do her homework, but I suspect she's keeping out of the way in case there's another argument.' He smiled.

'That's not going to happen,' Isabel said. 'I haven't got the energy for a repeat performance of last night.'

She retrieved a plate and some cutlery, and settled down to eat. 'Would you like some food?' she said. 'There's plenty. I'm happy to share.'

'No, thank you. Papa and I ate at the hotel this evening.'

'Is he all right?' Isabel asked. 'After the row last night? I wanted to call him, but I've been stuck in interviews at work. It's been a long day. We finally solved the case.'

'That's good news. You must be pleased.'

'I am,' Isabel said. 'So, how *is* Dad? Is he OK?'

'I'd prefer that you ask him yourself,' Fabien replied. 'I know he wants to talk to you. To apologise.'

'I'll go and speak to him in a while, when I've finished my food. I'm trying hard not to stay mad at him, but it's not easy. Things feel awkward between us. It's as though he's been manipulating me, telling me what I wanted to hear … and all the while having absolutely no intention of telling you the truth.'

Fabien shrugged philosophically. 'It's true that our father can be devious and slippery sometimes, but not necessarily intentionally, and certainly not maliciously.' He sipped his wine. 'Like you, I am angry with him, but you have to understand, this is how he is. Papa wants to be friends with the whole world – and sometimes, when he tries to please everyone, he ends up pleasing no one. His problem is, he doesn't know how to say no. That's probably how he ended up marrying your mother. Rather than hurt her with the truth, he went ahead and did a bad thing in order to please her.'

'You know him a lot better than I do, so I'm sure you're right – but that still doesn't excuse his behaviour.'

'And I have no excuse for my own behaviour either,' Fabien said. 'I would also like to apologise.'

'There's no need. Last night's quarrel wasn't your fault.'

'I'm not apologising for the argument,' he replied. 'I'm referring to my behaviour since I arrived. Nathan was right. I've not been as friendly as I should have been. Instead, I've been mistrustful

310

and rude, and you don't deserve that. *My* problem is, I'm not good with people. My mother used to attribute it to shyness, but I think I am naturally anti-social. I find it hard to make friends, but you're my sister and I should have made more of an effort.'

Isabel smiled. 'Don't worry about it, Fabien. We may be siblings, but we're also strangers with only Dad in common. We can't expect instant rapport. It going to take a while to get to know each other. Let's take it one step at a time, eh?'

'There's still another week before we fly home,' he said. 'Now that your case is solved, does that mean you'll be able to spend more time with us?'

'Yes, thankfully I should be around a lot more for the second week of your stay … assuming Dad doesn't decide to fly home early.'

'I'm sure he won't do that,' Fabien said. 'Although, he is considering checking out of the hotel. He knows how much you would like us to stay here, with you. That's fine with me, but I think we should leave the final decision to him, don't you?'

'I've already given up trying to convince him,' Isabel said. 'My powers of persuasion have failed miserably, so far. I'd forgotten how obstinate he can be.'

Fabien laughed. 'Perhaps that's something you and I have inherited from him, yes?'

'You're right,' Isabel said. 'I think he gave his stubborn gene to both of us.'

When she'd finished her meal, Isabel got up and headed towards the living room.

'Are you coming?' she said to Fabien.

'I think not,' he replied. 'It's best that you and he have some time alone.'

Nathan and Donald were watching an episode of *Silent Witness*. It was one of Isabel's favourite programmes, even if viewing it did sometimes feel like a busman's holiday.

She snaked an arm around Nathan's shoulders. 'You might want to join Fabien in the kitchen,' she said. 'He's opened a bottle of wine.'

'Aren't you having a glass?' Nathan said.

'No, thanks. Not right now.'

As he got up, Isabel slid down into the armchair he'd vacated. Reaching for the remote, she switched off the TV.

'Hey! I was watching that,' said Donald.

'It's on iPlayer. You can watch the rest of it later. Right now, I think we should have a chat, don't you? Fabien says you want to talk to me.'

'I do.' Donald linked his gnarled fingers and leaned forward. 'I'm sorry I've made a mess of things, Issy. I wanted this visit to be a success, but I realise I've let you and Fabien down. You were right – I should have told him and Pascal about my marriage to your mother. I'm not angry with Nathan for speaking out, not anymore. He and I have talked this evening, and we're friends again now.'

'I'm pleased to hear it,' Isabel said.

'I also want to apologise for giving you the impression it was Fabien's idea to accompany me on this trip. I asked him to come with me.'

'Why?'

'Because I was afraid.'

'*Afraid?* Of what?'

'Of seeing you again. I was worried you might still be annoyed with me, and I suppose I brought Fabien along as a foil. The trouble is, I'd forgotten how wary and curt he can be with people he doesn't know. He can be difficult, but I hope you'll give him a chance.'

'You know I will. He's my brother. Of course I'll give him a chance.'

'The other reason I wanted him to come along is that my health isn't as good as it was.'

Isabel's stomach flipped. What was he trying to say?

'Why didn't you tell me this before?' she said. 'What's wrong with you?'

'Don't panic, Issy. It's nothing serious, just old age playing havoc with my body.' He tilted his hands in a way that made him look very French. 'My heart isn't as strong as it once was. The doctor tells me I have an irregular heartbeat. I also have an enlarged prostate and, although the condition is benign, it does mean I have to get up several times in the night. That's why I asked Fabien to book the hotel. I didn't want to disturb you all … waking everyone up every time I needed a pee. The truth is, Isabel, I've become what your mother would call a doddery old codger – but my pride wants everything to be how it was before, when I was a much younger man. I didn't want our time together to be spoilt by you worrying about me, or thinking me feeble.'

Isabel got up and knelt in front of her dad's chair. 'I would never think that,' she said, taking hold of his hands. 'Don't you realise, Dad? I've waited years to see you. You're bound to be older … I'm not exactly a spring chicken myself. All I want is for us to enjoy being together again.'

'I know, and so do I.'

'We have to be honest with each other, though,' Isabel said, her expression serious. 'No more secrets, Dad. I'd rather you hurt me with the truth than with a lie. I'd also like you to move here for the second week of your holiday … you *and* Fabien. The case I've been working on has been solved, so we can finally spend some proper time together. It's my birthday in a couple of days … we could go out somewhere.'

Donald smiled. 'I can't believe my daughter will soon be fifty-seven years old.'

'I can hardly believe it myself,' Isabel said. 'I'm beginning to feel ancient.'

'Nonsense,' Donald said. 'No matter how old you are, Issy, you will always be my little girl.'

Epilogue

Eight days later, Isabel drove Donald and Fabien to the airport for their early morning flight to France. After an emotional goodbye at the check-in area, she returned to her car beneath a sky that was dark and heavy with clouds. There had been a light dusting of snow overnight, and the wind was cutting through her like a blade – but inside, she felt warm and at peace. She had renewed her connection to her dad, and had established a tentative, if somewhat unpredictable relationship with her brother. Things weren't perfect, but in her experience, perfection was a rarity in families.

By the time she sauntered into the CID office at nine o'clock, she felt as if she'd already been up for hours. She was greeted warmly by Zoe and Lucas, and Dan waved at her from his desk.

'Welcome back, boss. A little bird told us it was your birthday while you were on leave.' Zoe smiled and handed over a card. 'Sorry it's late.'

'Thanks, guys.' She was touched that they'd remembered, especially as her birthday wasn't something she advertised. 'Is everything OK? Have I missed anything?'

'Nothing exciting,' Zoe said. 'Same old, same old.'

'Good to have you back though, boss,' said Lucas.

'Your timing couldn't be better, actually.' Dan got up from his desk and strolled over to join them. 'There's an email just come through that you might want to look at. It's the results of the DNA comparison between Kevin Spriggs and Stella Mariner. When you've read it, I'm guessing you'll want to pay Stella another visit.'

Isabel arranged to see Stella at her place of work later that morning. Parking at the Derby Royal Hospital was always a mission but, after a couple of circuits, she managed to find a space a short walk from the main entrance. Stella worked on ward 101, and had agreed to take her break when Isabel arrived.

As she entered the ward, Isabel spotted Stella behind the nurses' station. She looked different in her uniform, older somehow, and more serious.

'How are you?' Isabel asked, as she approached the desk.

'I'm OK,' Stella replied. 'Work's busy, which is helping to keep my mind off things.'

'Is there somewhere we can talk? Somewhere quiet?'

Stella escorted her to a tiny, windowless room at the end of the ward. 'Has something happened with the case?' she asked, once they were both sitting down.

'Not exactly,' Isabel replied. 'I wanted to see you because we've received the results of the DNA comparison between yourself and Kevin Spriggs.'

'So, it's just a formality then?' Stella seemed relieved. 'You could have talked to me over the phone you know, rather than pay me a visit. I wouldn't have minded.'

'The thing is,' Isabel said, 'the results weren't what we were expecting.'

'Oh?' Stella crouched forward, instantly alert. 'What do you mean?'

'They show that you and Kevin Spriggs *were* related, but you weren't his daughter. He was your uncle.'

Stella pressed a hand to her forehead. 'How can that be?' She sounded breathless. 'There must be a mistake. Alfie Moss was

316

flagged up as a close match. He and I share twenty-three per cent of our DNA. The predicted relationship to me was either uncle, nephew or half-sibling.'

Isabel pulled a piece of paper from her pocket, something Zoe had printed out earlier. 'There's a disclaimer on the website,' she said. 'It states that predicted relationships aren't guaranteed to be accurate … they can differ.'

'And what exactly does that mean?'

Isabel concentrated, trying not to misremember the information she and Zoe had extracted from the website that morning.

'The *Tree of Life* assigns your match to a category based on the amount of shared DNA,' she explained, glancing at the printed note. 'The match is expressed as a percentage and in centimorgans … genetic markers, if you like. The small print on the website says that this predicted relationship – and I quote – *should be considered an "estimated relationship" and is not necessarily an exact description of your genealogical relationship to your match.*'

'So, they can tell you any old rubbish … Is that what you're saying?'

'Not at all. I'm sure they do their best to assign relationships to the right category, but it's a judgement based on the test results. The site recommends that members dig a little deeper to make sense of the results and give them context. Most people can compare family trees to pinpoint their common ancestors – but of course, neither you nor Alfie Moss had created an online tree.'

'That doesn't mean I didn't do my homework,' Stella said, her voice shaky and defensive. 'I double-checked the percentages and possible relationships before I sent the first message to Alfie. If what you're saying is true, then Alfie is my cousin, and not my half-brother, in which case we should only share around twelve per cent of our DNA.'

'You're right … in theory,' Isabel said. 'But there is one exception to the rule: double first cousins.'

'What the hell is a double first cousin?'

'Someone with whom you share both sets of grandparents,' Isabel explained. 'They're as genetically related to you as half-siblings. Usually, first cousins share about twelve and a half per cent of DNA – but *double* cousins share around twenty-five per cent, the same amount as half-siblings.'

'I don't understand.' Stella ran her hands over her face and let out a whimper. She looked tired and defeated. 'Are you saying that my *mother* was related to Alfie Moss?'

'Alfie's mother, Jessica Moss, is your mum's younger sister. DS Fairfax rang her this morning to confirm it. Jessica was fifteen the last time she saw or heard from your mum.'

Stella pressed her arms across her stomach. 'I knew mum had a sister and a brother,' she said, 'but that's all I did know. She'd completely cut herself off from everyone in her family and refused to talk about them.'

'Given her estrangement from her relatives and the circumstances of your birth, you obviously couldn't have foreseen the possibility of a double cousin scenario.'

Stella placed her hands either side of her temples. 'I still can't get my head around it,' she said.

'Kevin Spriggs married Jessica in 1993, a couple of years after you were born,' Isabel explained. 'It was pure coincidence that the two of them got together. Obviously, neither of them would have known anything about you, or had any inkling about what Kevin's brother had done.'

'So, my biological father is Kevin Spriggs' brother?'

'Yes. As far as we're aware, Kevin only had one sibling – Simon Spriggs. He's a few years older and he moved away two years before Kevin married Jessica. He lives in Leeds now. We're fairly sure Simon must be your biological father, but you'd need to confirm that with an official DNA test.'

Stella's expression crumpled. 'I don't think I want to know,' she said. 'This whole thing is like a nightmare I can't wake up from. It means Kevin Spriggs was killed because of something he didn't do, doesn't it?'

'Yes,' Isabel said. 'I'm afraid so.'

'Have you told Heather and Evelyn that he wasn't my father? Do they realise their stupid act of revenge was all for nothing? That they got the wrong man?'

'Not yet,' Isabel said.

Tears trickled down Stella's cheeks. 'This is all my fault.'

'It's not your fault. None of this is.'

'I can't believe the man who attacked my mother is still out there, walking free.' Stella shuddered. 'Will you be questioning Simon Spriggs? About the rape?'

'We might have done, if your mother had still been around. She could have reported it as a historic crime. Without any physical evidence, it would have been her word against his, and I doubt the case would have gone to trial – but by reporting it, your mother might have achieved a sense of closure.'

'She should have reported it when it happened,' Stella said, with a slow, sad nod of her head.

'I realise this won't be of any consolation, but it sounds as if Simon Spriggs is a changed man,' Isabel said. 'He told the family liaison officer that he stopped drinking years ago, when he moved away. Who knows, perhaps he made that decision because he was riddled with guilt about what he did to your mother. Maybe he wanted to make sure nothing like that ever happened again.'

'A reformed character?' Stella sounded unconvinced. 'There's no way of knowing that for certain, is there?'

'Not conclusively,' Isabel replied. 'However, when he died, Kevin Spriggs' DNA profile was already on the national database as a result of a previous arrest. When his profile was uploaded, it would have been automatically searched and compared against any unidentified crime scene samples. It didn't match any historic crimes.'

'Yeah, but that's *Kevin* Spriggs, isn't it? It doesn't put Simon Spriggs in the clear.'

'In a way, it does. During a search it's also possible to identify DNA profiles that are similar but not identical to an unidentified sample. When that happens, the senior investigating officer is informed and further inquiries can be made to establish whether the sample providers are related.'

'A bit like the matches on the *Tree of Life* site?'

'Yes, in a way,' Isabel said. 'A familial DNA search will throw up anyone who could be a parent, sibling or child to an unknown person whose DNA is being held in connection with a crime. Kevin Spriggs' DNA was never matched to any crimes and … more to the point, it's never been flagged as being similar to any unknown DNA connected to a case. In other words, Simon Spriggs doesn't appear to have perpetrated any unsolved crimes.'

Stella pressed her lips together. 'That's something, I suppose. He'll never be held to account for what he did to Mum though, will he?'

'No, Stella. I don't think he will. I'm sorry.'

'Mum's family should have been there to support her. She might have coped better if she hadn't had to bottle everything up.'

'It does sounds like she was dealt a poor hand when it came to her parents,' Isabel said, 'but from what my sergeant tells me, Jessica Moss is a nice woman. She's your maternal aunt. Would you be interested in connecting with her? I could put the two of you in touch, if you'd like me to.'

'I don't know,' Stella said. 'Maybe. I need time to think about it.'

'There's no rush … and no obligation.' Isabel stood up. 'Give me a call if you'd like to contact her. And, Stella … I'm sorry about today, having to deliver more bad news. I hope things start to get better for you soon.'

'So do I,' Stella said, swiping tears from her eyes. 'It's not even the end of January yet, and 2020 is already turning into a pretty crap year.'

'At least the worst is behind you,' said Isabel. 'Things can only get better. It's only a matter of time.'

Acknowledgements

Firstly, I'd like to give a big shout-out to everyone who took the time to read my debut, *In Cold Blood*, which was launched during the 2020 lockdown. It wasn't the best time to publish a first novel, but thanks to a wonderful blogging community and the team at HQ, lots of readers took a chance and bought the book. My thanks to each and every one of those bloggers and readers, and especially those who reviewed it. Knowing that people are reading and enjoying my work makes this whole writing 'lark' worthwhile.

I'm also grateful for the encouraging feedback I've received from family and friends. I truly appreciate your kindness and positivity, and your eagerness to read more of my work. My sister, Dawn, deserves a special mention: she has done a phenomenal job of spreading the word about my books. As well as being the best sister in the world, she's also a superb publicity champion!

Sadly, Dawn's husband, Dave, passed away as I was editing the final chapters of this book. Dave was a wonderful brother-in-law, and I'll always be grateful to him for loving my sister and taking such good care of her. He was a brilliant father to his three children, a doting grandad to six beautiful grandchildren, and a friend to many. This book is dedicated to his memory. We miss you, Dave.

Sending huge thanks to my amazing editor, Belinda Toor, for her ongoing support and the helpful editorial feedback on *Without a Trace*, and to Audrey Linton, Sian Baldwin and all of the wonderful team at HQ. Thank you for believing in my work and doing everything you can to spread the word to readers.

Thanks also go to Stuart Gibbon of the GIB Consultancy. Tapping into his vast knowledge of police procedures helped me to shape my fictional investigation and give it a ring of authenticity. Thank you, Stuart. If there are any errors in this book, I take full responsibility.

Several people have asked whether *Without a Trace* was easier to write than my first book. The answer to that question is yes … and no. Having successfully completed one novel, I did feel slightly more confident about tackling a second, but I definitely wouldn't say it made the process any easier. There was more pressure this time around – especially as I was working towards a deadline. Like many writers, I also experienced 'second novel syndrome'. Could I do it all again? Would novel number two be any good? In the end, I dealt with those niggling doubts in the only way I knew how – by writing the book, one word at a time. I sincerely hope you've enjoyed reading what I came up with.

Without a Trace continues and develops some of the story threads from the first book in the series. I do hope you like the Blood family's new canine companion, Nell, who is based on my own dog (also called Nell). She usually sits by my feet as I write, and she's such a loyal and loving old girl, I thought she deserved a place in the book.

It's always a pleasure to connect with other writers and readers, both online and in person, and those connections have been particularly important during the pandemic. Thank you to the people who've exchanged messages of support and solidarity, and to the authors who continue to share their help, knowledge and wisdom so willingly. There is always something new to learn about writing.

The final word goes to my favourite person on the planet, who also happens to be my husband. Thanks for cheering me on, Howard. I know I can always rely on your love, support and encouragement. Thanks also for the book of random names, which I will continue to dip into whenever I create a new character. Here's to lots more shared laughter, wine and coffee (our trinity of essentials). Love you lots.

Keep reading for an excerpt from
In Cold Blood …

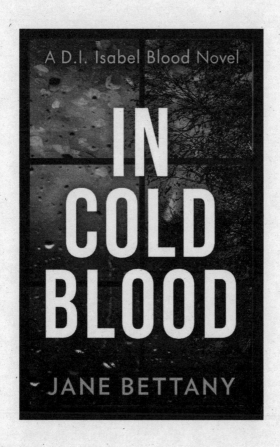

Chapter 1

The pantry was musty and airless and smelt faintly of curry powder and something that Amy couldn't identify. It was a tiny space, crammed with out-of-date food, a battered collection of saucepans, and containers filled with dried fruit and breakfast cereals. She emptied the shelves doggedly, thrusting everything into a heavy-duty bin bag.

Reaching into the corner of the highest shelf, she retrieved the last items: a jar of pickled onions and some homemade blackberry jam. Strictly speaking, she should throw the contents away and wash out the jars for recycling – but sod that. She had better things to do with her time. Instead, being careful not to break the glass, Amy placed the jars in the bag and tied it with a double knot ready to take to the bin.

It was as she turned to switch off the light that she noticed the marks on the wall. Height marks. Just inside the door.

A child grew up in this house, she thought, as she traced the pencilled scratches with her fingers. *An only child. One set of marks.*

The first measurement appeared in the lower third of the wall, alongside a date – 15th January 1965. The marks crept higher with each passing year. The last was dated 15th January 1977 and recorded a height of 5' 6".

Perhaps the 15th of January was the child's birthday, Amy thought. *There must have been an annual ritual to record his or her height on the pantry wall.*

She wondered why the marks had stopped in 1977. At 5' 6", a teenage girl would be fully grown. A boy might have gone on to gain a few more inches.

The measurements were a part of the history of the house that would soon be gone forever. When the new kitchen was installed, the pantry would be removed and replaced with tall, sliding larder cupboards. She and Paul had chosen a range of expensive, glossy units that would provide the kind of high-quality finish they hoped would sell the house.

Planning permission had been granted for a huge extension that would more than double the size of the existing kitchen. Amy's vision was for a light-filled, open-plan living space with shiny work surfaces, top-of-the-range appliances, and a vast dining area. There would be skylights and bi-fold doors opening onto the rear garden. Once completed, the bright, airy room would be the redeeming feature of the otherwise unremarkable 1960s house they had bought at auction eight weeks earlier.

Grabbing the bin bag, Amy took one last look at the height marks before switching off the light and closing the pantry door. It was cold, so she flicked the kettle on to make a hot drink. Paul had been outside for most of the day, digging out the foundations for the extension. He would be ready for another brew.

As she waited for the water to boil, the back door opened and Paul came in, shivering. He was pale. Unsmiling.

'What's up?' Amy said. 'Has something happened?'

'You could say that. I've only gone and found a fucking body.'

Amy tutted. 'Yeah, right. Very funny, bro.' Paul had been a wind-up merchant all his life. It was a trait he should have grown out of by now.

'Seriously. I'm not kidding, Ames.'

'Course you're not. What is it? A cat? Dog? Someone's long-dead hamster?'

'It's an animal, all right. Of the human variety.'

Dread tugged at Amy's stomach muscles. 'You'd better be joking,' she said.

'Come and take a look for yourself if you don't believe me.'

She followed him outside. They skirted the partially excavated foundation trench and stood next to what would eventually be the far corner of the extension.

'Down there.' Paul pointed at something protruding from the soil.

Leaning in closer, Amy realised it was the upper part of a human skull; the forehead and eye sockets jutted out from the damp layer of earth at the bottom of the metre-deep trench. If it had been buried a few inches lower, Paul would never have known it was there.

'Shit!' She blew air through her cheeks. 'This is awful.'

'You can say that again. It's going to delay everything. There's no chance of getting the extension finished before the new year now.'

Amy wrapped her arms across her body and glared at her brother.

'Paul! Are you for real? A body, *somebody*, has been lying here for God knows how long and all you're bothered about is the extension?'

'Come on, sis, don't give me a hard time. Our inheritance is tied up in this house. We need to get the work finished, sell up and move on to the next project. That' – he pointed into the trench – 'is a bloody disaster. The delay it'll cause is bad enough, but if word gets out, it's going to knock thousands off the property value. No one will be interested in buying this place, with or without a swanky kitchen. Who wants to live in a house where someone's been murdered?'

Paul's usual flippancy had vanished, replaced by a demeanour that was uncharacteristically sombre, almost hostile. He was obviously worried.

'Do you think that's what happened here then?' Amy said. 'Murder?'

'Of course it is. Use your nous. The body didn't bury itself, did it?'

'It could have been here for hundreds of years,' she said. 'A body buried during the civil war or something.'

'Civil war?' He scowled, shaking his head dismissively. 'What are you on about, Amy? This isn't an ancient battlefield.'

'OK. So maybe it *was* buried a lot more recently. Either way, the local paper's going to have a field day.'

Paul trailed the fingertips of his right hand along his jawline and studied the trench thoughtfully. 'Only if they find out about it,' he said.

'What do you mean?' She narrowed her eyes, staring at her brother in disbelief. 'Of course they'll find out.'

'Not if we don't report it.'

'What?' she said, incredulous. 'No way!'

'Think about it. If I hadn't dug such a deep trench, or the body had been buried a few inches further down, we'd have been none the wiser.'

Amy lifted her hands and locked her fingers across the top of her head. 'You're not seriously suggesting we keep quiet about this?'

'Why not? If I pour the concrete foundations now, this little problem will stay buried forever. No one will know but us.'

He leaned back and let the muscles in his shoulders relax. Just talking about a solution seemed to have calmed him. Paul's proposal offered a quick fix, an easy way out – but Amy was horrified by the idea.

She spun away from the trench, groaning with exasperation. 'Firstly,' she said, 'this is not a "little problem". Whoever it is lying down there was once a living, breathing human being. Don't you think they deserve some kind of justice, or a proper burial at least? And secondly, what if the person responsible for this is still around? They know what's hidden here. If they get away with it, what's to say they won't do it again somewhere else?'

'Bloody hell, sis.' Paul rubbed the back of his neck and kicked irritably at a clump of soil with his work boot. 'Why do you always have to be such a goody-two-shoes?'

Amy peered down at the skull – into the empty eye sockets from which someone had once looked out at the face of their killer. *Every house has its own secret history*, she thought, remembering the height marks scratched into the pantry wall. *Some things are best left hidden, but this definitely isn't one of them.*

She pulled out her phone and dialled 101.

Chapter 2

Detective Inspector Isabel Blood gripped the steering wheel of her car and drove through the streets of Bainbridge as fast as the speed limit would allow. She was heading to the secondary school where her youngest daughter was a pupil. At Isabel's age, attending a parents' evening should have been a thing of the past, but life had ricocheted off in an unexpected direction when Ellie was born.

It was damp and starting to get dark by the time she pulled into the school car park. She'd promised to meet Nathan outside the main entrance at five o'clock and she was already five minutes late.

There was no sign of him as she ran towards the school. He must have gone inside already. Pushing through the revolving glass door, Isabel dashed down the central corridor towards Ellie's form room. Nathan was waiting outside.

'I didn't think you were going to make it,' he said.

'Sorry. Something came up. You know what it's like.'

'You should have taken the afternoon off. They owe you enough hours.'

Isabel pressed her shoulder against a wooden locker and smiled. 'It's not always possible, as well you know.'

A door opened behind them and Ellie's form teacher, Miss Powell, beckoned them into the classroom.

They sat down and listened as the teacher began to deliver her verdict on how their fourteen-year-old daughter was doing in her lessons.

'Ellie is highly intelligent, self-assured, eloquent ...'

Nathan was unable to contain a grin.

'However ...'

Nathan's smile evaporated.

'Although Ellie is extremely capable, I'm concerned about her recent behaviour. She used to be a model pupil, but she's been acting very negatively since the beginning of term. She's become argumentative and she wastes a lot of time messing around with her friends.' The teacher paused to let her words sink in. There was a note of frustration in her voice as she continued. 'She's studying for her GCSEs now and she really needs to take her schoolwork more seriously, otherwise she'll fall behind. So far this term, she's handed homework in late on five separate occasions and she's not engaging in class like she used to. More worryingly, she's been turning up late for school in the mornings.'

'Late?' Isabel leaned forward, a sense of unease rippling somewhere beneath her ribs. This didn't sound like Ellie. Not at all. She'd always been a good kid.

'She's been catching the school bus, hasn't she?' said Nathan. 'Perhaps it's been running late, or she missed it.'

Miss Powell was unswayed by his line of defence. 'There have been no problems reported with the school buses. Besides, when I spoke to Ellie, she told me she'd been walking to school. That's fine, of course, if it's what she wants to do, but the school is a long way from where you live. If she's going to walk, she needs to set off earlier and get here on time.'

Isabel looked at Nathan, who appeared to be as baffled as she was.

'We had no idea she was walking to school,' Isabel said. 'We'll ask her about it.'

'Perhaps you could also find out why she's stopped coming to the after-school book club,' Miss Powell added.

Inexplicably, it was this final revelation that shocked Isabel the most. Ellie's love of books was legendary. The possibility that her love affair with literature might be over prematurely saddened Isabel inordinately.

'She still does plenty of reading at home,' Nathan said.

Miss Powell smiled. 'That's reassuring to hear, but I'm worried that Ellie is losing interest in her work here, at school. I'm disappointed. She could do so much better.'

'We'll talk to her … find out what's wrong. Won't we, Nathan?'

Although Nathan nodded supportively, Isabel knew that she would be the one who would have to deliver the reprimand. As far as her husband was concerned, their youngest child could do no wrong – and nothing the teacher said would change his opinion.

Having delivered the negative elements of Ellie's report, Miss Powell allowed herself a tight smile. 'There is one subject in which Ellie has been excelling …'

Nathan nudged Isabel and winked.

'Her art tutor is very impressed with the work she's been producing.' The teacher picked up the written report and read from it. 'He says … *Ellie is creative and talented and has a natural gift.*'

'She gets that from me,' said Nathan.

Isabel gave him a sideways glance and focused her attention back on the teacher.

Miss Powell put down the report and leaned back. 'There's an exhibition of artwork in the main hall,' she told them. 'Please take a look on your way out. Several of Ellie's pieces are on show.'

Isabel had switched her phone to silent, but she felt it vibrate in her pocket. Pulling it out, she glanced down at the screen. It was her colleague Dan Fairfax, her sergeant. He knew where she was. He wouldn't be ringing unless it was important.

'I'm so sorry.' Isabel stood up. 'Technically I'm still on duty, so I need to take this.'

She answered the call on her way out of the classroom. 'This had better be important, Dan.'

'It is, boss. I wouldn't disturb you otherwise. We've had word that a body's been found. I thought you'd want to know.'

Nathan had followed her out into the corridor clutching a printed copy of Ellie's report.

'Hang on, Dan. I need to have a quick word with Nathan.' Isabel turned to her husband. 'There's a body. I have to go.'

'Can you spare a couple of minutes to look at Ellie's artwork on your way out?'

'I'd rather not rush it,' she said, shame clawing at her conscience.

Nathan sighed, disappointed. Over the years, he had reluctantly accepted that sometimes her job had to take priority over family commitments. It was a regrettable reality they'd both come to terms with, but that didn't stop Isabel feeling guilty. Occasionally, being a good copper meant being a bad parent, or a rubbish wife. Mostly, Isabel loved her job, but there were times when she hated the way it screwed with her life.

'It's better if I come back another time and have a proper look,' she said, suppressing a flush of self-reproach. 'Sorry, Nathan. I'm needed urgently.'

She planted a swift kiss on his cheek before hurrying back along the main corridor towards the exit, the phone clasped to her ear.

'I'm on my way, Dan. Tell me where I need to be and I'll meet you there.'

'The property's on Ecclesdale Drive. Number 23,' Dan said. 'It's on that big, sprawling estate on the eastern side of town. Head for Winster Street and then turn left—'

'It's OK.' She cut him off. 'I know where it is.'

Isabel didn't need directions. She knew it well.

Ecclesdale Drive sliced through the centre of a housing estate that had sprung up in the early 1960s and had grown every decade since. The outlying fields that Isabel remembered from childhood had burgeoned into a confusing network of streets and cul-de-sacs, each one crammed with showy red-brick properties.

The houses in the original part of the estate were plainer, but built on bigger plots, with long gardens filled with well-established trees and shrubs. Isabel turned onto Winster Street, driving past the recreation ground she'd visited frequently as a child. The old slide was still there, as well as a vast climbing frame and a new set of swings. The flat wooden roundabout the local kids had called the 'teapot lid' had been removed on safety grounds in the 1970s, as had the conical swing that had been shaped like a witch's hat. Isabel smiled as she recalled the wild, spinning rides she had taken on that pivoted swing.

She took the second left into Ecclesdale Drive. The street was long and crescent-shaped, curving down towards an infant school and the newsagent's shop at the end. It was years since Isabel had been here. Ecclesdale Drive held lots of memories, but not all of them were good.

She pulled up behind two police vehicles that were parked halfway along the road. Her hand trembled as she switched off the engine, her fingers quivering involuntarily like the blue-and-white police tape that was fluttering around the outer cordon of the crime scene. Battling a growing wave of unease, Isabel took a deep breath and got out of the car.

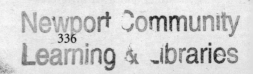

Dear Reader,

We hope you enjoyed reading this book. If you did, we'd be so appreciative if you left a review. It really helps us and the author to bring more books like this to you.

Here at HQ Digital we are dedicated to publishing fiction that will keep you turning the pages into the early hours. Don't want to miss a thing? To find out more about our books, promotions, discover exclusive content and enter competitions you can keep in touch in the following ways:

JOIN OUR COMMUNITY:

Sign up to our new email newsletter:
http://smarturl.it/SignUpHQ

Read our new blog www.hqstories.co.uk

🐦 https://twitter.com/HQStories

f www.facebook.com/HQStories

BUDDING WRITER?

We're also looking for authors to join the HQ Digital family!
Find out more here:

https://www.hqstories.co.uk/want-to-write-for-us/

Thanks for reading, from the HQ Digital team

If you enjoyed *Without a Trace*, then why not try another gripping mystery from HQ Digital?